THE THRONE'S UNDOING

The Throne's Undoing

Copyright © 2024 by Neena Laskowski

First Edition published December 2024

Published by Belles & Oats, LLC

Map Design and Internal Illustrations © Neena Laskowski

Cover Design © 2024 Moonpress

https://moonpress.co/

Identifiers:

ISBN: 979-8-9876368-7-9 (paperback)

ISBN: 979-8-9876368-8-6 (ebook)

ALSO BY NEENA LASKOWSKI

OF FIRE AND LIES

The Heir's Bargain: Fynn's Story (prequel)

The King's Weapon, book 1

The Crown's Shadow, book 2

The Throne's Undoing, book 3

The Kingdom's Reckoning, book 4

OTHER BOOKS

Between Blades and Vows

THE THRONE'S UNDOING

NEENA LASKOWSKI

OF FIRE AND LIES

BOOK THREE

To those who have ever felt broken,
lost, or caged within their own minds.
You will break free,
and you will become even stronger because of it.

THE SEVEN KINGDOMS OF VANERIA
THE MIST
THE WHISPERING SPRINGS
PONTIA
THE RED SEA
TETRIA
THE THREE LADIES
THE QUEEN'S CROWN
BORGANI

THE GLACIERS
RIVER OF ICE
RAGOLO
THE FROZEN LAKE
KADIA
THE NORTHERN SEA
LUCIAN R.
ALDERIAN MTNS
HIGH R.
TROJIAN MTNS
ZIA
LAKE OF TEARS
ARDENTOL

CONTENT WARNINGS

The Throne's Undoing includes elements that may not be suitable for all readers, such as references to alcohol consumption, mature language, violence, gore, manipulation, panic attacks, on-page death, assault, self-harm, and references to abuse. If any of these topics are harmful to you, please proceed with care.

PRONUNCIATION GUIDE

Please note: these are fictional characters and places. The following pronunciations are simply the way the author pronounces them. However, if you, the reader, have a different way of pronouncing the names, please do so.

<u>*People*</u>

Cetia - *ket-EE-uh*

Domitius - *do-mi-TEE-us*

Esmeray - *es-mer-ay*

Euralys - *ur-el-ees*

Fynn - *fin*

Graeson - *grey-sin*

Danisinia - *dan-i-sin-EE-uh*

Dronias - *dro-NEE-us*

Iro - I-roh

Kalisandre - *kal-ih-SAN-dra*

Kolen - KOL-en

Laurince - *lore-INS*

Lothian - loth-EE-in

Lysanthia - *lis-an-THI-uh*
Lystrata - LIS-chra-ta
Medenia - *muh-deen-EE-uh*
Myra - *MY-ra*
Mynhos - *myn-OS*
Rian - *RYE-in*
Sebastian - *sa-BASH-tin*
Sylvia - *sil-VEE-uh*
Terin - *TARE-rin*
Troia - *TROY-uh*

<u>Gods:</u>
Barinthian - bar-in-THI-an
Misanthia - *mis-an-THI-uh*
Nerva - *nur-VUH*
Pontanius - *pon-TAN-EE-us*
Ryla - *RYE-la*
Sabina - *sa-BEE-na*
Tanzia - *tan-ZEE-uh*

<u>Kingdoms:</u>
Ardentol - *ARE-den-tall*
Borgania - *bor-GAN-EE-uh*
Frenzia - *Frenz-EE-uh*
Kadia - *Cade-EE-uh*
Pontia - *Pont-EE-uh*
Ragolo - *ra-GOL-o*
Tetria - *te-TRI-uh*

PROLOGUE

KALLIE

Kallie tugged the cuff of her sleeve, pulling it over the blotchy purple and green skin peeking through. Every muscle in her body ached. Every time she took a breath, the corset squeezed her already bruised ribcage, sending a spike of pain coursing through her body.

Yet, as she stood on the other side of the oval table in the advisors' room from her father, Kallie tipped her chin up and pushed past the pain. She couldn't waiver, not now.

The bruises covering her flesh were nothing more than proof of her hard work and the work that still needed to be done to be perfect.

And Kallie would be perfect.

She had no other choice.

"Soon, this will all be ours," her father said, waving a hand over the map of Vaneria spread across the table. His blond hair was neatly swept back, and his impeccably tailored navy suit exuded an air of sophistication. "The seven kingdoms were never meant to be split into separate territories led by individual kings. But the future is near; I can feel it. I will become the king who reunited the kingdoms and pieced them back together."

Behind her back, she uneasily twisted her mother's gold ring around her finger as her eyes darted across the map. The small marble figurines representing the kings and queens of Vaneria stared back at her.

"What if the other rulers do not agree with your plan, Father?" she asked quietly.

"With you at my side, they will have no choice but to agree," he said, pressing his palms against the oak as he leaned over the table. "This is why the gods have blessed you, Kalisandre. You are the key to our success. Once you learn complete control of your gift, you will be stronger than you can even fathom."

Kallie nodded, yet doubt twisted her stomach.

They had been over the plan many times. She knew how important it was to strengthen her ability. If she wanted to be powerful, she had to be able to use her gift more than once or twice without suffering from debilitating migraines. Her next assignment would be a crucial step in achieving that, yet...

Releasing her bottom lip, she asked hesitantly, "Are you sure they will know how to strengthen my gift?"

The king sighed. "Yes, Kalisandre--as I have told you many times."

Kallie's gaze skimmed across her father's features. She did not know what she was looking for, for she knew she would find no comfort within his heavy, brown eyes. Yet she looked anyway.

Even though she had been training for months, she couldn't help but wonder if this was the right path.

"But how do you know?" The question slipped from her lips before she could swallow it.

Domitius straightened, and Kallie, unable to move, held her breath as he stormed around the table toward her.

She immediately dropped her attention to the floor, the shame dragging her gaze down.

Domitius snatched her face in his hand, squeezing her cheeks together as if she was once again a young girl running around the castle and causing trouble. "Do you dare doubt my wisdom?"

"No," Kallie whispered, dread making her voice sound hollow.

Cocking his head to the side, Domitius narrowed his eyes. "Are you sure? Because for someone who claims she does not doubt me, you sure have been asking a lot of questions."

Kallie's heart thundered in her chest. Her palms grew damp as her father arched a brow, awaiting her response. "I--I only wish to understand, Father."

His nose twitched. "Do you not trust me, Kalisandre?"

As his grip around her face tightened slightly, tears began to burn the backs of her eyes. Refusing to let them escape, she swallowed before saying, "Of course I trust you, My King."

The corners of his lips twitched upward, but the smile did not reach his eyes. It rarely did, though.

"Good," he said, loosening his hold on her. He patted her right cheek with his hand, pleased with her answer. "The choosing ceremony is in a few days. Until you marry the king, you must always be on guard, Kalisandre. Do you remember your training?"

Her answer was immediate. "Yes, Father."

"There is no room for error, nor room to question the plan. You were born to do this." Domitius's attention returned to the map and landed on the island on the northwestern coast. "Some kingdoms will be harder to convince than others, and war might befall us. But sacrifices must be made for the greater good.

"Once we're successful and I lead all of Vaneria, there will be no more wars. Kingdoms will no longer harbor resources and knowledge only for themselves. But to be successful, you must keep your walls up. Am I clear?"

Kallie nodded.

They'd had this conversation many times over the years. Whenever she was preparing to leave for a mission, her father had given her the same spiel.

Keep your mind focused.

Remember the mission.

Remember our goal.

I am trusting you, Kalisandre.

Do not let me down.

Every time, it was the same. Every time his doubt crept into his words and slithered into her mind. They spun and spun and spun.

All Kallie wanted was for her father to have faith in her.

All she wanted was for him to believe in her. To trust her. But he never did. He constantly questioned her and her faith in him.

Still, whenever the king of Ardentol demanded more of her, Kallie willingly obliged every single time. No matter the danger she faced. No matter the sacrifices that had to be made.

CHAPTER 1
GRAESON

"No!" Dani shouted through the tears streaming down her russet-brown cheeks as she sprinted to the pile of rubble, her dark brown braids flying behind her. She clawed at the rocks that had fallen from the ceiling, throwing them behind her and peeling away at the wreckage, bit by bit. "He can't get away. He can't get away!" she repeated like a desperate mantra, her voice mangled and throat raw.

Back throbbing, Graeson took in a sharp breath and coughed as he inhaled dust. He waved his hand as he tried fruitlessly to fan away the billowing cloud in the air. Yet dust motes continued to swarm his vision.

More coughing sounded behind him, and Graeson jerked around, ignoring the sharp pain in his back.

"Terin, you two all right?" Graeson asked, finding the Pontian prince huddled on the ground, his large form covered in a thick layer of dust. Time seemed to stand still as Graeson waited for a response, his lungs constricting.

Finally, Terin nodded, and ash fell from his brown hair.

Graeson's attention dropped to the delicate hand lying limp

beneath Terin's body. "Is she--" Graeson couldn't finish the question.

Thankfully, he didn't have to.

"She's all right," his friend said, assuring him as he pushed himself up with a groan.

Graeson stared at Kalisandre's unmoving form as Terin uncurled himself from her, having shielded her from most of the destruction. The evidence of Terin's gift still marked Kalisandre's pale face. The cotton wrapping around her forehead was soiled and stained red. Her wedding dress was shredded and smeared with grime and ash. But, Graeson reminded himself, she was all right-- she was alive.

"What the fuck was *that*?" Terin asked.

Forcing himself to look away from Kalisandre, Graeson studied the destruction from the explosion. Black soot covered the floor near the rubble, and an acrid smell lingered in the air.

"Seems like the same explosives the Frenzians used back home," Graeson said. "Maybe a toned-down version of it."

"Why would Domitius have one of those on him at a wedding?" Terin sputtered.

Graeson turned back to Terin and squinted at Kalisandre.

There were many questions spinning in Graeson's mind, and Terin's question was merely one of them.

"It seems like he had plans of his own," Graeson said.

"What do you think the chances are that Domitius was crushed?" Terin wondered.

Graeson snorted. "Not likely."

Terin's lips parted, but before he could say more, footsteps pounded down the hall, causing them to straighten.

"We need to go," Graeson urged, his mind spiraling. The Frenzian soldiers must have broken through the door to the tunnels beneath the temple. There was only one way out now, and based on the echo of the steps and the rattling of the cages, Graeson was not hopeful of an easy escape. He turned and called out, "Dani, enough."

But Dani didn't react. She kept digging as she repeated the same words over and over again. "He can't get away. He can't get away..."

She scratched at the wall, trying to get a hold of one of the fallen rocks in an attempt to reach the other side. Streaks of red smeared the stones from her bloodied nails.

Cursing under his breath, Graeson rushed over to her, pulling her up by the shoulders.

Mangled screams poured from Dani's lungs as she cried out, a desperate plea.

"Dani," Graeson rasped, tightening his hold around her. "He's gone."

"He can't be gone!" Dani shouted, twisting and clawing at Graeson's arms. "I have to kill him. I *have* to!"

As Graeson struggled to hold onto his friend without causing any harm, the pounding of the strangers' footsteps only grew louder. They had to move.

"We have more pressing things to deal with right now, Dani!"

"What could be more pressing than--" Dani choked on her words and froze in his arms.

The footsteps were now thunderous claps across the hard ground.

"Shit," Dani hissed.

With Dani finally regaining her senses, Graeson released her and swiftly drew the sword from its sheath. "If you want someone to kill, you're about to be in luck."

Dani wiped the tears away, leaving a wet streak through the thin layer of ash and grime that covered her brown cheeks. She pulled out a set of throwing knives from their holster, reeling in the rage. While Dani may not have a god inside her like Graeson, she was a born warrior--a fighter. She could turn off her emotions, bury the paralyzing anger, and transform it into something deadly.

This was the Dani Graeson had grown up with.

This was Fynn's wife--Danisinia Ferrios, the youngest general in Pontian history.

And by the gods, Graeson had forgotten how much he missed her. Even if he knew, deep down, that this face she wore was only a mask that hid the pain that was unfurling like a dark web inside her body.

Still, it was good to have her back, even for a moment.

"Terin, grab Kalisandre and get behind us," Dani commanded. "When we say run, you run. From the pattern of their footsteps, I would guess there are maybe three coming our way. Graeson and I will hold them off as you get out of here. You're weak--"

Terin bristled at the remark. "I'm not--"

"Protect her," Dani ordered, grabbing Terin by the collar as she cut him off. "We didn't come all this way for nothing. Got it?"

Frowning, Terin nodded in defeat, though his hand twitched at his hip where his short blade was sheathed.

Dani released him and turned to Graeson next. Sweat dripped from Dani's brow as she bounced on her feet. A glimmer of fear sparked in her hazel eyes, but she quickly hid it. "We strike first and ask questions later, yeah?"

"Works for me," Graeson said, twisting his sword as he readied himself.

Despite the exhaustion from the earlier battle that interrupted the royal wedding and the force of the explosion that had thrown them back, Graeson still had some fight left in him. If it meant Kalisandre and his friends could escape the temple alive, he would do whatever it took.

As the footsteps grew louder, his heart rate accelerated, hammering against his ribcage.

You would have nothing to fear if you just let go, the god whispered in the back of Graeson's mind.

Graeson snarled back, *Now is not the time.*

The god caged within beat against the mental door, demanding to be let loose, but Graeson ignored his pleas as his vision reddened with fury.

They had come too far for this to be over now, for things to end here in this decrepit space. Graeson would not die in a cramped tunnel beneath this temple, fighting for air among the dust motes and soot.

This would not be how his and Kalisandre's story ended.

Torchlight bounced off the walls, casting eerie shadows and revealing glints of steel. Dani shifted on her feet and took a tentative step forward, her fingers flexing over the hilt of the throwing knife.

Without hesitating, Graeson stormed forward, his sword gleaming in the flickering light. As their attackers rounded the corner, the shadows obscuring their features, he swung, only to have his arm knocked back. Then, in one breath, Graeson's legs were swept off the ground, and his back hit the floor with a loud *smack*.

Pain spiked through his body, and he hissed out, gritting his teeth. He tried to push himself up, but a weight came crashing down upon him, forcing him back to the ground.

The assailant, masked in shadows, grabbed the chest plate and slammed Graeson's back against the concrete, sending pain wracking through his body.

Graeson's fingers tightened around the hilt of his sword. But as he prepared to strike, Dani's shout ripped through the air. "Graeson!"

He snapped his head in her direction, the sound too urgent to dismiss despite the enemy atop him. When he found her still standing in front of the crumbled wall, not having moved an inch and with the throwing knife loose in her hand, Graeson's brows furrowed.

"Want to drop the blade, sunshine?" a feminine voice taunted.

Graeson turned his attention back to the person sitting on him. Their knees pressed into his thighs, and their hands locked his arms against the ground.

The rage faded from the corners of his vision as a nearby torch illuminated the person's face, revealing a halo of bright white hair that cascaded down and brushed his chest. A smudge of soot was smeared across her pale cheek.

Graeson blinked. "Ellie?" he exclaimed.

The Tetrian warrior winked, patting him gently on the face. "Glad to find you in one piece, Gray." Ellie leaned back, her knees still keeping him in place as if she didn't completely trust him.

As the god inside him seethed as Ellie stared down at him, Graeson didn't blame her.

"What the fuck are you doing here?" Graeson demanded, struggling to break free.

She shrugged. "Apparently, testing my luck with your blade."

The god tsked.

You knew, didn't you? Graeson asked.

Graeson could feel the god shrug. *I do not trust her.*

You don't trust her because she doesn't trust you.

Us, the god hissed in correction. *She doesn't trust us.*

She trusts me just fine.

The god cackled, the laughter sending a chill down Graeson's spine. *After all this time, you still think you and I are so different?*

"Gray?" Ellie called out, forcing Graeson's attention back to her.

He clenched his jaw but nodded.

Then, to the monster living within him, he said, *I am not you.*

The god chuckled but grew silent as he slipped back into his cell.

Ellie narrowed her eyes, assessing him. But after a moment, she stood and extended a hand. Graeson grabbed it gratefully.

"You're lucky we waited for you," Ellie remarked, helping him up. "If we hadn't come running when we heard the explosion, you would have been in a world of trouble if it was that easy to knock you off your feet."

Graeson grumbled but said nothing.

She was right, and they both knew it. He needed to get his head on straight, or else they would be in trouble the next time they came across someone *less* friendly.

"What happened?" Dani asked, having joined them. Terin stood beside her with Kalisandre's limp form already in his arms.

Graeson had the urge to reach out to Kalisandre and take her from Terin. But if he had almost hurt Ellie, who's to say he wouldn't hurt Kalisandre, too?

He folded his hands over his chest and peered at the other two who stood panting behind Ellie. Like the rest, the Princess of Tetria was covered in blood and soot. Medenia leaned against Emmett, her arm wrapped around the Pontian.

"We ran into some trouble on the way down," Ellie explained. "But we're mostly all right."

Terin shifted his hold on Kalisandre and asked, "Medenia?"

The princess's eyes widened as she pointed to herself. "Me? Oh, I'm perfectly fine," she said with a saccharine smile, the torch's flames reflecting vibrantly in her eyes. "I haven't had this much excitement in a *long* time. After sitting in so many council meetings, I was nervous that all my training would have been forgotten." She blew a raven-black strand of hair from her face. "Safe to say it hasn't in the slightest."

"You sure about that?" Dani asked, pointing to Emmett beside her.

"Oh, he's been better," Medenia said, adjusting her arm beneath Emmett's as he leaned more of his weight against her, his complexion a sickly hue. "He's not hurt, but he's not too keen on the sight of blood, apparently."

Emmett gagged, slapping a hand over his mouth.

"Got it," Dani said, grimacing slightly.

"Now that that's settled," Ellie said, "we really should get going. If the guards we ran into knew to check here, then others will surely follow. They've all filed out of the temple, so we should use the crowded streets to our advantage while we can."

Graeson nodded and turned to Terin.

"No, I've got her," Terin assured, holding his sister tighter to his chest. "I'm tired and draining quickly. I need to stay in contact with her, or else she could wake up sooner than we want. And right now, we don't need anything else to worry about. Just"--he adjusted his hold on her--"go."

Graeson hesitated, gnawing on the bottom of his lip in uncertainty. "Are you sure? I can--"

"I'm sure," Terin said, his words clipped.

Before Graeson could push the issue more, Ellie added, "Come on. We have no time to argue about this and no time to deal with your overbearing masculinity, Gray."

"My overbearing masculinity?" Graeson scoffed. "I'm not over--"

Ellie snatched his hand and pulled him after her, cutting him off. "Not the time," she snapped with a roll of her eyes.

Then they were running back through the halls, and Graeson had no choice but to follow.

When they came across the cells, the caged animals within thrashed against the iron bars, clawing at them. Rancid, hot breath filled the narrow hall as they snarled and hissed. Even though it pained him to leave them caged, Graeson kept his gaze forward. They couldn't afford to stop.

They retraced their steps through the tunnels beneath the temple. Their boots were a rancorous roar in the damp tunnel, and their breaths were heavy as their chests heaved to keep up with their need for air. As they neared the beginning of the tunnel, bodies littered the floor, and blood was splattered across the walls in a grotesque display of violence. Behind Graeson, Emmett whimpered. Even though Emmett was by no means a soldier, he should have known what he was getting into when he agreed to leave the safety of the island and accompany them. Then again, it was nearly impossible to prepare oneself for the way death wrapped its claws around its victims. No training could prepare you for the brutality and horror of a fight that ended in death. Or the way death tainted the air and lingered on your skin.

As they ran past the bodies, Graeson gave Ellie a side-eyed glance.

Ellie smirked. "What? Did you think I was joking?"

Graeson snorted, shaking his head. "Did you have to leave such a mess?"

Ellie cackled. "Oh, like we had the time to clean up?"

Graeson cocked a brow and glanced over his shoulder.

Kalisandre bobbled in her brother's arms. Her brows twisted at the center of her forehead while whatever dream Terin concocted consumed her senses. The urge to hold Kalisandre and ensure her safety himself filled his body to the point where it pained him not to reach out.

Yet perspiration dripped from Terin's face. Exhaustion was wearing on him quickly. After having knocked out so many guards in the temple when the attack began, Terin's well was depleting. Every ounce he had left of his gift needed to be focused solely on Kalisandre.

So, as much as Graeson wanted to take Kalisandre from Terin, instead he kept running, on high alert, his sword in his hand and determination weighing on his heart.

When they ascended the steps to the entrance, smoke seeped through the cracks, and Graeson skirted to a stop. Behind the door, the heat from the fire permeated the small space.

"This way," Ellie said, heading toward the hallway Graeson and Terin hadn't ventured down.

Inside the attached room, a single desk sat against the wall with papers strewn across it as if someone had quickly dug through them with little care. Tall stacks of religious texts sat atop a shelf. A priest's robe hung on the wall.

Ellie rushed past it all, heading straight for the door at the back of the room.

"Wait!" Dani called out as Ellie reached for the door handle.

"What?" Ellie asked, her hand pausing in the air.

Dani looked back at Kalisandre. "She's wearing a damn wedding dress! If we go out there with her like this, we'll be spotted in seconds." She turned to Emmett. "Can you cover her?"

Emmett shoved his hands into his pockets and shook his head.

"No?" Dani asked, eyes wide.

Emmet shrugged, offering an apologetic look. "I'm empty."

Graeson dragged Emmett by the back of his shirt. "What do you mean *you're empty*?" He spat, shaking Emmett by the collar. "You've hidden hundreds of identities at the cavern, yet you can't hide one person right now?"

"I'm drained. After the wedding--" Emmett exhaled, his skin thin beneath his eyes emphasizing the thin blue veins beneath. "I have nothing left."

Graeson's hand tightened around Emmett's collar, his knuckles blanching. "And you're just *now* telling us?" he demanded.

"It--it never came up," Emmett stammered, face pale. "It was hard to say anything when we were running for our lives!"

Graeson shoved Emmett away with a disgusted groan.

"What do we do now?" Ellie asked, glancing at their group in worry.

Graeson looked around the room, searching for anything that could help, but all he found was the priest's robe. If a wedding dress was bound to attract someone's attention, so would the priest's overly ornate robe.

"Is she wearing a slip?" Medenia asked.

Dani reached for Kalisandre's skirts, and the fabric rustled as Dani searched beneath the layers of tulle. "She is," she answered.

"Perfect. Terin, set her down," Medenia said.

Terin did as the princess requested and placed Kalisandre on her feet, holding her up by her shoulders.

Graeson stepped forward, hands clenched at his side. "What are you doing? She cannot go out there with nothing but a slip on."

Ellie snorted. "See? This is the overbearing masculinity I was referring to." She shoved Graeson aside as she went to help unlace Kalisandre's dress. "We have no other choice."

Graeson narrowed his gaze at the Tetrian, who only shrugged in response.

Medenia rolled her eyes and gave her back to Ellie. She pointed over her shoulder to the back of her dress. "Ellie, would you mind?"

"What are you doing?" Graeson asked, furrowing his brow in confusion.

Medenia waved him off. "Unlace me, Ellie."

"I was fine with making him angry, but fine," Ellie mumbled.

Once the dress was unlaced, Medenia stepped out of it, leaving her in nothing but a black slip that hit her mid-thigh. She bent over and swept the dress off the ground, then held it out to Dani. "Here. Put her in this, and let's go."

Dani turned to Kalisandre and began shifting her out of the shredded dress.

Cheeks aflame, Graeson swallowed and turned away. His attention quickly snapped to Emmett, who was still looking in the women's direction, and he snatched the man by the collar and spun him around.

"Hey!" Emmett shouted.

Graeson growled as fabric rustled behind them. With one seething glare from Graeson, Emmett quickly snapped his mouth shut.

As Graeson tapped his foot against the ground, the Frenzian armor he still wore grew increasingly uncomfortable and tight around his body. When he was about to say something, his patience waning, Dani said, "Let's go."

When Graeson spun around, a heaping pile of fabric covered in blood and soot lay across the floor. The extravagant wedding dress was unrecognizable with its edges torn and battered. Kalisandre now wore a simple sage green dress, which hung over her feet when Terin lifted her into his arms once more.

The door creaked open, calling Graeson's attention away from Kalisandre.

Ellie held up a finger as she peered out. "All clear," she said a moment later.

They filtered through the door and into a shaded alleyway. Smoke filled the air, tainting their lungs and coating their skin in ash. Somewhere nearby glass shattered, and people screamed. Timber burned as destruction besieged the kingdom.

As Dani stepped beside Graeson, she looked around and asked, "Where's--"

"Here!" a voice said down the alley. Sylvia's freckled face appeared, their auburn hair flying behind them as they rushed toward the group, waving a hand. Excitement twisted their mouth into a wicked smile. "Took you all long enough."

"We ran into some trouble," Dani admitted, walking to her friend.

Sylvia grabbed Dani's arm, their amber eyes widening at the sight of the binding wrapped around it. "Are you all right?"

Instead of answering, Dani snatched her arm from Sylvia's grasp. "What's the outlook, Sylv?"

Concern drew Sylvia's brows together, but they didn't question Dani's change of subject. Instead, they sighed and said, "Not great. It's going to be tricky getting out to the horses. More and more soldiers are crowding the streets. They're all searching for the lost bride while struggling to maintain some semblance of order as they try to usher the crowd away from the spreading fire."

"Just what we need," Dani grumbled, face twisted in a scowl.

"Bright side? The streets are fucking crazy. Everyone's panicking and running around like their heads have been cut off." Sylvia raised a brow, shifting on their feet. "Speaking of, were you able to...?"

Dani shook her head. "The bull king lives."

Sylvia bit down on their lip but nodded. They scanned the group, and their brows twisted. "Where are Moris and Armen?" they asked.

Graeson brushed his fingers through his hair. "Armen ran when things started going south."

"He *ran?*" Dani spat, spinning around. "You didn't tell me that!"

Graeson's hand fell, slapping his thigh. "When did I have the time, Dani?"

"That fucking bastard." Dani spat on the ground. "I knew he was no good."

"And Moris?" Sylvia pressed, quieter this time with more hesitancy filling their voice.

Graeson and Terin exchanged uneasy glances, and the truth hung heavy in the space between them.

Finally, Graeson shook his head. "He didn't make it," he said quietly.

Dani squeezed Sylvia's hand, and a moment of grief passed between the pair.

When Graeson and the twins decided to come to Pontia months ago, the first people Dani wanted to join them were the two soldiers who had been at her side since she was a private in the military. Moris, Sylvia, and Dani had been in the same squadron when they initially enlisted.

Outside of Graeson and the twins, Sylvia and Moris were Dani's closest friends. They were strong-willed and good company.

Moris deserved more than to be abandoned in a burning temple. He deserved more than a silent moment between friends. He deserved so much more; however, there was no time to grieve the dead. The gods would not grant them that opportunity.

If the day was any indication, Moris would not be the last friend to meet an untimely end in the coming months. This was only the beginning. The two soldiers before him knew that all too well.

So, when water filled Sylvia's eyes, they blinked it away and straightened. "His sacrifice will not be in vain," they said, voice laced with determination.

Dani nodded in agreement and peered down the alley, where the streets were flooded with panicked wedding guests and civilians. She crossed her arms, tapping a finger along her arm. "Sylvia, do you have any more of those explosives?"

A devious smile lit Sylvia's face, shifting the freckles on their pale face. "Let's burn this fucking place to the ground."

CHAPTER 2
MYRA

A GUTTURAL SCREAM RIPPED THROUGH MYRA'S LUNGS AS THE WALL collapsed. She cowered on the floor, her arms covering her head. Tears filled her eyes, but she could not decipher whether it was because of the dust and smoke surrounding her, the king's nails biting into her arm, or the sight of Kallie disappearing before her eyes.

Myra had betrayed her closest friend.

She had lied to her and pretended to be someone she wasn't.

She, like Kallie, had been strung along by the king for years. The only difference, however, was that Myra was all too aware of the king's hold on her, while Kallie had no idea.

However, Myra had no time to dwell on the consequences of her actions, not while King Domitius was dragging her down the tunnel and away from the collapsed wall.

"Move!" the king shouted through a fit of coughs, his voice dripping in vitriol she had come to know intimately by now.

"What about Kallie?" Myra asked, voice shaking as she looked back at the wall through tear-stained eyes.

Anger and terror poured from the wall as muffled screams

seeped through the cracks of the pile of rocks. Yet, beside her, the only emotions coming from the king were determination and fury. Not a trace of fear tainted Myra's tongue.

"She will do what needs to be done. Now, run," the king commanded, his fingers tightening around her forearm so hard it hurt.

With tears streaming down her cheeks, Myra obeyed the king and ran.

She ran despite her body screaming at her to disobey. That alone was enough.

She ran despite her heart shattering.

She ran because there was *no other choice.*

Torment and agony dripped from the walls of the tunnel, but there was no time to process the emotions spinning around her as the king dragged Myra through the winding halls, past more cells of malnourished animals and corpses.

The creatures Myra had seen on their way into the tunnels as Dani had run after them would haunt Myra's nightmares for the rest of her days.

Since Myra and Kallie arrived in Frenzia, Myra had felt something strange within the castle's walls. A feeling that crept over her skin and clawed at her throat, but she hadn't been able to place it. It lurked in the halls, twisting and turning.

The moment Myra stepped foot in the temple that morning, however, the feeling overtook her, almost forcing her to her knees.

Now, she knew why.

The Frenzians were doing horrible, unspeakable things. Things that Myra couldn't even begin to fathom.

When a humanoid creature with wings and ruby eyes slammed against its cell's bars earlier, Myra had shrieked in horror. She had looked urgently toward the king, yet he only kept running, nearly dragging Myra across the floor behind him as she lost her footing.

She felt no fear, no surprise, no curiosity from him. At first, Myra was astounded. How could the king not have reacted? How could he have kept going after seeing the wild creature? A creature that, by all accounts, should not have existed.

There were many things Myra did not understand about the king, but one thing had always been crystal clear: he was a monster. Of course, seeing another monster would not frighten him. Like calls to like.

Then, the tunnel split into two paths, and the king tugged Myra to the left. And it was the lack of hesitation, the lack of thought in which the king chose which path to take that told Myra everything she needed to know.

The king did not react because he already knew about the creatures beneath the Frenzian temple.

Myra peered at him as he dragged her through the tunnels in the opposite direction from which they had come. "The creatures in the cell--" she began, but the king interrupted before she could continue.

"The Frenzians will create more of them."

"Create? They *created* them?" Myra asked in horror.

The king scoffed. "Of course. How else would they exist?" he retorted.

Myra's mouth hung open in shock. "They're...they're monsters."

His lips curled into a cruel smile. "Yes, they're magnificent, aren't they?"

But Myra knew then that they were referring to two different things. While the king admired the rabid creatures living in captivity, Myra couldn't help but feel immense empathy for them-- for the pain they must have undergone and the cruelty they faced. Only a portion of it lingered in the tunnel, dampening it.

The creatures within the cells were not the monsters; the

Frenzians were. The beasts were simply a result of the Frenzians' monstrosity.

As their anguish polluted the air, crawled across her skin, and seeped into her pores, Myra could do nothing but put up her walls and cut off her ability to identify the emotions as best she could. Yet, even as they reached a door at the end of the tunnel and Domitius yanked it open, tossing Myra over the threshold, emotions continued to linger as if she had crawled through a spiderweb and the sticky threads still clung to her flesh.

Myra blinked at the light streaming in from the windows high above.

The tunnel had led them back to the castle, where guards were running across the halls in a frenzy.

King Domitius shouted at the nearest guard, "You, stop!"

The guard jerked to a halt, startled as his eyes bounced from Domitius to Myra. "Your Majesty," he said, bowing. "We've been looking everywhere for you. They just got the doors of the temple open not too long ago. We found King Rian injured from the fray but could not find you nor the princess."

The guard looked at Myra again. He glanced at her blonde hair, a stark contrast to Kallie's brunette waves, and turned back to the king with a furrowed brow. "Have you...have you seen the princess, Your Majesty?"

Domitius merely shook his head. "Sound the alarm and send all soldiers to the streets. My daughter, King Rian's bride, has been taken again."

CHAPTER 3
GRAESON

SOMEWHERE IN THE VILLAGE, A BELL RANG LOUD AND PIERCING--A warning for the flames licking at the sky. The people in the streets picked up their pace, bumping into each other as names were shouted in an attempt for friends and family to locate one another.

Panic rang in every voice, in every fearful, wide-eyed gaze as heads swiveled over the crowd. Mothers and fathers ushered children forward, some picking up the children who were too small to keep up as they raced through the streets.

The wedding was said to be the largest gathering of Vaneria since blood poured down the city during the Great War. And for once, Graeson was thankful for the throng filling the road. To navigate the streets more easily while attracting less attention, they split into three groups: Graeson with Terin and Kalisandre, Dani with Emmett and Sylvia, and Ellie with Medenia.

All around them, people ran past, shoving one another as everyone raced to escape the fire and smoke. Usually, Graeson would have despised weaving between the panicked people, their bodies pressing against his, their heat suffocating him and ringing around his neck as the world grew smaller and smaller.

But at that moment, Graeson was thankful for the chaos pressing in on him from all sides. Their clothes, torn and burned from the kiss of the flames, which would have turned heads in any other scenario, blended with the rest of the disheveled crowd.

Adrenaline pumping through his veins, Graeson scanned the endless sea of people, his eyes sweeping over the faces rushing past. Up ahead, the sun hit metal, catching his attention.

Several soldiers walked against the flow of the crowd, their gazes sweeping across the pedestrians with an intense focus that had Graeson clenching his jaw. They tugged every woman that neared them to a stop. With rough hands, they yanked the women's faces up, turning them side-to-side. When they noted the eyes were too brown, the hair too light, the features not quite right, they moved to the next one.

While Kalisandre might have shed the bustling white gown, the change of clothes would only give a guard a momentary pause. If they were familiar with her, she would be recognized quickly. Graeson held back a curse.

Terin inched closer to Graeson as they weaved between the clusters of people and whispered, "Are you sure this is a good idea?"

Graeson's palms grew slick with sweat.

They cannot have her, the god inside growled.

As if Graeson would let them.

Graeson peered at Terin from the corner of his eye. Kalisandre was strewn across Terin's shoulder, and his arms were wrapped around her waist. The back of her head was matted with blood, her skin was covered in soot, and the sleeves of Medenia's dress hung loosely off her shoulders. She was far from the picturesque bride she appeared to be only an hour ago.

Now, to the people in the crowd, the princess would look like any other guest who had suffered an injury during the mayhem, and maybe they could use that to their advantage.

As much as seeing her in such a state sent Graeson's mind spiraling, she was alive, and that was what mattered. Everything else they would figure out later.

Still, Graeson couldn't help but think something was off--that something was incredibly, painfully wrong about the situation.

Domitius had let them go. He had let *Kalisandre* go.

While a gnawing feeling of unease nagged at Graeson, there was no time to decipher the king's motives, not now.

So, instead of driving himself insane, Graeson dragged his gaze away from the princess and focused on the path ahead. "I guess we will find out, won't we?"

The guards inched closer, inch by inch.

Graeson peered up at the clock tower.

They had five minutes for Dani and the others to make their move.

But five minutes could also spell their deaths if the guards spotted them before then.

Only a few people separated the nearest guard from them now. The guard's attention went to the next woman in the crowd, but his attention quickly passed her when he noticed her blonde hair. He began searching the crowd again, and Graeson turned on his heel.

"This way," Graeson ordered, tugging Terin behind him and dipping down the nearest street.

Graeson led them down the alley and into the thick shadows. His hand fell atop the hilt of his sword, his body abuzz with new energy.

"This looks like a dead end," Terin said, confusion and fatigue flooding his voice.

"That's because it is," a stranger remarked behind them.

Terin cursed, his steps faltering and pebbles skittering across the ground.

But Graeson was already spinning around, his sword drawn and at the ready. He stepped forward, putting Terin and Kalisandre protectively behind him.

The guard looked Graeson up and down, his lip twitching. "Where's your helmet, soldier?" he asked.

Graeson feigned looking around for the helmet that he had discarded in the temple before shrugging. "I never really cared for the tacky thing."

The guard's hand tightened around the hilt of his sword, his eyes darting to Kalisandre. "Where'd you get the armor?"

"One of your buddies, probably." Graeson smiled at the guard. "He's dead, or else I would ask his name."

The guard snarled, taking another step closer. "Give me the princess."

Rage rose in Graeson's chest, but he tamped it down just enough to hiss, "She is not yours to take."

The guard merely laughed, skillfully twirling his sword as he adjusted his stance. Then, he lifted his weapon and charged, his blade slashing through the air.

"This will only take a moment, Ter," Graeson said as he rolled his neck, cracking it.

Metal hit metal as their weapons collided. The man cried out in fury, eliciting a low chuckle from Graeson.

"How long have you been in the guard?" Graeson asked, as his heels dug into the ground, not moving an inch as the guard tried to press forward.

The man blinked. "Excuse me?"

"I would wager only a year or so. Is this your first fight?"

The man's lips parted, but no response came.

Graeson nodded in understanding, and with a flick of his sword, he sent the man stumbling back into the side of the building. "Thought so. Only a fool would not call for support."

The guard slammed into the wall with a loud *oomph*. As he

pushed himself away from the wall, he rolled his shoulder, causing his shining armor to creak.

"At least now you won't look so fresh," Graeson said, eyeing the new scratches marring the man's armor.

"Come on, Gray. Stop messing with him. We don't have time for this."

Graeson rolled his eyes. They still had two minutes at least by his count, but if Terin wanted him to end this quickly, so be it. "Let's get this over with, shall we?"

Standing, the guard growled in rage, and Graeson struggled to hold back his laughter.

"You're a cocky bastard," the guard seethed.

Graeson deflected the guard's strike and twisted around, pressing his blade against the man's neck. "So I've been told," he taunted with an amused smirk.

Then, the earth shook as a loud *boom* rocked the capital.

Screams erupted across the city. Dust fell off the rooftops above them, coating Graeson's shoulders and making him cough.

The guard gasped. "What the fuck--"

"About time," Graeson muttered. Then in one fell swoop, Graeson removed the blade and knocked the man out with the butt of his hilt.

"That's our sign," Graeson urged, propping the unconscious guard against the wall. "Let's go."

Then, they were running.

CHAPTER 4

KALLIE

*O*N HER HANDS AND KNEES, K*ALLIE HEAVED*. H*ER BREATHS CAME IN A torrent, rushed and labored. Each intake of air threatened to burst through her ribcage. But no matter how much oxygen she pulled into her lungs, it wasn't enough.*

Kallie didn't know how long she had been training, but every muscle screamed at her to take a break. Nonetheless, she couldn't stop. Not when her father wrapped his hand around her arm and demanded she continue, his shouts drowning out the intense ache shaking her to her core.

The king yanked her off the floor, and Kallie's very being begged to fall back to the ground as her legs shook beneath her. Sweat dripped down her neck beneath the haggard braid and coated her back, dampening her blouse.

He tightened his grip, his fingers pressing deeper against her skin, bruising. "If your body is weak, your mind will be too!" Domitius shouted at her, the whites of his eyes streaked with red.

Kallie's eyes watered, but she kept her mouth closed and silently begged for the tears to vanish.

The king shoved her forward with a snarl, and Kallie fell to her knees.

"You are despicable! You must push through the pain. Have I taught you nothing?"

She struggled to answer, "I--I'm--"

"No excuses!" he roared.

Kallie dropped her gaze, landing on her arm where the red imprint of her father's fingers slowly faded.

"Again!" The king's command echoed in the large, cold space beneath the marble castle.

Kallie's arms trembled beneath her, and she bit her lip. She took a deep breath and began to count silently to herself.

One.

Two.

Three.

Exhale.

Four.

Five--

"I said again!" he spat.

Kallie wiped the bead of sweat from her forehead. Every muscle cried out for her to take a rest. But she couldn't until she had proven herself-- until she had shown her father what she could do.

On trembling limbs, Kallie pushed off the floor and wiped the sweat from her palms onto her trousers. Then she ran, head-first. Her arms pumped at her sides as she weaved through the obstacle course the king had built beneath the castle.

"Faster!" the king shouted. Although Kallie could no longer see him because of the walls of the maze, she heard his words clearly enough, as if he were beside her.

She ran faster.

She ran harder.

She dove as the triggered arrows came for her, biting back tears as an arrow whizzed by too close to her head.

KALLIE GASPED, her eyes shooting open.

The waterfall of the Whispering Springs roared, a rush of noise filling her ears. But the sound of the water was not the reason for her body growing more numb by the minute. It wasn't the reason her hands trembled or her teeth chattered. Neither was it the reason for the buzzing that filled her head.

No, it was the person sitting cross-legged atop one of the boulders at the edge of the small lake--the man who should not have been there at all.

Kallie knew in every bone in her body that her brother was dead. However, Fynn looked just as alive as the night they were on the ship before everything went wrong. Before Sebastian and his crew surrounded him and slaughtered him.

His brown hair was disheveled as if he had been running his hands through it incessantly, a habit not unlike him. His clothes were as immaculate as always, perfectly pressed with his collar angled. A smirk plastered across his face. Yet when she met his deep brown eyes, a chilling emptiness caused her to shiver despite the brilliant, warm sun overhead.

"I don't understand," Kallie whispered, her body shaking and her feet sinking into the sand. She wrapped her arms around herself.

Fynn sighed and raked his fingers through his chestnut waves. "That's because you do not wish to hear the truth."

"No," she argued. "I already know the truth. My father--"

"Is a liar," Fynn said, interrupting. "He has been manipulating you, sister. He never cared about your well-being, only what you could provide him."

"You're wrong," she spat, nails biting into the sides of her arms as she squeezed herself tight.

None of this made sense.

Not Fynn being here, not this lucid dream that felt all too real.

Nothing her brother said made sense--not the words he claimed to be true--the words attempting to unwrite her story, tangling what she once thought true. Fynn claimed that her father was not to be trusted and was not the person she believed him to be--that he did not care about her.

But her brother was wrong, so incredibly wrong.

Kallie pressed her palms against her temples and rocked back and forth. Her chest tightened with each loud thud of her heart. Her breaths grew more shallow as her lungs constricted and the world threatened to close in around her.

Her father would never lie to her.

He would never betray her.

Kallie couldn't breathe. She couldn't think. She couldn't make sense of anything anymore.

As hot tears burned the back of her eyes, she coughed, trying to clear her throat and steady her racing heart. However, as she inhaled, smoke filled her lungs and only made the shaking worse as she tried and failed to breathe in fresh air.

None of this was right, *she thought.* Everything was wrong.

From the way the sun beat down upon the sand, to the picturesque clear skies, to Fynn staring at her, to the very words coming from his mouth.

It was all wrong.

Wrong.

Wrong.

Wrong.

"Terin?"

Kallie blinked as Fynn's voice cut through the air like a knife, piercing and sharp. Through tear-stained eyes, she stared at her brother. Her hands fell from her head, and she pressed her palms into the sand in a feeble attempt to ground herself.

"Wh-what are you doing?" Kallie asked, her voice trembling.

Fynn stood upon the boulder, looking up, his eyes bouncing across the sky as if searching for something. As if Terin was looking down upon them.

For a moment, Fynn's gaze remained fixed on the too-blue sky.

Then, he nodded once before returning his attention to Kallie. Sorrow filled his gaze, every curve of his features seeping with pity.

Kallie hated it, yet she could not erase the expression from Fynn's face.

"I already told you, Kallie," he murmured. "You are not listening. I thought that..." Fynn sighed and shook his head, his gaze dropping to the sand momentarily. When he looked at her once more, something flashed across his countenance, stirring an inexplicable emotion within her. "It is clear that you are not ready to see the truth."

"What truth?" Kallie asked, furrowing her brows in confusion.

"Once you are ready, you will know. But you need to gain control of yourself first."

"I am in control," Kallie shouted.

Fynn offered her a sad smile. "Unfortunately, dear sister, you are gravely mistaken."

Kallie dug her hands into the sand, the grains filling the space beneath her nails. "What are you saying?" she demanded.

But before Fynn could respond, a sharp pain spiked at the back of her head, and Kallie squeezed her eyes shut.

This isn't real, *Kallie told herself.* It can't be real. Fynn isn't here. Fynn is dead.

"Kalisandre, look at me," Fynn's voice beckoned her.

Kallie ignored him, though, keeping her hands pressed into the sand as if she could will the sight away. She sat there, reeling as the confusion spun in her stomach and gave way to nausea.

Fynn was wrong.

He had to be.

Because if he was right, her entire life had been a lie.

But that could not be possible.

Even contemplating that what he spoke was the truth made her sick to her stomach. He didn't know what he was talking about. He didn't know her father. He didn't know her.

"Kallie," he whispered, voice pained.

Then, as the seconds passed, ever so slowly, Kallie peeled her eyes open. As she looked up at the man who shared her blood, the golden hue around Fynn's head began to fade as the colors of this world melted.

Dark shadows were now cast across Fynn's face. His eyes had since dulled, and his brown waves had lost their sheen. When she looked at the sky, she noticed even the sun had dimmed, its brilliance having dulled to a muted hue as if a film covered the world.

"You must fight it, Kallie," Fynn said.

"Fight what?" Kallie screamed, slapping a fist against the sand. "What are you talking about?"

A smile flicked at the corner of Fynn's lips, and sadness coated his eyes as he said, "The truth is always hard to hear, especially when we have spent our entire lives looking the other way, not knowing what stood before us. But Kallie, you need to look. You cannot hide from it anymore."

"Hide from what? Speak plainly!" Anger rose in her throat, and her body began to shake again.

Fynn sighed, his chest rising as he brushed a hand through his hair. "When you're ready, perhaps I will explain, but for now, there is no use. You will only push the truth away and bury it far too deep where you cannot reach it."

"Ready for what? What truth?" *Tears streamed down her face as she begged for an answer, for an explanation, for* anything *that didn't feel wrong.*

Every limb, every ounce of her blood screamed at her, shouting about the wrongness of his words, his voice, this place. And yet, the wrongness didn't prevent the tears from falling. The wrongness didn't keep her from reaching out a hand.

"I have already told you," Fynn said with a shake of his head. "I cannot do anything for you until you're ready."

Kallie attempted to stand, but her legs failed her, sending her crashing to the ground.

Still, she would not give up. She needed answers.

Kallie crawled, her nails clawing at the sand as she hurried forward. But every yard she gained, every inch she came forward, the more Fynn seemed to fade away.

With her panic rising, Kallie reached forward, her anguished cry filling the air, "Fynn!" Tears continued to fall down her face as she struggled against time to reach him before he vanished. "Don't--Don't leave me!"

Fynn made no move to reach out to her, nor did he take a step toward her. Instead, he only gave her a small smile that struck her in the chest.

"Please, Fynn!" Kallie yelled. "I'm ready! Whatever it is, I'm ready!" Yet, as loud as she shouted the words, they were heavy on her tongue. As if even her voice knew she was lying. Because how could she be ready if she didn't even know what she needed to be prepared for?

Kallie pushed herself onto shaking legs but couldn't gain purchase and fell face-first into the sand. The sand began to melt beneath her, and Kallie's eyes widened in horror. The more she struggled and the more she tried to reach him, the deeper she sunk.

She looked up at Fynn, pleading, begging.

Still, Fynn did not move, his body slowly fading from existence. As he stared down at her, no light shone in his eyes. No sparkle, no smirk.

"You are more capable than you believe yourself to be, Kalisandre," he said, his voice growing more distant, just like his form. "I only hope that you will realize that before it is too late."

Fynn's voice swept over her, wrapping around her like a warm blanket.

Kallie tried to grab it and hold onto it, but it slipped through her grasp. Desperate, she lunged, screaming as she attempted to wrap her arms *around her brother and force him to stay. But her foot sunk further into the sand, and the edge of the rock slammed into her stomach, knocking the wind out of her.*

When she blinked and pushed herself up, Fynn was gone.

Then, the world was inked in black once more.

CHAPTER 5
GRAESON

GRAESON AND TERIN WERE THE FIRST TO REACH THE HORSES NEAR the Draconian River. As they made their way out of the inner city, detonations erupted as Sylvia and the others set off their explosives. Dani's plan had worked perfectly. Buildings crumbled, people screamed, and Frenzia fell into chaos. The guards were pulled away in every direction, the lost bride only a secondary thought as small fires threatened to consume the capital in earnest.

Even as the fire continued to roar behind them, Graeson knew Domitius would not rest until he had Kalisandre back. Graeson was not so foolish to think that the king's game was over just because Domitius caused the tunnel to collapse and separated himself from Kalisandre.

On the contrary, everything in Graeson's body told him this was just the beginning. Soon, the king's men would come for them.

Thankfully, as Graeson and Terin took the opportunity to rest and shed the Frenzian armor, the others quickly joined them. When Graeson spotted Sylvia, the same wicked gleam coated their amber eyes. When Sylvia spotted the last two unclaimed horses, a mix of anger and somberness filled their expression.

"Come on," Graeson said, cutting through the silence as his footsteps crackled fallen leaves and detritus. "We should get going before we lose our advantage."

Sylvia nodded, wiping their cheeks with the back of their hand and mounting their horse.

"What do you want to do with her?" Ellie asked, nodding in Kalisandre's direction.

Terin shifted his sister in his arms as he eyed Graeson wearily. "Kallie will remain in a coma for a while if I am not in contact with her, but it will drain me faster if we're separated for too long."

"There is no discussion to be had. She'll ride with you, Terin," Graeson said. "She is small enough."

"It doesn't matter if Terin's horse can handle her weight. Riding two to a horse will still slow us down," Ellie argued, folding her arms over her chest.

"We have no other choice," Graeson retorted, heading to Terin.

"He's right, Ellie," Medenia sighed, guiding her horse toward them by its reins. "We will have to make do."

Ellie's lips thinned, but she didn't argue further.

Graeson tipped his head to his friend. "I've got her, Ter," Graeson said, his hands outstretched.

"Thanks," Terin mumbled, passing Kalisandre to Graeson before getting atop his horse.

Graeson tenderly brushed a stray wisp of hair from Kalisandre's face. Her soft features were smeared with dirt and blood, and her brows were drawn slightly together. He hesitated, his grip tightening around her. When she didn't stir, though, Graeson carefully hoisted her onto Terin's horse.

Soon, he promised.

THEY RODE HARD and fast through the forest, only stopping for short periods to let the horses rest and to relieve themselves. Time passed slowly in the woods, every snap of a branch or rustle of leaves making them jump with paranoia.

Although they seemed safe, the entire Frenzian military would be after them soon enough. The destruction left in their wake would only keep the Frenzians distracted for a limited time.

Dani made frequent loops around the area, ensuring no one followed. When she returned from her latest lap, she said to Graeson, "Tell me what happened with Armen."

"What is there to tell?" Graeson asked, focusing on the woods ahead.

"Come on. You obviously feel some way about it," Dani said, peering down at Graeson's hands, where he gripped the reins so tightly that his knuckles turned white.

Graeson loosened his hold slightly and sighed, but the tension in his neck remained. He shrugged haphazardly. "Armen and I have never been the best of friends. The man is a prick who can't see over his ego. It was only a matter of time before he betrayed us."

"Is that what you think happened? That he betrayed us?" Dani pressed.

"Armen is many things," Terin said ahead of them, joining in the conversation, "but he has always been loyal to the Crown."

Graeson snorted. "Apparently not as loyal as we thought."

However, Graeson couldn't deny that he had trusted Armen enough to bring him along. Despite his personal feelings toward Armen, Graeson had believed he was loyal. Even though Armen had spoken against Kalisandre, Graeson didn't think Armen would have been so selfish as to abandon them and their kingdom.

Graeson should have known better.

He should have listened to the god within. Because after all this time, when it came to mortals, the monster was right. More often than not, humans only cared about themselves.

"I just...I find it hard to believe," Terin finally mumbled, breaking the tense quiet.

"I do not know what to believe anymore," Graeson said, his voice growing cold. "But I do know this: whether Armen intentionally betrayed us or whether he simply ran to save his own life is only a matter of semantics. Either way, Moris is dead because of him."

Dani and Terin fell silent, the only sound accompanying them being the clatter of hooves as they continued their trek through the foreboding forest toward Tetria.

The sun slowly moved across the sky, casting rays of light pouring through the canopy of leaves above.

As they rode, Graeson struggled to keep his focus on their surroundings. His eyes kept drifting to Kalisandre, unable to resist stealing glances at her. His mind was consumed with too many questions and worries. How would they explain why they had taken her against her will a second time? Would they be able to undo whatever damage Myra had inflicted on Kalisandre's mind? Would Kalisandre be able to trust them? Would she ever be able to forgive them? The weight of the conversation weighed heavily on him as they traveled.

When the horses began to slow their pace, Ellie called out, "We need to rest. Night is coming soon. If we keep going, we will run the horses--"

"No," Graeson interrupted, snapping his attention away from his wayward thoughts. "We must keep going."

Ellie kicked her boots against the horse's sides and raced ahead. Turning suddenly, she brought the horse to an abrupt halt, forcing Graeson's mount to stand on her hind legs as she cantered.

Graeson gripped the reins and squeezed his thighs as the horse's front hooves smacked the ground, "By the gods! Are you--"

"We're stopping," Ellie shouted over him, looking past him and toward the others.

He bristled. "No, we need to--"

Ellie's gaze locked onto his, her intense black eyes meeting his piercing silver stare. "We're *stopping*," she hissed. "The horses need to rest, just as we do. Running ourselves ragged will do us no good."

Graeson clenched his jaw, his teeth grinding together as he glared at Ellie. She wasn't going to budge, and Graeson knew it.

By now, they had been traveling for several hours. The sun was dipping down in the sky, teetering just above the horizon. Shadows slithered quickly across the uneven terrain as evening neared.

He released a heavy sigh and glanced over his shoulder. "Dani?" he prompted.

Dani was already moving, guiding her horse around him and Ellie. She jerked her chin to the right. "I already found a place to lay low and rest until morning."

Graeson shifted his gaze toward Terin, biting his lip.

The prince was pushing his limits. Anyone could see that by the way his skin had dulled and his movements had slowed; just a bit longer and he might collapse.

Analyzing his options, Graeson returned his attention to the two women with a resigned sigh. "The moment dawn comes, we ride."

WHEN THEY HAD ENTERED the cave, Emmett practically threw himself onto the ground as he stretched out his limbs. "Gods, I never thought I would be thankful to be lying on stone."

Sylvia chuckled, but the light sound was short-lived as sorrow once again filled their gaze.

Without Moris' jokes cutting through the ever-present silence, his absence rang heavily in the cave with nothing left to distract them.

Moris was a good man. But Graeson had realized long ago that good men were often easiest to kill. Because the ones who didn't deserve to live--the people who destroyed, conquered, and slaughtered for their own advantage--were always the ones who refused to die.

Dani, sitting beside Sylvia, nudged them with a shoulder. Sylvia leaned into her, and Dani wrapped an arm around them. Dani's brows pinched in pain, though. The wound Dani had suffered earlier in the tunnels still caused her some grief. Graeson frequently found her wincing and touching her side, her palm sweeping over her stomach before she caught herself. She wouldn't be able to hide her pregnancy forever. However, it was futile to mention it since Dani would likely dismiss his concern and counter it with some spiteful retort.

So, Graeson kept his mouth shut as Sylvia and Dani silently mourned their comrade. He followed Terin as he placed Kalisandre gently on the ground.

"Here," Graeson said, quickly taking a seat on the other side of Kalisandre. He lifted her head and cradled it in his lap, gently brushing his knuckles across her forehead and sweeping away the loose strands of hair.

"How is she?" Graeson asked as Kalisandre remained asleep, lost in whatever dream Terin had woven for her.

Terin sighed as he slumped to the ground on the other side of her. "I am not sure what the king did to her, but her mind is a mess from what I can tell." He grimaced.

"How do you know that?" Medenia asked as she settled on the opposite wall of the cave.

"While I cannot read her mind like my brother could," Terin began, his gaze quickly flicking away from Dani as she flinched at the mention of her husband, "her mind has clearly been tampered with. It's a tangled mess, more so than before even." He furrowed his brow, stroking the scruff on his chin. "It's hard to explain if you haven't experienced it. I can still shift her dreams, but it's...harder. Finding the memories to call forth feels like I'm digging through piles of thick, heavy mud."

Graeson's brows twisted together as he observed Kalisandre's unconscious form. The torn piece of white fabric from her dress was now stained a muddied red color. He shifted her slightly and unwrapped the makeshift bandage from her head. As he peeled it back, he noted that the wound on the back of her head was no longer actively bleeding. Still, seeing her blood spread across the cotton sent a spiral of cold anger rising through his chest. This was all his fault. He shouldn't have fought her.

He should never have let her go when Domitius had first attacked them all those years ago. He should have held on tighter. If he had, then none of this would have happened.

"Here, Gray, use this," Ellie said, pulling a small square of fabric from her bag and calling Graeson back to the present. She poured liquid from one of the canteens on it before tossing the soaked rag to Graeson.

Emmett perked up from his spot on the ground, sniffing the air. "Is that liquor?" he asked eagerly.

Ellie scoffed, tucking the canteen back into her bag. "Not for you, it's not."

"What? Like it magically changes or something?" Emmett asked with a huff.

With an exasperated eye roll, Ellie placed her bag behind her, ignoring him.

Emmett let out a frustrated groan and flopped back onto the ground, throwing an arm over his eyes.

Shaking his head, Graeson gently patted the damp cloth against the back of Kalisandre's scalp, cleaning the wound. Once satisfied that the wound wouldn't get infected, Graeson set the rag aside and carefully readjusted Kalisandre. He leaned on his palms.

"Must she remain unconscious?" Medenia asked with a frown. "Why is she anyway? Hasn't she already been through enough?"

Before anyone else could respond, Dani mumbled, "Because she'll kill us when she finds out what we have done."

"Why take her in the first place then?" Medenia asked.

Graeson didn't need to raise his gaze to know Dani had turned to him. This was a question only he could answer.

He cracked his neck. "Taking her this way was not the original plan."

"You mean your intentions were *not* to force the woman you claim to love unconscious and drag her across the seven kingdoms unwillingly for the *second* time in the past year?" Ellie remarked, leaning against one side of the cave.

Graeson rolled his hand into a fist, an ember of anger growing into a spark inside him as the god stirred. "It's more complicated than that, and you know it."

Ellie eyed him quizzically as if she could hear the god's voice rearing its ugly head.

Graeson forced himself to look away from her when Medenia asked, "So, how long must she remain passed out?"

"Until she is ready," Terin answered with a sigh.

Medenia tilted her head in response. "What do you mean until she is ready? Ready for what?"

Terin rubbed his palms over his eyes in exasperation. "The last time I put her to sleep, it was easy to keep her unconscious. But this time? She's been fighting me almost every step of the way. If I release her completely, she will fight us."

"Are you sure?" Medenia raised a brow.

"Unfortunately, yes," Terin said. "Even if I wasn't, I do not think it is worth the risk. Not yet."

"How long can she remain like this then?" Ellie asked as she unfastened the leather strap that wrapped around her torso and held a series of throwing knives. As she placed it on the ground, the small weapons clattered together. "What's the longest you've kept anyone unconscious?"

Terin was quiet for a moment, his gaze fixed on the rough contours of the cave's ceiling. Although the evening was fast approaching, Graeson could still see the faint purple hue around Terin's eyes and the tiny web of green veins in the dim light.

"Two days," Terin whispered.

"*Two* days?" Ellie repeated in shock.

Terin cleared his throat and shrugged a shoulder. "Well, *almost* two days. When we were on the ship back to Pontia, Kallie hadn't handled the sea sickness well. I helped her sleep through a good portion of the trip."

"Was her mental state impacted because of that?" Medenia asked.

"She was slightly disoriented when she awoke but fine overall," Terin said.

"Is it safe to keep someone knocked out for so long?"

Dani shifted against the wall and said, "A couple of years ago, I suffered a major injury during a mission in Kadia. I was unconscious for a couple of weeks. My mind was intact, but it was my body that suffered the worst. Being dormant for so long made my muscles weak." Dani shrugged. "Whether or not it is safe is debatable, but I managed."

"What's the worst-case scenario then?" Ellie asked as she inspected one of her throwing knives. She ran a long finger over the blade as she pursed her lips.

"The worst case?" Terin's gaze flicked to Graeson.

Ellie twisted the knife and nodded. "We have about a week's journey ahead of us. What if she must remain unconscious for the remainder of the trip?" She raised her head and swept her gaze around the room. She cocked a brow. "Or do you expect her to go along with being captured *again* if you release her in a day or two?"

The muscles in Graeson's jaw ticked at the remark.

"If she is a danger--" Dani began, but Graeson interrupted.

"If she is *in* danger, we must be aware of it."

"Terin?" Ellie prompted.

Tugging on the ends of his hair, Terin said, "The worst-case scenario is that she falls into a coma and..."

"*And?*" Graeson prompted, his body tensing, his mind racing with endless possibilities of what could go wrong. His hand froze in Kalisandre's hair, unable to move until he knew what fate might await her.

A cold breeze swept into the cave as Terin met Graeson's stare.

Terin swallowed and dropped Graeson's stare to look at his sister. "And she doesn't wake up."

Dread coiled in his stomach. "But we're not going to let that happen," Graeson spat, swallowing down the thickness of his words.

"And what will you do to stop it, Gray?" Dani retorted. "Scare her mind back to normal?"

"We will figure it out," Graeson snapped in return. "Kalisandre is stronger than you give her credit for." Of that, he was certain.

Dani clicked her tongue. "You forget that she remains loyal to that man."

Graeson's jaw tightened briefly. "Only because of the hold he has on her."

"Why do you think Domitius just let her go then?" Dani asked, anger beginning to fill her voice. "He knows something that we do not. She is a danger to all of us."

"What do you suggest we do then, Dani?" Graeson challenged. "We cannot let the sacrifice of those who have died in the hopes of rescuing her be for naught."

Dani was standing now, and even from across the cave, Graeson could see the fire blazing in her hazel eyes. Sylvia tried to pull Dani back down, but Dani struggled against them. She spat on the floor before sitting down when Sylvia refused to let her go.

"I know all too well what has been sacrificed," she hissed, her lips curling into a sneer. "I am not willing to let more people die because of her or because of your carelessness."

"She will remain asleep until we are somewhere safe," Terin said. "I promise you that, Dani."

Graeson bit down but remained silent, aware he would be outnumbered if he argued. Nevertheless, it did not mean he had to agree with Terin's decision.

"And how long is that?" Ellie asked. "A day? A month? Terin, are you prepared for that?"

Terin grabbed his sword and whetstone and began sharpening his blade. "For my sister, I will do what I must." He shrugged, gaze determined.

Ellie arched a brow. "Even if that is true, we cannot keep her unconscious forever."

Nodding, Terin continued to work his blade. "You are right. At some point, we will have to do something."

"We cannot trust her," Dani argued, still seething.

"No one is disagreeing with you, Dani," Ellie said, crossing her arms over her chest.

"He is," Dani said with a disgusted grimace as she pointed at Graeson.

Graeson placed his hand atop Kalisandre's shoulder. "She is not to be harmed," he commanded.

"No harm will come to her, Gray," Ellie promised, expression guarded. "But we must proceed with caution."

"Ellie is right," Terin said, holding his blade up and inspecting his work. "Although, I am hopeful she will stop fighting me soon. Once she stops, I'll be able to let her mind rest while I sleep."

"But until then?" Dani asked, brow cocked.

Terin placed his sword beside him and settled against his bag, propping his head up slightly with his arm. "Until then, don't let me sleep for too long." Terin closed his eyes, attempting to get some rest.

Sylvia whispered something in Dani's ear that made Dani finally settle as well. Dani leaned her head against the wall, closing her eyes as she spun her wedding ring around her finger.

Medenia leaned forward. "You care for Kalisandre, do you not, Graeson?"

Graeson dragged his gaze from the floor to the Tetrian princess and nodded.

"Yet you are all right with taking her against her will and rendering her unconscious?" It was the same question Ellie had asked but held no judgment or ridicule; only bewildered curiosity filled Medenia's words.

"What do you wish for me to say?" Graeson asked, brushing a hand through his hair. "Every moment that passes, every second that Kalisandre remains in this coma, pains me more than the last. It is not a choice I make easily."

"Yet you make it all the same," Medenia murmured.

"Because she cannot make her own choices, not when Domitius has poisoned her mind."

Medenia leaned back, flipping a crystal within her palm as she peered at Kalisanre. "She has been made to believe the bull king was her father. And for better or worse, he has played that role for as long as Kalisandre can remember. It is understandable that--"

"No," Graeson said, cutting her off. "That is not the main problem here. While it is terrible that he has fed Kalisandre a lie her entire life about who he is to her, when the truth was revealed to her, she ignored it. Think about it: if you were to discover that your parent was killed by the person who raised you, would you forgive them so easily?"

Medenia shrugged. "Families can be complicated."

Graeson knew that all too well, but it did not explain everything. Not in this case. "While that may be true, it does not mean you would forgive him so easily if you were in Kalisandre's position."

Medenia paused, then said, "I cannot say what I would do." She tilted her head, her brows furrowing. "You keep saying that Domitius has messed with her mind, Graeson, but how do you know that? What proof do you have?"

Graeson cracked his knuckles. "He confessed it in the tunnels."

"What did he say exactly?"

"He said that her mind has been manipulated."

"Manipulated *how*?" Medenia asked. Then, as her gaze flicked from Kalisandre to Graeson, she gasped, eyes widening. "Does Domitius--"

"No," Graeson said, anticipating the question. "Domitius doesn't bear an ability. If he did, Armen would have discovered it and told us. While he is the one pulling the strings, Domitius is not the one with a gift."

"Then who?" Medenia asked, forehead creasing in confusion.

"The handmaiden."

"The handmaiden?" she repeated.

Graeson nodded. "Kalisandre's handmaiden and best friend is a woman named Myra. She was the other woman we had brought to Pontia originally."

"Wait," Sylvia said, snapping their eyes open. "*That* handmaiden?"

"Yes?" Graeson said, but by the way Sylvia's eyes had widened, the response came out more as a question. Graeson leaned forward. "What is it that you know, Sylvia? Did she say something when you were traveling with her?"

Sylvia shook their head. "Not quite."

"But?" he pressed.

Sylvia's shoulders dropped. "It's more of a hunch. When we were traveling south together, she was...off."

Ellie snorted as she used one of her knives to pick the dirt from her nails. "Why you all expect these women to react positively to being kidnapped is beyond me."

Graeson, ignoring Ellie, asked, "Off how, Sylvia?"

Sylvia tipped their head in Ellie's direction. "Ellie is right, actually. I had expected some sort of reaction from the handmaiden while we traveled--whether that be anger or a form of disassociation. I recall you saying that on your trip north with Kalisandre, the princess fought back. She tried to escape. But the handmaiden? She was...compliant. Friendly even."

Graeson waved a hand dismissively. "That's how she was with the rest of us when we arrived in Pontia. She was sweet, kind, and endearing, especially to Kalisandre. Maybe it's merely her personality? Or perhaps it's what she thought she needed to do to survive when she still believed us to be the enemy?"

"That's just it," Sylvia said, shaking their head. "Who acts that way to their captors? Before we had separated, I recall the handmaiden and Kalisandre whispering. Fear was written all over the handmaiden's face; she was practically dripping in it. But once we split ways? Something changed.

"Myra was...different. She was quiet, yes, but it was almost as if a weight had been lifted off her shoulders. The only time the fear came back was when we arrived at the southern port, where Ardentolian guards were everywhere. She acted scared. At first, I thought nothing of it. I had reasoned that it was because she was afraid of what we would do to her if they discovered her, but now..." Sylvia shook their head. "Now, I can't help but think she was afraid of returning."

"Did Domitius explain what Myra did to Kalisandre's mind?" Medenia asked.

"He said that she manipulated her emotions, twisting them," Graeson said.

Medenia was silent for a moment, but Graeson could see her mind at work. She cocked her head to the side as she observed Kalisandre with an intensity that Graeson wasn't sure what to make of.

Finally, Medenia hummed, nodding. "It makes sense now."

"What does?" Graeson asked, perplexed.

Medenia slowly dragged her attention from Kalisandre to meet Graeson's eyes, but it was almost as if she struggled to pull her focus from Kalisandre.

She blinked, her eyelashes brushing across the tops of her round cheeks. "I've been trying to figure out what's been off about her since I met her at the welcome dinner. If the handmaiden truly has warped her mind, that would explain the oddness I have felt. Her aura has been tampered with."

"Her *aura*?" Graeson said hesitantly.

Medenia nodded. "We each bear an aura: a general feeling that emits from one's presence. You can learn a lot from someone just by inspecting their aura."

"And this is something you...see?" Dani surmised, apparently sharing the same reservations Graeson did regarding the matter.

To Dani, Medenia asked, "You once explained that you are a huntress, correct?"

"Yes," Dani answered hesitantly.

"And because of this, you are more attuned to signals that might appear insignificant to others?"

Dani nodded once more.

"But sometimes it is not simply something you merely *see*. It is a feeling, an insight. The shift in the air, an unannounced silence," Medenia said.

"I suppose," Dani mumbled skeptically.

"It is a similar thing that I experience, that many of my people learn to identify in our queendom."

Still unsure, Graeson asked, "But what made you come to believe her aura was tampered with?"

Medenia offered him a small smile, but it did little to soothe his doubts. "Call it an instinct if that makes you feel better."

He frowned. It did *not*. "How does this help us exactly?"

Medenia blinked at him as if the answer was as clear as the sky. But did she not realize the sky was filled with ominous gray clouds that swallowed the sun?

"It helps because it proves that you are right," Medenia said, placing the crystal she had been rolling in her hand back around her neck. The white crystal disappeared beneath her slip. "But more than anything, it tells me that there is *hope*. Because beneath the murkiness of her aura, beneath the shadows and the darkness that threaten to consume her, something else lies there. Your Kalisandre is still there. We just have to find her and pull her out before it is too late."

With Medenia's words, a seed of hope was planted within Graeson's chest, yet he did not let it bloom.

Despite hoping that whatever Myra had done to Kalisandre's mind was reversible, Graeson also knew that there were some things one could not get rid of.

Especially when it came to one's own mind.

HEAVY SNORES FILLED the small space as Graeson lay awake, staring at the ceiling, his mind murky with thoughts he couldn't avoid. Darkness had long since enveloped the cave, yet sleep evaded him.

Unable to bear it any longer, he stood and slipped outside, carefully and quietly, tiptoeing around the slumbering bodies scattered across the cave's dusty floor.

Once outside the cave, Graeson felt the crisp night air brush his skin and tangle in his black hair. He gazed up at the shimmering new moon. As the glow of the new moon bathed him, the back of his neck prickled, and a sense of unease crept over him.

In the stillness of the forest, something akin to a chuckle sifted through the trees, causing Graeson to straighten, every muscle in his body tensing. Even the god inside him bristled, sensing something *other*. Slowly, he turned toward the direction of the sound, but only trees and brush greeted him. And yet...

"You are still fighting your true nature, I see."

Graeson's hand twitched at his side despite knowing a mere blade was useless against this intruder. "I am not fighting anything," he said through clenched teeth.

"Do not lie to me!" the voice roared, and Graeson struggled not to flinch as the ground shook and the leaves rustled around him. "I can sense the wall within you, the pitiful cage you have built. Do you think locking the so-called monster away will make you more human?"

Graeson couldn't speak, his voice trapped in his throat as he searched for the owner of the voice concealed within the woods.

"You still do, don't you? After all this time, I thought you would have given up that pursuit."

Graeson's sharp voice cut through the still air. "What are you doing here?" he demanded, scanning the forest.

The leaves rustled as a breeze swept across him, and the once-loud chirping of crickets fell silent. When no response came, Graeson clenched his hands into tight fists and hissed, "Show yourself."

More laughter echoed through the trees, sending a spiral of chills skittering down Graeson's spine.

"You do not command me, son."

"I am not your son." Ice-cold fury rose within Graeson. Even though Graeson could not see him, Graeson knew Barinthian, the god who claimed to bear his blood, was there. The deity lurked somewhere among the trees and shadows, hidden but undeniably present.

"Are you not?" Barinthian's voice surrounded him, low and haunting and *searching*. "You sure act like me."

"I am *nothing* like you, " Graeson spat in disgust.

The gold rings around his fingers hummed as the beast roared within.

"Short temper? Lethal with a blade? A craving for blood to soak the earth? How are you *not* like me?" the god laughed.

A feeling akin to a finger trailing down the side of Graeson's cheek scorched his skin. Graeson quickly shook it off, only to be met with the mocking laughter of the god.

The ethereal voice crooned, "You are the spitting image of me. Vengeance runs in your blood."

"At least, I care for human life," Graeson seethed. He was

nothing like the God of Retribution and Spite. Graeson would never abandon a child or his mother.

Graeson would never abandon those he loved.

"Do you truly, though?" Barinthian asked. "Or do you just care about *hers*?"

Graeson whipped his head around at the sound of the voice, his blood boiling beneath his skin. "Do not dare speak of her."

"Oh, right. How could I forget? Your dear Kalisandre is off limits." The god clicked his tongue. "A pity, really. She is a sight to behold. It is no wonder you wish to claim her."

"She is not one to be claimed," Graeson growled, stalking slowly around the shadows that beckoned him closer.

"Is that not how those precious bonds my dear brother created all those years ago work?" Barinthian asked. "How do you think she will react when she discovers the truth about the bonds? Do you think she even will accept you? After all, how can she accept you when you don't even accept yourself?"

Graeson squeezed his eyes shut, forcing the red seeping into the corners of his vision to vanish. "You do not want to push me right now," he warned.

Wind swept across Graeson's face. When the god spoke next, his voice was right at Graeson's ear. "Oh, I think that is *exactly* what I wish to do." Strong fingers gripped Graeson's shoulder, and warm breath brushed across Graeson's neck. "Let the rage out, son. Show the world the beast you truly are. Show them the *real* you."

Graeson spun, but the god was nowhere to be found.

CHAPTER 6

MYRA

MYRA TRIED TO MELT INTO THE WALL OF THE DARK, COLD ROOM beneath the Ardentolian castle. In the damp cells, the shadows loomed large. Melancholy coated the walls and oozed from the stone, making the air thick with agony and misery.

Since Myra was a child, she had struggled to contain her ability. Many thought their powers were gifts from the gods, but Myra's could only be described as a curse. Bearing one's own emotions was already a burden enough for many, but to experience the emotions of every person you touched? It was a torment Myra would never wish on anyone.

Humans were not the only ones whose emotions she could sense, either. Buildings also thrust their emotions at her. If Myra was lucky, some structures had a warm and inviting aura. When she visited homes filled with laughter and love, it was reminiscent of the sun shining down on a field of freshly bloomed daisies in late spring.

But Myra was rarely lucky. These days, those kinds of places were few and far between.

Instead, the buildings Myra had to frequent often reeked of

death and dread. And this humid dungeon beneath the Ardentolian castle was the worst of them all.

The air beneath the castle was sticky with agony, torment, and rage. The stone walls were soaked with the cries of the victims who had been tortured in the cells. The ground had been watered with the tears and blood of the dying, so much so that Myra could barely remain standing.

The call for death was too strong here, and it tugged on her very limbs.

Unlike the emotions of humans or animals, Myra could not manipulate the emotions of the walls or floors. Those emotions were etched in the very stone. Permanent and unbendable. The very infrastructure of a building would have to crumble for the stories melted into the concrete or the memories buried inside the walls to disappear. Even if the building was demolished, there was always the chance that the earth remembered.

An emotion's effect was always worse when Myra's memories were personally tied to the place. And here, in the dungeons, grief wrapped around Myra's lungs, agony twisted around her limbs, and rage coated her throat.

However, Myra wasn't the one bound to the wall this time. Now,, she stood behind the king, her hands trembling, while an unfamiliar woman sat chained to the cement floor.

Myra wondered what the stranger had done to be imprisoned beneath the castle. Although, perhaps the better question was *why* Myra was bearing witness to it. This was the first time in years she had been dragged down to the cells, and the last time . . .

Myra swallowed the memory, forcing it back down. *Not now.*

Domitius crouched before the woman. Her black hair hung in thick, grease-coated strands down her face. Her skin was nearly transparent, as if she hadn't seen the sun in years. She wore a ragged dress, stained and worn thin with holes throughout the fabric.

Domitius snatched her chin with his hand, jerking her face upward and squeezing her sunken cheeks together. "You said the fates were aligned," he hissed.

Though frail, the woman wrenched her chin free from his grip. As lifeless as she may appear, there was still some fight left in her.

"How many times must I tell you?" The woman pulled at the manacles keeping her bound. "The fates can change."

"What is the point of having a seer if you cannot tell me the truth? You *said* it would work, that my plans would come to fruition if I had the girl!" the king thundered.

Myra's eyes widened in fear. *A seer? But if she's a seer, how did she end up here?*

The prisoner rolled her eyes, and something about the woman's features felt familiar, but Myra couldn't quite place them. This room--the memories and feelings that dripped from the walls--clouded her judgment.

Here, she always saw the ghosts of her past. Phantoms that would not so easily let her go.

"Time is an illusion. The world shifts," the woman sneered. She sank against the wall, exasperated, as if her current circumstance of being chained to a cell was not her primary concern but rather a simple annoyance. "My visions can only be so accurate, as I have told you many times."

Domitius pulled on one side of the chain, the links tightening around the women's limbs. "Then make them *more* accurate."

Myra forced herself to remain still despite the screaming desire to run away. But there was no running from the bull-king. She had learned that a long time ago.

The woman tipped her chin up, snarling. "It doesn't work like that. My visions are not meant to be forced out as you so often seem to forget, *Kage*."

Domitius pulled at the chain once more, and the woman reeled.

"My *King*," she spat in defiance.

He tossed the chain onto the ground, and the metal links clattered against the stone floor as he pushed himself up into a standing position. Turning around, he began pacing in the small cell.

His feet wore a line in the dust-covered ground; Myra on one side, the woman on the other.

Myra couldn't help but find the similarities despite the line between them. They were both the king's prisoners. Only the woman wore chains, while Myra did not.

However, Myra wondered if it would be easier to rot inside of a cell instead of being given a false sense of freedom. Freedom that was frail, fickle, and false. A privilege she knew could be taken from her at any minute. A privilege that had resulted in Myra betraying her best friend.

The choice, however, had never been hers to make. Once Domitius discovered what Myra could do, her path was set. There was no going back now.

As Domitius paced back and forth, the woman lifted her head, and her eyes locked onto Myra. She cocked her head to the side. Her eyelids fluttered, and her head swayed. Then, she abruptly straightened, and an eerie chill crept over Myra's skin as the corner of the woman's lip twitched.

When she turned her gaze to Domitius, her eyes narrowed. "You still don't get it, do you?" she challenged.

He rolled his eyes. "Get *what*, woman?"

The woman grinned, her teeth yellowed and rotten. A rancorous sound that made Myra wonder how long the woman had been in Domitius's captivity poured out of her mouth. "You'll never win. The fates may appear to be in your favor one minute, but *they* have one thing that you lack."

Domitius lunged forward, brandishing a blade to her throat. "What could they possibly have that I do not?" he demanded.

There was that laugh again. Then, a deafening silence filled the room as the woman quirked a brow.

The prisoner raised her chin as if to dare Domitius to kill her.

"Love," she whispered, and he scoffed.

Domitius laughed bitterly. "*Love?*"

"Mhm."

"How does that have to do with anything? Love is nothing. Love is--"

"*Everything*," the woman spat, interrupting the king. "Why do you think the fates have changed?" When Domitius didn't respond, she continued, "It is because, despite everything that has happened, the Pontians still have love in their hearts for that girl. You have manipulated your false daughter's mind and her emotions countless times, but the one thing you cannot manipulate--the one thing you cannot falsify--is love.

"You thought making Kalisandre fear love was the answer, but that is far from the truth. It is because Kalisandre craves to love and be loved in return that you will never win. Despite everything you have done, she still has love in her heart for them, for *her*."

Myra pressed her back against the wall, wishing she could disappear as the woman stared at her. But she was stuck in here. The door was locked, and Domitius was the only one with the key.

The king looked over his shoulder at Myra, then back at the woman. "What are you talking about?"

"The future is not a straight line, but rather it is like the knotted roots of a tree, and we seers stand at the base of it. There is always more than one path to choose from, and while we can sometimes predict which route a soul will take based on past decisions, the future is never certain. It branches and splits out in different directions.

"As relationships change, so too do our paths. The fates are ever-changing for this reason. A tangle of choices waiting to be unraveled. You never know what you'll get until you pull, until you tug. Until you *choose*."

"Enough of the riddles. Speak sense, seer," Domitius hissed.

She shook her head, licking her chapped lips. "The handmaiden cares for your false daughter. Up until now, her love for her family has been leading her decisions, but something has changed."

The woman paused, her nearly white eyes staring at Myra thoughtfully.

Her lip twitched. "Multiple forces now guide her," the prisoner surmised.

Myra's body went rigid, and before she knew it, Domitius was pressing the heel of his palm against her throat.

"So, this is your fault!" he shouted, his voice ringing in the cell so loud it pained her ears.

Myra never wanted Kallie to get hurt. Despite betraying her trust since she entered the princess's employment, Myra had grown to care for her.

Kallie was troubled, her emotions twisted and torn. But Myra saw what lay beneath the battered mess. She knew Kallie's heart. Even so, she did not know what the seer meant. As much as Myra hated that Domitius forced her to manipulate Kallie's emotions, she had no choice but to obey.

"I--I don't know--" Myra choked on her words as he squeezed her throat.

Her eyes watered as her lungs begged for air. She tried to focus on the king and bite back the fear bubbling to the surface, but her vision was clouding. Black splotches pulsed in her blurry gaze as he tightened his calloused grip.

Anger painted the king's face when he glared down at her. He had lost. He had lost, and the Pontians had won. They had taken Kallie and escaped.

And now Myra was forced to reap the consequences of his failure.

She couldn't defend herself. She couldn't explain, for Domitius wasn't here for answers.

He wasn't here for an explanation.

He was here for an outlet for his anger, for a release.

The spots in her vision grew, and before she knew what she was doing, she pulled from the pit of her stomach. She instinctively followed the iridescent string that floated in the air, invisible to all but her. She tugged on it, grabbed it, tried to bend it to her will.

She tried to coax it, soothe it. Snuff out the fire that coated its strands.

But as she sent the emotion down the string that ran from the fingers wrapped around her throat to the nerves in his mind, Domitius's nose twitched.

His fingers dropped from her throat, and Myra wheezed, gasping for air.

The oxygen struck her lungs in an icy and painful burst. Sharp and bitter. Before Myra could catch her breath, she was thrown across the room, and the wind was knocked out of her as she hit the wall.

Domitius's mouth was moving, but Myra couldn't make out the words as the room spun around her. The back of her head throbbed. Pain shot down her spine, and her vision pulsed.

She couldn't breathe. Her body had gone stiff as pain erupted all over her.

The door creaked open behind the king. Two figures entered the cell, but her vision was still too fuzzy to make them out. One of the figures shoved the other forward, and the second, shorter figure fell to their knees.

Myra inhaled, but her body couldn't process the intake of oxygen. It stopped short, lodging itself in the middle of her throat, choking her.

She tried to move.

She tried to crawl, but her limbs were too weak, and they folded beneath her weight. She slipped, her face smacking against the floor.

Still, she tried. Even as the tears blurred her vision and drowned out her voice. Even as a sharp pain seared through her body. Even as a burst of poisonous laughter echoed in the cell, Myra crawled.

She needed to touch him. She needed to make sure he was real. She needed proof that this wasn't an illusion Domitius had somehow concocted.

But the man on the ground didn't look at her, his tired gaze fixed on the floor.

"Mynhos?" Myra whispered, the single word scratching her vocal cords. It was a name she hadn't said aloud in over a decade, a name she called out for in her dreams.

Her brother was alive.

Alive and in front of her.

But *why* was he here?

Her fingers brushed his shoulder, and he flinched back from the touch.

Domitius stepped forward, blade in hand. "Perhaps you need to be reminded about what you are *truly* fighting for."

The king snatched Mynhos's wrist, and her brother at last looked at her with anguish swimming in his hazel eyes. Domitius pressed Mynhos's hand flat against the stone floor.

In his ear, Domitius whispered, "Don't bleed on my floor."

He struck.

And all Myra could hear was her brother's screams echoing in the small, stone room as he bled. Mynhos hurried to bury the severed limb in his clothes as he rushed to fulfill Domitius's command

Myra reached for him, but she was being dragged back by her braid. She tried to fight it as pain wracked through her skull. She tried to wiggle out of Domitius's hold, but she couldn't.

She couldn't fight him.

She couldn't grab hold of anything.

The door shut behind them, the locks clicking into place. Mynhos's agonized screams rang in her mind on repeat as she was dragged down the hall with tears streaming down her face.

She couldn't save Mynhos's hand, just like she couldn't save her parents all those years ago. Myra had barely even saved herself.

But saving herself had come with a price, one she was still paying.

CHAPTER 7
GRAESON

As the group rode north the next morning, Graeson's focus constantly strayed from the path ahead, lingering on Barinthian and the consequences that awaited him once they arrived in Tetria. Finding Kalisandre and stopping the wedding, he realized, was the easy part. The hardest part was yet to come.

"We should stop here," Ellie said after a while of riding. "The horses need a break, and we need to refill our canteens while we can."

Graeson peered through the towering oak trees that littered the landscape. The leaves rustled softly, disturbed only by a few birds bouncing between the branches, their delicate melodies light in the air.

"I'll scan the area," Dani said, grabbing the reins. "We should be quick about it."

As Dani and her horse disappeared within the brush, everyone else dismounted.

When Emmett's boots hit the ground, he groaned in discomfort as he kicked out his legs. "Have I mentioned how no one bothered to tell me how much horseback riding would be needed on this little escapade?"

"It's better than walking," Sylvia countered with a shrug. They brushed their hands through their auburn hair, plucking a leaf from it. "On a mission to Kadia a couple of years ago, we had to walk most of the way once the river ran dry."

"And the knowledge of this factoid is supposed to help me how?" Emmett asked in response, rubbing his thighs in discomfort.

Graeson rolled his eyes and made his way toward the trickling stream, leaving the two to prattle back and forth. When he reached the water's edge, he dropped to his knees and scooped up a handful of water. Splashing it onto his face, he washed away the dust and weariness and took a calming breath.

"We'll have to boil this," Ellie said, having joined him at the stream.

"We don't have the time," Graeson sighed, running his damp fingers through his jet-black hair.

"How much water do you have in your canteen?" Ellie asked, brow arched.

Graeson unbuckled his canteen from his belt and shook it near his ear. Water sloshed against the sides of the container. He pursed his lips. By the sound, he was nearing empty.

"That's what I thought."

"Fine," he said, giving in. "If Dani gives us the all-clear, we'll start a fire."

Ellie nodded. "We should cook some fish while we're at it. While Medenia may be happy living off berries, I know the rest of us are not."

"I do not live off berries," Medenia called back, having heard them further down the stream as she plucked red mulberries from a thin branch.

"Sorry, I stand corrected," Ellie said with a playful jest. "Let's not forget your endless supply of nuts."

Licking the juice from her fingers, Medenia said, "Don't forget mushrooms, eggs, and--"

"Yes, yes," Ellie said with a wave, chuckling softly.

Soon, they were all resting along the riverbend. Ellie and Medenia were rolling their eyes at something Emmett said. Terin sat against a tree while Sylvia stood by, watching over him and Kalisandre.

Graeson remained by the river. Although he wanted to go to Kalisandre, he felt pulled to stay where he was. As he stared at the water sloshing by the shore, his thoughts twisted and turned.

Fighting this only makes it worse.

Graeson gritted his teeth. And yet, the god's words only made memories Graeson wished would disappear rise to the surface.

His KNEES *and palms pressed into the wet concrete as the sound of the waterfall flooded his senses. Then, all at once, there was nothing.*

A cold breeze brushed Graeson's neck, sending a chill creeping across his skin.

"Pontianius," Graeson said in greeting, keeping his head low and eyes fixed on the ground.

The god laughed, the sound bouncing off the walls. "Why do you fight it? Giving in would be so much easier."

Graeson shook his head, tousling his hair as shame and anger colored his cheeks. "Because I am not him.*"*

Pontanius sighed. "I understand your distaste for my brother--"

"Distaste?" Graeson hissed with a scoff. "Barinthian abandoned my mother when she was pregnant with me. He only cared to produce a replica of him."

"Are you?" the god drawled.

"Am I what?" Graeson asked, his brows furrowing.

"A replica of my brother."

"No," Graeson snapped.

"Then why do you fight it?"

"Because!" Graeson shouted despite being in the presence of a god.

Pontanius was different from the other deities. Unlike Graeson's father, Barinthian, Pontanius did not constantly lash out in anger, did not pit mortals against one another, and did not seek to take over the mortal world. Graeson actually liked Pontanius. However, whenever the topic of Graeson suppressing his godly nature arose, he couldn't bear to be around his uncle.

Still, he kept seeking Pontanius's guidance.

"Because if I let go of my control, who's to say I won't become him?" Graeson asked, his voice barely above a whisper. "Who's to say I won't--" Graeson swallowed, unable to ask the question that plagued him.

"You won't what?" Pontanius prompted.

Graeson rubbed his hands over his face. "Who's to say I won't lose the piece of her I have left?" he whispered.

A hand, cold and almost nonexistent, brushed Graeson's shoulder. "You will not lose your mother by becoming who you were born to be."

"You do not know that," Graeson argued.

The god corrected, "Nor do you know whether you will turn into Barinthian. But that does not mean you should continue to torture yourself."

When Graeson said nothing, Pontanius sighed. "When will you learn?"

"Learn what?"

As water dripped from the ceiling, time seemed to stand still as he waited for the god's reply. For a moment, he questioned if Pontanius had left him. However, even though his eyes were still fixed on the ground, Graeson could still sense Pontanius's presence. Goosebumps skittered across his skin as the god watched him.

At last, Pontanius clicked his tongue. "Fighting this only makes it worse."

"COME ON, GRAY," Ellie called out, dragging Graeson's attention from the river coiling through the woods before him. "You need to rest, too."

Graeson snorted but said nothing.

"That's not a suggestion," Ellie added.

Graeson frowned at the river but trudged over to Ellie before she could harp on him any further. He had barely slept last night, and while he was exhausted, he wouldn't be able to rest until everyone he cared about was safe.

Suddenly, hooves pounded the ground, and branches snapped one after another. His hands instinctively reached for his scimitar on his back.

A few seconds later, Dani burst through the trees. But while the others sighed in relief, Graeson's grip did not waiver.

A stray braid hung in front of Dani's face, having fallen from her bun. Sweat dripped from her furrowed brows. But her frazzled appearance was not why Graeson pulled his weapon from its sheath. His attention was locked on the blood-stained dagger hanging from Dani's hip.

"We've got company!" Dani shouted.

Medenia hurried toward Kalisandre. "Let's get her on the horse."

"No time," Dani argued, tugging on the reins of her mount only a couple of yards away before jumping off. Dust motes flew into the air as her feet hit the ground.

"We're staying to fight?" Sylvia asked, causing Emmett's face to pale.

Ellie pulled two throwing knives from the belt strapped over her right shoulder.

"It's our only choice," Dani said.

"How many?" Graeson asked, taking out his second scimitar.

Sylvia tried handing one of their daggers to Emmett, but he shrunk away from the blade, refusing to take it.

"Shut up and take it," Sylvia spat, forcing the dagger into Emmett's hand and folding his fingers over the hilt.

"Two squads," Dani said in response to Graeson, "about fifteen in total."

"Shit," Emmett hissed and cradled the dagger closer to his chest.

Graeson's jaw flexed as he glanced at Kalisandre's unconscious body from the corner of his eye. "How long?"

"Only a few minutes, if that. I tracked the group to the river south of us. I ran into one of their lookouts and quickly dispatched him before he could alert the others. Unable to take them all by myself, I hurried back. But a horse galloping through the woods isn't the most discreet form of escape. They'll be on us sooner rather than later."

"Best we take them head-on anyway," Ellie determined, bouncing on her toes. "They were bound to catch up to us at some point." She shrugged.

"How did they even find us? I thought we covered our tracks?" Medenia asked, short sword in hand.

Dani stepped forward, teeth bared. "Are you questioning me, Princess?"

Graeson spun the scimitars in his hands. "It doesn't matter how they found us, only that they *did*."

"Medenia, you good to fight?" Ellie asked.

"Always," the princess said, her expression hardening.

Dani nodded. "You and Sylvia will stay close to the three of them," she ordered, pointing to Terin, Kalisandre, and Emmett.

Terin stepped forward. "I can fight. I don't need someone to--"

She snapped, "Do not argue with me about this, Terin. Not right now. By the gods, fight if you are attacked, but we do not need you running into the fray."

"Dani's right. You and Kalisandre must be protected," Graeson said.

"And what about Medenia?" Terin argued.

Medenia snorted, a look of pure steel shining in her eyes. "I can handle myself."

Dani peered into the forest, as if expecting intruders at any moment. "With that settled, Ellie, you and I will take the borders. Graeson?"

"I know my place," Graeson said, twirling his two blades. Dani nodded before walking toward the perimeter of the area they occupied. He looked to Terin and the others. "Stay safe."

"We've got her," Terin assured him, but Graeson wasn't sure if he felt any better.

Graeson turned away and closed his eyes as the others prepared themselves. At some point, the birds had grown silent.

The soldiers were close.

He could feel it in the way the air shifted around him, and the hair on the back of his neck stood on end.

For years, Graeson had envisioned the moment he would save Kalisandre.

The queen had warned him that it would be more complicated than he thought. While he hadn't doubted Esmeray, Graeson had never imagined that he would also lose some of his closest friends in the process. He never imagined so much betrayal and so many secrets to reveal themselves, either.

He trained to be stronger; he trained to be better. He had done everything *right*. He had gained control over the beast within, learning to lock the god inside him where he couldn't harm anyone.

Back home, everyone feared him because of the rumors that weaved their way through the kingdom. Because of that fear, Graeson hid who he was. He tamped it down. He shut it away.

He shut *himself* away.

But Graeson was so tired of hiding who he was.

He was so fucking tired of locking that part of himself away. Because as much as he detested the god within, it was a part of him. There was no hiding from that.

In the distance, hooves and boots pounded the ground.

Graeson exhaled and opened his eyes.

Ellie and Dani crept forward ahead of him, weaving through the forest on either side of the small camp to cut off the enemy.

He once told Kalisandre that he would not be merciful to those who tried to take her away from him, and he had meant every word.

Graeson's fingers flexed around the handles of the scimitars, and a rumbling stirred in the back of his mind. Red coated the corners of his vision, but this time, instead of pushing it away, he welcomed it.

When the first soldier appeared, brandishing a longsword, metal armor shining in the sun, and the Ardentolian crest brandishing it, Graeson didn't hesitate.

He attacked.

He raged.

He became the monster he was born to be.

CHAPTER 8
KALLIE

Kallie gasped and choked on the air that filled her lungs.

Her fingers dug into the ground as her heart thumped within her chest, ricocheting against her ribcage. A blinding white light covered her vision. As she tried to blink it away, fragments of scenes bombarded her senses.

The images collided together, smashing into one another and shattering into pieces. One moment, arrows were whizzing past her. Then, Fynn appeared, peering at her with his soft brown eyes as a glittering waterfall roared behind him. A second later, fire poured from the ceiling.

Various scents tickled her nose: lavender, salt, smoke, charcoal, and burnt lumber.

As she tried to make sense of it all and distinguish reality from her nightmares, Kallie's head pounded, and her ears rang, the sound sharp and piercing. But beneath the incessant ringing, she heard something else.

Shouting.

Yelling.

The *ting* of metal clashing together.

Kallie squeezed her eyes together, willing the pain and noise to vanish, to free herself from whatever torment plagued her bones. But all it did was cause more pain to spike her head.

She tried to open her eyes, but her eyelids were too heavy, as were her body and mind. Still, she took a deep breath and forced herself to focus. She tried to concentrate on her senses.

When she inhaled again, she noticed the smell of iron and moss tainting the air.

She identified the chaotic clang of metal, the grunts, and the nonsensical shouts that filled the air amidst the fray of battle.

She could feel her heart hammering in her chest.

Then, when she focused harder, she felt sharp prickles poking her palms. She wiggled her fingers, and her brows twisted together.

Was that...grass?

Why was there grass? Why was she outside? Her wedding was the last thing she could remember clearly as her mind finally stopped spinning. She should have been in the temple marrying Rian. She should have--

Then Kallie recalled the heat of the flames as a fire spread across the temple and chaos erupted.

Had someone taken her outside? Had the temple burned down?

Slowly regaining control over her muscles, Kallie swiped her palm across the thin blades, trying to ground herself as she finally peeled her eyes open. Clouds filled the sky, and the sun shone down, blinding her. No smoke in sight.

Before she could adjust to the brightness, darkness filled her vision once more.

Her head lolled to the side, and she blinked.

A bead of blood dripped from a blade of grass, bending under the weight of it.

Kallie's eyes darted from left to right, her vision blurring with fear. She tried to scream, but her voice was gone, her throat too dry to produce a sound.

Was the blood hers?

Someone else's?

She couldn't tell. She didn't know.

Her body was heavy, too heavy as if she had been asleep for days. Her chest rose, her lungs expanding. It was all too much.

She was losing control.

Deep breaths, she told herself. *Deep, slow breaths. Control it. Fight it.*

The ringing in her ears slowed, and the sound of grunts and groans surrounded her, drowning her.

Kallie tried to push herself up but struggled to move her limbs. She tried to call out, but the words refused to leave her tongue, her mouth sealed shut.

A flash of metal whizzed by as someone ran past her.

"Behind you!" someone shouted, the voice familiar and sending a chill down her spine.

A whistle kissed the air, sharp and crisp, followed by a loud *thud.*

Black muddied boots stopped in front of her face, sending a plume of dirt flying into the air.

Kallie twisted her head up, trying to make sense of what was happening around her. Her gaze trailed over light brown trousers, stained and soiled.

Silver flashed, swiping through the air--a blade.

Then a grunt.

And Kallie screamed--or at least tried to. The noise that slipped from her raw throat was mangled.

She stared at the spot beside the pair of mud-covered boots as a head slapped upon the ground and rolled toward her, the eyes of the victim wide open and staring at her, lifeless.

Vibrant blood pooled on the ground as yet another head appeared next to her, the rest of the corpse falling to the ground shortly after in a heap.

The boots turned, and a shout ripped through the air, "Graeson!"

Kallie's lungs collapsed. Her heart thumped in her chest as a surge of panic crept up her throat.

"Shit," another man growled in a low voice as more boots pounded on the ground and swords clanged together.

She couldn't just sit here.

Not if Graeson was here.

She had to do something.

Her father would want her to do something.

Kallie pushed through the soreness coating her bones and moved past the heaviness soaking her limbs.

The scene unfolded before her: men and women fought all around her, their faces glistening with sweat and their muscles straining. Almost immediately, she found Graeson among the fray, as if some inexplicable, magnetic force she could not deny pulled her toward him.

The sunlight struck his jet-black hair as he wielded his scimitars as though they were an extension of him. Dirt and gore stained his clothes, though Kallie knew unequivocally that none of it belonged to him. He was too skilled for that.

She mustered the strength to lift herself up and onto her elbows. While she may have admired his technique, Kallie only felt one thing as she stared at Graeson: absolute rage.

CHAPTER 9
GRAESON

F**URY ROARED THROUGH** G**RAESON'S BODY AS HE SWUNG HIS SCIMITARS** with practiced ease. With each clang of metal, the god inside seeped out a little more, pushing his humanity back bit by bit.

All the anger Graeson had been holding back bled from his hands and into the blades. Each opponent he met fell, their life spilling onto the earth, which greedily ate it up as he moved on to the next victim.

An energy flowed through him as he twisted and slashed. He was unhinged, unstoppable, and completely unmerciful.

Then, as Graeson lifted his blade, something called to him, beckoning him to turn around. When he tried to spin around to the call, his feet were swept from under him, and his back hit the ground with a hard thump. Dirt flew in the air.

Before Graeson could clear the ringing from his head, a weight pressed on him, flattening him against the ground. Sharp nails dug into his hair and yanked his head up before slamming it into the ground again.

Graeson hissed, eyes springing open in anger. But for the first time in his life, he was helpless as he stared at the assailant.

He swallowed the vitriol sitting on the tip of his tongue the second he took in the brown, chestnut waves falling around his face. The thick halo of hair blocked out the battle happening around them. And though his friends struggled, he was speechless as deep blue eyes swimming with shadows stared at him.

Graeson pushed past the god taking hold of his body as the woman he would do anything for sat atop him, regarding him without mercy.

"Kalisandre?" he whispered, awestruck. She shouldn't have been awake. Had something happened to Terin? Had he been--

"You bastard!" Kalisandre shouted, wrapping her hands around his throat, strangling him, and forcing his previous thoughts back.

A raging storm brewed within her sea-blue eyes. Yet, despite the wrath roaring, he wanted to get lost in the sea. He would gladly drown within them.

Kalisandre's slim fingers tightened around his throat, and for a second, Graeson let them.

He let her rage fuel the storm. He let her release her wrath and pour it into him because at least this, the anger burning in her eyes, was better than the lifeless body they had been carrying across the Frenzian lands.

He would happily take her anger, her rage, over watching her wither away before him. He would rather face her wrath than wonder what would become of her if they took too long to reach safety.

And perhaps Graeson let Kalisandre's grip tighten around his throat longer than he should have because, more than anything else, he deserved it.

He deserved her fury, her anger, her hate, for he had taken the one thing she had always strived to gain: a choice.

Again.

All Kalisandre wanted was freedom--a choice in this puppet life of hers, yet Graeson had ignored her. He hadn't returned home when she had told him to. He hadn't listened to her even though he knew she had promised to marry the king.

So, yes, he deserved her fury.

Because even if he had the choice to redo things, he would do it the same way again and again.

Kalisandre deserved her freedom. She deserved to make her own choices, to know the truth, and to break free from the king's control. Graeson would do whatever it took to give her that. He made a promise, and he intended to keep it. No matter what.

In the back of his mind, a roar sounded from the god, but Graeson ignored it.

"Graeson!"

Terin's voice snapped Graeson out of his stupor. Panic surged through him, and he grabbed Kalisandre's wrists.

With a growl and determination twisting her features, she tightened her grip around his throat, squeezing.

He wiggled beneath her hold, loosening her fingers just enough to shout at Terin, "Don't touch her!" His voice was gravelly and raw, but he knew Terin had heard him when the footsteps stopped.

Kalisandre screamed, her cheeks turning red as she shifted atop him to tighten her hold. Although Graeson was still stronger than her, something *other* was fueling her.

For a woman who had been more or less unconscious for a while, she had the energy and strength of the kraken. Graeson couldn't shake her hold off, not without hurting her.

Using his legs, Graeson tightened his core and twisted, rolling them around. Kalisandre's back hit the ground harder than he had anticipated. Her grip loosened, and Graeson flew into motion. With one hand, he gathered her wrists and held them above her head.

Kalisandre thrashed beneath him. "Get the fuck off me!"

Her hair was spread across the dirt and draped carelessly over her face. Her skin was pale, her cheeks hollow and stained with mud.

She was far from the princess he had seen standing in a diamond-covered ball gown months ago in the marble castle of Ardentol, or the seductress dripping in blood-red rubies inside the Frenzian castle. Out here, in the forests of Frenzia, Kalisandre was not a princess or gemstone for the bull king to parade around.

Her truth was laid bare. She was a woman betrayed by the people she trusted the most. A woman enraged who craved freedom more than anything.

And yet, the words that Kalisandre cried suggested otherwise.

"Where is my father?!"

She will never be free if the bull king's hold remains, the god hissed.

He shouted back, "He is not your father!"

Outraged, Kalisandre kicked, and, as much as Graeson hated himself for it, he shifted and forced her legs flat. She struggled beneath him, but Graeson kept his grip firm.

"He is more my family than any of you," she spat. "He is the only family I have."

Graeson flinched. "He lied to you. He's *been* lying to you! How do you *still* not see that?"

"And you all haven't?" she scoffed.

All around him, his people met blow for blow from their enemies, their blades slashing through the air. He needed to help them. Graeson had already slayed three of their assailants before he was pulled away by Kalisandre waking up, but his friends were quickly being overtaken.

"Go ahead," Kallie snapped, drawing Graeson's attention back to her. "Call Terin. Force me unconscious again. That's what you did, right? He's been messing with my head again?"

Graeson shook his head in frustration. "If you listened, you would understand."

But Kalisandre still wasn't listening. "Tell me where he is! If you killed him, I'll--"

"He got away," Graeson cut her off.

Kalisandre stopped struggling then, her gaze flitting between his eyes in search for the truth, but it had already been laid bare.

If she still believed Domitius cared for her, he would have to prove that he didn't.

Graeson pressed on. "He abandoned you as the temple burned. He left you to die."

"You're lying," Kalisandre spat, but her expression warred before him.

Despite the hatred she spewed, Graeson saw a flicker of doubt in her features. It was brief, and if Graeson hadn't been staring at her, he would have missed it. But it was there, and that was all that mattered.

He just needed to deepen the fissure. "Where was he when the glass shattered? When the fire started? Where was he when you fell to your knees?" he pressed.

A deep crease formed in the center of Kalisandre's forehead as she tried to recall the events.

How the ceiling came crashing down and how she was abandoned on the altar as her father fled through the tunnels and her fiancé ran toward the door to help break them open.

"He--" She shook her head, unable to finish her sentence. The answer would only prove that Graeson was right.

"When the fire started, he ran and didn't look back," Graeson said. "Dani went after him. When Terin and I followed after her with you in our possession, you know what Domitius did?"

Kalisandre remained silent, her throat bobbing as she swallowed.

"He did *nothing*, Kalisandre. He let us take you. He brought the ceiling down over our heads with little care for your wellbeing and ran."

Red streaked the whites of her eyes, and tears puddled at the bottom, hanging precariously on her lashes.

Still, she held to her truth, as stubborn as ever. "You're lying. He would never let you take me if he was alive."

"Do you truly believe that?" Graeson blinked at her, eyes wide. At that moment, he pitied her more than he ever had before as she lay there with blood on her face and dirt in her hair, crying for a man who did not care about her.

More than anything else, Graeson wanted to kill Domitius for causing her this much pain and forcing her to believe that he was someone she could trust.

"He's my father," Kalisandre rasped. She hung onto those three words as if they could save her, as if her very life depended upon them.

Graeson shook his head, huffing a mangled laugh void of any humor. "Believe what you want, Kalisandre, but Domitius only cares about his own survival."

"You're lying!" Kalisandre shouted as she tried to slip from his grasp.

"Then why did he let us take you? Why did he drop a tunnel on our heads while you were still in your brother's arms? If he cared about you, why did he let *you* go, Kalisandre?" he challenged.

She tried to speak but struggled to utter a single word when she found no sign of deception on Graeson's face. Then, as if she could not meet his eyes any longer, Kalisandre looked away, her long eyelashes brushing her sunken cheeks.

Graeson knew they weren't the words she wanted to hear, that the man who had put her in this position--manipulated and betrayed her--had gotten away without punishment.

Nevertheless, she needed to know the truth, no matter how much pain it caused. It should have been a relief that she finally understood the truth. But when Graeson looked down at her agonized face, he only felt deep empathy for Kalisandre.

When she finally lifted her gaze, she looked over his shoulder. Her expression hardened, the last remnants of emotions disappearing. Her pupils dilated and then contracted quickly.

An alarm rang in the back of Graeson's mind, but before he could react, hands were wrapped around his throat once more.

CHAPTER 10
GRAESON

Kalisandre slipped from Graeson's grasp as he was dragged back, his legs scraping against the ground. As he reached up and tried to yank the hands from his throat, the stranger only tightened his grip.

"Restrain him," Kalisandre commanded, scrambling to her feet.

The hands around Graeson's throat vanished before quickly twisting Graeson's arms behind his back, causing his shoulders to pop. When Graeson attempted to glance over his shoulder to identify his assailant, familiar brown eyes stared back at him.

Graeson gasped. "Terin, what are you doing?"

"Twist his arm harder," Kalisandre called out, her voice cold and detached.

Searing pain shot through Graeson's arm and up his neck as Terin obeyed Kalisandre. Graeson didn't understand how she had manipulated Terin in the first place without uttering a word, yet somehow she had him under her spell.

Despite the danger they were in now, the god within Graeson hummed in appraisal. While Graeson didn't doubt her inner strength, he wished he wasn't the one in peril because of it.

He looked around but found no one in a position to help. Sylvia and Medenia fought back-to-back as three soldiers circled them, taunting them. Further away, Ellie fended off three men, diving beneath a swing that came straight for her head. Although he couldn't see Dani in his peripheral, he heard her grunts from somewhere farther away. He would need to deal with this himself, then.

Without hurting his best friend or the woman fated for him.

Kalisandre stood, her legs trembling slightly as if the spike of adrenaline was quickly draining from her body.

Noticing where Graeson's gaze had gone, Kalisandre tilted up her chin and snarled, "He warned me you would do this. He warned me you would try to sway me to betray him!"

"Whatever he told you," Graeson said on his knees, "you can't believe him."

Kalisandre stalked closer, pointing at him and cutting him off, "You do *not* get to tell me what I can or cannot do."

Baring her teeth, she dropped onto her knees in front of him. She snatched the collar of Graeson's shirt and yanked him forward, Terin's hold remaining firm.

With just a few inches between them now, Graeson could feel her breath on his face as she bristled with anger.

Mine, the god whispered.

"But Domitius does, is that right?" Graeson challenged, voice low as he cocked his head.

Kalisandre blinked but immediately shook her head, dispelling the brief flicker of emotion spanning her countenance. "He does not control me."

Graeson smirked. "Are you sure about that, little mouse?"

"Yes," she hissed.

"Then why were you going to marry the Frenzian king?"

"Because--" Another hesitation, another slip in her demeanor and Domitius's manipulations.

Marrying the Frenzian had never been Kalisandre's choice. It was one of the many made for her; they both knew she could not deny it.

Still, the slip was short-lived.

Kalisandre rolled her shoulders back and steeled her expression, her lip curling. "I was going to be queen. I was going to have power."

Graeson huffed. "You mean you were going to be Domitius's puppet."

"I am *not* his puppet; I am his daughter."

"You are his *weapon!*" Graeson shouted, the anger pooling over through what had been a previously calm facade. "To be used and swung whenever he demands. Do you truly not see what he has made you become? Even now, you take your anger out on me when all I wish is for you to be free!"

Kalisandre lunged, snatching him by the collar. "You speak of my freedom?" she hissed. "You tie my wrists and knock me out; *that* is not freedom, Graeson. That is--"

Without warning, Kalisandre crumpled to the ground, her words dying in the air in an instant. Without a second thought, Graeson wrenched himself free from Terin's grasp and lunged for Kalisandre before her head could hit the dirt.

"You stupid, lovesick fool!" Dani said, spitting on the ground beside Graeson, her dagger in hand a mere foot away.

With Kalisandre cradled in his arms, Graeson snapped his gaze up. But before Graeson could yell at Dani for knocking Kalisandre out, someone clawed at his arms, trying to pull him back.

"Terin!" Dani shrieked. "What are you doing?"

"Shit," Graeson hissed, setting Kalisandre on the ground. "He's still under her command!"

He quickly rolled away, shaking Terin off. His friend did not stop his pursuit, though, driven by the remnants of Kalisandre's command. She had indeed gotten stronger since they first found her and took her to the Whispering Springs. And Graeson only had himself to blame for that.

Terin lunged again, grabbing Graeson and sitting on his legs, stilling him. With blind ferocity, Terin smashed Graeson's face into the ground, and dirt and grass filled his mouth.

"Just hold still!" Dani shouted.

Graeson released a muffled groan as Terin yanked Graeson's arms, twisting them behind his back.

Graeson winced as the sharp pain shot through his body. Behind him, he heard a loud *thump*, followed by a groan. In an instant, his hands were free.

Rolling onto his back, his shoulder throbbing, Graeson found Dani brandishing her dagger, the blade pointed to the sky. With her other arm, she caught Terin as he slumped over, unconscious. Dani huffed as she lay the prince carelessly beside Kalisandre on the ground.

"Playtime is over, don't you think?" Dani cocked a brow, swiping up Graeson's scimitars from the ground and tossing one of them at him as he stood. "Perhaps now you can do something useful?"

Graeson caught the first blade by the hilt, then the second. "You just knocked out--"

"Kill now, talk later," Dani snapped, spinning on her heel as a soldier came barreling forward.

Graeson looked at Terin and Kalisandre, hesitating briefly. But as more soldiers flooded from the nearby treeline, Graeson knew Dani was right. There was no time to argue.

Joining the fray, he ran toward Sylvia and Medenia. Sliced one of the soldiers at the ankles, Graeson pulled him to the ground and stabbed him straight through the chest.

"Hey! He was mine," Medenia shouted, her voice a near whine.

"You can thank me later! Protect them," Graeson said, not bothering to stop as he changed directions and headed toward Ellie on the other side of the camp.

One soldier had Ellie's back pinned to his chest while his friend waved a blade in front of her, taunting her with her untimely demise. Graeson didn't wait to hear the man speak before charging forward.

Jabbing his shoulder into the man, he sent them both crashing to the ground. The soldier was quick, though; he rolled, forcing Graeson under him. As the soldier raised his dagger, poised to strike, darkness swept over the area and the wind picked up. A sound akin to a screech filled the air.

The man stilled, his face rife with fear.

Graeson's mouth curled into a sinister smile as he peered at the sky. Enormous wings flapped against the backdrop of the sun, their nearly translucent membranes nearly glowing. Sharp claws shimmered in the sunlight as the creature circled overhead.

"What is that?" someone nearby asked as Emmett's high-pitched scream ripped through the forest.

As the soldier looked up, Graeson did not waste time to question why the dragon-wolf was here or how it found them. He twisted the soldier's dagger around and drove it straight through his heart.

Quickly tossing the man's lifeless body off him, Graeson stood just as the dragon-wolf dug its claws into one of the soldiers running for Dani. The creature crushed him flat against the ground, muffling the victim's scream.

It swiped its tail across the forest floor, knocking one of the soldiers Ellie was battling off his feet.

Just when Graeson thought maybe the wild animal was on their side, its black-feathered wings flared out, and Graeson ducked, narrowly missing them. When Graeson tried to push himself up, the dragon-wolf's tail came flying towards him. His chest smacked the ground, pushing out a groan. Air whipped over his head. Just as quickly, a scream ripped through the air behind him, followed by a thunderous *crack*.

Cautiously, Graeson lifted his head and peered behind him, his stomach curling with dread for what he may find.

Pressed against a tree, a soldier struggled to get up, his limbs shaking and fear sparkling in his eyes. With a snarl, he grabbed a dagger from his belt, his gaze dripping with anger. Glaring at the dragon-wolf, he reared his arm back, preparing to strike.

Before he could release the blade, though, a black throwing knife pierced his neck.

The man's blade fell from his hands as blood spurted from his lips, mouth gurgling as his life force swept out of him in currents of crimson. He scrambled to apply pressure to the wound, but it was no use; he fell limp to the ground moments later.

Across from Graeson, Medenia grabbed another throwing knife, rage drenching her stance as she turned away from Graeson and the soldier, who now slumped dead against a tree.

The massive creature stood on its hind legs, roaring as several soldiers ran towards it from multiple directions, their swords raised.

As the animal stomped down, it lashed out with its wings, sending a powerful gust of wind whipping at the men, knocking one of the men to the ground.

A blood-curdling scream left his lips, but another soldier came charging in his place.

Graeson sprang to his feet, and from the corner of his eye, he spotted Medenia aim another blade. She threw the knife, but it was a second too late.

The soldier drove his dagger through the creature's large wing, piercing its membranes, right before Medenia's knife found its mark.

The dragon-wolf screeched, loud and ear-shattering, as it retracted its wing with the blade still lodged in its flesh.

Knowing the beast was now wounded, the third soldier ran harder as the dragon-wolf retreated several steps, hissing its displeasure.

Graeson ran, sliding past the dragon-wolf and cutting off the man. The color drained from the soldier's face, and Graeson didn't feel an ounce of guilt as he drove his blade through his stomach with a sickening squelch.

When Graeson turned around, he halted, a shout lodged in his throat as another soldier charged.

But this time, the creature was faster, and the man soon met the God of Death as his body was chomped in half by the beast's harrowing array of sharp teeth.

Struggling to catch his breath, Graeson quickly scanned the area. All around him was destruction.

The ground was littered with bodies and blood. But thankfully, and by the blessings of the gods, none of the corpses belonged to any of their entourage. He breathed a sigh of relief.

With the battle over, Ellie hurried to Medenia, checking for any wounds as the princess shoved her away. Sylvia knelt beside Terin, who was still knocked out, checking his head. Even Emmett had managed to stay alive, his dagger stained red.

He heard someone retching as Emmett asked, face drained of color, "What--what is that?"

The creature snarled, exposing fanged yellow teeth as it turned toward Emmett. It spread its wings, and the muscles in its legs flexed as it crouched as if readying to pounce.

"That," Dani said, wiping her mouth with the back of her hand

and pressing her stomach with the other, "would be the infamous dragon-puppy."

A sad smile twitched at the corner of Graeson's lip at the mention of the name Moris had given the wild creature.

"Fucking balls." Emmett gasped in horror and took a step back. "You all did not mention how terrifying it is."

Graeson observed the animal. Although its lip curled into a snarl, the creature did not move toward Emmett as everyone seemed to hold their breath.

The dragons of old, the god within said, *were born with strong instincts.*

Graeson wasn't sure if he trusted the god's assessment, but perhaps the dragon-wolf could tell friend from foe. Many animals could sniff out a human's intentions.

"As long as you don't piss it off, you'll be fine, Emmett," Graeson said warily.

He took a handkerchief from his pocket. He wiped each blade clean before returning them to their sheaths on his back.

"I'm not too sure about that," Emmett remarked, his legs trembling. "It's staring at me like it wants to eat me." He swallowed, and his knuckles turned white around the hilt of the dagger as he glanced from the creature to Graeson.

The dragon-wolf's lip curled higher as it sniffed, its nostrils flaring. Even from yards away, Graeson could smell the scent of iron and decay on the creature's breath as it snarled. As Graeson cocked his head to the side, the animal flicked its blazing eyes toward him. He swallowed hard.

Perhaps he was wrong. Maybe the creature would kill them all.

But as he looked more closely, he noticed something else within the animal's expression: *pain.*

The animal shifted, and that's when Graeson saw it. Its right wing was curved closely to its body as if shielding it. A glint of metal flashed in the sunlight, and Graeson's eyes widened.

He cursed under his breath. The dagger was still stuck in its wing.

Tentatively, Graeson took a step forward, slowly but not as hesitantly as he had the first time when he freed the beast from its chains.

He heard Emmett gasp and whisper, "Are you insane? We just saw it slaughter those guys."

Graeson ignored him, though. He could sense the god watching from its cage, too. Not with fear but curiosity.

I told you, the god said, *the dragons know when they are in danger.*

When he was only three yards away, Graeson put out a hand.

The dragon-wolf recoiled and snarled, its hot breath smacking Graeson's face.

Holding his ground, he pointed to the dagger. "I can help," he whispered gently.

With flared nostrils, the creature flexed its paws, and sharp, ivory claws dug into the dirt.

Most would have retreated then, but the creature couldn't heal if the dagger remained lodged in its wing. It couldn't fly or enjoy the freedom it only recently obtained access to.

As Graeson stood there, waiting for the animal to relax, unease washed over him. Despite his determination to provide aid, he wondered if some things could not be helped. Just as he was about to give up, the creature shifted, spreading out its injured wing for him to inspect it.

With a quick nod, Graeson slowly approached. His hand gently ran over the membranes of the wing. Outside of the wound, the beast looked healthy--or at least better than it had the first time Graeson had seen it a couple of weeks ago when he freed it.

The recent freedom had transformed it quickly, though, as if the mere taste of it was power enough. No longer captive and under the Frenzians' hold, the dragon-wolf looked like it could finally breathe, live, and flourish.

And yet, if today had gone differently or if there had been more soldiers, what would have happened? Would any of them have survived?

Humans will do anything to get what they want, the god inside whispered.

Or was it Graeson's voice, *his* words?

Because despite fighting it at every turn, Graeson was slowly realizing that the two were not so different. Both were monsters in their own right. The corpses across the field proved that.

Clearing his throat, he wrapped his fingers around the hilt of the dagger and pulled the blade out.

The animal screeched, loud enough to send any birds that remained in the nearby trees scurrying deeper into the forest. Even he had to wince, the sound piercing his ears.

Graeson stepped back, tossing the weapon onto the ground as he gave the animal a wide berth.

"How did it even find us?" Dani asked quietly as if afraid to disturb the animal.

"I have no idea," Graeson whispered.

The beast stretched its legs first, then spread its wings, testing them. A pained expression immediately crossed its face as the wounded wing twitched. With a frustrated huff, the animal crouched down, the muscles in its hind legs flexing as it prepared to take flight.

Graeson's stomach churned as he watched the animal struggle. The moment the dragon-wolf jumped and tried to move the wounded wing, compensating by flapping the other wing more furiously, it crashed. A thick cloud of dirt flew into the air.

Graeson coughed and waved the cloud away, clearing his vision.

The creature whined, curling its wings against its sides as it stared at the sky with agonized longing.

"What's wrong?" Medenia asked quietly, approaching.

Dani hissed at her, but Medenia waved her off.

"Its wing is too damaged," Graeson said. "I don't think it can fly."

The creature snapped its head in Graeson's direction, growling as it peeled its lip back over its teeth. Medenia hummed in acknowledgment and kneeled in front of the creature's head.

Graeson quickly stepped closer. "What are you doing?" he asked warily.

Medenia waved him off as she reached out her other hand.

Graeson glanced at Ellie, but she shook her head, holding up a finger for him to wait.

When the creature extended its head, Medenia caressed its cheek. With a soft smile, Medenia crooned, "You will fly again, little one."

"Little one?" Dani whispered.

Medenia ignored Dani and continued petting the dragon-wolf. "Would you like to travel with us?" she murmured.

"What did she just say?" Emmett shrieked in disbelief.

A quiet grumble came from the dragon-wolf as it looked at Emmett, its ruby-red eyes narrowing.

"Do not listen to him," Medenia chided, calling the animal's attention back to her. "He is just scared of the unfamiliar. But you're not so different from my dog at home, now are you? I can even see you have the same snout." She grinned.

The creature puffed up its chest and lifted its chin from Medenia's hand. Dumbstruck, Graeson could do nothing but watch the interaction.

Medenia clicked her tongue. "Oh, don't be like that. I think you and Beau would get along swimmingly if you met." She tipped her head closer and chuckled. "As long as you promise not to eat him. But you wouldn't do that, would you, Nyrri?"

The creature scoffed.

"That's what I thought."

"Wait, now she's naming it?" Emmett gasped, clutching his hair.

Medenia scowled at him. "Of course not. She already has a name. Everyone does."

Graeson eyed Medenia curiously as Dani asked, "Wait, are you *speaking* to the animal?"

"It is not that hard if you simply listen," Medenia replied, her voice still containing the same melodic lilt she used with the dragon-wolf.

Mouth agape, Dani turned to Ellie as if she would be the one to admit that the princess was on the verge of losing her mind.

Arms crossed, Ellie merely shrugged with a look of indifference. "What? Medenia is particularly in tune with the Goddess Nerva."

"But she's the Goddess of Strength," Dani argued, still skeptical. She looked at Graeson, but even he was at a loss for words.

Ellie sighed. "The gods do more than what some mortals claim. You should know that by now. Take the Goddess Misanthia, for instance. She may be the Goddess of War and Strife, but she is also extremely strategic and gentle when it comes to protecting those who cannot protect themselves.

"Nerva may be the Goddess of Strength in your kingdom, but to us, she is so much more. She is the Goddess of Motherhood and Femininity."

"So...because of this, Medenia can speak to animals?" Dani asked, incredulous.

Ellie rubbed a hand across her face, exasperated. "First off, if you think that your little island is the only kingdom a god has favored and provided with *gifts*, you are wrong and more ignorant than I first thought. Second, Medenia does not simply *speak* to the animals; she *understands* them. Many people possess this skill, but Medenia is particularly talented."

Medenia patted the top of the dragon-wolf's head and stood, wiping the dirt from her palms. "We should get going. Nyrri believes more soldiers will come soon if we stay too long," she explained.

"You cannot possibly be serious?" Emmett sputtered, eyes wide.

The animal snarled at Emmett, and he raised his hand in response. "See! It's a wild creature, not a pet!" He looked around in a frenzy. "The horses surely will have issues traveling along it."

"*She* is no danger to anyone," Medenia argued with a growl.

"How can you be so sure?" Dani asked.

The princess raised her chin. "She told me."

Dani glanced at Graeson. "Come on. You're telling me that you believe her?"

The gods were more powerful than any of the myths gave them credit for. The god within him was one beast; Pontanius, another. But the rest? The rest were so much *worse.* Despite how fondly Ellie spoke of Nerva, most of the high gods were brutal and unyielding. They were not beings that Graeson wished to deal with if he could help it.

Graeson turned to the god within for an answer.

Now you wish for my opinion? the god asked, voice dripping with annoyance.

Does she speak the truth?

The god huffed but did not deny it. If the god did not question Medenia's ability to communicate with the animal, Graeson wouldn't either.

"I believe Medenia," Graeson said finally. "If she says we are safe, we are safe."

"I should mention," Medenia interjected, dusting off her soiled slip as she stood, "that the previous humans Nyrri has interacted with have not been kind to her. If Nyrri senses that you wish her harm, she will not hesitate to act upon her instincts."

Nyrri pushed herself up, and though she held her wounded wing closely to her, the sharp teeth she revealed warned that she was still utterly a threat.

Emmett squealed.

Dani groaned, mumbling, "Yes, because *that* is comforting."

"There is nothing to fear. Even dogs were once wild creatures," Medenia assured, surveying the group. When her gaze caught on Graeson, she cocked her head and offered him a soft smile. "Sometimes we only need someone willing to understand us to help shed our cold exterior, do we not?"

Graeson shifted but remained silent.

"Very well," Dani said, though the skepticism was still present.

"What are we going to do with them?" Sylvia asked, calling everyone's attention to them. Sylvia pointed to Terin and Kalisandre, who remained unconscious on the ground.

With her arms crossed over her chest and brandishing a smug look, Dani turned to Graeson. The faint traces of the bruise around his neck heated beneath her gaze.

He pursed his lips. The bruise would fade quickly. He walked over and picked up Kalisandre. Once in his arm, her head slumped back, but otherwise, she did not stir.

In his arms, she was safe.

He inhaled, blowing it out slowly.

Turning toward his horse, he said to the others, "We ride onward and hope that Terin wakes up before she does."

CHAPTER 11

MYRA

*M*YRA *CHOKED ON HER TEARS AS SHE LOOKED AT HER PARENTS KNEELING on the ground of the throne room. Mynhos leaned against her, her little brother's sobs shaking them as they sat helplessly with the king's guards at their backs.*

Mynhos hadn't stopped crying since the guards, clad in armor, had kicked down their front door that very morning. When their father had spotted the men heading for their house, their mother immediately peeled open the hidden door beneath the pantry, urging Myra and Mynhos to hide in the hole in the floor.

Afraid of what was to come, the children had begged their mother to stay with them. But the space was too small and could only fit the two children.

With a quick kiss to each of their cheeks, their mother shut them inside, and darkness swept over them, whispering of the coming danger. The siblings gripped each other as boots pounded atop them and shouts filled the humble bungalow.

Somewhere, porcelain shattered, and Myra could imagine the men throwing her mother's beautiful pottery across the dining room.

As the guards ransacked the home, Myra tried to reach out and shift the guards' emotions, but her brother's fear and her own consumed her. To keep his tears at bay and his sobs silenced, she poured all her energy into settling Mynhos's emotions. She tried so hard to keep them both silent. Sweat dripped from her forehead, mixing with her sweat. Her arms ached as she tugged Mynhos close.

But despite her efforts, the guards had still found them.

All the way to the castle, as their hands were tied behind their backs, their mouths gagged and eyes covered, Myra could only think one thing: if she was stronger, she could have saved them all.

But her well of power had long since dried up. Not an ounce of the gift granted to her by the gods--a gift that was quickly becoming a curse-- remained.

Even still, Myra refused to give up.

As Mynhos and Myra were forced to sit and watch their parents be interrogated, Myra mustered all the strength she could. She reached out to her parents, to the guards, to the king, but they were all too far to reach.

When she pulled onto the fading threads floating in the air that connected to her brother beside her, Myra's own fear and anguish caused the thread to slip from her grasp. She yearned to hold onto him--to do something. But with her hands bound, she could only scoot as close as possible.

"We must give credit where it is due," the king said to her parents, kneeling shoulder to shoulder in front of him. "Your ability to escape the Crown's notice for so long is commendable."

Her father tipped his chin up, his blond curls soiled with dirt and blood, but it was her mother who spoke. "Do whatever you want to us, but please, leave them alone. They're just children."

King Domitius smiled, but the twisting of his mouth only unsettled Myra even more.

"You are traitors to the Crown. Your fates are sealed."

He raised his gaze, his brown eyes falling upon Myra and her brother, cowering at the guards' feet.

Myra, unable to help herself, latched onto the invisible thread before her. It thrashed with an untamable darkness that burned at the touch. Still, she tried to coax the king's emotions, to bend them to her will.

But when Domitius cocked his head to the side and chuckled, she knew it was useless.

She was helpless. Too weak to save her family.

"On second thought..." The king spun the sword in his grasp, his eyes locked on Myra for a moment before returning his attention to her parents. "I can offer you this. I was going to take the one child, but I suppose I can make use of both."

"Please!" her father begged. "They're only children!"

"You're a monster!" her mother said, spitting on the floor.

"Enough!" King Domitius shouted. He looked at two of the nearby guards and nodded his head. "Turn them around. Let them get one last look at their precious children. Because if I am anything, I am considerate."

The guards stepped forward and yanked Myra's parents around. Her parents immediately met Myra's and Mynhos's gazes.

"We're sorry," her father croaked, his eyes glistening with tears.

"Take care of him," her mother whispered.

Myra bit down on her trembling lip as a tear slipped down her mother's cheek. Her mother never cried, and Myra knew then that there was no stopping the king.

The king shifted, and metal caught the fading light spilling across the floors from the windows. Myra immediately turned to Mynhos, pressing her head against his.

The sword slashed through the air, followed by a thud, then a strangled cry from her mother and a scream from Mynhos.

"Don't look!" Myra urged her brother, her eyes springing open for a second before she squeezed them shut as the blade whipped through the air again.

Yet even with her eyes closed, Myra could still see her mother's head fall to the floor, landing beside her father's.

The king's orders were no more than a distant buzz in Myra's ears as her ears rang. She kept her head pressed against Mynhos, her cheeks soaked with tears and throat raw from her screams. At some point, a guard yanked Myra and Mynhos up. Myra forced herself to look away from her parents' crumpled bodies as the guards dragged her away.

Down, down they went.

Mynhos screamed and shouted, his limbs flailing. Before long, a guard grabbed him, throwing the four-year-old over his shoulder and storming away.

Myra desperately yelled after them, trying to go after her brother. She had to be with him. She needed to be with him. She promised she would take care of him. Yet the other guard merely snatched her wrist and tossed her over his shoulder as well, carrying her through the dark, damp halls beneath the castle.

They passed cell after cell before the guard finally stopped in front of one. Keys jingled in his hand. He ripped open the door. Then Myra was flying in the air, the cell door slamming shut behind her as she crashed onto the ground.

A click ripped through the room, a piercing echo that solidified her fate.

Wiping her tears away, Myra hurried toward the cell door, her heart pounding. She slammed her fists against the door, shouting for her brother.

For hours, she screamed for Mynhos. Her throat was ripped to shreds, but she did not care.

Soon, though, her voice gave out. She pressed her forehead against the cold, grimy door, and her tears fell into her lap.

In the damp cell of the marble castle that dripped with anguish, Myra was completely and utterly alone with only her thoughts to entertain herself as time ticked by.

Her home had been destroyed, her parents were dead, and her brother had been taken from her.

Why was she still alive?

Why had the king not ordered her death, too?

Myra didn't know how much time had gone by.

For the first few days, she could barely manage to push away the grief from her limbs to stand, letting the day's rations go to waste. Soon, her ribcage poked through her stomach, her limbs grew feeble, her body became frail.

Myra tried to have hope. She tried to recall happier days: playing with Mynhos in their garden while their mother sat on a bench embroidering and their father chopped wood for the fire.

But as each day passed, those memories became harder and harder to dredge up.

She dreamed of escaping, clawing through the ground and digging her way out.

She latched onto the single strand of hope that she would see her brother again. She had heard the king saying he would keep both of them alive.

Yet if Mynhos was alive, where was he?

As the last ounce of hope she clung to began to slip through her fingers, the door creaked open, blinding light pooling across the floor of her decrepit prison.

Myra lifted a frail, shaking hand to block the bright flame as a guard shifted, making room for another to enter.

Every muscle in her body tensed as the stench of the individual's emotions draped over her. Myra knew who the man was before her vision steadied.

King Domitius crouched in front of her. The king's blond hair shone bright white in the flickering flames. Half of his face was cast in shadow. When Myra met his gaze, he quirked a brow in befuddled amusement.

She knew she was supposed to drop her gaze; it was what her mother had always told her when the king's guards patrolled the streets. It was a sign of respect--but more than that, it was to deter the crown's attention.

Yet she had no energy to move. She had already failed to avoid the king discovering her, so what was the point of hiding anymore?

"Do you wish to see your brother?" he asked.

"Mynhos?" The first word she had spoken in months left her lips on a gasp. "Where--where is he?"

Myra's heart hammered in her chest. As the king tipped his head to the side, she was sure he could hear it pounding, too.

The corners of Domitius's lips tipped up, but his smile brought her no comfort as darkness swirled within his irises. "What would you do to ensure his survival?"

"Anything."

Boots pounded against the ground, pulling Myra from her slumber. She blinked her eyes open, but darkness blanketed the cell. As the guards neared, the usual clatter of keys did not ring at her cell door or any other.

Fear flooded Myra's body, but the emotion didn't belong to her. This fear was tainted with pain and was bitter on her tongue.

A chain scraped against the floor, metal scratching against the stone outside her cell. But the guards didn't stop; instead, the guard and whichever prisoner they led kept walking, the manacle continuing to screech.

The fear that slipped through the tiny cracks around the door filled Myra's cell until she felt like she was drowning in it.

Her hand flew to her throat as it lodged itself there and overwhelmed her senses. She gasped for air, for a reprieve. Pressing her palm against the wall, she begged the cool temperature to soothe the agony consuming her.

But no reprieve came.

The fear strangled her, like thick black smoke filling a room. It wrapped its tendrils around her body and yanked her to the ground.

Her nails bit into her palms as she struggled to regain her breath.

On her hands and knees, Myra heaved.

Only once the sound of the grating chains and footsteps vanished further and further into the depths of the dungeon was Myra at last released from the torment.

Her limbs shook beneath her as her breathing slowly returned to normal. When she tried to push herself up, her arms and legs collapsed beneath her weight. She fell onto the stone floor, her cheek smacking against the ground with a hard *thump*. Pain spiked her jaw. As her ears rang, nausea twisted at her stomach until the pain was too much to handle, and Myra retched the little nutrients she had been given.

She knew she should get up but couldn't force herself to.

So instead, she curled on her side, her body trembling and tears streaming down her cheeks as she heard the faint whisper of screams rip through the halls.

As darkness swallowed her, she could no longer tell whom the screams belonged to.

CHAPTER 12
KALLIE

ALL SENSE OF TIME VANISHED.

Kallie didn't know how many hours or days had passed or even where she was when she opened her eyes. When she woke, she didn't even know whether she faced reality or some figment of her imagination. Every time she came to, a different sight greeted her.

Sometimes, she awoke to trees above her, as golden rays of sunlight seeped through the forest canopy and birds hopped from branch to branch. The breeze kissed her cheek, and the calming scent of cedar and oak brushed her nose. Other times, the sound of a roaring waterfall was the first thing she heard before she felt the kiss of the too-vibrant sun on her skin.

Right before dread filled her bones once she took note of the rock where Fynn sat.

And then there were the other visions and sounds that flashed before her--ones she could barely make sense of before they vanished.

The mazes the king built beneath the castle, the sweat soaking her limbs as she ran through them.

The plethora of bruises that covered her arms and ribcage in a macabre design only her father could dare hope to fashion.

Graeson beneath her, her hands wrapped around his throat.

The screams that ripped from her lips as she was dragged away from a home she had long-since forgotten.

The countless fires that she had survived but now threatened to take her.

Every time one of those nightmares appeared, Kallie pushed them away as fast as she could, fighting them at every turn before they had a chance to swallow her whole.

Yet they persisted. They came at her, one after another, endlessly.

But she could do nothing to stop them, although she tried.

So, whenever the sky appeared, the brilliant green leaves rustling in the wind, and a comforting warmth pressed against her back, Kallie tried to hold onto those moments for as long as she could.

But without fail, voices would soon sound, though her senses were still too disoriented to parse them.

"She's waking," a familiar voice would shout.

Followed by another more melodic voice saying, "On it."

When the darkness swept over her and the heaviness of sleep covered her bones, Kallie could do nothing but sink into that feeling, welcoming the never-ending shadows.

KALLIE HEARD the waterfall before she saw the water's surface sparkling in the sunlight, unnaturally blue and blinding. She squinted at the foam that formed where the water rushed into the lake and sighed.

"Why is it always here?" she asked, not bothering to look for her brother, for she knew he would be here. When Fynn was near, the world

was different: a little brighter, a little lighter, as if his very spirit soaked the earth.

"That is what you wish to ask me?" Fynn asked incredulously beside her. "Why we are at the Whispering Springs?"

Kallie shrugged. "It is as good of a question as any, is it not?" she asked, without bothering to turn around, her gaze fixed on the waterfall.

She could almost make out the entrance of the cave behind it. The ghostly outlines of the statues of Pontanius and Sabina loomed inside.

It had only been a few months since she had first visited the springs with Graeson, yet so much had happened since then. And yet, it felt as if nothing had changed. She still didn't have a crown, nor had she proven herself worthy of one.

Instead, here she was again, being dragged across the continent.

When her brother remained silent, she wrapped her arms around herself tightly and muttered, "You have told me little as it is, Fynn. You can at least answer that."

"I have told you plenty, Kallie, but you refuse to listen."

Kallie groaned and strolled forward, her feet sinking into the cool, damp sand along the shore. Although Kallie hadn't heard him approach, Fynn now stood beside her.

Brushing a hand through his hair, he sighed. "We are here because this place is embedded with Pontanius and Sabina's spirits."

Kallie's brows furrowed. Perhaps that was why there was a strange energy here. "Is this a dream?" Kallie wondered.

He paused, then said, "Of sorts."

"How can it be a dream of sorts? Are we here, or are we not here?" Kallie asked, perplexed as she stared out at the water.

Whatever this was seemed unlike any of her other dreams. It was visceral and vivid in a way she couldn't quite fathom. The water looked and felt real. She could feel the coarse grains of sand scrape her skin. She could smell the moss in the air. And yet...

"In the physical sense of the word? No, we are not here, *Kalisandre."*

He peered at her from the corner of his eye and smirked, his brows arched. "I am dead, after all. I no longer walk the mortal plane."

"The mortal plane?" she repeated, sparing him a glance.

Fynn hummed, folding his hands behind his back. "There is the world of the living, the world of the dead, and the world of the gods."

"Am I dead then? Is that it?" The very thought filled her with dread as she shifted uncomfortably.

Fynn chuckled. "No, you are not dead, sister." He tilted his head toward the sky, smiling softly with amusement. "Although from what I have gathered, my wife did knock you out cold."

Hesitantly, Kallie reached up and felt a bump on the back of her head where Dani must have struck her. She couldn't remember the incident clearly. But as she tried to recall it, anger bloomed.

Her hands fell to her sides, her nails biting into the flesh of her palms and knuckles blanching. Kallie could sense Fynn's eyes on her, but she refused to meet them as the memory of the fight resurfaced.

But the more she mulled the fight over, the more she realized she could do nothing about it. Not here.

By the gods, Kallie still didn't even understand where here *was.*

Fynn kicked at the sand. "You and Dani would have been best friends, you know. Always looking for logic rather than accepting things for what they are."

Kallie recalled thinking the same thing once upon a time, how the two of them would have grown up together, how they would have studied and trained together with the twins and Graeson.

But that was in another life, one that Kallie could never return to. One she never truly possessed.

"Her forgiveness will not be easy to earn," Fynn said after a moment.

Folding her arms over her chest, Kallie scoffed. "I do not want her forgiveness. I do not wish for the forgiveness of any of them."

Her brother snorted. "That is a lie."

"It is not," Kallie spat. "I do not care what they think of me."

Fynn laughed, and the sound bounced off the cliffs as if to haunt her. "You care more than you think."

Kallie rolled her eyes. "And you call me the liar."

Fynn turned to her, then took a step closer, staring at her with an intensity that Kallie could not ignore despite her efforts. "Tell me this: why do you believe you don't want their forgiveness?"

"I don't believe it; I know it, Fynn," she said pointedly.

He brushed his hair back and looked at Kallie with such sadness. "By the gods, Domitius really does have his claws deeper in you than I first thought."

"What?" Kallie exclaimed, stepping back. "No, he doesn't."

"Then why is it that the first thing you ask me is why we are in this place? Why isn't it about the dreams you've been having? The memories that Terin has been pulling from the back of your mind?"

"Terin can't--" Kallie swallowed, her eyes narrowing. She retreated another step. "Terin is not Esmeray. He cannot access my memories."

"He can't while you are awake, but when you are asleep?" Fynn smirked, the twitch of his lip sending a spike of anxiety spiraling through Kallie's bones. "The mind is a pliable thing, sister. You should know that better than most.

"It is why you can manipulate people and bend them to your will. It is why I could read people's thoughts, why our mother can strip one's memories. People often underestimate Terin because, on the surface, his gift appears to be just the ability to knock people out and slip through their dreams. But they are gravely mistaken to underestimate him. He can manipulate their very dreams. He can bring another person--dead or alive--into one's dreams, for he can open a world between the living and the dead.

"That, dear sister, is why we are here. Terin has made it so. But that is not the extent of his gift. Our dreams often reflect our past. Our nightmares are the tragedies we wish to forget, the mistakes we wish never to relive.

"It requires immense concentration, but Terin is able to grab someone's memory and weave it into a dream." Her brother gazed over the waterfall, at the roaring water crashing down.

Kallie shook her head in denial. "You speak nonsense."

With a sad smile, Fynn peered back at Kallie. "I speak the truth."

Kallie bit down, the muscles in her jaw twitching.

Fynn cocked his head to the side. "What have you been dreaming about, Kallie?"

"Nothing," Kallie mumbled, dropping her gaze to look at the sand.

Fynn stepped closer. "Dig deeper. Recall the dream before this. Where were you?"

"I don't know," Kallie whispered, hugging herself tightly as a gust of wind swept over her and tangled in her hair.

Fynn gripped her shoulders, shaking her slightly. Without meaning to, Kallie looked up, but it was a mistake. His brown eyes seared into hers as if Fynn was trying to look into her very soul.

"Yes, you do. Think back, Kallie." Fynn squeezed her shoulders harder. "Where were you? Who were you with?"

Kallie blinked.

"I--" The words were caught on her tongue as she riffled through her mind. But no matter how much she tried, she couldn't remember.

"Come on, Kallie," he whispered, his gaze skimming across her face, searching, pleading. "If you still remain loyal to Domitius and truly believe he cares for you, then why are you afraid to recall the dream?"

Kallie took a jilted step back, causing Fynn's hands to fall from her shoulders. Fynn, however, took a step forward as well, matching her.

A scene flashed before her eyes, but she shook it away. She didn't want to think about it. She didn't want to see whatever it was he was trying to make her remember.

Kallie retreated further, but the moment the sole of her foot hit the sand, her ankle rolled.

Kallie hissed in pain as she fell to her knees.

"Kallie," Fynn said warily.

"I don't remember!" Kallie shouted, squeezing her eyes shut.

"Yes, you do!"

Kallie flinched, but it wasn't Fynn's voice she heard.

"You are weak, Kalisandre!"

She pressed her palms against her ears in an attempt to block out the noise. But no matter how hard she pressed or how hard she tried to ignore it, her father's words slipped through, ripping through her palms and filling her eardrums.

He shouldn't be here, *she thought.* He can't see me like this. He shouldn't--

"Despicable!" her father shouted.

Tears burned her eyes and rushed down her face as she shook her head. But even as her head pounded, as she pressed her palms harder against her ears, her father's words kept coming.

"You are pitiful. Yet you want a crown? Ha!"

This was wrong.

All wrong.

Whatever her brothers were trying to show her was a lie--a facade, a charade. A fabricated story to get her to believe them and convince her to betray her father.

"This isn't real. This isn't real!" Kallie shouted.

"Just because you refuse to remember does not make it false," Fynn said, his voice a faint whisper in her ear as if he were yards away. "You cannot keep running from your past, Kalisandre."

"You're wrong!" she cried. "You're lying! He wouldn't--he loves me!"

She tried to hold onto the truth, to the father she knew, the man who raised her, cared for her, and trained her.

Her brother's tone was sad, distant now. "A true parent does not need you to prove your worth to them. You have to know that."

Kallie shook her head. Agony ripped at her lungs as she screamed, a blood-curdling noise pouring from her throat. Still, her father's voice seeped out and wrapped around her limbs, strangling her.

"You want power? You desire a throne? What kind of ruler falls to their knees? What kind of ruler crumbles at the sight of blood? Sacrifices must be made, Kalisandre!" he roared.

Her cheeks were damp, and her screams became mangled as her father's words surrounded her broken body.

They squeezed, twisted, and pierced her heart.

"You are weak," he spat.

Her mind felt as if it was being torn apart as past assignments from her father resurfaced: various names written in elegant handwriting on slim envelopes, a vial of poison given to a lord who had disagreed with a ruling; another poison given to a man who had spoken aloud a name which should have stayed forgotten; a dagger pressed into the hand of a guard who had seen too much.

"No, no, no," Kallie repeated, gripping her hair.

Her brothers didn't understand.

"Sacrifices must be made for the--" Kallie groaned in pain as she tried and failed to repeat the words she had been trained to say.

"You are unworthy."

"No!" Even though she knew he could not hear her, she shouted anyway.

"You are nothing.*"*

Pain seared through her head as if her very mind was on fire.

What were her brothers doing to her?

"Stop it! Stop!" But no one listened, and the pain continued as her brothers rifled through her mind.

With her arms wrapped around her knees, her body shook, and her lip quivered as tears ran down her face and the screams continued to pour from her lungs.

Someone tried to reach out.

Fynn? Terin? Her father?

She couldn't tell. Either way, they tried to cut through the noise, beckoning her.

But her name was no more than a whisper on their lips. They tried to shake her, to stir her, but she threw them off as panic overtook her body.

Kallie kept rocking as she continued to cry and scream into the air.

Then, when she thought she couldn't scream anymore, darkness consumed her whole.

CHAPTER 13
MYRA

THE WALLS WERE CRYING, AND MYRA COULD DO NOTHING ABOUT IT besides sit there with her head against the floor as she wrapped her feeble arms around her knees.

When she had initially agreed to assist the king, Myra had never imagined that she would be right back where she started nine years later. So much had changed since then, yet so much remained the same.

Among the shadows within the cell, a stench that Myra couldn't shake slithered across her skin. No matter how much she tried to rub it off, the horrid residue of the dungeons stuck to her flesh. Iron, moss, and something putrid filled the air of the cell just as it had before.

As she sat, the insides of her stomach gnawed at her, yet she had no desire to consume the half-eaten porridge that sat abandoned. The portion she had managed to eat earlier, she retched soon after.

Throughout the day, the guards came and went, sliding her meals through a small compartment at the bottom of the cell door. Occasionally, they came inside, poking her with needles to take her blood and check her vitals.

Every time a guard pried the small door open, the torchlight spread across the floor, illuminating the blood that stained them.

As soon as the door closed and the cell became swathed in shadow once more, the stains faded into the stone. Yet, while the darkness might have hidden them, it couldn't erase the anguish that seeped up through the ground and soaked her skin.

Since she had been in his employ, Myra had manipulated Kallie's emotions to the king's will.

In the beginning, Kallie was no more than a stranger. The guilt, although present, was minimal and a consequence Myra would easily swallow if it meant protecting her brother.

But then, as the years wore on, Myra never saw Mynhos.

Whenever Myra asked about her brother, the king would supply some elaborate excuse that Myra didn't dare question. And perhaps that was her downfall: never asking questions, never seeking the answers she wished.

Instead, she naively obeyed. Because as long as she never made the king mad, she and her brother would be set free one day.

But that day never came, had it?

At the time, Myra believed the choice she had made was the safest one--the right one.

She couldn't have been more wrong.

Her brother's supposed safety was only a bargaining chip.

And as Myra sat in the cell, she wished she could justify her actions solely in the pursuit of her brother's freedom. But at some point over the years, she had begun to question Mynhos's survival. Years went by, and she never saw him.

Still, she had continued to manipulate Kallie. Perhaps she continued because Myra didn't wish to anger the king out of fear that he would not only hurt Myra but Kallie as well.

Because despite knowing she shouldn't, Myra had befriended Kallie.

Myra had tried to stay away, of course. She had tried to distance herself. Yet when Kallie opened up to someone, it was as if she was letting them in on a secret--one that Myra desperately wanted and craved while alone in the castle.

Their friendship was one she had not predicted, but one she had learned to cherish. As a result, she tried to do what she thought best.

She did not wish for Kallie to suffer.

There were several mornings when Myra witnessed the bruises marking Kallie's skin and the haunted expression she wore after spending an evening training with the king. Kallie would startle at the smallest of noises or an unexpected touch.

Myra had thought that by altering Kallie's emotions and taking away the pain, she was helping her friend. When Myra erased the pain, Kallie's smile returned, the jumpiness vanished, and the bruises soon disappeared. But not all suffering could so easily be wiped away.

As time passed, fissures appeared in the careful tapestry Myra had woven within Kallie's mind. Stitches unraveled, holes appeared, and threads became too fragile. All it took was one misstep, one event, one training session with the king to undo Myra's work. But now that the tapestry was so tightly crafted, Myra feared there was no undoing it. Not without the risk of completely destroying Kallie's mind.

Especially not after what Myra had done to Kallie the night before the wedding.

Myra had completely wiped Kallie's emotions and replaced them with the false ones that Domitius had ordered Myra to weave together.

Therefore, unless Myra wanted to face the king's wrath and doom both of their lives, Kallie's emotions had to stay in check.

The king would have killed Myra if she failed and Kallie

disobeyed him. But first, he would have tortured Kallie in front of her, forcing Myra to watch the consequences of her failure unfold. Myra had lost too many people to let that happen again.

Forcing herself to believe it was better than the alternative, Myra kept helping hide Domitius's true self. She continued to enable the cycle.

Myra now knew that living in ignorance only delayed the inevitable. Now, Myra had all the time in the world to rethink the choices she had made to get to this point.

One evening, as Myra stewed in her guilt inside the dark, damp cell, a couple of guards passed by, their low, muffled voices seeping into the room. Myra crawled over to the cell door and pressed an ear against it.

"Has there been any word about the princess?" one of the men asked.

Myra inhaled sharply as she waited for the other guard's response.

"No, nothing," another guard said. "The Frenzians have sent soldiers in search of the princess, but none have been successful in their quest."

"I heard one of the squadrons was completely slaughtered at the edge of the forest; only their bones were left."

"This is one time I am grateful for having this post. I would rather deal with the prisoners and traitors than deal with whatever creature ripped those soldiers to shreds."

Myra didn't know if she should be relieved or not that the king had failed to retrieve Kallie thus far. If Kallie remained missing, Domitius would not be able to use her. The king had always been so confident about his success, but the seer suggested that he could fail.

And if Myra could not escape the king's hold, maybe Kallie could. One of them deserved freedom, at the very least.

Her thoughts turned to her brother.

She didn't know how much time had gone by since she had heard her brother's screams.

She should have found solace in the fact that Mynhos was alive.

That truth gave Myra little reprieve, though.

While the king may have kept her brother alive while she did his bidding, it did not make Myra feel any better.

What kind of life must Mynhos have been living over the years? Was he, too, locked in one of these cells? Had he been here the entire time, living in the dungeon while Myra felt the sun kiss her cheeks?

Did the brother she once knew even still exist?

When Myra had seen him, Mynhos had refused to look at her. Did he even recognize her?

It had been nine years since Myra had last seen him. Many things had changed since then. He was only a boy, no more than four years old when they were first captured. When the king had taken them captive and killed their parents, Myra had promised that they would escape this place as she held her brother close and as his tears fell upon the marble floors of the throne room.

She could only imagine how much he hated her now.

If he had lived in the dungeons for the entire time, Myra would not have blamed him for hating her.

After everything she had done and the betrayal that coated her hands, Myra was no longer a person *she* even recognized.

Myra forced her gaze away from the shadows.

She tried to ignore everything else: the stench, the ache in her limbs, the iciness coating her fingers. Within the cracks of the ceiling, she tried to find an ounce of sunlight seeping into the cell. Anything that she could latch onto.

But all around her, death bloomed, and it had long since spread its infestation, bleeding into the cotton of her dress, latching onto her skin, and melting into her bloodstream.

So, the walls continued to cry, and Myra sat there, holding back her tears despite no one being able to hear her sobs.

CHAPTER 14
MYRA

Myra grunted as a boot kicked her in the side. With the fog of sleep slowly evaporating, she raised a shaking hand to her face, shielding herself from the bright flames of the torch before her.

She squinted up at the guard but couldn't identify the man beneath the full-faced helmet he wore.

For almost a decade, Myra had lived among the Ardentolian guards. She had walked the halls beside them, exchanged pleasantries, and even ate among them on the rare occasion.

While she never considered the guards true friends, most of them had been kind to her or looked upon her without malice.

Now, the guards treated her as if she was nothing more than the last dregs at the bottom of a barrel of ale.

Myra had sacrificed her friendship, ignored her morals and values, and lied to everyone close to her by the order of the king. And where had it gotten her?

"*Now,*" the guard roared, slamming his foot into her side again, eliciting a grunt of paint from her lips. "The king has requested your presence."

Myra's stomach turned, the nausea returning and rendering her immobile.

The guard released a groan and yanked her up by the crook of her elbow. Myra's legs trembled as she attempted to stand. With her head spinning, she failed to steady herself and collapsed.

The guard cursed, anger spewing off him as he pulled her up again. "We cannot keep the king waiting."

"I'm sorry," Myra mumbled.

The guard tightened his grip on Myra's arm and yanked her forward, dragging her behind him. Outside the cell, a second guard nodded and turned, leading them down the hall.

Myra narrowed her gaze at him and stumbled. "Where are we going?"

"The king has decided it is time," the first guard said.

She blanched, her face paling. "Time for what?"

"Time for you to be of use."

Her lips parted.

But as if the guard felt another question brewing, he halted and spoke before she could. "You have been in the king's employ for several years. I should not need to tell you this, but I will: save your energy on futile questions. You will need every ounce of energy you possess for whatever task the king needs you to perform."

Trepidation dripped from the guard walking ahead, giving her pause. Although it was not his anxiety that had made Myra bite her tongue, but rather the emotions coming from the closest guard. Unlike the second man, malice and anticipation slithered from the guard gripping her arm.

Myra stayed silent as they led her deeper into the dungeon and through parts of the castle she had never known existed in the years she had lived there.

The torch in the guard's hand was the only source of light in the tunnel. Its flames danced across the stone walls, dispersing the shadows. Still, darkness followed them, chasing after the light like a starving beast.

They passed several cells barred with large iron doors not unlike the one she had come from. The further they went, the more decrepit the hall became. Shredded cobwebs hung from the ceiling. A scattering of footprints covered the hall, disturbing the dust on the ground.

Myra looked at one of the cells from which the foul emotions were most potent. Both guards' postures had changed slightly as they passed the cell.

"What's in there?" Myra whispered.

"If I were you, I'd stay as far away from those cells as you can. You never know what beast will crawl from them."

"What do you mean?" Myra asked, recalling the creatures lurking beneath the Frenzian temple. Could it be possible that Domitius was harboring his own?

"Stop trying to scare the girl more than she already is, Kolen," the other guard said over his shoulder.

Kolen merely chuckled and leaned closer to her. "The king likes his toys. While some may look like you, others are not as easy on the eyes."

Myra shuddered as a chill ran down her spine.

The guards remained silent the rest of the way, their heavy footfalls reverberating through the quiet hall. When they finally reached the end of the hall, an iron door blocked their path.

Kolen dug into his pocket and pulled out a set of keys. Dozens of keys clinked together as he rifled through them with one hand.

Picking out a slender one, he twisted the ancient key inside the lock. Goosebumps crawled across Myra's arm as he pried the door open, its metal hinges protesting with a spine-chilling screech.

With a rough push, Kolen forced her inside the small, square room. A single torch flickered on the far wall, revealing two doors facing each other. The air crackled with anticipation.

"Iro," Kolen said, tipping his head to a door inside the room.

The second guard nodded and knocked on the door to the right, fear wrapping around his ankles.

Sweat coated the back of Myra's neck. She wasn't sure if it was because of the heat or the unease spilling from Iro as he waited by the door. Either way, every muscle and nerve in Myra's body screamed at her to run, to flee, to escape back down the hall from which they came.

Yet Myra did not move a muscle.

She couldn't.

She stood frozen as the door finally cracked open from the other side. A low moan sounded from somewhere in the room, a noise that crept across Myra's skin and sent a shiver down her back.

"Finally," King Domitius said, and his sinister voice had Myra yearning for the cell she had just escaped. "We have been waiting for you."

The king, despite his impeccably tailored suit, looked slightly distraught. To anyone else, he might have seemed sick with worry because of his missing daughter, but Myra knew better.

Domitius did not care about Kallie's well-being. He only cared that she remained in his possession and remained loyal.

Myra had caught the flicker of wildness within his eyes before he had composed himself and she had dropped her gaze. Although the emotion was fleeting, she easily recognized the underlying panic.

More than anything, Myra wanted the king to feel that he was not all-powerful--that he could not control everything. But after years of being in the king's employ, Myra knew that the king was not easy to shake. Once his mind was made up, there was no turning back. He would not stop until he succeeded.

"Your Majesty," Kolen said, bowing deeply and forcing Myra to follow suit.

Myra could feel the king's gaze press down on her.

"You couldn't have cleaned her up before coming?" Domitius drawled.

Kolen tensed beside her and cleared his throat. "We did not want to waste any time, Your Majesty."

"Is this conversation not a waste of my time?"

The guard tipped his head in penance. "Yes, Your Majesty. My apologies, My King."

"We will have to make do." Domitius huffed and turned on his heel. "Come."

Kolen straightened and pushed Myra forward.

Myra stumbled forward, her footsteps unsteady. Without anything to stop her, she collapsed onto the floor, her knees hitting the stone. She bit her lip to stifle the cry of pain.

"What the--?" the king began, spinning back around. He groaned in annoyance.

Suddenly, a rough hand snatched her chin and jerked her face upward.

Domitius's gaze bore into hers, his lip curling as his fingers dug into her cheeks.

Myra blinked away her tears and cleared her emotions, hiding them away as best she could. She held her breath as King Domitius scrutinized her.

"So, this is the prized handmaiden?" a new voice wondered, one much too familiar.

Myra's eyes snapped to the man appearing behind the king, and her breath caught in her throat as she locked eyes with the Prince of Frenzia.

She tried not to jerk out of the king's grasp or show any kind of emotion at all. But it was hard to keep still when Sebastian's small, green eyes observed her with too much interest as they skated down her body.

Sebastian's deep maroon suit jacket hung over his arm, the rich hue clashing with his red hair. The sleeves of his cotton blouse were rolled up to his elbow, and the hem of his shirt was tucked into the top of his black trousers.

Months ago, when they sailed the Red Sea from Pontia to Frenzia, Myra was thankful that she hadn't been required to interact with the prince.

Even in Frenzia, Myra rarely interacted with Sebastian, much to her relief. She had been around Frenzia's staff long enough to know their distaste for the prince, no matter how many titles he held. Sebastian Dronias was nothing but cruel, unkind, and wretched.

"Indeed, it is," King Domitius supplied, his lip curling as he released her. "Stand up," he commanded.

Myra tried to obey, but her limbs shook, and her attempt was feeble at best.

Sebastian chuckled in amusement, and Myra bit down on her tongue as tears burned behind her eyes. She had never been physically fit, not like Kallie, whose training had shaped her body. Still, Myra had never felt so weak as she did now. She pitied herself as the four men watched her struggle.

"Your Majesty," Iro said, his fear a tangible thing.

Myra squeezed her eyes shut as a wave of annoyance came from the king.

"Is there a problem?" Domitius asked.

Kolen stilled, his breathing quieting because even he knew that one did not interrupt royal affairs.

Still, the fear-filled guard stepped forward. "Your Majesty," Iro said, "the girl is weak. Getting her here was more cumbersome than we had anticipated. Are you sure--"

"Do you *dare* question me?"

Iro lowered his voice. "No, Your Majesty. Of course not. I just--I know how important this task is to you. I do not wish for anything to interfere with its progress."

The king hummed, the tension in the room growing taut. Domitius cocked his head and said, "I am feeling generous today, so I will let you leave this room with your tongue still intact. But do not question me again lest you wish never to speak again. Now get her off the ground."

"Of course, Your Majesty," Iro said, yanking Myra up by the elbow. "Thank you, My King."

Sebastian strutted forward with his hands folded behind his back. He stalked around her in a circle, clicking his tongue as he observed her. "I say this with the utmost respect, Your Majesty, but she does not seem all that special."

"Ah," the king tsked, "and that is why she has been such a splendid tool to have in my employ. Sometimes, those who hide in the shadows prove to be the best weapons."

Crossing his arms over his chest, Sebastian peered at the king inquisitively. "But I thought Kalisandre was your weapon, is she not? After all, you paraded her around as such."

The muscles in the king's jaw twitched at the mention of Kallie, but he pressed forward, hiding his dismay from those in the room. "While that is in part true, Kalisandre's *obedience* wouldn't be possible if it wasn't for her handmaiden." He smiled.

"Is that so?" Sebastian asked, doubtful.

"Indeed."

"If only all members of one's staff were as useful."

The two men laughed, the cruel sound making Myra's skin

crawl. Then, someone cleared their throat, silencing the laughter as everyone turned toward the door from which the king and prince entered.

A man stood at the doorway, his hands folded together in front of him. He wore a stained white apron, a sight which made the blood leave Myra's face. Black gloves stretched over his arms, stopping at his elbows. Through silver-rimmed spectacles balancing precariously on the tip of his nose, the man observed her with beady eyes.

"Your Majesty," the man said, shifting his attention to the king. "Apologies for the interruption, but I am ready when you are."

"Thank you, Dr. Thorne," Domitius said. He turned to Sebastian. "Let's get started then, shall we?"

"Are you sure we can trust her?" Sebastian replied, his gaze flicking from the king to Myra with suspicion.

King Domitius merely shrugged. "She is just a woman--and a handmaiden at that. No one would believe her if she uttered a word." Fixing his gaze on Myra, the king arched a brow. "Though she won't, now will she?"

Myra understood the king's unspoken demand: if she wanted to see her brother again, she would obey.

Myra bit down on her tongue as Mynhos's screams came to the surface of her mind.

While she might have failed to keep him safe over the years, she was determined to keep him alive. Whatever Domitius wanted her to do, she would do it if that meant she would save her brother.

Sebastian hummed in agreement, scratching his chin. "I suppose it is worth the risk to be able to boast about our success."

"A king does not boast," King Domitius said with a click of his tongue.

Sebastian's jaw twitched, but he tilted up his chin. "And some kings do nothing at all."

King Domitius smirked. "It is a wonder you were able to make any progress with the research."

"My brother may be pretty on the eyes," Sebastian said, "but that is all he is good for. He has always been soft, and his head is constantly in those old textbooks. Knowledge, however, is only powerful if one knows how to use it and is willing to push the boundaries of what is possible.

"My father knew this, and he knew who Rian was. So, when the time came, I was the one who my father had confided in and entrusted. Since his untimely death, I have taken it upon myself to continue my father's research."

Domitius nodded. "And you have made great strides."

Sebastian nodded. Then, he pursed his lips, his eyes narrowing slightly. "But we made a deal. This knowledge does not come freely."

"You will get what is owed," the king said with a flick of his hand. "You need not be hasty. You still do not sit on the throne."

The back of Myra's neck grew damp as the heat of the room increased. She tried to hide her interest as the conversation continued.

"Not yet. Though that will be solved soon enough. I cannot say the same for your side of the deal, though. The princess is still nowhere to be seen," Sebastian argued, quirking a brow. "From what I've heard, she is still gallivanting with the Pontians."

Myra's heart thumped in her chest, and she swallowed down her relief. She could only hope that Kallie was hidden and as far away from the king's reach as possible.

"Do not worry yourself over them," King Domitius said. "They mean nothing in the grand scheme of things. We have ensured they will not be a problem for long."

"And if they are able to thwart your plans once again?" Sebastian asked.

"They won't," King Domitius said, his nose twitching.

"How can you be sure?"

"Steps have been taken to ensure their demise."

Myra tensed when she felt the king's gaze land on her. Guilt stirred within her for the actions she was forced to take before the wedding. She could only hope she had somehow failed to twist Kallie's mind.

Sebastian shrugged. "Well, let us hope your little pet is as successful with this experiment. After all, I didn't come all this way for nothing. Let us see if she is truly the answer we have been searching for."

He turned around and followed the other man into the room, where waves of fear and dread poured from in macabre waves.

A flurry of emotions twisted in the air and washed over her. Myra's stomach grew sour, and her skin became clammy and cold.

The king stepped in front of Myra. He tipped her chin up with a finger and lowered his voice so only she could hear. "You have failed me once. Let us see if you can redeem yourself, shall we?"

Myra swallowed the rising lump in her throat and said the words she had been trained to say, "Yes, My King."

He released her chin and followed Sebastian.

As the guards pushed her forward, an overwhelming sense of fear enveloped her. It soaked the wall, spilling onto the floor and threatening to drown her. But only some of the fear belonged to Myra. The rest emanated from whomever remained in the room from which the king had emerged.

The intensity was unbearable, consuming her and overtaking her senses.

Sweat coated her neck and dripped down her back. Her entire body trembled, and she grew light-headed as the room spun.

Her fingers dug into Iro's arm as her legs turned to liquid and her head spun, her vision darkening.

But before she lost consciousness completely, she heard the king's disapproving voice as he chided, "Take her away and do not bring her back in this state next time. We cannot afford any more delays."

CHAPTER 15
KALLIE

Kallie coughed, spitting out a cool liquid that dribbled down her throat.

"Gods," a nearby voice hissed.

"She needs water," someone else said.

"She'll choke."

"No, she won't," the second individual argued, voice tense and stern.

Kallie tried to take in her surroundings, but when she blinked, black splotches crowded her vision. In the hazy darkness, she could barely make out the two silhouettes hunched over her, their identities hidden. Even their voices were foggy in her ears, distant and undistinguishable.

"Kalisandre," one of the voices beckoned, her name rolling off the man's tongue like a sweet lullaby sung to soothe a temperamental child. "Can you hear me?"

She hummed, her tongue too heavy to voice a response.

"Can you take a sip for me?" he asked gently.

Kallie tried to shake her head in dissent. She was too tired.

"You can sleep after you drink something," one of the men murmured.

His voice was familiar, but when she tried to match it with a face, her stomach twisted, and pain shot through her mind, heat rising in her veins.

"Please drink."

Cold metal touched her lips, pleading for her mouth to open.

She groaned but opened her mouth, allowing the crisp water to pool inside. She lazily swished it around, and when she swallowed, the man put the flask to her lips again. But the cool water did little to sedate the rising fire building within her veins.

There was something wrong--something she should have been doing. Yet she had no energy to act upon it.

The flask disappeared, and the man said, "Now you can rest."

A slight smile tugged at her lips as her eyelids grew heavy once more.

KALLIE HURRIED through the marble halls of the castle with her head down as she bit back the tears threatening to slip free.

She passed several guards and servants who bowed and curtsied at the sight of her, but Kallie ignored them all.

Her father's words were an incessant hiss in her ears: Never let them see you weak. If they see you are too emotional, if they can identify your weakness, they hold all the power.

If they saw her crying, word would get back to her father, which would only worsen matters. She wouldn't let a single tear drop in their presence despite how much her throat seized and her eyes burned.

When she finally reached her quarters, she burst through the door and slammed it shut behind her. Her back hit the wall, her chest rising hard and fast. And still, even in the safety of her room, she tried to refrain from crying.

If she cried, there would be no denying that her father was right.

But as her fingers wrapped around the doorknob, her knuckles blanching, Kallie could no longer hold the tears back. Immediately, she swatted them away from her face before they could fall and stain the silk corset she wore.

Afraid of someone overhearing her sobs, she pushed herself away from the door and scurried to her bed. She dropped onto the mattress, the plush quilt consuming her.

She quickly snatched a pillow and muffled her sobs. The fabric was soaked in seconds as the tears rushed out, unrestrained. Throat burning, Kallie sat up and tossed the pillow onto the ground, opting to sob into her hands instead.

Soon, the door's hinges creaked open, the high-pitched squeak ripping through the quiet, and Kallie tensed as soft steps hit the floor.

"Leave," Kallie commanded, her voice strained and wobbly as she tried to swallow the cry in her throat.

The footsteps stopped.

When the door clicked shut, Kallie's shoulders sagged in relief. She rubbed her fists against her eyes, the tears smearing across her knuckles.

Through the sobs, however, Kallie heard the faint tap of heels and stiffened once more.

She lifted her head, her hair falling in front of her face. "I told you to--"

"Kals," Myra interrupted, the handmaiden's voice a soft plea.

"I wish to be left alone," Kallie said through her hands. Myra might have been her friend, but Kallie did not want anyone to witness this moment of weakness.

Despite the request, the bed dipped as Myra sat beside her.

"No one should be left alone while they are hurting," Myra whispered. "You are in pain. Let me comfort you." She wrapped an arm around

Kallie, tugging her close, and instantly, some of the tension in Kallie's body released.

Still, Kallie fought the comfort offered to her. She tried to shrug Myra off. "I don't need to be comforted. I am fine," she insisted.

Myra only pulled Kallie closer.

Kallie inhaled in an attempt to extinguish the trembling that had overtaken her body. Notes of lavender and mint wrapped their sweet aroma around her.

She took another breath, focusing on the scent, allowing it to pull her mind elsewhere.

After a few more steadying breaths, Kallie relented as if a deep part of her needed her friend's presence. Kallie peeled her hands from her face, then wrapped her arms around Myra, leaning into her embrace despite knowing she shouldn't.

"You push yourself too much, Kals."

Kallie bit her lip, then released it. "I have to, Mys."

With a delicate hand, Myra brushed a strand of hair from Kallie's cheek. "One day, it will get better."

She almost laughed. "When?"

Myra did not respond, for they both knew there was no clear answer.

Myra squeezed Kallie, and her handmaiden's mere presence was enough to soothe the ache in Kallie's chest and dry the tears upon her cheeks.

As they sat, Kallie's breathing steadied, the trembling settled, and logic returned.

Her father pushed her because he knew Kallie could take it. He pushed her to make her better. The intense training, the grandiose speeches about plans and sacrifices, the assignments--they were all to make Kallie become the best she could be.

She was enough and would make her father proud.

Even if it was the last thing she did.

Light beamed above her, bright and stabbing. Kallie tried to peel her eyes open, but her head pounded from even the smallest twitch of her muscles.

Soft voices floated above her.

"It has to be done," a woman added.

"If we do this, he will be mad," a man said.

"It does not matter. We can't risk--" the woman gasped. Then louder, she called out, "She's awake!"

Shuffling sounded, and then Kallie felt a hand upon her chin, tilting her head upward.

Kallie groaned, swatting the hand away from her face.

"Eat," the man commanded.

For a second, Kallie thought her eyes were playing tricks on her. Because by the gods, that face made something move within her.

But she was wrong.

She had to be wrong.

He wasn't here. He couldn't be.

The hand pried her mouth open, and she felt a spoon slide into her mouth. She had no energy to fight them despite how demeaning it felt. She was utterly exhausted, so when sleep called for her again, she happily obliged.

CHAPTER 16
GRAESON

"I STILL CAN'T BELIEVE WE LET IT COME WITH US," EMMETT MUMBLED as they trotted down the stone path, his brown face a sickly hue.

The dragon-wolf's tail whipped in the air as her feet stomped on the ground of the Tetrian swamps. Emmett yelped as the tail almost knocked him off his horse.

"I already told you *her* name is Nyrri," Medenia called back with a roll of her eyes.

As if in response, Nyrri gently curled her tail around Medenia's shoulders.

Medenia smiled fondly at Nyrri as the animal puffed up her chest. "Plus, I told you already, Emmett, she needed time to heal," she said.

Nyrri tipped her head up and continued strutting forward, causing a small smile to twitch at the corner of Graeson's mouth. Nyrri's wing had healed quickly, but she was still not fit to fly long distances, as her balance was still off-kilter.

Emmett shivered atop his horse. "Pontanius, please watch over us," he called out to the sky, praying to the god.

After several days of traveling alongside the dragon-wolf, most of the party had grown accustomed to Nyrri's presence; even the horses had become less skittish as they traveled. Still, while Nyrri might have been tame, Graeson did not blame Emmett for his continued fear.

Despite Medenia's assurance that Nyrri was not a danger, at the end of the day, the creature was still a wild beast foreign to all.

As they traveled through the woods of Borgania and then the swamps of Tetria, Medenia always walked closely to Nyrri. Every time there was an unexpected noise or movement nearby that made Nyrri either bear her teeth or thrash her head, Medenia would pet the animal and whisper unintelligible words into her ear, calming the beast.

Still, the creature was certainly deadly. They had all seen her rip the soldiers to ribbons. Even when the beast hunted and tore apart a deer, its wild nature was as clear as day.

"Medenia's right," Graeson said, the reins loose in his hands. "If we had abandoned Nyrri, who knows who would have found her next? We did not free her once already, only for her to be captured again."

Medenia nodded. "It is not merely enough to free her. If those tunnels showed us anything, there are bound to be more like her somewhere. The Frenzians will pay for what they have done," she said.

Graeson looked to his right, where Kalisandre lay unconscious atop Terin's horse. Thankfully, when Terin had awoken, Kalisandre's command of him had dissipated.

They were still unsure how she had been able to manipulate Terin, for neither Graeson nor Terin recalled her saying anything to him. Therefore, the group did not want to take any further risks.

For the rest of the journey, Kalisandre remained unconscious, only being woken up to eat and drink. Thankfully, Terin would soon get his reprieve.

Once they arrived in Tetria, Terin would finally release Kalisandre. Then, they would finally discover the actual damage the king had done.

"Frenzia and Ardentol will pay for everything," Graeson said as they continued on.

WITH APPREHENSION, Tetrian warriors clad in leather and sharpened swords guided Graeson and the others down the trodden path toward the stone castle.

As they rode past storefronts and market stalls, Graeson was all too aware of the sideways glances from warriors and civilians alike. Initially, the people of Tetria greeted their princess with warm smiles and excited waves, but as their attention turned to the rest of the group and the beast by their side, their eyes widened in sheer horror.

Medenia stuck close to Nyrri, sensing the unease spreading through the city. Parents grabbed their kin, pulling them closer, as their children's expressions filled with a mix of wonder and excitement.

When they reached the castle, the iron gates creaked open. Ivy and moss stretched across the stone walls as if the earth was trying to pull the building underground and swallow it whole. From outside, the stained glass that decorated the castle's walls only marginally paled in comparison to how they sparkled across the floors inside. Inside the gates and away from the overcrowded streets, the guards led them to the royal stables, where they all dismounted and handed their horses' reins to the stable hands.

Graeson placed his horse Darling's reins in the waiting palm of a freckled-faced boy who scratched the horse behind the ear with his other hand, whispering into Darling's ear. Joy sparked the boy's eyes, and Graeson smiled.

"She's a good steed," Graeson remarked, scratching behind Darling's other ear.

The boy grinned widely. "Don't tell the others, but she is my favorite."

Darling preened, her tail sweeping the air at the compliment.

Graeson leaned over to the boy and whispered, "Your secret is safe with me."

The boy looked away, his shaggy hair falling into his face.

As the stable hand led Darling away, Graeson headed over to Terin, who was struggling to lift Kalisandre from his horse. When a guard took note, Graeson hurried toward Terin, cutting the Tetrian off.

"Here," Graeson said, reaching up. He lifted Kalisandre from the horse by the waist, folding her over his shoulder.

"Sir, I can--" one of the warriors began.

Graeson shook his head. "Please, go help Dani," he urged, nodding toward Dani, who was struggling to direct her horse into one of the stables.

The guard groaned, shaking her head. "Winter hates that cell. She's never going to get her to go inside," the Tetrian said, already walking away and shouting orders at one of the nearby boys.

"Thanks," Terin remarked with a yawn. "I was afraid I'd drop her."

"It's nothing," Graeson said, securing Kalisandre in his arms and feeling a sense of calm with her near. "We should ask to see a healer."

"My sister's mind still seems to be intact if that is your concern," Terin said wryly, running a hand across his tired face and pushing back his tousled brown waves.

Graeson arched a brow. "While I think Kalisandre should see a healer as well, I was referring to *you.*"

"I'm fine, Gray." Terin took a step away from the horse and stumbled.

Graeson arched a brow. "Sure."

Despite having rested throughout their journey, the bags beneath Terin's blood-streaked eyes were more prominent than ever. Sleep had never come easy to him, but after the extraneous use of his ability, the man needed to rest now more than ever.

He was a walking paper bag, disheveled and weak. His beard had grown more haggard, and his hair was past his chin.

"All right. I've seen better days," Terin admitted, stuffing his hands into his pockets.

"The healers could at least give you a sleeping tonic to help."

Terin huffed. "If they do that, I'm afraid I'll be asleep for days."

"You need the rest, Ter."

Terin looked towards Kalisandre, and his brows drew together. Thoughts Graeson couldn't quite decipher deepened the wrinkles forming in the middle of his friend's forehead. "I'll think about it," he said after a moment.

"That is all I ask," Graeson said as they walked toward the group gathered outside the stables. "I need to bring you both back in one piece, remember? Or else Esmeray will have my head." The mere thought made him shudder.

Terin snorted. "I think it's a little late for that."

Graeson shrugged, even though he knew Terin was right.

If the queen wasn't already storming through the halls in a mad fury, she would be soon enough. Even the sea separating Pontia from the rest of Vaneria couldn't keep the whispers from reaching the kingdom. Gossip always found its way over.

As Graeson and Terin left the stables, they watched a boy who must have been no more than sixteen take a hesitant step toward Nyrri. The boy lifted his chin as he held his hands steady at his sides. But while his posture was sturdy, a hint of fear coated his deep brown eyes.

"Bengi," Medenia called with an amused smile.

The boy hesitantly turned toward the princess. Trepidation sparkled in his eyes as if he feared giving his back to the creature would only increase his chances of being eaten whole. "Yes, Your Highness?"

"No need to take Nyrri into the stables. The queen will want to see her first."

"Oh," Bengi mumbled, blinking. He cleared his throat and bowed again, his brown hair falling in front of his face and hiding the flush quickly spreading across his warm, brown cheeks. "Of course, Your Highness."

Medenia ruffled Bengi's hair. "Where's Ophelia?"

"She was out hunting, but word has already been sent about your return."

Medenia frowned but quickly wiped it away before squeezing his shoulder and nodding to the guards. "Let us see the queen."

As the group walked away from the stables, Graeson heard Bengi mutter under his breath, "Bless the goddess and the stars."

Beside Graeson, Ellie chuckled and leaned toward him. "I thought Bengi was going to shit his trousers there for a second," she whispered.

"Brave of him to step forward," Graeson said.

Ellie shrugged. "Oh, I'm sure he only offered because Medenia was there. He's had a little crush on her since he could barely walk."

"Truly? Doesn't he know she is with Ophelia?" Terin said, leaning forward slightly.

Ellie chuckled. "Of course. He's Ophelia's little brother, after all."

At the base of the steps, a line of Tetrian warriors stood with their sheathed swords mere inches from their fingertips. All eyes were on Nyrri as the small group approached.

In the middle of the line of warriors and a few steps up, Queen Cetia stood with her chin tipped up. She balanced her hands on a crystal sphere sitting atop a wooden cane. Her long nails, dipped in black, clicked against the orb.

With two guards flanking her, the queen stepped down, and her sage-green dress whipped in the billowing wind.

"I hear that you have not only brought one dangerous creature into my queendom, but two," she drawled. "Rumors scurried through my streets the moment you stepped foot on Tetrian land about a foreign beast and a captured bride. The warriors seem to fear the beast, but I have heard other rumblings that make me question who we truly should fear here."

Graeson, unable to stop himself, said with an even but firm tone, "Kalisandre is not a danger to anyone, Your Majesty."

They hadn't come all this way and sacrificed so many lives for the queen to turn them away now because of some supposed threat.

The queen raised a brow. "You claim she is not a danger, yet you knew exactly who I was referring to," Cetia smirked. "I could have been referring to you."

"But you weren't," Graeson retorted. As the corner of his vision reddened, the anger rising within him, he exhaled, long and heavy.

"Peculiar, though, is it not?" Cetia asked, tilting her head. Although Graeson knew the blind queen could not see him, her gaze bore into him, as if she could perceive more than even he could.

The question and the queen's tone only increased Graeson's anger. However, before he could say anything more, Ellie stepped forward.

"Your Majesty," Ellie said, curtsying low with respect. "The princess is unconscious and has been so for most of our journey.

Whether or not she is a threat yet is to be determined. Either way, we request a healer for both the princess and prince."

"Is the prince harmed?" Cetia asked, forehead creased in concern.

Terin cleared his throat. "No, Your Majesty, I am well."

Cetia tapped her staff against the ground. "Do not lie. I can hear the exhaustion dripping from your tongue."

Terin shifted on his feet uncomfortably.

Cetia snapped her fingers. "Laura and Galia, take them to the infirmary, then place the princess in a holding cell."

Graeson clutched Kalisandre closer to his chest as two warriors stepped out of the line. "You will not touch her."

"Do not forget, child, that this is my queendom. I do not care who, or *what*, you are," Cetia commanded, her words quiet but authoritative.

Ellie placed a hand on Graeson's shoulder, with a look urging him to stay quiet.

Reluctantly, he did. But this conversation was far from over. Still, when the warriors reached for Kalisandre, he was slow to give them her. His unease was only marginally settled when Terin nodded at Graeson, silently promising to watch over Kalisandre. Graeson watched Kalisandre's limp body all the way to the castle's main doors, longing to go with her.

Ellie squeezed his shoulder, beckoning him to stay, before letting it drop.

The queen descended the rest of the steps, her heels rapping against the stone, two guards following. As Cetia reached the bottom, the guards faltered as Nyrri's claws scratched the cobbles below.

"Your Majesty," one guard said, a hand near the queen's arm, "the creature--"

"The *creature*," Cetia snapped, turning her head to the side, "has a name. Does it not, Medenia?"

"Her name is Nyrri," Medenia said, joining the queen. She wrapped an arm around her mother's arm and guided the queen forward.

Nyrri shifted as the women approached, and metal screeched as a warrior drew her sword, the sound ripping through the courtyard.

A low rumble vibrated in Nyrri's throat, and Graeson snapped his head in her direction. The dragon-wolf's eyes darkened, the red nearly snuffing out as her pupils enlarged.

Her top lip curled, revealing sharp, yellow canines.

"Put your sword away, Fallon," Medenia scolded.

"But, Your Highness..." the warrior who had pulled out her sword began to say before the queen interrupted.

"Fallon," Cetia warned, pausing her approach. "That was an order."

Fumbling an apology, Fallon returned her sword to its sheath and stepped back into line. Her fingers, however, still flexed over the hilt. As did a few of the other warriors, Graeson noticed.

"Mother, it is safe," Medenia assured. "Nyrri has not hurt any of us."

Ellie cleared her throat, her hands folded behind her back. "Do not paint a lie with misguided truths simply because you are fond of the creature, Medenia. While Nyrri has not hurt one of *us*, we would be remiss if we did not relay the entire truth. She is dangerous, Your Majesty, deadly even. She mauled several soldiers we encountered on the outskirts of Frenzia."

"Is this true?" Cetia asked.

Medenia sighed. "Yes, Your Majesty."

"Yet you all have remained unharmed?"

"Yes, Your Majesty," she repeated.

"Now, *that* is peculiar. Do you have any theories, Medenia?"

Medenia straightened, pride coloring her face. "Many animals can smell fear and anger. The same goes for Nyrri but at a more heightened level. Nyrri is well-attuned to humans' intentions."

Cetia hummed in acknowledgment before slipping her arm out of Medenia's and taking a step forward. Then, slowly and carefully, the queen reached out a hand.

Nyrri's wings flared out, and a gust of wind blew back the queen's raven-black hair. Movement flickered down the line of warriors, a couple of women stepping forward. Cetia, however, held up a hand, halting the guards' approach.

Graeson watched with curiosity as Nyrri leaned forward, her long snout nearing the queen's hand. The creature sniffed, nostrils flaring. And for a moment, time stilled.

Then, Cetia lifted her hand and felt for the creature's nose. "What did you say Nyrri is exactly?"

Nyrri tilted her head, leaning in as the queen stroked her snout. A breath of relief echoed down the line of warriors.

"We're not sure exactly," Ellie admitted. "She has some of the features of a wolf, such as her snout and paws. But she also has wings that span past the length of her body and the ruby red eyes of the dragons of old."

"Interesting," Cetia murmured, deep in thought.

"When we were in the tunnels beneath the Frenzian temple," Graeson explained, "we came across several animal and human carcasses inside cells."

"Human?" Cetia repeated, voice pitched in disbelief.

"Yes," Graeson began, but he paused as he scanned the crowd. He shifted on his feet. "We have been traveling a long time, Your Majesty. Perhaps we could discuss this inside?"

Ceita patted Nyrri's nose. "Of course. Where are our manners? Rooms have been prepared for you all, and dinner shall be served in a couple of hours," the queen said, waving Graeson and the others forward.

One of the nearby guards cleared her throat, causing the queen to halt.

"Your Majesty, what shall we do with..." the guard hesitated, her gaze flitting between the princess and the creature. "*Nyrri?*"

Cetia flicked a dismissive hand in the air. "Lizbeth and Phoenix, take Nyrri to the stables."

"The stables? But what about the horses?" the guard asked incredulously.

"Mother, the stables might not be the best place," Medenia interjected. "She would feel confined. She was held in captivity for who knows how long."

Cetia nodded, pursing her lips. "Very well. Take her to the courtyard then, Lizbeth, and keep watch."

"Keep *watch*?" the guard asked, trepidation shadowing her features. But Cetia was already walking up the steps, Medenia at her side.

Graeson stood near the windows overseeing the eastern courtyard where Nyrri lounged in the grass. Occasionally, the dragon-wolf would open an eye and let out a menacing growl, frightening the nearby guards. As soon as their faces blanched, Nyrri would close her eyes, and Graeson could have sworn he saw a flicker of amusement twitch at her lips.

When Graeson had attempted to slip away to the healer, Ellie had pulled him back, claiming he would only get in the way. Despite every bone in his body telling him not to, Graeson begrudgingly listened, knowing Ellie was right.

Besides, it would take the healers some time to check on Kallie before they were able to transfer her to a holding cell anyway.

Sylvia and Emmett had opted to retreat to the guest rooms to wash up and rest. Sylvia tried to persuade Dani to see the healer, but she refused, saying she would go later. Still, Dani bounced her knee as she sat, her nervous energy filling the room.

"You wished for privacy, and I have given it to you," Cetia mused, after giving them time to fill their stomachs. "Now, tell me, where exactly did the animal that is now scaring half of my guards come from? The animal feels...other. Explain."

Crossing his arms over his chest, Graeson faced the queen and recounted the creatures they had seen in the temple when they had pursued Domitius. When he described the thin child with horrid wings, his stomach churned in horror.

"Whatever the Frenzians have been doing secretly beneath their kingdom is neither natural nor humane," Graeson said.

On one of the plush couches, Medenia gripped her tea cup firmly. "They are clearly preparing for a war, Mother. Why else would they be partaking in such horrendous experiments?"

The queen's black nails tapped along the timber of the chair's arm. She nodded thoughtfully. "The motives of the other kingdoms will always remain a mystery. However, the Frenzian kingdom has always proved to be a wealth of knowledge; knowledge that they have decided to keep to themselves for centuries. But I do know this, the Dronias line has ruled over Frenzia since before Vaneria split into the seven kingdoms. The family is rumored to have once been dragon tamers."

"Dragon tamers?" Dani repeated over a sip of tea, peering over the rim of her cup.

"Yes," Cetia affirmed. "While dragons became extinct centuries ago, the Frenzians--the ruling line, specifically--believe that dragons came from the skies, ripping through the very stars and carrying the gods upon their backs."

"How does their origin have to do with the experiments?" Medenia asked.

"You call Nyrri a dragon-wolf, do you not?" her mother replied.

"With no other known creature existing, it is the closest comparison."

Cetia folded her delicate hands in her lap. "If I had to guess then, it would seem that the Frenzians are trying to recreate the dragons."

Graeson looked outside, where Nyrri was curled up. Several yards away, a bird circled above her, and she sat eerily still, watching. When the bird swooped down, Nyrri snapped her head out, snatching the small critter with her sharp teeth.

"How can they recreate them? Can they even do that?" Dani asked with a shudder.

"I do not know if we will ever know *how*," Cetia said, her brows twisting together. "But if what you say is true, they are already doing it. So it seems that yes, they can."

"Do you think Domitius knew?" Medenia asked. "Is that why he sought a marriage alliance with them? Was the choosing ceremony just a ploy?"

Graeson tensed, his rage rising as he realized that the marriage alliance was an even bigger ploy than they had thought. The king wasn't just after Frenzia's army, but their knowledge as well. And he planned to use Kalisandre to get it. Was there no end to his deceit?

"I think it is safe to assume that he was aware of the ongoing events or knew something about them. I think it would be foolish of us to believe otherwise," Cetia remarked.

"How could he have known? Neither of our kingdoms did," Ellie asked.

"How has Domitius known anything?" Cetia inquired. "How did he know how to get into your kingdom seventeen years ago? Why did he take the princess to begin with? Why has he kept her *alive* this entire time? There are many things we do not know about that man and the knowledge he possesses." The queen shrugged, taking a swig of tea.

"There is one way," Dani said, exchanging a knowing glance with Graeson. "Domitius has been conversing with a seer."

"We do not know that, Dani," Graeson argued. "Seers are rare. Therefore, the possibility of Domitius knowing one and having one in his possession is highly unlikely."

"But not *impossible*," Dani said, peering at him.

"Whether he has a seer or not matters little at this point," Cetia said. "A war is coming, and Queen Esmeray will need to make a choice."

Graeson turned toward the window and gripped the ledge as he looked at Nyrri, his knuckles blanching. "There is no choice to make. There is only one answer."

CHAPTER 17
MYRA

Myra should have been grateful for the king's silence.

She should have been even more grateful for the increase in rations, for her body no longer ached to the point of exhaustion. But Myra knew it wasn't the blessing she begged for it to be, for kindness from the king never came without a price.

She had learned that years ago.

Still, she forced herself to eat as much as she could. Because even though the king had not yet sent for her, she knew he would in due time.

And the next time she faced Domitius, she vowed she would not crumble to her knees before him.

Myra couldn't fathom what use the king and Sebastian still had for her. With Kallie being taken again by the Pontians, Myra at least knew she would not be manipulating the princess. However, Myra wasn't sure if she could afford to wonder what was to come. Whoever was in that room with the healer caused a wave of pain smacking into her and leaving her breathless.

Every day and night, she prayed to the gods for some sort of solace. But even the gods could not prevent the inevitable, it seemed.

Soon enough, the rattling of keys approached, and the cell door creaked open. She pressed her back against the wall.

"Come," the guard, whose voice she recognized belonging to Kolen, ordered. "It is time."

Myra debated saying no. She wanted to fight back. She wanted to scream. Myra begged her body to do anything at all as her gaze flicked to the door.

Even Kallie had fought when the Pontians had come to take her.

In the end, Myra only nodded and followed as she always had. Fighting, she knew, would only make matters worse--for both her and her brother.

Although the second guard waiting outside the cell hadn't spoken, Myra quickly realized he was not Iro, for he was too tall.

"Where's Iro?" Myra asked, breaking the tense silence.

Kolen peered at her. Though shadows from the helmet bled over his eyes, Myra sensed the vile spilling from them.

"The king does not take kindly to those who question him. Remember that, handmaiden," Kolen grumbled.

Myra bit her tongue. She shouldn't have been surprised.

While the king might have shown mercy to the guard before, no one ever escaped King Domitius's wrath for long. It was only a matter of when his ire would be released.

Jaw clenched, Myra squeezed her hands in front of her, and the three walked silently through the halls, taking the same path as before.

The healer, Dr. Thorne, was the first to greet them. He peered at Myra over his glasses, which were balanced precariously on the bridge of his nose. With a humph, he said, "She looks better than the last time, I suppose."

"*She* is right here," Myra spat, her brazenness surprising her.

The healer smirked. "And spritely this evening." He looked at the two guards. "Wait outside."

The guards nodded and turned on their heels. The iron door slammed shut behind them, and Myra startled, her heart thumping as sweat soaked her palms.

"Ready, Dr. Thorne?" King Domitius asked, appearing behind the healer.

"Of course, Your Majesty," Dr. Thorne said with a short bow before disappearing into the room.

The king's smirk sent a nerve-wracking spiral crawling down Myra's spine as he turned around. At least Sebastian wasn't there this time. A small blessing.

The emotions seeping from the room were rancid. Familiar bouts of suffering soaked the air, but something else twisted along with it--something bright yet poisoned.

Excitement.

Myra pressed a hand to her stomach in an attempt to settle the newfound nausea, but it did little to help.

Her other hand began to shake at her side, and she pressed it atop the other, steadying it. She glanced at the iron door that was now closed as sweat saturated the back of her neck. Her leg twitched, her foot lifting from the ground--

"I would think twice before deciding to run."

Myra froze. Her attention snapped to the king before she quickly diverted her gaze, bowing in submission.

She cursed herself for thinking even for a second that she could run and escape whatever awaited her in that room.

Once Domitius had a hold of you, there was no going back.

"My King," Myra mumbled, her voice shaking. "I wasn't--I--"

He scoffed, his lips curling into a sneer. "Save your energy on your pitiful excuses. You will need every ounce of it if you wish to return to my good graces. Perhaps if you are successful, I will even let you see your brother."

Myra gulped, yet hope blossomed in her chest.

"Would you like to see him, Myra?" King Domitius taunted, stepping forward, his toes nearly touching hers.

Myra nodded, unable to utter a word.

He tipped her chin up. "Then you will do exactly as I say," he hissed. "You have already wasted precious time with your dramatics the other day. I will not be made a fool of again. Do you understand?"

She nodded again.

He tightened his hold, squeezing her face. "Good. There is more at stake here than your worthless life. What we are doing will change the course of Ardentol's history--*Vaneria's* history." He released her face with a hard flick and stepped back, smoothing the front of his jacket. "Now, there is no time to waste. We have work to do."

He seized her by the crook of the elbow and pulled her into the room. As the door clicked shut behind them, she gulped as a whirlwind of emotions engulfed her.

Everything from agony to excitement permeated the air, coiling around her limbs and ensnaring her. As it threatened to strangle her, she fought to push through the rising panic.

Dark stains covered the stone walls. From what exactly, Myra could not tell. In the corner of the poorly lit room, Dr. Thorne was rifling through various items on a small metal table: needles, scalpels, perforates, saws, gags, and various ghastly instruments foreign to Myra.

Myra wondered just how much *healing* Dr. Thorne did within the castle's dungeons.

Dr. Thorne picked up a vial filled with a milky liquid that made bile rise in her throat. He turned to her, a wide grin splitting his wicked face.

Myra's back slammed into the wall as she stumbled. Her body shook as she pressed her hands harder against her stomach, and the words tumbled from her lips before she could stop them. "What-- what are you going to do to me?"

King Domitius chuckled, and the discordant sound sent goosebumps skittering across Myra's skin. "Oh, my dear. We are not doing anything to *you*."

"Then why--" Myra swallowed, her gaze bouncing across the room from the man to the king.

The king lifted a brow as an amused grin spread across his face.

"Why am I here?" Myra whispered, unsure where the gumption to question the king came from. She knew better, yet the questions continued to spill from her tongue before she could stop them. "What do you want from me?"

Regret spun in her stomach, but Myra needed to know.

She needed to know why she was here and still alive. She could no longer avoid the reasoning, not when she was in this room.

King Domitius folded his hands behind his back. Not an ounce of rage dripped from the king, yet the sinister glint in his brown eyes was even more frightening. But perhaps she was used to it by now.

"You see, Myra, due to your failure, Kalisandre is no longer in my hands. She is somewhere gallivanting with the Pontians. Although, if all is going according to plan, the Pontians will only taste victory for so long. I suspect that they are already seeing the consequences of their audacity.

"Nevertheless, because of the current circumstances, we have had to change our plans. You will do whatever I say, or else it will be your brother who will pay the consequences for your failure. You do not want him to lose another limb, do you?"

Myra's eyes widened, her skin turning clammy.

"Are we clear?" he pressed.

"Yes, Your Majesty," Myra said, voice shaking with untamed terror.

Domitius turned around and nodded to the healer.

Dr. Thorne walked toward the ivory curtain covering one side of the room. When he pulled it back, the metal rings screeched as they slid down the rod, revealing a large metal table sitting behind it.

Myra struggled to hold back a gasp at the sight before her.

A man lay chained to the table, bound by tight restraints at the wrists, ankles, and torso.

Myra's gaze flicked to Dr. Thorne, who wheeled the table over. The wheels creaked with every turn over the cement floor, but the man atop the table did not move.

It only took Myra a moment to realize why. He was unconscious.

Still, even with the blanket of sleep over his face, the stranger's expression twisted with agony. His features were familiar, yet Myra could not place him, though she knew she had seen him before.

His brown skin was a sickly hue. He wore only a pair of trousers. Across his bare chest and arms, ghastly bruises and scars marked almost every inch of his body that was visible. The skin around his eye was thin, and the veins protruding from his arms were prominent. His short black curls were matted and frayed at the edges.

Myra pressed her palms against the cold wall behind her as if she could force her body to slip through it.

"I am no healer," Myra whispered. "I cannot heal him."

"*Heal* him?" King Domitius laughed. "Oh, no. We do not need you to heal him."

Myra's brows drew together. "But he's in pain. He's clearly suffered immense injuries."

She was speaking too much, but she didn't understand what he wanted from her. She could not help this man.

The king waved a dismissive hand in the air. "His injuries are a result of his own insolence. They will heal in time, but that is not why you are here."

"Then why am I here, Your Majesty?" Myra forced the last two words out of fear of angering the king.

The table on wheels ran into the makeshift bed. The man inhaled, jolting awake. Fear immediately poured from his body, a tsunami of alarm and trepidation rushing from him and falling onto the floor, soaking Myra's feet.

And within its wave, pain and anguish mixed, tainting the flood of emotion. The man jerked, tugging at the restraints that held each limb to the table.

His bloodshot brown eyes widened as he screamed around the gag lodged into his mouth. When Myra's gaze met the stranger's, he strained against the restraints, a plea slipping from his eyes and muffled in his throat.

Myra tried to take another step back, but her legs were frozen.

She couldn't move.

She couldn't speak.

Then, in the corner of her eye, she saw Dr. Thorne remove a needle from the man's neck. The stranger's head fell to the side.

The king snatched her wrist and tugged her close. "This is why you are here," he hissed.

Only a hint of annoyance showed on the king's face as if this man's outburst was not unordinary. As if her entire body hadn't felt like it was frozen in ice. Who was this stranger?

Terror coated her limbs as she looked from the king to the man.

"The creatures we saw in Frenzia were only the beginning. With the combination of my research, Frenzia's advancements, and your gift, we will make history. Kalisandre's gift needed more fine-tuning before I could get her involved. You, on the other hand," the king mused, his brown eyes brewing with malice and greed. "Your gifts are similar enough. You will do what Kalisandre could not."

Myra's eyes widened, but she kept her mouth shut out of fear of making things worse for her brother.

"All we need you to do is calm his mind. Think of it as bringing him peace."

Myra swallowed as she was forced to accept the hand she was dealt.

"Who is he?" Myra asked quietly.

"Who he *is* does not matter. What matters is what he will become."

CHAPTER 18
KALLIE

"It's not fair!" Kallie shouted, her fists slamming against the ground.

"What's not fair?" a boy much taller than her, with shaggy black hair, asked. He peered at her with silver eyes, his brows drawing together and a wrinkle creasing the center of his forehead.

"I'm too little!" Kallie said through the tears that began to roll down her cheeks.

"Little?" the boy repeated, brow arching curiously.

Kallie nodded, biting her lip.

Her brothers had already sprinted ahead, their legs longer and stronger than hers. Even though she had tried to run faster, Kallie couldn't keep up. They were four years older than her and over twice her size.

It wasn't fair. She wanted to play with them, to be as fast as them.

But every time she ran after them, they hurried away, faster and faster than she could force her feet to go.

The boy looked at Kallie. Unlike when the adults around her peered at her, he didn't look down at her. He sank to the ground, propping himself up on one knee.

While he wasn't her brother, he lived in the castle with them. When

Kallie had asked her mother where his family was, her mother said they were his family since his mother had left this world long ago. Although Kallie didn't understand what that meant, she didn't mind him being around, for he was always kind to her.

When her brothers would push her down or run away from her, he was always at her side, pulling her up. He didn't have to. She wasn't his responsibility.

Her brothers were the ones who were supposed to be taking care of her; at least, that's what her mother and the caretakers reminded the young princes before they traipsed through the castle's forest like hooligans.

Yet the boy with the sad silver eyes and raven-black hair was always the one who made sure Kallie didn't get hurt and left behind.

"Kal, you're not little," he said softly.

"Mhm! Little like... like..." Kallie bit her lip, looking around the forest. A gray furry critter scurried across the ground, over the roots and leaves. "A mouse!"

The boy chuckled. "You're little like a mouse?"

She nodded frantically.

He reached out a hand and pulled a leaf from her long brown waves. "Well, little mouse, do you want to know a secret?"

Kallie looked at him with wide eyes as if he held the entire world in his palm. "Yes!"

"Shh," he said, raising a finger to his lips. "Do you remember what we do with secrets?"

Kallie nodded enthusiastically, mimicking his gesture. She listened with eager ears as he wiped the tears from her cheek.

"A mouse may be small, but it is a mighty little creature."

"Mighty?" Kallie repeated the word, chewing on it. She didn't know what it meant, but the way he said it made it sound like it was a good thing.

"Mhm. Mighty," he said, nodding. "It means strong."

Kallie narrowed her eyes as she pursed her lips. "Small but mighty?"

"That's right. And you'll grow taller eventually."

Kallie perked up. "Taller than Fynn and Ter?"

The boy chuckled. Long strands of hair fell in his face, and he pushed them back as he leaned on his heels. He shrugged. "Probably not."

"Taller than Gray?" she asked, poking him in the chest.

Shaking his head, he chuckled more this time, his eyes alight with amusement. "Most definitely not."

Kallie pouted and sank into the dirt.

"Come now, princesses do not pout."

Kallie shook her head. "Little mouse," she whined.

Gray stood, his body towering over hers. But when he looked at her, he neither looked at her as if she was smaller or weaker than him, nor as if she was just some annoyance that followed after them.

"You may be small, little mouse, but you are mighty and fierce." He reached out a hand. Kallie wiped away the last remnants of her tears and wrapped her fingers around his. He murmured, "Never forget who you are."

Never forget who you are.

Kallie's eyes shot open.

Sharp, cool air burned her lungs. The stench of smoke was long gone, replaced with the faint smell of moss and bergamot. While the fresh, clean air should have been a relief, it wasn't.

As various images flashed across her mind, anger quickly filled her veins.

A bloody, severed head.

A scimitar gleaming in the sunlight.

Sharp silver eyes staring down at her.

Terin's hands wrapped around Graeson's throat.

As each image passed, a spark ignited in her mind. At first, it was small--a puff of smoke, a strike of a match. But then, a breeze swept across her, and the flames burst to life, consuming every inch of her body.

She had been taken. *Again.*

Her entire body vibrated with red-hot fury.

How long had she been out? Where had the Pontians taken her?

Although her memory was hazy, she couldn't recall the nauseating rocking of the ocean, only the faint memory of horses' hooves pounding the ground. She had to have been on the mainland still. At least, she hoped.

No matter where she was, she would wreak havoc.

For the past few months, Kallie had blamed herself for everything that had ensued. She had blamed herself for the death of Fynn, for the homes of innocents burning to the ground on the shore of the Red Sea.

She had blamed herself for failing her father time and time again.

She had forgotten *who* she was. But she was Kalisandre Helene Domitius, and she had vowed to set the world aflame.

Despite knowing exactly what Kallie could do, the Pontians seemed not to have learned their lesson last time.

Because when Kallie twisted her wrist slightly, she found her hand unbound.

They trusted too easily, and their mistake would be their undoing.

Kallie's limbs felt heavy, and a prickling sensation crept over her skin, freezing her in place. She refrained from moving, lest she rouse someone's suspicions, and contained her rising terror. Panicking would only get her killed.

No, she needed to assess the situation first.

Her vision was slow to adjust, however. In the thick darkness that enveloped her, her surroundings slowly came into focus as she listened.

Muffled noises echoed from somewhere outside the room. Although Kallie couldn't make out their words, she could identify several indistinct voices. Somewhere nearby, an owl called out into the night, and a chilly breeze kissed her neck, the smell of moss and mold growing stronger.

Quietly, she looked to her right and spotted a cracked window. Moonlight seeped into the room, casting a faint glow across the floors. Small tables were scattered across the large space, the moon's rays catching on the glass vials. A couple of small, empty beds sat between her and the window.

Kallie's brows twisted together. She wasn't in a bedroom then, but rather what appeared like an infirmary.

Close by, there was a slight creaking of wood.

Kallie stilled, her heart hammering. Soon, the creaking disappeared, the sound falling away, and she waited with bated breath.

When nothing came of it, she reached down to the pit of her stomach, and tendrils of her gift stirred eagerly as if her power had been waiting for her to wake.

It's now or never, she told herself.

Gently, she pushed herself to a seated position. Her vision blurred, the familiar warning of a migraine stirring.

Although her limbs ached as if she had been sedentary for much too long, Kallie pushed through it. She looked to the right and quickly muffled her gasp with a hand. Her other hand gripped the stiff cotton sheets, her fingers curling as her chest rose.

There, on the last bed, lay a ghost.

The moon's glow through the window brushed upon her brother's face. But despite the constant back and forth between dreams and reality, Kallie knew she was not sleeping or imagining things.

Fynn was not lying on the bed but rather Terin.

Terin's hair was disheveled and strewn across his face, cutting across his features. In the moonlight, his tan skin had a sickly green hue. The skin beneath his eyes was a deep purple as if he hadn't slept in weeks.

Pain spiked her head, and she balled the sheet tighter within her palms.

Kallie shook away the rising pity she felt for the Pontian prince. He may have shared her blood, but blood meant nothing when the person abandoned and lied to you.

Terin's bed, however, was right next to the door.

He had yet to stir, his breathing still even.

Kallie's hand went to her thigh where she had strapped the dagger before the wedding, but it was gone, of course. She scanned the room for anything she could use as a weapon.

If this was an infirmary, there had to be a scalpel or something else she could use. Cabinets lined the wall near the cracked door, and she bit her lip.

She would have to be quick and quiet.

Tossing her legs over the bed, Kallie stood. When she straightened, her legs wobbled, and she grappled for the wall, her palm pressing against it for stability.

Being quick, unfortunately, would not be an option if she could barely stand.

She took a deep breath in and counted to four in her mind. She held the oxygen in her mouth for five seconds, steadying herself and calming her raging thoughts before she exhaled.

Then, on quiet, unsteady feet, Kallie crept toward the nearest table. She searched through the instruments but found only strips of cotton, gauze, and miscellaneous herbs. She sifted through several drawers, finding only aprons, linens, and flimsy gowns.

"Shit," Kallie hissed when she pulled open the last drawer and discovered only more sheets. She shut the dresser, the vials on top shaking slightly from the force.

Cursing, she looked over her shoulder but found Terin still asleep. She sighed in relief.

Hurrying to the cracked window, she pried it open. The wood creaked as the hinges turned. Her heart thundered, but she didn't dare waste any more time. She pushed open the window the rest of the way and quickly surveyed the environment.

All around the property, tall, foreign, white-barked trees covered the area as far as she could see through the darkness of night.

Kallie looked down.

Shit!

Her fingers curled around the window's ledge. She was too high to jump without hurting herself in the process. Her eyes widened, an idea spinning together.

She hurried to the dresser and pulled the sheets out, constantly checking if Terin had awoken. Quickly tying the sheets together, Kallie tossed one end of the makeshift rope out the window and tied the other to the nearest bed anchored to the floor.

Kallie lifted herself onto the windowsill, her legs dangling from the ledge. Sending a silent prayer to the gods, she twisted around and grabbed onto the sheet with a deadly grip as she began her descent.

Just one foot after another. That's all she needed--

A tear in sheet ripped through the silence, the top of the sheet snagging on a jagged piece of metal that Kallie hadn't seen. If she was quick enough--

The tear spread even further the moment she shifted.

Quickly, Kallie reached for the window ledge, trying to find purchase, but her nails only clawed at the wall. As the fabric ripped, Kallie squeezed her eyes shut as she prepared for the inevitable fall.

A hand suddenly gripped hers, and Kallie's eyes sprung open.

Eyes sharp as steel stared down at her. "Going somewhere, little mouse?" Graeson said, his voice low and sending a vibration through her core.

"Let me go," Kallie spat.

"I don't think so."

Before Kallie could argue more, Graeson was yanking her up and back through the window. His large hands wrapped around her, pulling her inside.

He pressed her back against the wall, his hands gripping her arms.

"What was the plan, Kalisandre?" Graeson asked, his voice low and cold. "Jump out the window and hope the swamp cushioned your fall?"

Kallie jerked against his hold, but that only caused him to tighten his grip. Her gift stirred within the pit of her stomach, but she knew it was useless. Graeson was immune to her manipulations.

"Oh, come on, Kalisandre, don't act like you aren't at least a little happy to see me."

"Happy? You kidnapped me!" Kallie frantically scanned the wall, searching for anything she could use to aid her. From the corner of her eye, she saw the flicker of light. "*Again.*"

His lips parted, but the words struggled to come out.

Kallie, however, didn't waste the opportunity his pause provided her. She wiggled a hand free from his loosened grasp and struck the mirror on the wall beside her. Before the shards fell, she snatched a piece of glass.

"You should have gone home when you had the chance," Kallie

said, gripping the glass. The sharp edges cut the inside of her palm, and warm blood began to drip down her wrist, but she ignored it.

"And you should have never left," Graeson said, briefly observing the shard of glass before returning his cautious silver eyes to her.

Everywhere Graeson touched, hot fury heated her skin, burning her from the inside out. Her fingers wrapped tighter around the glass, the edges piercing deeper into her flesh. Even the pain slicing through her hand couldn't sedate the rage that rose within her blood.

"The last thing I remember was that I *was* home."

Graeson scoffed, his leg pressed against her thigh. His eyes were a brilliant silver in the moonlight, as bright as a scorching fire. "Frenzia is not your home."

Kallie reared her hand back. Graeson dogged. Then, in one quick maneuver, he gripped her wrist, shaking her hand free of the glass. Kallie struggled against him, her arm pushing back against his, but his grip was too tight.

"You do not want to play this game with me right now," Graeson warned, his words clipped. "You're not yourself. I do not wish to hurt you."

"Hurt me?" Kallie laughed, the sound bitter and cold, even to her. "You think you have that much effect on me?"

"Kalisandre."

The rising spikes of a headache began to form, and she tried to shake it away.

Graeson was her enemy, not her savior.

She seethed, "If you cared for me as much as you claim to, you would have never taken me in the first place."

"I took you *because* I care for you! Can't you see that?"

Regret and sorrow glistened in Graeson's gaze, but Kallie

refused to accept it. Not when his words never seemed to line up with his actions.

"You care, so you kidnapped me? Is that it?" Kallie looked at the wrist, which he was still gripping. "Did you finally run out of your supply of rope?"

Confusion contorted Graeson's features as he looked at Kallie's wrist. His grip loosened momentarily, and she let her body become dead weight suddenly. She sunk to the ground and slipped between Graeson's legs before he even had the chance to register what had happened. Adrenaline pumped in her veins as she snatched the shard of glass and faced Graeson.

"Kalisandre, you don't want to--"

Graeson shouted in pain as Kallie drove the shard of glass into his side.

Kallie didn't waste time. She spun and ran.

"Leaving so soon, Princess?"

Kallie skirted to a stop as she nearly ran into Dani, who appeared at the door.

A sneer ripped across Dani's face, her golden-hazel eyes aflame. Kallie's lips parted, the command on her tongue. But before she could utter a word, Dani spun Kallie around, locking her arms behind her back and placing a gag in her mouth.

"Your gift is useless without your voice, is it not?" Dani spat as Kallie hit the floor, and Dani's knees pressed against her spine.

Kallie struggled against Dani's hold, a muffled scream bursting from her lips.

Graeson said something across the room, but Kallie couldn't hear it as her anger roared in her ears.

She would not let them win. She couldn't.

Flashbacks of Kallie beneath the tree flooded her mind.

She would not be rendered helpless.

She kicked, struggled, and made it as hard as possible for Dani to get a hold of her.

Ahead of her, Graeson ripped the shard of glass from his side, and sticky blood coated his fingers. He pressed his hand against the wound and stepped forward, doubling over.

Kallie's heart thundered, sweat beaded at the base of her next, soaking the back of her hair.

She had to get out of here.

Kallie grabbed onto the tendrils of her gift, tightening them within her hold as Dani snapped metal cuffs to her wrists, the chain connecting them clanging together.

"Grab him!" Dani shouted.

As chaos erupted around her, Kallie released the command, and the sound of pounding boots filled the air as figures dashed past her.

CHAPTER 19
GRAESON

Most thought rage was like drowning in flames. But true rage was a pool of ice--a numbness coating your skin and blinding you from all sense.

A flood of Tetrian guards ran into the room, running past Dani and Kalisandre on the floor.

"What do you think you are doing?" Graeson spat as the guards tugged him backward.

No one answered him, though. Instead, Ellie stepped between Graeson and Kalisandre. Her fingers flexed around the hilt of a throwing knife, and her expression was cold as she commanded the guards. "Dani, take her now!"

"Ellie," Graeson warned, voice grave.

Kalisandre's muffled screams filled the room as she struggled against Dani's hold. Then, suddenly, Dani stood, her hands falling from Kalisandre.

Ellie gasped as Kalisandre struggled to her feet. "Dani, what are you doing? Grab her!" she demanded.

A sound akin to a laugh fell around the gag lodged into

Kalisandre's mouth. Her brown locks fell in front of her face, and she stared at them with an ire-filled gaze, a storm roaring.

Graeson's eyes widened in horror. "She's manipulating her!" Graeson shouted.

"What? That's not possible," Ellie shrieked. "Guards!"

At her command, more guards immediately barreled into the room as if they had been waiting outside.

Graeson jerked from the guards' grip, his shoulder twisting and popping with a sickening sound. But before he could escape, another guard lunged forward, grabbing onto him.

One of the women came at Kalisandre and snatched her arm. Kalisandre swiftly spun around, her tangled brown hair swirling through the air. In an instant, the guard released her and redirected his attention towards Ellie.

"Ellie!" Graeson yelled as the guard ran toward her. Ellie spun, blocking the woman's swing and then knocking her out.

"Get off me!" Graeson shouted at the guards holding him. "I'm the only one she can't control!"

The guards did not let go of him. Their grips only tightened.

Guards continued to attack Kallie, snatching her limbs and tugging her. Each one though, quickly fell under her command, releasing her and charging after Ellie. But not without twisting her limbs and forcing out a high-pitched scream from her lungs.

A deep rumble vibrated through his throat as he was forced to watch. He had promised that she would not get hurt.

"Fucking knock her out already!" Ellie shouted as guards surrounded her, their swords unsheathed.

"We're trying!" a Tetrian cried in dismay.

"Do not touch her!" Graeson roared.

A river of icy rage flooded his body. And that was all it took for the logic, the sense, to be cast to the wayside as Graeson unlocked the door and set the god free.

THE HUMAN SLIPPED into the shadows of his mind with little to no fight against the god's pursuits.

As a warrior clad in leather shifted Kalisandre in her arms, the god acted. He ripped his arm free from whatever mortal held onto him.

But as he ran toward her, the humans were relentless, their determination an annoyance and hindrance all at once.

"Grab him!" someone shouted.

More hands wrapped around his limbs, but he easily shook them off as if they were no more than flies buzzing around his head. Grunts and curses flew in the wind, but the god did not care who he hurt. He did not care who fell. All he cared about was the woman who was promised to him.

They would not take her.

He would not let--

The god hit the ground, his cheek smacking into the floor as someone knocked him to the ground with a boot to the back.

Before he could get up, someone's knees dug into his spine. Hands locked around his wrists and forced his arms against the floor, spreading them. A heavy weight pressed down on his legs, flattening him to the ground.

The god tried to push up in vain, but he couldn't get any leverage as the warriors drove him down. Nails dug into his skull, digging and piercing. His head was yanked up, and a cold blade was pressed against his throat, eliciting a snarl from his lips.

The Tetrian princess's face came into view, a fire burning in her light gray eyes.

"What do you think you are doing?" the god roared, anger filling his voice.

"We are doing what must be done. What we agreed upon," Medenia said.

"What who agreed upon? Because I do not recall granting anyone the authority to touch Kalisandre or me."

But it was not the Tetrian who answered him.

"All of us, Gray."

Although the god could not see him, the god knew whom the voice belonged to before the man even came into view.

The prince knelt, his hands hanging over his knees and a heaviness soaking his countenance. Terin dug his fingers through his shaggy brown hair, the ends sticking in different directions.

A stab of betrayal struck the man inside in the chest, sharp enough for even the god to feel.

This is why you do not trust mortals, *the god hissed at the man within.*

"Get her out of here," Terin said, the cold metal still pressed against the god's throat. "Now!"

"She is your sister," the god growled, his gaze flicking to Kalisandre in rage.

Terin nodded, sorrow filling his features. "I am doing this because she is my sister. It is the only way we can help her."

"And if you do not?" the god challenged. "If you are unable to fix her?"

Terin and the Tetrian princess exchanged glances, but their silence spoke louder than any words could ever dare.

The god snarled, anger flooding his system.

He couldn't decipher who the anger belonged to anymore--him or the mortal, for the line between the two was quickly disintegrating. Either way, it fueled him, empowered him. He pushed against the warriors whose weight pressed on him.

Twisting his limbs, he pushed and pushed--

"Now!" someone shouted.

The blade disappeared from his throat.

But before he realized what was happening, a sharp thump hit the back of his head, and the mortal body fell onto the ground. As black smoke fluttered at the edges of his visions, he spotted Kalisandre being dragged away, her body limp in a guard's arms.

Yet the god, as powerful as he might have been, was helpless to save her.

CHAPTER 20
MYRA

Mynhos's screams still haunted her dreams. They were the only thing that kept Myra returning to that wretched room without fighting the guards who tugged her down the halls.

She would do whatever she had to in order to protect Mynhos, even becoming a person she hated and despised. Because if Myra was being honest with herself, after everything she had already done, she already hated who she had become long ago.

Still, she couldn't get herself to ignore her morals completely.

Every day, Myra made every effort to hinder any progress without raising the king's suspicions. As Dr. Thorne prepared to inject the poison into the man's neck, Myra let her influence fall from the victim. She flinched as the man thrashed and screamed against the gag in his mouth. Myra hated herself every time the stranger blinked up at her, the pain a thin layer over his brown irises. A desperate plea spread across his features, but the man did not understand what he was asking of her.

While Myra could take away his pain, it would only further his demise with whatever horrid concoction resided inside the vial.

Even though she hated watching him in pain, she told herself it was better than the alternative--than becoming one of those horrid creatures.

According to Dr. Thorne, for the medication to be taken, the victim's heart rate had to be even, and their mind had to be willing. During the trial period, if the victims fought, it prevented the poison from infiltrating their bloodstream.

It was why forcing them unconscious with medicinal herbs wasn't a viable option. There had been too many failed experiments with unwilling patients, and King Domitius wasn't taking any more chances.

So Myra delayed as much as possible. And for a while, her delay went unnoticed.

Abilities like Myra's were temperamental at best. To manipulate one's emotions and weave new ones took time and energy. It was why Kallie had struggled to gain control over her powers for so long. Therefore, the king would not expect success right away.

After all, based on the information Myra had gathered, Domitius had been working on this project for decades. He would not rush it if that meant risking its success.

Every day, Myra gritted her teeth as the man's screams ripped through the room like a strike of thunder shaking a stable. They pierced Myra's eardrums and sent her head spinning, causing her hands to tremble at her side.

But no matter how loudly he yelled or how much he fought against the king's experimentation, no one would come for him. No one would save him.

Even the other prisoners in the dungeons would have had a hard time hearing the screams. The secluded room muffled the noise, making it so faint that some would think they were merely losing their minds. Outside the room, the screams were surely no more than a figment of one's imagination.

And yet, Myra still heard the screams every night as she lay her head down to sleep, as the shadows filled her cell and drowned her. She found herself questioning if the cries belonged to Dr. Thorne's victim, her brother, or if they were simply a nightmare she couldn't possibly escape.

Myra had tried her best, but it wasn't enough--it never was.

Because when Kolen came for her late one day, the chains in Kolen's hands told her everything she needed to know.

"Are those really necessary?" Myra asked, her stomach turning.

"King's orders." Kolen motioned for her hands.

Reluctantly, Myra held them up, trembling.

The metal was freezing against her skin. When he released her hands, they fell, the chains a heavy weight on her frail wrists.

"Ankles, too," Kolen said when Myra made to move.

Her mouth fell open to protest, but the guard was already snapping the cuffs in place.

As she walked out of the cell, a short chain ran from one ankle to the other, scraping against the floor.

Holding back tears that began to sprout, Myra turned toward the usual path.

The guard snatched her wrist. "This way," he ordered.

"What? Why? Where are you taking me?" Myra asked, frantically looking over her shoulder in the other direction.

Was she walking to her execution? And if so, why was she not more afraid?

"The king thinks you need a little motivation," Kolen said, tightening his grip around Myra's arm.

The fear settled in her stomach then. Because if this was not her execution, she was terrified of what awaited her.

They took the steps that led to the main floor, the chains rattling with every step. At the top of the staircase, Kolen peered down at her. "Don't bother screaming. No one will hear you. The king has sent everyone out of the castle this evening just for this little visit. Doesn't that make you feel special?" He smiled wickedly.

Myra gulped as the guard pushed open the door. She squinted when a flood of light streamed in from the torches lining the halls. As Kolen dragged her through the side entrance of the throne room, she looked longingly at the moonlit windows. Salvation was so close, and yet so far out of her reach.

The guard flung Myra to the floor in front of the steps leading to the throne. Her knees slammed against the white marble floors, and the heavy chains cut into her ankles.

Domitius lounged on his throne, his chin resting on his propped-up hand as if bored. With a quick snap of his fingers, the main doors creaked open.

As the newcomers entered, a wave of emotions washed over Myra, sending chills down her spine and setting every nerve ablaze.

Myra turned and nearly toppled over as the chains restricted her movements. "Mynhos?" she croaked, gasping for air.

As a guard led him down the walkway, her brother didn't react, his head remaining slumped and his gaze fixed on the ground.

His blond hair was shaggier than before, and greasy, dull strands stuck to his forehead. Wearing an oversized jacket that sagged over his frail body, the sleeves too long for his arms, and ill-fitting pants, Mynhos was no more than a walking pile of bones. A shadow of the brother she once knew.

Myra's brows twisted together as her heart pounded in her chest.

"What's wrong with him?" she asked in horror, turning to the king as tears burned the back of her eyes.

The king rolled his eyes as if her question was an annoying fly he wished would disappear. He looked past her. "Mynhos, your sister wishes to see you. Lift your head," he ordered.

But when Myra returned to look at her brother, Mynhos raised his head.

With a blank, tired expression, his complexion was as white as the marble walls that surrounded them. A near ghost.

Tears burned her eyes. "What--what happened?"

Mynhos's gaze flicked to the king.

"Go ahead. Tell her," King Domitius said.

"You," Mynhos said, his voice low and haunting. "You did this."

Myra gasped, her heart shattering as she looked up at her brother.

"You left me," he whispered.

"No! No, Mynhos. I never wanted to leave you. I--I--" Myra choked on her tears. Her eyes darted to his injured arm, where the jacket's sleeve was draped loosely over it, shielding it from view.

"You forgot about me," he seethed.

"Mynhos, please," Myra begged through her sobs as she crawled forward. Every word that left Mynhos's mouth was another dagger to her heart.

"If you cared about me, you would do as the king says."

Then, the guards were dragging Mynhos away.

"Wait!" Myra shouted, reaching out. "Wait! Mynhos! I'll fix this. I promise I'll fix this."

But Myra wasn't sure if her brother heard her as the guards disappeared through the side doors. She stared after him, the river of tears falling down the contours of her face. Her throat was on fire as she struggled to breathe.

A hand snatched her jaw, tugging her gaze away from the door.

The king snarled, his calm composure melting away and revealing the true anger beneath it. "*That* is what happens when you waste my time."

This was all her fault.

She had delayed too long.

CHAPTER 21
GRAESON

When Graeson awoke, his head spun. The line between him and the god within was growing thinner by the day. It was becoming far too easy for him to let the beast out.

Yet such ease did not make it less jarring, nor did it prevent the ache in his bones.

As Graeson finally reoriented himself into his own body, he first thought he had imagined the entire event. It was one thing for Kalisandre to turn against him, but to discover that his own friends had betrayed him and conspired behind his back to take Kalisandre was unfathomable.

And yet, as he lay in a cold, dark cell, the reality of the situation hit him. The god roared, and Graeson's blood ran ice-cold as he stared at the iron bars, realizing the depth of the betrayal.

Soon, boots rapped against the cement, and Graeson pushed himself off the hard mattress on the gritty stone floor. Medenia and Ophelia appeared in front of his cell, and Graeson's lip curled from the taste of betrayal as he saw the princess's sad expression. He wasn't surprised that Dani and Terin weren't the first ones to see him, instead sending the Tetrians to play peacemaker, but it hurt all the same.

The princess parted her lips as if to speak, but the anger forced Graeson forward. He clutched the iron bars within his fists. "Where is she?" he demanded.

Eyes widening, Medenia stumbled back, and Ophelia stepped in front of her, shielding her.

"Watch it, Graeson," Ophelia said with a snarl, brandishing a sword.

"Let me see her," Graeson hissed, losing his patience with each passing second. He needed to know Kalisandre was safe, and he would not rest until he got the answers he sought.

"We have no intention of keeping you inside this cell," Medenia said, tilting her chin up as she quickly regained her composure. "Your actions last night, however, left us no choice. In your rage, you injured several of my guards. Once you have calmed down, we will let you out."

"Once I've calmed down? I *am* calm," Graeson spat. "But if you keep me in this cage, if you keep me away from her, I will show you true rage."

"The princess has come to you out of her good graces, yet you snarl like a ravaged beast." Ophelia shook her head, her dark brown curls flying from the movement. When she met Graeson's gaze again, a look of disgust colored her countenance. "Get a hold of yourself."

Graeson's nose twitched. "Where is she?"

Medenia gave Ophelia's hand a reassuring squeeze. Ophelia released a sigh, but she did not stop Medenia from stepping closer to the bars. The warrior's knuckles, though, blanched as she tightened her grip on the hilt of her sword.

"You cannot see her right now," Medenia said with an apologetic look. "If you interfere, you may cause more harm than good."

"Tell. Me. Where. She. Is."

Medenia was unfazed by Graeson's anger though and sighed. "She's with the queen and Ellie."

An icy fire surged through his veins and his hands flexed around the iron bars. "Why?"

"She is a danger to everyone right now. The utmost caution must be exercised." Medenia said, but something in her voice led Graeson to believe there was more than what she was saying.

"What are they doing to her?" Graeson asked, his fingers curling around the pole, the metal growing hot beneath his hands.

But Medenia was silent as Ophelia glanced at her.

"Tell me!" Graeson roared, his scream echoing down the hall and making the floor quake.

Another set of footsteps approached, and Terin came into Graeson's view.

In the torchlight, some color had returned to Terin's face, yet a heaviness still coated his expression as his gaze met Graeson's.

"She tried to *kill* you, Graeson," Terin said.

Graeson slammed his fist against the bars. "I do not care! How are we supposed to convince her to trust us when at every turn she is knocked out?"

Ophelia snorted. "Perhaps you should have thought about that before bringing a monster into our kingdom."

At Ophelia's words, red bled into Graeson's vision.

"*What* did you say?" Graeson asked, his knuckles turning paper white as he tugged on the iron bars.

"Graeson," Terin hissed, calling his attention. "The queen and Ellie are handling it."

"Handling *it*? Handling *what* exactly?" he demanded.

"Look," Terin said, "we had to do something! She is my sister, and I do not want any harm to come to her just as much as you don't. But we cannot risk everyone's lives! We must understand what is going on in her mind before we can even *think* about trusting her. She has betrayed us once already. I will not let her harm anyone else I care about."

Graeson scoffed. "She is a human, too, Terin. She deserves to be treated as such."

Terin rubbed a hand across his face. "I know that! By the gods, do I know that!"

Graeson glanced between the three people who stood before them. The people he once considered to be his friends. The same people who put him in this godsforsaken cell.

"How long?" he demanded.

Terin blinked, his brows drawing together. "How long what?"

Graeson pressed his chest against the bars. A sharp pain from the wound in his side shot through him, but he pushed through it. Though the bleeding had stopped, the bruised and tender skin still throbbed. Graeson paid it no heed. He would get his answers. "How long have you been planning to betray me?"

"We never planned to betray you," Terin said, digging his fingers through his hair.

"But did you not go behind my back? Did you not lie to me about your intentions?"

"We didn't..." Terin's lips parted, but he closed his mouth shut once, twice as he struggled to find the words. "That's not--you have to understand! We were running out of options! You saw her! Kallie has more control over her gift than we thought. She didn't even have to say anything aloud to get the guards to turn on us."

"How *long*?" Graeson spat, each word containing the anger threatening to burst from his body. He was hanging on by a thread, and the god's rage pressed against his cage. If Graeson relinquished his control now, he feared he would be unable to regain it.

"Graeson," Terin said calmly, "please."

Graeson did not wish to hear his excuses, though. "How long, Terin, has this been the plan?"

"We didn't want to do this! But when my sister tried to kill you when we were attacked..." Terin swallowed, and he wiped the sweat from his forehead with the back of his hand. "We had to do something. We had to ensure everyone's safety. Fynn--"

"Fynn is dead!" Graeson shouted.

"I know, I know, but he..." Terin raked his fingers through his hair with an exasperated sigh. He turned his gaze to the ceiling. "I can still reach him."

"What the fuck do you mean you can still reach him?"

The color drained from Terin's face as Dani stormed forward, snatching him by the collar.

"Dani, I--" Terin was slammed into the wall before he could finish his sentence.

"What the fuck did you just say, Terin?" Dani bellowed. "And do not lie to me."

Terin looked at the others, but no one dared move. It seemed Terin had been keeping secrets from them all.

Terin gulped. "I--I don't fully understand how it works."

"But you can speak to him?" Dani demanded, her nails biting into his biceps.

"It's not that simple."

"He is my *soul bond*, Terin!" she shouted. "You cannot even fathom how it feels to lose your other half, how it feels to be ripped from the one person who makes you feel whole! He is my godsforsaken soul bond, yet you have kept this secret from me?"

Terin's gaze danced across Dani's face, but he would find no salvation within them. "He--he didn't want you to know!" he sputtered.

"*He* didn't want me to know?" Dani laughed, the sound mangled and harsh. "Even when he is dead, you still follow him at every turn, don't you? How can you lead our kingdom when you can't even make your own damn choices!"

"Dani, please!" Terin begged.

"Tell me how," Dani commanded, her fingers gripping the fabric of his shirt. "Tell me how to speak to him."

"I promised," he whispered.

Her lips curled into a sneer. "That is not your choice to make!"

Graeson huffed a laugh. At the sound, Dani snapped her head in his direction, and a blazing fire roared in her hazel eyes.

"Did you know?" she snapped.

Graeson rolled his eyes and twisted his hands around the metal bars. "No, Dani. I did not know Terin could fucking speak to the dead."

"I'm not *speaking* to the dead," Terin countered, but Dani ignored him, her attention fixed on Graeson.

Dani cocked her head. "Then what's so funny, huh?"

"It's just ironic, don't you think?" Graeson asked with a smirk. "You're pissed at Terin because he has stripped your choice away from you, and yet you turn around and do the same thing to Kalisandre."

"That is not the same thing, and you know it," Dani deadpanned. "Kallie is a danger to *everyone*."

"Like you're so innocent?" Arching a brow, Graeson glanced at Terin. "You have the heir to the Pontian throne in a chokehold."

Dani released her grip on Terin, who sighed in relief. But Dani was far from done. Her rage was only beginning to boil within her.

"You wouldn't listen to us!" she shouted, rattling the bars.

"You didn't have to intervene. I had her," Graeson spat.

"You did *not* have her," she scoffed. "She fucking stabbed you with a shard of glass! She was running away from you. What were you going to do? Let her continue to run her mouth? Let her run free?" Dani challenged, pointing her blade at him. "You were staring at her like a lovesick puppy. The moment she opened her mouth, you were done for. She's a viper, and you would have gladly let her sink her teeth into you."

Graeson clenched his jaw. "I would have done what needed to be done."

"We both know that is a *lie*, Gray. You are not fooling anyone," Dani snapped.

He didn't want to think about what would have happened if Dani hadn't come into the infirmary when she had. He wanted to believe that he would have stopped Kalisandre from escaping. But at the same time, his heart had been beginning to crack.

It seemed that with every step he took to get closer to Kalisandre and help break her free from Domitius's grasp, the further away she was from him.

"How are you supposed to help her break free if part of your mind is still locked in a cage?" Dani asked.

Ophelia cocked her head to the side, her deep brown eyes narrowing. "Perhaps we should have them try with him first?"

Graeson snapped his attention to the warrior. "Try *what*?" he balked.

"No," Medenia said, shaking her head and ignoring Graeson's question as if he hadn't even asked it. "His cage is not the same as hers. Kalisandre's has been weaved and carefully crafted, while his has been made simply out of his own denial."

The god within sneered, snapping its jaws.

Ophelia nodded. "I suppose you're right. Is it not risky, though?" she pondered.

"What are you talking about?" Graeson snapped, his gaze flitting uneasily between the two women.

Medenia shrugged. "It can be, but it is still worth trying. I believe they're almost done preparing."

Graeson's gaze bore into Medenia's. "*Try what?*"

Dani stepped into his view. "You have two choices, Graeson. Option number one: you let us do what needs to be done. Option number two: you stay within this cell for the foreseeable future."

Red tipped the edge of his vision as concern and anger rose in his throat.

"What are you planning to do to her?" Graeson asked.

"We already told you," Medenia said. "We are doing what must be done."

"Which is?" he pressed, his entire body trembling with the raw fury that scorched his skin.

The god clawed at the walls, saying something, but Graeson was too focused on the words pouring from Dani's mouth.

"Breaking Kalisandre's mind apart, of course," Dani said with a sinister smile.

The bars snapped in Graeson's hands.

CHAPTER 22
MYRA

Myra pressed a light hand upon the patient's head, just as she had for the past week. Tears rimmed her eyes as she grabbed onto the threads of pain and agony coming from him. Tugging them taut, she reached deep into the pit of her stomach and pulled.

She poured every ounce of tranquility down the thread--as much of it as she could, as much as she had to offer him before the guilt and nausea rose in her stomach. Before the hate and doubt settled in her bones.

The invisible black and red threads turned golden, transforming in seconds.

The deep wrinkles that previously creased the man's forehead softened, and the screams ceased. The tension in his jaw lessened as the new emotions took over. And for a moment, the man could pretend like he was anywhere else.

Myra could at least grant him a moment of bliss. As short as it might have been.

Dr. Thorne stepped forward, flicking the syringe with his fingers.

The bitter taste of ash coated Myra's mouth. Guilt and

trepidation flooded her system. Tears burned at the back of her eyes, but she held them back. She didn't deserve to cry. She didn't deserve to feel anything.

Yet, while Myra might have been able to alter everyone else's emotions, she had never been able to change her own.

And despite how much she wished to close her eyes, despite how much she wanted to look away, Myra kept her eyes on the needle as Dr. Thorne poked a vein protruding from the man's neck and deposited the murky liquid into his bloodstream.

CHAPTER 23
KALLIE

THE WARMTH OF THE CANDLES LICKED KALLIE'S SKIN, YET HER fingers grew cold despite the heat surrounding her. She tried to remain calm. She tried to breathe, but the air in the room was stifling, suffocating, and all-consuming.

Mistake, a voice in the back of her mind screamed.

Mistake.

Mistake.

When she had awoken, she had been moved to a new room with two strangers. Kallie had tried to get answers from two women, but they had ignored her. When she tried to use her gift, she found herself utterly drained.

One of the women sat in the darkness, her sharp black nails tapping along the wooden arm of the chair.

Click.

Click.

Click.

And even though the woman sat in the shadows, not saying a single word, power oozed from her fingertips.

Meanwhile, the second woman with striking white hair glided

around the room, placing crystals between the candles encircling Kallie. With a swift brush of her hands, she declared, "We're ready."

The hairs on Kallie's arm stood on end as the woman cloaked in darkness nodded.

"Ready for what?" Kallie asked, looking between the women. She shifted on the hard metal seat beneath her, and the restraints around her wrists and ankles dug into her flesh.

The white-haired woman finally turned to look at Kallie then. Her piercing black eyes narrowed as if she were peering into Kallie's soul. The woman's eyes were the darkest hue Kallie had ever seen, as dark as the pits of the Beneath.

Kallie couldn't help but wonder how her manipulation would affect them.

Would the haze of her gift look like a cloud sweeping over the night sky?

Or would the darkness consume it and swallow it whole?

Even though Kallie knew her well had been used up, she tried to test her theory and reached for her gift, pulling at her core. But as Kallie felt for the source of her gift, there was a wrongness that coated her veins.

She was not merely empty but completely closed off from her power as if it wasn't even there.

"Do not think about using your mind tricks on us, Princess," the white-haired woman said with a satisfied smirk. "They will not work here."

Kallie stared at the woman, panic coloring her face and heating her cheeks. She scanned the room.

There had to be a way out.

There was always a way out.

She pulled at her restraints, but they didn't budge, only rattled and dug into her flesh.

The woman with black eyes stepped closer to her, a haunting

look glistening in her gaze. She brushed a hand across Kallie's hair. "This will only hurt if you fight it."

"Fight *what?*" Kallie demanded, tugging on the restraints again. "What are you going to do?"

The woman dragged her nail across Kallie's cheek before tipping her chin up. Then, in a soft, chilling voice, she whispered, "We're going to set you free."

"Unhand me!" Kallie roared, shaking and fighting against the bindings. "You do not know who you are messing with. He will come for you! He will come for you all!"

"No can do, Princess," the woman said, releasing Kallie's chin and taking a step back. "You see, your friends have reason to believe your mind is not your own."

"They are *not* my friends," Kallie hissed, already knowing who the stranger was referring to.

The woman shrugged and grabbed a torch from the wall. "Makes no difference to me what you consider them. Either way, Domitius has dug his claws into your mind, and we intend to release them once and for all."

"You have no idea what you are talking about!" Kallie screeched as the metal cuff dug deeper into her skin, rubbing it raw. "My father has done nothing. My father--"

"--is not the man you think he is," the older woman said, standing from the chair across Kallie. She took a step forward, and the light from the torch kissed her face, illuminating her features.

The woman's eyes were nearly white, and the flames bounced off her raven-black hair. She wore a gold crown with black and translucent crystals woven through the metal. A single emerald stone dropped from the center point and sat against the woman's forehead.

Kallie's mouth hung open, speechless. It was not just some stranger who stood in front of her. It was Cetia Perseianes, the

Queen of Tetria. She recognized the crown and the queen from her years of studying the seven kingdoms.

"Domitius has manipulated entire kingdoms into believing a lie," the queen continued, her voice calm but assertive, refocusing Kallie's attention, "beginning with you. As you are very well aware, he is not your birth father, and yet he has somehow convinced the seven kingdoms that he is. Do you know how that can be?"

"His blood is of no concern to me. He is my father in every other right," Kallie spat.

"Ah, so you don't know. Yet you do not question it? You are not at all curious?"

Kallie's hands rolled into fists, her nails biting into her palms.

The queen cocked her head ever so slightly. "If it was anyone else in any other circumstances, I would agree with you about the importance of blood, or lack thereof. But the truth is a precious thing, my dear. Do you not wish to uncover it?"

"I already know the truth," Kallie argued.

The queen tsked, shaking her head in dismay. "I've been told that you desire power, yet you dismiss the ability to gain knowledge. My dear, if you wish to be powerful, if you wish to rule, it would be wise to learn the power of knowledge."

Kallie's brows twisted as she recalled Tessa, the former queen of Frenzia, saying the same thing to her. Knowledge might have been powerful, but what Cetia claimed was a treacherous lie. And yet...

While Kallie knew Domitius well, she couldn't help but admit that she didn't know everything about him.

He hadn't told her that he had taken her from her parents as a child.

He hadn't told her that she had brothers.

He hadn't told her that she was to marry Rian because of the knowledge Frenzia possessed.

What other secrets, then, could the King of Ardentol be harboring?

"You want power, Princess?" Cetia asked. "Then it is time you stop letting the men around you dictate what you do. It is time for you to step out of the shadows."

The other woman stood beside the queen and held out a wooden bowl. Kallie squinted at it as the queen dipped two fingers into its contents. Then Cetia stepped forward, her fingers dripping in a white liquid.

Sweat coated Kallie's skin as Cetia stretched out her hand.

Kallie's breathing picked up, and her heart pounded against her ribcage, threatening to break through it. Kallie trembled against the chains. She pushed against the wall blocking her gift, but it was no use.

The queen drew a line down Kallie's forehead, the liquid freezing against her warm skin.

Cetia's searing white eyes fell upon Kallie, and panic rose in Kallie's throat as the queen leaned down in front of her.

This is a mistake.

Fight it.

Fight *it.*

Kallie tugged at the restraints. She pulled, she screamed, she roared. The chair rattled beneath her. The rope burned around her wrists and ankles like a fire singing her skin--hot, searing, and piercing.

Kallie's attention flicked to the other woman, whose pitch-black eyes bore into her with an intensity that threatened to consume her.

The woman stepped outside the circle of candles and crystals that surrounded them. She cracked her neck, the sound thundering in the silent room. Then, she dipped the torch into a water basin, snuffing out its flame and blanketing them all in a sea of darkness.

Cetia placed her palms on either side of Kallie's face, calling her attention back to her. A flicker of movement flashed in her peripheral.

"This will only hurt for a moment," Cetia whispered.

The younger woman knelt on the floor and twisted her hands above the candles in an unfamiliar gesture.

All around her, flames stirred to life, twirling and dancing around the room, rising and falling as they swept across the small space.

And like a moth to a flame, Kallie fell into them as a scream ripped through her throat. But Kallie knew no matter how loud she screamed, no one would rescue her.

CHAPTER 24
GRAESON

Graeson slid around the corner, his hand scraping the wall as his feet skidded across the corridor. He slammed into several guards, handmaidens, and bystanders as he dashed along, his heart racing and sweat trickling down his back.

He would not stop until he reached Kalisandre. Not until he saved her from whatever insanity Cetia and Ellie were performing.

When Graeson realized what the Tetrians and his friends planned to do, rage overtook him and unleashed the god within. The iron bars of his cell bent within his grasp, his inhuman strength fueled by anger breaking them apart.

As his friends screamed and shouted, Graeson did not stop.

He didn't care what they did to him. Nothing would prevent him from reaching Kalisandre.

He noticed nothing. He heard nothing.

He cared about *nothing* besides getting to her before they tore her mind out and destroyed her.

Did they even know how dangerous it was to mess with one's mind? Did they understand the consequences or the damage they could cause?

Kalisandre had never agreed to this level of invasion. *Never.*

But did the others care? No.

His friends, this queendom, they only cared about the greater good. But Kalisandre deserved more.

As if an invisible string connected his soul to Kalisandre's, he let his instincts guide him through the halls.

More and more guards littered the harrowing corridors the deeper he ventured.

Graeson was close, though. He knew it in his heart.

When he turned a corner and saw the queen's warriors standing guard, their hands folded behind their backs, his stomach lurched.

He sprinted forward. This was it.

One after another, the guards' attention quickly turned to him, their confused expressions turning into fear as they grabbed their weapons. But their blades would not stop him.

The god shouted at him in protest, but Graeson ignored his slur of angry words and shoved him back.

This was Graeson's task to do, and his alone.

The guards' eyes widened as they stepped before the door and shifted their stances. One of the guards held up a hand, her sword hanging low.

Graeson barreled forward, his mind consumed with thoughts of saving Kalisandre.

The shouts of the guards were brushed aside, and something within him stirred, the god's shouts becoming louder.

But Graeson's desperation clouded his judgment. He didn't notice the shadows dancing across the floor and spreading from the crack beneath the door.

As Graeson neared the door, a sudden surge of intense heat overcame him and beat against his head.

His knees buckled, and he crashed to the ground in front of the guards.

Brilliant, stark pain Graeson had never experienced before laced the back of his head, rendering him immobile. He screamed, his vocal cords ripping apart as the floor began to quake beneath him.

He called out for Kalisandre, begging for her to hear him.

But he knew that she was beyond his reach as the hall erupted into thick darkness, and he was helpless to stop it.

CHAPTER 25
KALLIE

THE ROOM SPUN, AND KALLIE CLUTCHED THE EDGE OF THE SEAT, HER nails biting into it.

Ribbons of red and orange streaked across Kallie's vision, as if an artist had dipped their hand in paint and spread them across a canvas with no sense of direction. Her bones vibrated as the colors whirled around her, faster and faster with each passing second.

She bit down, her teeth squeezing together and her jaw popping as nausea rose inside her. Rising, rising, *rising*.

The moment Kallie questioned if she could hold on any longer, the world jerked to a stop.

Her body jolted forward, and the restraints yanked her back, the chains rattling on the floor.

Peeling her eyes open, she shook her head.

No...This isn't right.

Kallie squeezed her eyes shut, then opened them once more.

The candles and sea of color were gone as if they had never existed. A darkness thicker than the midnight sky blanketed the world surrounding her.

She looked around the room--or at least she thought she did, for she could not tell. There were no discernible shades of gray, no shadows, no pricks of light.

Kallie couldn't make out a single thing around her. It was as if all of the light had been completely sucked out of everything she could see.

The only thing that grounded her was the chair she sat on. She tried to take a deep breath, but smoke and sage filled her mouth, choking her.

A wave of panic rose in her throat, and her skin prickled.

Kallie blinked again and again, trying to wash away the darkness that permeated her vision. No matter what she did, however, she couldn't *see* anything.

What had Cetia done?

What world had she dropped Kallie into?

Was this a dream? A nightmare? Some weird plane she did not know existed?

Kallie recalled her father speaking about the strange happenings within the Tetrian queendom and the witch who ruled its land. But Kallie hadn't given her father's claims much thought. She had dismissed and ignored them.

But now...now she regretted not listening more closely when he spoke of the queen's wickedness.

What poisons had the queen--

Kallie stilled as a whisper kissed the air, making the hair on her neck stand on end. The words, however, were unintelligible, too quiet to parse.

She tried to grasp onto the faint syllables and hold onto them, but they slipped through her fingers like the sand on the shore. Whatever the words were, Kallie knew they were important. She could feel it within her bones, yet she couldn't prevent them from flying off into the spinning air.

"Who's there?" Kallie asked, voice shaking as goosebumps spread across her skin.

"Kalisandre."

Kallie jerked to the right, but she still couldn't see anything, only a single shade of darkness smeared across her eyes.

"Kalisandre."

Her name was even clearer and more urgent this time, yet Kallie still could not identify to whom it belonged.

Then, more voices joined in the fray, repeating her name round and round. It was as if a hundred voices spoke her name into the air simultaneously, varying tones layered on top of one another.

Kalisandre. Kalisandre. Kalisandre.

Her name was a hiss on their lips, a whisper in the air, a shout in her ears.

But as her name spun around her head, one voice stripped itself from the others.

"All you had to do was listen, Kalisandre. Was that truly so hard?"

The frigid air nipped at her ankles, causing a shudder to run down her spine as she recognized the voice by the disdain dripping from it.

"Father?" Kallie croaked, her throat dry. "What--what are you doing here?"

But Kallie received no answer as an ice-cold breeze swept in, sending a chill over her flesh.

"Father?" Kallie called out into the void, her heart pounding.

This time a second voice called out to her. "What did you do, Kalisandre?"

She could almost pinpoint the owner of the voice. But when the name was at the tip of her tongue, a finger brushed her chin and swept it away. Although she could not see him, she felt her father staring at her with disapproval as the scent of whiskey drowned out the other scent lingering in the air.

"Such potential," her father hissed in her ear, and she shuddered.

Kallie could feel him tip her chin up, yet she saw nothing. No distinguishable shadows danced before her face. Yet he was there. She knew it.

"If only you listened..."

Kallie tried to swallow and clear her throat, but her mouth was too dry. "Father, I didn't--"

"Do not lie to me!" Domitius's voice roared throughout the tenebrious space.

The cold air licked Kallie's legs, and frost wrapped around her ankles. She didn't know where it was coming from. All she knew was that its icy tendrils were creeping up her calves and twisting around her limbs.

"Do you not remember what I have done for you?" Domitius demanded, his breath cold on her neck.

"Father, please. I--"

"Kals," a pair of voices whispered, one feminine and one masculine, both soaked with sorrow.

When Kallie turned toward the pair, her father called her attention back to him. "Who has cared for you all this time, Kalisandre?"

"Kals," the voices repeated.

Kallie's head swiveled. She searched the darkness for the source, but there was nothing. No one.

Notes of lavender and mint wrapped around Kallie.

"Trust me, Kals," a voice as sweet and bright as the first morning in the spring said.

"Myra?" Kallie croaked.

"This is for your own good," Myra whispered. And as sweet as her words were, they were sour in the air.

Suddenly, something tugged at her core, and Kallie blinked, straightening, as another voice spoke. Although it was quieter than the others, it sounded even louder in her ears.

"Never forget who you are."

Kallie's throat seized as her heart ricocheted against her ribcage.

"I have given you everything!" her father shouted, jerking her head back. "I have raised you as my own. I have trained you, shaped you. And yet you still yearn for their attention? Why? Because they share your blood?"

Kallie bit her lip, shaking her head as the ice coating her calves spread over her knees and thighs. "They're nothing. No one."

"That's right," her father whispered, gripping her shoulders. "Blood is only as thick as one makes it."

Kallie nodded, although she did not know if her father could see the movement.

"You've betrayed me once, Kalisandre. But you only need to do one thing to earn my trust again."

That was all she wanted: to have her father's trust, to have his approval.

"Anything, Father," Kallie begged, tears pooling at the bottom of her eyes.

"Fight it," one of the other voices called out. Their voice sang of summer and fresh air, of laughter and joy. But as it flew past her, it grew heavy and quickly turned to mud on her ears.

Kallie gripped the chair, her nails cracking against the metal frame.

"Sacrifices are a necessity," Domitius hissed as he dug his fingers deeper into her shoulders. "Their lives are nothing when it comes to the power you will have."

The scent of lavender and mint calming the rising nausea.

"It's going to be all right." The warmth of the sun filled Kallie's veins the moment Myra spoke. Gentle fingers landed on Kallie's shoulder and squeezed. "I promise."

"You have come so far, Kalisandre. Are you going to let them take everything you have worked for away?" her father demanded.

"No," Kallie whispered, shaking her head and holding back tears. "I won't let them."

"They do not know you," her father taunted. "They do not know what you could become, *who* you could become. They only wish to make you weak, to stifle your power. They *fear* you. They believe you are a monster."

His words slithered into her mind, soaking into her skin and coating the veins that ran through her body. As he continued, Kallie saw the truth in every word he said.

These people were strangers. They were the *enemy*. Their selfishness had torn Vaneria apart. Pontia was full of secrets and lies, and for centuries, their rulers had only wished to harbor that power for themselves.

Her father had always been right about them. He was right about everything.

Kallie might have shared their blood and been born a Pontian, but she wasn't one of them.

She didn't *belong* with them.

"They do not want the best for you," he continued as the frost rose higher and higher. "They only care about themselves. They always have. Pontia has not changed for decades, centuries even, and it never will."

She nodded. "I know, Father."

The frost slipped up Kallie's torso and across her ribcage. It squeezed her abdomen and froze her arms to her chest.

Her breathing became shallow, and her heartbeat raced as her legs grew more and more numb.

"Kals!"

Kallie turned her head at the sound of the voice that had haunted her dreams.

"Fynn?" Kallie called out, her heart hammering. Pain pierced her bones, cracking the ice.

"Whatever means necessary," her father hissed.

"Don't listen to him, Kals!" Fynn shouted as the king said, "He was a sacrifice, Kalisandre. A sacrifice we needed to achieve our dream."

Kallie's face twisted as she swiveled her head between the two men pulling her in different directions.

Soon, more voices joined in, the chorus returning and spinning around the room.

Round.

And round.

And round.

A sea of shouts spread across the room, slithering over her sweat-slicked skin.

Still, her father's voice was the loudest of them all.

"Who has trained you all these years?" he thundered.

Kallie sobbed, no longer able to hold back her tears. They streamed down her face as her father's disappointment laced each word.

For years, all she had wanted was to prove to her father that she was more, that she was capable, that he could trust her. But now, all of her work began to crumble in the darkness.

Brick by brick, the pieces fell.

Each training session, each sacrifice, each mission--they fell from the tower she had spent her entire life building.

Kallie tried to scramble forward and catch the falling pieces, but the chains yanked her back.

"Who has promised you power, the power you otherwise would not have access to?" Domitius challenged.

Kallie's lips began to tremble, and the tip of her nose burned as the frost rose.

"You did," Kallie said at last, but the words were ash on her tongue. Still, she wanted to believe them. She *needed* to believe them. Because if they were not true, then why had she done everything she did? Why had she tarnished the servant's reputation in Frenzia? Why had she manipulated all of those civilians? Why had she betrayed her flesh and blood?

If they weren't true, then who was she?

Who would she *become*?

"If the truth within is not found," another said, their voice miles away. "Then--"

Before the stranger could finish, her father interrupted, "Do not let your emotions get the better of you, Kalisandre!"

Lavender and mint mixed with whiskey. It swarmed around her, sweeping across her face and her neck. The scents wrapped around her throat, forcing the words out. "I--I won't."

Her hair flew across her face as a gust of wind smacked into her.

"Kals!" Fynn shouted through the darkness.

Kallie tried desperately to reach for him, but her hands were frozen to her sides.

"You have to fight it, Kallie," Fynn urged, his voice sounding farther and farther away.

Kallie struggled to turn as the ice held tight around her body. She tried to break it apart, but her entire body was quickly growing too numb to move.

Her father chuckled, and the sound had the hair on the back of her neck standing.

"I can give you everything," Domitius crooned.

"Fight it!" Fynn pleaded.

Her heart raced faster.

"He's lying to you, Kal," another voice said, ripping through the noise.

Kallie shook her head to calm the heavy patter of her heart. Yet, no matter how hard she tried, it only beat faster.

"Why didn't you tell me?" Kallie croaked at last.

"You dare question me? The man who raised you, who cared for you?"

Tears streamed down her cheeks, but Kallie forced herself to push through the pain and asked, "Why did you take me away from them?"

"I have treated you like a daughter all these years, Kalisandre. Is that not enough?"

Kallie blinked, her tongue growing heavy with frost.

Was it enough? It had been once. But why did it feel as if it wasn't now?

"Kals," Myra said, her voice as sweet as candy. "It's going to be all right."

Kallie wanted to believe Myra. After all, how could she not? Myra was her best friend--her family.

As was Domitius.

They were all Kallie had needed for so long. They were the only two people she could ever count on. They were the only ones who cared what she--

"They're lying, Kallie," Fynn shouted, his voice faint though powerful enough to break through the endless void.

Hands fell onto her shoulders, one light and one heavy, both familiar.

So much had changed within the past few months. All she wanted now was to sink into the familiar.

"Show me the weapon you were meant to be," her father whispered. "Show me the weapon I have raised you to be."

This was what she wanted: to be wanted and needed.

To have power.

This was what she was born for.

The chorus started again, all shouting her name as she spun around the room. With each repetition, she spun faster and faster, her hair whipping across her face.

The darkness began to dissipate as flashes of color bled across her vision.

"Kalisandre."

"Kalisandre."

"Kalisandre."

The ice crawled over her skin, its frigid touch burning into her flesh as it rose higher and higher.

Soon, the coldness became a welcome companion as Kallie whirled around the room. It seeped into her bones, stabilizing her and keeping her from rocking in the chair.

She wanted to sink into it, to let it consume her. It would have been easy to do just that. Because as its frigid touch enveloped her, it numbed her from her head to her toes.

It would be much easier if she just let go, if she gave into it. It would be so much easier to be numb to it all. To let the emotions *go*.

Kallie had always been too emotional. Her father had told her that too many times to count. But the ice on her skin promised to get rid of those emotions, to relinquish that pain she felt in her chest.

She nodded to herself. *Yes*, she thought. *It would be so much easier to care less.*

"Little mouse, you are smarter than this."

Kallie's breath hitched as Graeson's voice broke through the roar of voices.

"You can still fix this, Kalisandre," her father said. "Come home."

Home.

Where was her home?

Ardentol was Domitius's kingdom; its people were his, not hers.

Was that not what she wanted--her own throne, her own kingdom to rule?

But then...

A thought seeped through the cracks of the thickening ice.

Her father had tried to sell her to Frenzia to gain their kingdom. Kallie was supposed to sit on the throne, but she would not have ruled. Not really.

She would have been just another figurehead, another queen for a man to manipulate.

Kallie's brows twisted. "Pontia was once my home."

"That island?" her father asked with a snort. "What good--"

"Ardentol was my home once, too," Kallie whispered, her voice shaking as she continued, ignoring his interruption. "Until you sent me away." She blinked, struggling to make sense of it all. "How are you better than any of them?"

"I have treated you as if you were my own!" Domitius shouted.

Had he, though?

Various memories rose to the surface.

Kallie walking into the center of a ballroom, her hand in her father's, her diamond-covered dress sparkling beneath the chandelier.

Kallie running through mazes, her lungs threatening to burst.

Her knees hitting the ground as she struggled to breathe. A hand gripping her arm, bruising her flesh.

Green, hungry eyes boring into hers as a hand wrapped around her throat and another skated up her thigh.

For her entire life, Kallie had strived to be the perfect daughter, the perfect *weapon.* She pushed her body, broke her bones, and sacrificed her morals. She let Domitius's dreams become hers. His goals had morphed into hers.

Nothing she did was ever in pursuit of her desires.

She lied to the people she cared about because he told her to.

She manipulated innocents because he commanded it.

She sacrificed an entire kingdom's safety to advance his political agenda.

What had Kallie ever done that was just for her?

Even her romantic exploits, which were few and far between, resulted from assignments to test her abilities.

Diamond. Weapon. Pawn--*that's* what Kallie was to Domitius. Not a daughter, and by no means an equal, not even close.

She was merely a tool for him to use.

The ice around Kallie's fingers cracked as her fingers strained against it, her muscles flexing.

Enough was *enough.*

But then, all around her, more whispers swam in the air.

"Traitor."

"Liar."

"Snake."

"Manipulator."

Each whisper and insult wrapped its smoky tendrils around her body, curling around her frozen frame. The syllables snaked around her throat, strangling her tighter and tighter with each repetition.

And one by one, Kallie finally recognized the voices: guards whom she had sacrificed, innocent lives whose homes were destroyed in Pontia, the victims her father had her manipulate in Ardentol, the servant whose life she had tainted by following her father's plan, her allies, and friends.

Rian.

Dani.

Terin.

Esmeray.

Graeson.

Fynn.

Their voices joined in unison as they hissed one insult after another.

Kallie squeezed her eyes shut, bit her tongue, and dug her nails into her palms, hoping the pain would drown out their voices. Still, their words sunk into her skin.

"Who are you to them but the enemy? A liar, a traitor, a manipulator?" Domitius drawled with disdain. "They will never trust you. They will *never* forgive you."

Guilt coated Kallie's stomach, twisting and turning over and over.

He was right.

Of course, he was right.

They would never forgive her. She could never earn their trust after everything she had done and all the pain and irreversible destruction she had caused. Not after--

"Kals," Fynn said as he placed a gentle hand on her shoulder. He squeezed once. "It's okay."

Tears sparkled in her eyes at her brother's words, but she could not accept them. She had never deserved his kindness when he was alive, and she didn't deserve it now.

"It's not okay," Kallie said as the tears fell. "It's not--"

"Kal," Graeson soothed, joining Fynn. "This isn't you."

Kallie shook her head. Graeson didn't know what he was saying. He had said the same words to her before, but he didn't *know* her.

How could he possibly know who she was when she didn't?

"Kalisandre," another man said. This voice, however, was foreign yet familiar, as if she had heard it in a dream once before. "You have to fight it, fight him."

A protective warmth exuded from the man's voice. Despite not being able to see him or even identify who he was, she felt safe. Yet, simultaneously, her heart ached, for somehow, she knew she would never experience his safety again--as if the man was beyond her reach.

"Our father is right, Kals," Fynn whispered gently.

Kallie gasped. *Our Father?*

"You are weak," the king spat, forcing her to return her attention to him.

She gripped the chair harder as her head pounded.

"You are *nothing*," Domitius said.

"Kalisandre," a woman murmured, breaking free from the rest of the group, strong and fueled with fire and honey.

Kallie straightened. It was the same feminine voice that had spoken to her in the cave at the Whispering Springs.

"Find it, Kalisandre, and destroy it before all is lost," the goddess Sabina warned.

The voice brushed across her face, a heat that was unrelenting, and Kallie jerked back as it scorched her skin.

"Come back to me," her father said. "Come take the throne. Show the world what we have spent years building."

Yes, My King.

The phrase was on the tip of her tongue, yet she couldn't pry her mouth open to say it.

It should have been an easy answer. It should have been simple to utter the three syllables she had grown up saying. Yet it wasn't simple. Not at all.

"Destroy it, Kallie. Destroy the link," the voices around her said in harmony.

Something tugged at her mind and urged her to obey Domitius's command, to tell her father *yes*.

Kallie didn't want to disappoint him.

She didn't want to betray him.

She didn't want to make him angry.

"Kalisandre," her father beckoned. "Listen to me."

Yes.

It's what she should say, yet she couldn't.

How many times had Kallie told him yes? How many times had she quieted her voice? How many times had she sewn her lips shut for the sake of appeasing him? Biding by his rules? His plans?

And for what? What did Kallie stand to gain? A pretend crown that held no actual power? A kingdom that did not respect her?

Was that what she wanted? To sit on a throne while speaking his commands?

What kind of life would that be? Living as his puppet?

Once Domitius claimed the entire realm, what would happen to her then? What would he do with her when he had no more use for her?

For her entire life, Kallie craved power. But now, as the world was ripped away from her and the ice threatened to consume her, Kallie questioned that desire for the first time.

Power was supposed to set her free. Power was supposed to release her.

Instead, Domitius promised her a chain around her neck that grew tighter and tighter the higher she climbed onto the throne.

Kallie was not a pawn for him to maneuver.

She was not a weapon for him to use.

More than anything, in that moment, all Kallie wanted was power over herself.

"No!" The single word ripped through her lungs and poured out her mouth like a torrent. She didn't care if the word shredded her dry throat or if it mutilated her vocal cords.

Fire erupted through the darkness. Its golden tendrils and brilliant flames wrapped around her, melting the ice and bringing life back to her frozen limbs.

Within the wild flames, black and white eyes sparkled. In a flash, the fire was swallowed whole.

Then, there was nothing.

CHAPTER 26
GRAESON

A BOOT NUDGED HIS SIDE, AND GRAESON GROANED. HE TRIED TO PRY his eyes open, but the light bleeding behind his eyelids was too bright and painful. His head throbbed as if he had drunk his weight in alcohol despite not having had a single drop.

"How long?" a familiar voice asked.

"An hour or so," another said, their voice slightly muffled as if Graeson's ears were clogged. When he opened his eyes to identify the person, the world was a blur around him. "We tried to stop him, Your Majesty, but he wouldn't listen."

"Typical," another person said with a snort--Ellie, perhaps? "Do you think he was impacted, too?" she said.

After a beat of silence, another person, whom Graeson recognized as the queen, said, "It is possible. One cannot be certain, though. Get him up and take him to his room. We will have to wait until he wakes to see what damage has been done, if any."

Several sets of footsteps sounded around Graeson. Then, hands were upon him, lifting him and placing him on what he presumed to be a stretcher.

"Were you...were you successful then?" Someone--Terin, Graeson thought--asked.

The queen let out a heavy sigh. "That remains to be seen as well."

"He will not be happy when he wakes up," Terin mumbled.

"We only did what you asked. If we were successful, he will be thankful," Cetia said.

"And if you were not?"

"Then we have bigger concerns than his inflated ego."

"When do you think she will be awake?" Terin asked.

"Whenever she decides to. She fought me the entire time while I tried to unweave the damage the bull king and the girl had done. Her mind was an absolute mess. I must say, the girl did a number on your sister. That, tied with the training she received from the king over the years, made it difficult. While we did our best to untangle the coiled threads, I will not give you empty promises."

Graeson groaned, his limbs and tongue heavy, yet he forced the words out of his mouth anyway. "If you hurt her--"

A hand pressed down on his shoulder, and sharp nails immediately dug into the space between his shoulder and collarbone.

"Are you threatening my queen, Graeson?" Ellie demanded. "Because I know you are not that foolish. If Kalisandre was hurt, it is her own fault."

Graeson pried his eyes open and squinted at Ellie. His vision was slow to focus, but he could see her black, void-filled eyes staring down at him, unblinking.

An inaudible roar sounded in the back of his mind as she continued to glare at him.

Then, someone pulled her back, forcing her to step away and unpeel her claws from his shoulder.

Cetia's blazing white eyes were unfocused as she gripped Graeson's shoulder. "Sometimes we must experience pain to be set free." She cocked her head to the side. "You felt it as well, though, did you not?"

Graeson huffed. He attempted to push himself up onto his arms, but his limbs were weak, the energy drained from him. "Yes," he gritted out.

"You experienced the pain because you, too, have been holding back a part of yourself. But where Kalisandre's mind was manipulated, yours is simply ignorance. I can sense the twisting of your mind, the confliction and hesitation. You hold yourself back." Cetia raised a curious brow. "Why? Do you fear the truth? Do you fear what you may become?"

Graeson shook the queen's hand from his shoulder. "Do not speak of things you do not understand," he mumbled, a heaviness coating his mind again.

Cetia pressed her palm to his forehead and clicked her tongue. "Oh, child, do not think me fooled. You do not even understand the things going on in your mind."

CHAPTER 27
MYRA

After days of silence, Myra followed Kolen down the dark, cold hall. Anxiety pounded in her throat as she twisted her hands together, and her footsteps echoed around them.

While Myra had been held inside the cell, she felt the presence of those outside, striding down the hall toward Dr. Thorne's work rooms. Excitement swept across the ground.

At first, Myra had struggled to identify it as such, for she had been deprived of the emotion for so long. Yet it came at her like a lightning strike, piercing and blinding. And she knew then, without a doubt, that the experiment had been successful.

She couldn't help but wonder what she had started.

For days, she waited for the king to call her again. During that time, guilt ate at her. It gnawed on the insides of her stomach and twisted in her throat.

Myra tried to reason with herself. She tried to find the silver lining--that at least with her help, the man wouldn't be in pain and could live in ignorant bliss.

But Myra didn't deserve to identify a reason that would grant her peace in the decisions she had made. Because although she told herself she obeyed the king to protect Mynhos and prevent him from experiencing further harm, how was Myra supposed to live with herself knowing she had aided the king once again?

The truth was, she deserved to suffer inside a cell for the rest of her life.

WHEN MYRA and the guard reached Dr. Thorne's work rooms, the king was already waiting for them. If the emotions wafting from the king and staining Myra's skin didn't give away Domitius's excitement, the wide smile would have.

The stretch of his lips made Myra's stomach turn, and bile rose in her throat.

"Your Majesty," Myra said with a short bow. "Did it work then?"

"Oh, it worked wonderfully."

Myra swallowed, shifting on her feet as she kept her gaze rooted to the floor. If the king was in a good mood, perhaps now was the best time to ask. "Can I see my brother again?"

"In due time," Domitius said.

Lips parting, Myra finally lifted her gaze. "But you said--"

At his fierce look, Myra snapped her mouth shut and reined in her irritation as she folded her hands behind her back and dug her nails into her palms.

"You may have done well, but your job is far from over. Your brother is safe," the king said, walking to the door as he reached into his pocket and pulled out a key. "For now."

"Is there...is there more *coaxing* that the man needs then for the experiment to be complete?" Myra asked, hating that she didn't even know the previous man's name. But since he had been either unconscious or unable to speak due to the gag whenever she had seen him, there had been no time to gain his name.

"No. The Pontian's transformation has been completed."

"The man was Pontian?" Myra breathed.

"Indeed." The king smiled, but rather than soothing her concerns, it only made them worse. "We are creating something spectacular together. I have been trying to discover a way to accomplish this transformation for decades. With access to Freniza's abundance of scientific research on hybridization and your gift, I have finally succeeded."

"Hy-hybridization?" Myra asked, stammering over the word as the fear dripped into her voice. The nausea rose, and she had to press her hand against her stomach to stifle it.

Domitius nodded.

"Among rulers, it is a well-known fact that the Frenzians hold deep wells of knowledge within their castle walls. But this knowledge expands beyond their advancements in armor and weaponry. The research Sebastian has taken over in his father's absence deals with genetics. Hybridization, to be exact.

"Over the centuries, many farmers have done this accidentally by cross-pollinating different plants, producing new variations. The former King Lothian, however, was particularly interested in the hybridization of animals, specifically dragons."

"I thought dragons were only legends?" Myra asked, dumbfounded.

"Perhaps they are merely legends *now*, but there was a time when they roamed the world freely. Lothian had made great strides in his research, but what he lacked in gumption, his son excelled at. When he showed Sebastian his research, his son went beyond the research and started experimenting.

"Sebastian has been able to create something akin to a dragon by morphing the genetics of other animals. He calls it a drakonis. While I do not care so much about their pursuit to recreate the legendary beasts, I have found their research beneficial in other ways."

Myra's heart hammered in her chest as Domitius cocked his head and continued.

"You see, I have studied gifts like yours and Kalisandre's for decades, ever since my father informed me about them when I was a mere child. Your gifts are a result of the gods' blood within your veins. But I could never understand why these gifts have always been concentrated in Pontia.

"After all, when the gods came to the mortal world, they traveled and lived throughout Vaneria. And yet, only Pontians have been found to have these unique abilities. For centuries, the Pontians have kept their secrets by secluding themselves from the rest of Vaneria. They have harbored their gifts and kept them from the rest of the world.

"Many think the Great War started one hundred years ago because of a dispute between lords. However, it was actually because the rulers on that little island were afraid their truth would be revealed to the world. They wanted to keep the power to themselves. Selfish of them, don't you think?"

"But I am not a Pontian," Myra whispered, the words slipping out subconsciously.

Domitius smirked, the sinister twitch of his lips only increasing Myra's anxiety. "Ah, you see, that is where you are wrong. Your mother, in fact, was a Pontian."

Myra's brows twisted together. She didn't believe a word the king was saying, and yet...

She thought back to when she first stepped onto Pontian soil. Once on land, as the salt in the air twisted around her, the kingdom felt...familiar. It reminded Myra of her mother, as if spring bloomed there every day.

Myra had thought it was because Domitius hadn't tainted the

island, but perhaps she had been wrong. Maybe there was more to it.

"But how do you know that?" Myra asked in disbelief, voice shaking.

"The details of the matter are unimportant. You and Kalisandre are similar in that sense. Always looking for the details. Always wanting to know everything and wanting to understand everything." Scoffing, Domitius waved his hand in the air. "This is the only thing that matters. For decades, I have tried to figure out a way to replicate the abilities, but I have been unsuccessful until now."

The king stepped toward Myra, and she had to force her feet to stay in place as the fear drifting from the room twisted around her ankles.

"You have proven to be most useful. And now that we know that you can do what we need you to, we have rewarded you." He smiled from ear to ear.

"Rewarded me?" Myra repeated, her stomach turning.

"Come." The king turned to the door and opened it, ushering her forward. "Let me show you."

Aghast, Myra stared at the door, blinking.

She did not wish to see whoever it was that lay inside. Her mind was already spiraling.

Somehow, her feet carried her forward even though every nerve in her body screamed for her not to listen to the king. To stop the madness and stop aiding him, for if Myra couldn't break the cycle now, there would be no hope for her ever.

Dr. Thorne set down the syringe and bowed low as Myra and the king entered.

"Your Majesty, everything is in order. We are ready to begin when you are," he announced.

"How is his temperament today?" King Domitius asked brightly.

"It is..." Dr. Thorne hesitated and squinted through his glasses at the ceiling as he searched for an answer. Finally, he sighed. "It is the same as it normally is, Your Majesty. However, I am hopeful that he will tire himself out soon enough. One can only fight for so long as we have seen."

His beady eyes landed on Myra. But before Myra could retreat, Domitius stepped behind her, his presence overwhelming her.

"Isn't that the truth?" King Domitius said in agreement.

Dr. Thorne nodded and turned toward the curtain dividing the room. As the curtain was drawn back, Myra's tongue turned leaden, and her jaw dropped at the sight of the new man strapped to the table.

And for a fleeting moment, relief washed over her because it was not her brother who lay upon the table as she feared but rather the King of Frenzia. Rian's wine-colored hair stuck to his forehead, his brown skin was ashen, and his green eyes were wide and bloodshot as he swept his gaze across the room in a panic.

"Your Majesty?" Myra whispered in horror, her voice no more than a faint breath. "I--I do not understand. He is not a Pontian."

"Good observation," Domitius mused. "I admit, that has been my goal for so long that I did not fathom that there could be other possibilities. But Sebastian's youth has enlightened me. We do not simply seek to harvest powers; we wish to transform normal civilians."

He folded his hands behind his back as he peered at Rian. "The king here has been asking too many questions, and it is time we give him some answers. What better way to do that than to let him go through one of the transformations himself? Let his research and fixation for the legendary creatures finally be of use."

"Does--does the prince know?" She swallowed.

King Domitius chuckled darkly. "The prince delivered King Rian here himself."

CHAPTER 28
KALLIE

KALLIE STARED AT THE CEILING. SHE WAS BACK IN THE INFIRMARY, but this time, she was strapped to a bed with no desire to escape.

She didn't know how much time had passed.

She didn't know how many days had come and gone.

She barely listened to those who visited her. Some would talk over her, above her, beside her. They spoke to her, about her, and for her.

And Kallie remained silent through it all.

Sometimes, she wondered if she would ever be moved to speak. She wondered if she even *could* speak. She did not try to find out.

In truth, Kallie couldn't muster the energy to care.

She was no more than a corpse at this point.

It was worse than when she had been in and out of sleep while she was dragged across the kingdoms. It was worse than when she had sailed across the sea, her stomach turning and the heartache of what she had done pressing heavily on her heart.

Because in those moments of fleeting consciousness, Kallie at least cared. She at least felt *something*, whether that was guilt or rage or hurt or nausea.

But as Kallie lay there in a foreign castle, she felt nothing. Absolutely nothing at all.

CHAPTER 29
MYRA

Despite the rod in his mouth, Rian's screams ripped through the room, vibrating Myra's very bones and rattling the healer's instruments. The rush of fear, agony, and anger pierced through the shields Myra had spent so long building over the years.

In a matter of seconds, however, Rian tore through them as if they were nothing, and Myra was helpless to stop him.

She sat beside the frail king as he continued to fight.

Fighting, however, only ever made things worse. A fact she knew only too well by now.

She wiped the sweat from her face. Then, she took a deep breath before reaching for the Frenzian king again. Her gaze dropped to their joined hands where blood stained the back of her hand.

CHAPTER 30
GRAESON

Graeson jerked upright, his fists digging into his mattress as his breaths became ragged, pouring out of his chest in a rush. His blood pumped through his veins, an icy fury rising within him as the need to find Kalisandre overtook him.

A rod fell over his chest, pressing against him.

He blinked and looked down, following the wooden cane to the side of his bed where Cetia sat, her face even and near-white eyes downcast.

Her straight, raven-black hair fell down her back in billowing tendrils. She wore a simple moss-green dress and a black lace shawl that hung loosely over her shoulders.

"She is fine," the queen said, pressing the wooden cane more firmly against Graeson's sternum, her expression still calm.

Graeson's features twisted, confusion rushing over him as he tried to get his bearings. "I didn't say--"

She lifted a shoulder in a shrug, then dropped it. "You speak in your sleep."

With a narrowed gaze, Graeson pushed the cane away from him.

"Let her rest."

"I need to see her," Graeson argued, throwing the blankets off him.

The queen poked him in the ribcage.

"Ow," Graeson grunted, swatting the cane away. "What was that for?"

"For not listening," Cetia hissed, setting her cane in front of her. Folding her hands on the large emerald globe atop the twisted cane, the queen leaned against it, her long, wrinkled fingers curving around the stone.

"You are not my queen," Graeson grumbled. "I do not need to listen to you."

Cetia arched a brow. "From what I have gathered, you do not listen to your queen, either."

Graeson grunted, and the god within roared.

We do not bow down to rulers who wear makeshift crowns.

Graeson bit down on his tongue, refusing to speak the god's words aloud in the queen's presence. Despite agreeing with the beast within, Graeson did not wish to insult the queen in her own home.

At least not more than he already had.

"I need--" Graeson began, but Cetia cut him off with a quick bop of her cane against his head.

"No, what you need is to face your own problems before you can even think about helping her." She gave him a pointed look.

"I do not have any problems," Graeson argued, rubbing his temple where the emerald bruised his skull.

"Tell me about your father then."

Graeson grew silent.

The queen sniffed. "Ah, see. Silence often speaks louder than words if you dare to listen. And your silence speaks volumes."

Graeson rubbed a hand across his face, and the gold rings he wore were cold on his skin. He sighed.

The chair Cetia sat in creaked as she stood. "I will not force you to speak to me. Ellie told me who your father is, though it comes as no surprise to me. Although you may be similar in many ways, you are not Barinthian. Nor must you be. We are often granted things when we are born that we would have never sought out for ourselves otherwise. Therefore, while you can fight the power that you were born with all you want, you will have to face it sooner or later." She shifted her weight on the cane.

Graeson glared down at the bed, his fingers curling into the sheets. "I have faced it."

Cetia shook her head as she released a heavy, tired sigh. "No, child, you have not. You have only pushed it away. That is not the same. How do you expect to help Kalisandre if you cannot even face your own demons?"

Cetia did not give Graeson a chance to answer before she took her leave.

Then Graeson was left alone in his room, the monster within him stirring.

WHEN GRAESON COULD NOT RETURN to sleep a few days later, he found himself wandering the halls. He hadn't known where he was going until he arrived outside the infirmary.

He gripped the wooden door frame, his fingers curling around the pine. It was nearing midnight, and the healers had since disappeared to their rooms further down the hall, leaving only a guard to watch over the lone patient who lay motionless on the thin mattress.

When Graeson had stopped at the room, the guard had

immediately raised a brow at him, her fingers twitching at her side near her sheathed sword. But Graeson had never made it past the threshold, his feet remaining in the hall as if an invisible block prevented him from stepping any closer.

After several moments, the guard eventually realized Graeson wasn't an immediate threat and relaxed...marginally so.

Night swept over the room, but the moon's glow shone directly on Kalisandre, as if a beacon on her slumbering form.

He pressed his palm against the wall, anchoring him to the spot as something stirred within him.

Terin's voice broke through the silence soaking the hall. "You still haven't gone to see her."

Graeson steeled his expression, wiping the tension from his forehead as much as possible before shifting away from the infirmary's entrance and facing Terin.

Graeson folded his arms over his chest and leaned against the wall beside the door. "I am here, aren't I?"

"But are you going to go inside?" Terin asked.

"She needs time to rest." He shrugged, feigning nonchalance when he felt anything but.

Terin peered into the infirmary, his fingers tapping along the doorframe. With a sigh, he shook his head. "All she does is rest."

Graeson's fingers dug into his biceps. "Her mind isn't--"

"Gray," Terin interrupted, tilting his head toward the infirmary. "Go see her."

"Has she asked for me?" Graeson asked, arching a brow.

Terin hesitated. "No, but--"

"But nothing," Graeson said, shaking his head. "I promised that I would set her mind free and let her live her life."

"Is that what you are doing then?"

"Yes."

"Not sulking?" Terin pressed, arching a brow.

The muscles in Graeson's jaw went taut. "I am *not* sulking."

"If you say so, pal." Terin patted Graeson on the shoulder, which Graeson immediately shrugged off. Terin released a heavy sigh as he brushed his chestnut brown waves back. "I'm sorry, Gray."

Graeson snorted and pushed himself off the wall. He started walking down the corridor, but he didn't make it more than a few steps before Terin was tugging his arm, calling him to a stop.

"Graeson, wait."

He spun. "Is that an order, my *prince*?"

Terin's lips parted, his features contorting. "Gray, what--"

But Graeson didn't let Terin finish as his anger propelled him forward. "That's what led you to believe that you didn't need to inform me of your plan to betray Kalisandre and destroy her mind, right?"

The muscles in Terin's jaw flexed, his gaze hardening. "Watch yourself, Gray."

"Or what? Will you name me a traitor?" Graeson took a step closer, the toes of his boots nearly touching Terin's. "You forget who I am."

Terin huffed, rolling his eyes. "I do not forget who you are, Graeson. It is because of who you are and what she means to you that we did not include you in this decision."

"Is that so?"

"Yes!" Terin shouted. But as if recalling the time of night, he straightened, brushing a hand over his face and wiping the slip of anger from his expression. When he spoke next, his voice was calmer, quieter. "You are stubborn, Graeson. And that stubbornness can blind you. If we had spoken to you about letting Cetia and Ellie look at Kallie's mind, you would have said no and done anything you could to prevent it."

"Of course I would have prevented it! As you should have. She's your sister!"

"As you keep reminding me," Terin mumbled.

Graeson stared at him. "Do you not care for her safety?"

"It is not only her safety that I must look after," Terin argued.

Graeson huffed and flicked his hand in the air. "Oh, right. Because now that you are heir, her safety does not matter when it comes to the kingdom." He shoved Terin in the chest. "You are just like Esmeray."

Terin pushed his hand. "You're not listening, Graeson."

"No, *you're* not. What if it hadn't worked?"

He spun in a circle, his anger and frustration compiling on top of one another without anywhere to go. Graeson pressed his hands against his temples before flinging them out wide. "Fuck! What if it didn't? She hasn't even spoken yet!"

Terin grabbed Graeson by the shoulders, forcing him to a stop. Graeson snarled, his nose twitching, but Terin only gripped Graeson's shoulders tighter, not painfully but with enough tension to coax Graeson to meet his gaze.

For a moment, Terin didn't say anything as his dark brown eyes bore into Graeson. Then, Terin shook him gently. "She has been through a lot. I only saw a sliver of her memories, but the things Domitius did to her..." Terin shook his head, his words trailing off. "She will get better, Gray. She only needs time."

"You do not know that." Gods, none of them did.

Terin offered him a sad smile. "My sister is many things, but she is not a quitter."

Graeson scoffed, but he knew Terin was right. Even as a child, Kalisandre was too stubborn to quit.

Sensing Graeson's shift in emotions, Terin pressed his forehead against Graeson's before pulling away. "I am sorry for keeping our intentions from you," he said softly.

Graeson exhaled a heavy sigh, forcing his shoulders to relax. He shook his head. "No, you are not."

Terin chuckled. "You're right. I'm not, but her state is not your burden to bear."

Graeson shifted further away. "Neither is it yours."

Terin shrugged. "These days, I have many burdens I must carry. What's another?"

Graeson took a step back to observe Terin. "Are you at least sleeping?"

He lifted a shoulder. "A little. The healers gave me a supplement to take to help."

"Have you taken it?"

"Once."

Graeson snorted. "Seems like it. The bags beneath your eyes are only *slightly* purple now."

"Was that a joke, Gray?"

Graeson rolled his eyes.

"What?" Terin asked, shoving Graeson lightly. "You've been so uptight since we got Kallie from Frenzia that it's nice to see you normal for a change."

"I am anything but normal," Graeson countered.

"Perhaps, but I mean it all the same." Terin shifted on his feet, his gaze flicking quickly to the infirmary down the hall. "Look--"

"Terin, don't. Not right now."

But the prince only crossed his arms and arched a brow.

Graeson sighed and moved to the wall, pressing his head against it.

Terin turned to him. "You have traveled the seven kingdoms. You have stormed through fire after fire for her. Whether or not she accepts the soul bond, you were friends once, were you not?"

Graeson rubbed a hand across his face. "That hardly counts. We were both no more than children."

"She looked up to you when we were children, when Fynn and I wanted little to do with our annoying little sister. But you were always there, helping her up. You don't have to be more than that now. You can be her *friend*."

Graeson arched a brow. "And if she doesn't want me to be her friend?"

Terin sighed, fatigue bringing down the corners of his mouth. "Now more than ever, she needs to be surrounded by people who care about her."

He tilted his head as he looked at Graeson, a flurry of emotions that passed too quickly for Graeson to parse.

"And perhaps you do, too," the prince added. "Because whatever is going on in your head, you need to talk to someone about it if you won't talk to Dani or me."

"Have *you* tried talking to Dani?" Graeson snapped.

While he hadn't seen her yet, he did not doubt that Dani was beyond pissed about Terin hiding his ability to speak to Fynn from her.

Terin narrowed his eyes at Graeson. "I see what you are trying to do, but changing the subject only hurts you in the end." When Graeson only stared blankly at him in response, Terin dug his fingers into his hair, pulling at the end of the strands. "I have tried, but she only wishes to yell right now. I cannot talk sense into her."

"Do you need to? Perhaps giving in to her request is what she needs the most right now."

"I do not know if that is true. She needs to move forward, not backward."

Graeson snorted. "Are you that daft, Terin? Fynn was her soul bond, but even more than that, she bears his child."

Terin's eyes widened, his face paling. "Has she...has she confirmed this?"

Graeson offered him a sad smile.

"Fuck," Terin whispered, the dire syllable ringing through the hall.

Graeson stepped forward and squeezed Terin's shoulder comfortingly before the prince walked away.

Once Terin's footsteps faded, Graeson looked down the hall. He could picture Kalisandre lying on the hard mattress almost perfectly. Her chestnut waves a mess and spread across her pillows. Her skin was pale, and her cheeks hollow.

Terin was right, of course. Kalisandre needed support right now.

But every time Graeson looked at her, he only saw his failure to protect her, time and time again.

While he knew Ellie and the queen had only acted in Kalisandre's best interest, Graeson had felt the world shift as they ripped apart her mind. He could only imagine the torment Kalisandre had experienced.

Still, he couldn't get himself to enter the room. Not now.

She needed time to heal. She didn't need him hovering over her and making things worse. And right now, that's what Graeson would do. Because as he felt the fragile invisible thread stretching from him to her, Graeson was barely holding himself together.

His bones vibrated beneath his flesh, his muscles strained, and his vision blurred.

Now, more than ever, he needed to keep a hold of himself and keep the beast contained. Because if he listened to the voice in his head for even a second, there was no going back.

Graeson, however, didn't know how much longer he could keep fighting himself.

CHAPTER 31
KALLIE

"She won't get up, Your Highness. We have tried encouraging her to walk around the room at least, but she refuses," one of the nurses, whom Kallie hadn't quite caught the name of, whispered a few yards away. "Well, in truth, she isn't even refusing because that would imply that she showed some sort of emotion or desire to do *something*. She will hardly even sit up unless we force her to."

Kallie's back was turned away from the healer and whomever she spoke to, but Kallie had no energy to turn around and identify them. They would make their presence known to her whether she wished to acknowledge them or not soon enough. That's how it always went, it seemed.

Even the queen had stopped by at one point. But all Cetia did was press the back of her wrinkled hand to Kallie's forehead before shaking her head in disappointment and leaving without a word having passed her lips.

The woman with stark white hair had also visited several times. She wouldn't say much, only sit in the chair at Kallie's bedside, watching in eerie silence that unsettled her.

Terin would come, too. He had spewed a lengthy apology for

kidnapping her for a second time. But when Kallie only blinked at him, pain glazed his brown eyes. Kallie, however, could not offer him the forgiveness he sought.

She wished it was simply because he did not need her forgiveness, not after everything she had done. But rather she could not speak the words because she had no words to give, kind or otherwise.

Still, Terin kept returning. At first he, like the rest, had sat there in silence.

Kallie could feel his discomfort when he would shift and fidget within the straight-back chair, as if he finally realized that while they might have shared the same blood, they were still strangers.

Eventually, the uncomfortable became comfortable, and Terin began talking.

He told her what happened after the temple erupted into flames. He told her what the king had revealed to them in the tunnels. He told her of her best friend's betrayal.

A far-off pang echoed somewhere inside as he revealed the truth about Myra: that she had manipulated her emotions and most likely had been doing so for longer than anyone thought.

Yet Kallie was numb to it all.

And perhaps it was because she did not wish to admit her ignorance of her own failing.

Then, Terin started to tell her stories of their childhood, the games they would play together, and the days they would run barefoot through the castle grounds.

But the memories with Kallie in them were few and far between, and soon, he began to tell her other stories.

The ones of the life she had missed out on.

A spike of pain should have filled her chest at these memories she did not possess, of the people she had never gotten a chance to know, but instead, there was nothing.

Just a void, an emptiness she didn't know what to do with.

So, Kallie did nothing with it.

By the time Terin was called away, he would look at her one last time before he left, his gaze falling to her finger where their mother's ring still encircled before his smile fell.

But Kallie did not care if her silence hurt him.

She couldn't get herself to care.

Because while the Pontians were thrilled that the queen was able to rip Kallie's mind apart, what was Kallie supposed to do with what was left of her?

The rage was gone.

The anger had vanished.

The craving for power was nonexistent.

Everything Kallie had once cared about--the crown, the power, the king's approval--felt nonsensical now.

"Come on."

Kallie's gaze flicked to the woman before her, and she immediately recognized the princess of Tetria.

A constellation of freckles smattered Medenia's nose and cheeks. Her midnight hair was twisted into an elaborate braid that was draped over her shoulder. A string of emeralds hung from the black satin ribbon that held the braid together.

Now that Kallie had seen the queen, she couldn't help but see the resemblances.

Although Medenia's eyes were a smidge darker than the queen's near-white ones, they were just as hypnotic.

When Kallie looked upon the princess, fear was only a passing thought.

The queen had already destroyed Kallie's soul. There was nothing left for Medenia to take from Kallie, even if the princess wanted to.

Medenia folded her arms across her chest, blowing a strand of hair that had fallen from the plait. "I suppose Opal wasn't kidding about you being stubborn, huh? I had hoped the healer was exaggerating about your...lack of enthusiasm. Well, that's just not going to work for me. It's time to get up, Princess."

Kallie's forehead creased with wrinkles at the title.

She *was* a princess; she used to own a title. But now? Now what was she?

Who was she?

Medenia rolled her eyes. "Fine. I'll get you up myself then, but if I hurt you, you only have yourself to blame," she said snidely.

Medenia bent over the bed, digging her hands beneath Kallie's shoulders and tugging her up. Kallie's head spun, and she tossed out a hand, gripping the sheets as she attempted to steady herself.

"Some fresh air would do you some good, I think," Medenia muttered as she continued her torture. She pulled Kallie's legs from under the blankets and brought them over the edge of the bed.

Kallie groaned as her knee cracked, pain blossoming through her leg.

Medenia flicked a brow up. "If you wish to stay in this room, all you have to do is say so." The princess waited, her hands folded in front of her stomach.

Kallie dropped her gaze, too tired to fight her.

"Then it's settled." Medenia clapped her hands together.

Pulling Kallie up by the crook of the elbow, Medenia guided her out of the room. Well, more like dragged her out of the room.

Outside the infirmary, the sound of rapid, clumsy footsteps drew Kallie's attention. A large, shaggy, brown dog bounded toward them, its tongue lolling out the side of its mouth as it panted eagerly.

"Hi, Beau!" Medenia greeted the dog with a cheerful smile, reaching down to pet its head. "I can't play right now. Go find Ophelia, all right?"

Beau cocked his head and let out a sad whine.

"Beau," Medenia scolded gently.

The dog released an exasperated huff before dashing down the hall.

"He's been so needy since we returned," Medenia said, shaking her head and guiding Kallie through the corridor. "I missed him of course, but right now is not the best time to play fetch."

Kallie said nothing in response, her attention solely focused on staying upright.

Their walk was slow and laborious, but their pace didn't seem to bother Medenia even as they made the trek down the steps at a torturous pace.

"It's unfortunate that you tried to escape the first night. If you hadn't, perhaps they would have been more inclined to set you up on the main floor," Medenia remarked as they descended the steps. "But they were worried that you'd take off again when you woke. Maybe we can convince them to move you now. It doesn't seem like you're going anywhere anytime soon."

Kallie gave Medenia a cursory glance. The Tetrian princess was rather...peculiar. But peculiar or not, Medenia had shown Kallie nothing but kindness when they had met at the welcome dinner and then again before the hunt started.

Yet sometimes, the princess's words, if twisted a certain way, sounded like an insult. Kallie wasn't sure if she should have been insulted or not at that moment. Still, she remained silent nevertheless.

Medenia shrugged and helped Kallie down the last few steps. "Come on," she said before guiding Kallie to a set of glass doors leading outside.

Kallie wasn't quite sure if a stroll outside was what she needed.

Then again, she didn't know exactly *what* she needed, or even what she wanted, for that matter.

The sun kissed Kallie's skin as the doors cracked open, and the fresh air tickled her nose. As Kallie scanned the enclosed garden, she inhaled a sharp breath at the sight of a foreign creature resting in the middle of the flowers beside a fountain and stopped dead in her tracks.

"Oh!" Medenia squealed, squeezing Kallie's arm. "I don't believe the two of you have formally met. Unless..." she trailed off, peering at Kallie, a brow arched. "*Have* you seen her before?"

At the sound of Medenia's voice, the beast lifted its head and peered in their direction, and as its ruby-red eyes landed on her, Kallie stumbled backward and shook her head as she kept her eyes on the beast.

The sun bounced off the animal's irises so vibrantly that it looked like a roaring fire was aflame within them. Yet, as the creature looked upon Medenia, nothing but kindness sparkled within. Kallie could sense Medenia observing her intently as if the princess wasn't sure if she believed Kallie's answer. But while Kallie may have lied about many things over her lifetime, she was not lying about this.

When Medenia tugged Kallie forward, Kallie was tempted to dig her heels into the dirt. But alas, she did not. She trudged forward, reluctantly and helplessly.

Kallie could not understand what she was seeing. One of its paws peeked out from beneath its stomach as it lay on the ground, and it was larger than Kallie's head. The animal had the snout of a wolf, but as the two women approached, it stood, stretching its wings out wide. And as it pressed its paw against the ground, large, sharp talons protruded from it.

Kallie gasped in horror, yet Medenia led them closer. The creature cocked its head, its eyes narrowing and nostrils flaring as it scrutinized Kallie.

"This is Nyrri," Medenia announced, smiling and looking

adoringly upon the animal that could quite possibly eat them whole. She released Kallie's arm and approached the deadly beast. "We found her when we were traveling, and we are fortunate to have found her when we did. Without her, all of us might have died. Isn't that right, Nyrri?"

The creature nuzzled into the princess's hand in response.

Medenia continued, "Since we have taken her in, she has scared many of my guards away. But you have nothing to fear. Although she can be dangerous, she is sweet at heart."

"How?" Kallie croaked, the question slipping from her lips.

Medenia glanced at Kallie, astonishment registering across her face at the question. But while the princess may have been shocked at hearing Kallie's voice, Kallie's attention was purely on the animal. The more Kallie observed Nyrri, the more she quickly saw the beauty of the beast.

Nyrri's eyes were so expressive that Kallie could see almost every emotion drip from them as she experienced the world around her.

The creature spread her wings out again as she nuzzled Medenia's hand before tucking them against her sides. But before Nyrri tucked them away, Kallie glimpsed the scars across the membrane of the wings that the sun's glow illuminated. It was clear that the creature had suffered a great deal of pain throughout her life.

Without realizing it, Kallie had taken a step forward, a hand extended. Nyrri shifted closer as well, extending her snout toward Kallie. When Nyrri did not bite Kallie's hand off and instead closed her eyes before nudging her hand, Kallie stroked the bridge of her nose.

Medenia offered Kallie a sad smile and said, "We're not sure how she came about or what she is exactly. Based on the information we have gathered, the Frenzians seem to be partaking in some sort of experiment. During the attack at your wedding, Domitius--" She paused abruptly.

Kallie stared at her unmoving hand as a ghost of an unidentifiable emotion came and went. She could feel Medenia's gaze boring into her but refused to meet it.

Instead, she swallowed and continued petting Nyrri's nose.

Medenia cleared her throat and continued, "He ran off into an underground tunnel. When we found you and the others down there after the king had caused the tunnel to collapse, we saw...things. Terrible things. Malnourished animals that had clearly undergone some sort of horrific testing. We believe they're trying to create a weapon from them."

As Kallie stared at Nyrri, her eyes widened as she finally realized what the creature reminded her of. A worn illustration in an ancient text surfaced in her mind, depicting an animal with brilliant scales, a long tail, and a large snout. Even the red eyes made her think of the helmets the Frenizans wore.

"Dragons," Kallie whispered, her hand falling.

Medenia grabbed Kallie's hand. "Do you know something? Did--"

Kallie shook her head as she blinked at the princess. She hadn't meant to say anything, but she couldn't take it back now.

"No, I..." Kallie cleared her throat. "I had spent a lot of time with Rian in the royal library. He has a deep interest in the creatures and believes they aren't truly extinct. When I had mentioned it to my fa--"

Kallie's brows twisted as the word got stuck in her throat.

Nyrri gently shoved her hand, and Kallie returned to petting the beast as she pressed forward. "When I had mentioned it to Domitius, he dismissed Rian's interest, thinking it a mere childish obsession."

Medenia hummed. "Well, now we know it was not merely some childish obsession."

Kallie nodded absently, unsure of what to think of the beast.

She was unsure of many things. She had known that the Frenzians were protecting important knowledge, but she had never imagined that the existence of this creature was part of that.

Were these experiments that Medenia spoke of the reason that the king wanted Kallie to formalize an alliance with the Frenzians? To gain access to whatever knowledge created Nyrri? But then why had he dismissed it when Kallie brought up Rian's research into the legendary creatures? None of it made sense.

"How did she end up with you again?" Kallie asked after a moment of pondering.

"On our way to Frenzia before the wedding, we found her caged among a group of Frenizan soldiers near the Borganian border. From what Graeson and the others relayed, most of the soldiers did not make it out alive."

"Most?" Kallie repeated, ignoring the twisting of her stomach at the mention of Graeson's name.

Medenia nodded. "According to Graeson and Dani, two men managed to escape, fleeing by horseback."

A previous conversation with Rian the day before the welcome ceremony resurfaced. Rian had mentioned that his soldiers had been slaughtered and that he and Sebastian had to flee.

Was this what he was doing then? And if so, how could he have allowed it?

Based on her interactions with him, Kallie wouldn't have thought that Rian would partake in something like this. He was kind, modest...but he was also ignorant. His soft green eyes always seemed troubled and soaked with sorrow.

Kallie had never seen any malice within them.

But perhaps the young king was not whom Kallie had imagined.

Maybe she wasn't the only one who had been wearing a mask all this time.

Medenia grabbed a piece of meat from a nearby bucket, and Kallie quirked a brow, recalling a detail the princess had revealed to her during the hunt.

"I thought you were a vegetarian?" she remarked.

"I am," Medenia said with a small smile. She shrugged and threw the meat into the air. "But Nyrri is not."

Nyrri jumped, her wings spanning out as she caught the raw meat with a quick snap of her jaw. When she landed, the ground around her shook, causing Kallie to stumble back several steps. However, even as Kallie's heart beat rapidly in her chest and she got a good look at Nyrri's sharp canines, Kallie wasn't afraid of the wild creature, despite logic telling her she should have been.

How long had the animal been held in captivity? How long had she had to endure the Frenzians' cruelty before she finally gained her freedom? Before she found someone who did not wrap a chain around her neck?

Before the Tetrians stopped fearing her?

The creature might have been born to kill and destroy, but hidden within the dragon-wolf's gaze was a yearning for security and companionship. She bumped Medenia's thigh, silently begging for affection, for connection.

As Kallie watched Nyrri, she felt at ease for the first time in a long time, even as she felt the eyes of dozens of guards watching her in the garden.

CHAPTER 32
MYRA

THE ROOM CARRIED MANY STORIES, STORIES MYRA COULDN'T EVEN begin to peel from the bricks and detangle. So much torture had transpired within this cell. In this entire godsforsaken castle.

The pain soaked the ground beneath her. It was so embedded into the very foundation of the castle that Myra didn't know if it would ever disappear.

Some scars were so deep that even when no marks were left, there was no erasing them.

Yet Myra was learning to find comfort in the agony that swathed the cell in shadows. Because, to an extent, the company of the pain wrapping around her was better than the fear and anguish of the living.

King Rian had fought the healer the entire time they were in that wretched room.

But more than that, he was fighting *her*. After the Frenzian King had screamed and fought Myra's attempts to soothe his mind, Domitius had left disgusted by Myra's failure.

Dr. Thorne and Myra were forced to stay, though. The hours

were long and slow to pass. Only when the healer had enough and Myra could barely keep her eyes open as blood dripped from her nose from exertion did they stop. By the time the guards had led her back to her cell, her mind was weary, her limbs exhausted.

She had never encountered such a strong-willed mind before. Every time she tried to soothe his emotions, to break him down, his anger and rage came back tenfold.

To some extent, she was glad that Rian was fighting it, for she did not wish for King Domitius to succeed.

Yet, she did not wish to see Rian in pain either.

Days later, Myra leaned her against the wall, dreading the day the guards would come to retrieve her once she had recovered. She squeezed her eyes shut as she tried not to think about the experiments, what became of the Pontian, or what would become of her brother if she failed.

But she had to believe Mynhos was still safe. Because if he wasn't...

Taking a deep breath, Myra attempted to steady herself. She brushed her palms against the rough concrete and focused on the pebbles scratching her skin. She let the cold ground seep into her flesh and fill her body.

She exhaled and counted to four.

Then, she repeated the process.

As she exhaled and her heart rate began to settle, a rattling at the door sounded, jolting her. Her heart thundered in her chest, the panic quickly returning as if it had never left.

She pressed her back against the wall, her nails scratching her palms as she curled her fingers inwards.

The door creaked open, and a guard stepped forward, balancing a tray in his hand. Myra's shoulders dropped, and she quietly sighed in relief.

It's only dinner.

The guard set the food down in front of her. As Myra reached for the porridge and took a small bite, her stomach turned when the door clicked shut and the guard remained inside the cell.

With the bland porridge thick in her throat, she cautiously peered at the guard. The man, however, continued to stare ahead at the back wall of the cell, his hands curling and uncurling at his sides.

Although Myra had not fully recuperated yet, she reached out to his mind, to the emotions at the surface. Fear, concern, and hesitancy tainted her tongue.

"Is there--" Myra swallowed as the guard turned his attention to her.

Although armor covered his form and prevented Myra from identifying him, there was something familiar about the guard and his presence all the same.

She forced out, "Is there something I can help you with, sir?"

"That depends," the guard said. "Why do you not eat?" he asked, pointing to the bowl in her lap.

Myra blinked. "What do you mean?"

"You have only taken one bite. Are you not hungry?" Concern dripped from the man's words, yet Myra could not understand it. The guards never cared about her well-being, not more than the king made them, anyway.

"I--I do not have an appetite," Myra admitted.

The man nodded. Shifting on his feet, he glanced at the door, his armor creaking.

Then, he did something that surprised her even more: he squatted in front of her. And although Myra could not see his pupils beneath the shadows of the helmet, she could feel his stare boring into her, as if he were searching for something.

She pressed her back further against the wall, sweat beading on her neck. "Why are you here?" she whispered.

His breathing was heavy, and a dense apprehension spilled around him. After a moment, he shook his head. "I shouldn't have come," he muttered to himself.

He pressed his palms against his knees to stand, but something overtook Myra, and she reached for him. He halted, staring down at her small fingers wrapped around his wrist. She didn't know what stupidity had made her do it, but something in his emotions twirled in the space between them that had her reaching out.

The man slowly sunk back down onto his heels. He grabbed the collar of his armor and scratched at his neck beneath the metal, revealing skin rubbed raw.

He muttered a curse under his breath, then removed his helmet entirely.

Myra gasped, her eyes widening in disbelief before she could catch herself.

The captain of Rian's guard stared back at her. The whites surrounding his dark brown eyes were stained red, and the golden-brown skin beneath his eyes was tinted purple.

"Shit. I really shouldn't have--"

Laurince tried to stand again, but Myra only tightened her grasp around his wrist.

"Wait, please," Myra said, the words nearly a plea.

Laurince observed her for a moment. But then he must have seen something within her face, for he sank back down. Still, he remained silent, staring, pondering, hesitating.

Myra might not have known Laurince well, but she knew he cared deeply for his king. If he was wearing an Ardentolian uniform, perhaps there was a reason for him being here other than delivering her food.

Jaw twitching, Laurince's eyes flicked to the door. Dread filled the room as his attention remained on the door for a second too long.

He mumbled, "I shouldn't be here. It was risky to come. Even riskier to show you who I am." He brushed a hand through his short black waves, his fingers shaking slightly as he ran them through the silky strands.

Myra loosened her grip around his wrist and folded her shaking hands in her lap. "Why are you here?" she said lowly.

One of his hands rolled into a fist, his knuckles blanching. "I just"--he took a deep, steadying breath--"I need to know." His determined gaze met hers.

"Know what?" she asked, confused.

"Is he alive?"'

Her lips parted then closed before finally asking, "You do not know?"

Laurince shook his head. "He..." His brows twisted with pain.

Myra knew very little about Laurince and what kind of man he truly was beneath the armor. But she did understand people's emotions, and his fear and pure concern were potent. "You can tell me," Myra whispered.

Laurince rubbed a hand across his face. "The king has been missing from the public eye since the wedding. They said he was injured and then had fallen ill, needing to be isolated. But I saw him leaving the castle and followed. I was surprised to find him taken here of all places. I was even more surprised to learn he was locked in the dungeon. When I discovered that you were being taken there...I had to find out." Laurince wrung his hands together, peering at her. "You have seen him, though?"

Myra nodded. "He is alive, but I cannot say he is well." She swallowed and forced the words out, no matter how hard they were to say or how confusing they were in her mind. "The other man--they took him, and I don't know what happened to him. I do not think he is dead, but I am not sure that is a blessing either."

Laurince's brow creased. "What do you mean? What man?"

Myra, however, held her tongue as she narrowed her gaze. Laurince was the Frenzian king's guard. He had to know the truth. How could he have not?

Was this some sort of trap? Was this another ploy of King Domitius's?

She wasn't sure. Even though she felt no malice or treachery spilling from his emotions, she proceeded carefully.

"Have you been in the tunnels beneath the royal temple in Frenzia?"

"The tunnels?" Laurince asked, eyes narrowing. "What do they have to do with anything?"

Myra pursed her lips. "So you know they exist."

"Well, yes. They're ancient, but they are no longer in use. From what I've heard, they're no longer passable after centuries of decay." He shrugged.

Myra's gaze flitted across his face as she tried to find traces of a lie.

She found none.

Swallowing, she said, "There are creatures that live in cages within the tunnels."

"Creatures?" he repeated.

Myra nodded. "Prince Sebastian and the late king were conducting experiments. King Domitius somehow got wind of it, and now he has begun his own experiments with the prince's assistance."

"Fucking Sebastian," Laurince hissed. "I knew something was amiss when he was the one I saw getting out of the carriage." Laurince shook his head and returned his gaze to her. "Do you know what these experiments are?"

Myra bit her lip. "They tell me very little," she said at last. "Though I fear the results."

"Yet you help them?" he pressed, his gaze turning cold.

Myra shifted uncomfortably and said, "I have no choice."

He scoffed then. "Everyone has a choice."

Guilt wrapped around her throat. She felt sick as she thought of what she had done for the king.

Laurince cocked his head to the side as he observed her, his eyes narrowing slightly. "What does he have over you?"

Her eyes widened. "I--I never said--"

"You do not have to. It is written all over your face."

Myra gulped. Then, as she exhaled, she whispered, "My brother. He has my brother."

Laurince pursed his lips, the muscles in his jaw flexing. "He has my king."

Myra squirmed at the mention of King Rian.

"Did you only come here for answers?" she asked.

Laurince observed her for a moment. "Tell me this first: do you agree with what the king is doing?"

Myra looked around the cell illuminated by Laurince's torch. "If I agreed with everything the king did, I wouldn't be here, now would I?" she muttered, gesturing towards the cell around them.

Laurince shrugged. "I still don't know if I can trust you."

"Yet you came in here anyway?"

"Obviously," Laurince said, his gaze narrowed.

"Why?" Myra asked again.

He scratched the scruff covering his jawline. "I...I don't know. I guess I came here because I didn't know who else to go to."

"But you don't know me."

"You have a point," Laurince said, assessing her. "Back home, when you were with the princess, you seemed...caring, kind, honest."

Myra snorted before she could catch herself. All lies.

Laurince raised a brow. "Are you not those things?"

"It's complicated," Myra mumbled.

He hummed as if it was that simple. As if Myra hadn't betrayed everyone she cared about. Then he said, "Most things in life are complicated."

"I suppose that is true," Myra agreed bitterly. "Are you an honest, kind, and caring person, Laurince?"

"I like to think that I am." He pursed his lips and grimaced. "Then again, I was not kind to the man I stole this uniform from, nor did I care for his life."

Myra's eyes widened.

"At least I am honest," he said, lifting a shoulder before dropping it in indifference.

Myra twisted her hands in her lap. To an extent, Laurince had a point. Nor could she pass too much judgment for the wrongs he may have committed to get here. Although Myra had never killed a man or even physically harmed one, she had done heinous things during her lifetime. She was *still* doing terrible things, things that went against all her morals.

She may have been kind, but she was not a good person. Not in the slightest.

At least Laurince wasn't pretending to be someone he was not. He never claimed to be a good person.

Her gaze swept over the cell. Too many weeks had passed inside this decrepit place. How long would the king keep her locked up? Would he ever let her go? Doubtful.

For years, Myra had looked the other way.

Enough was enough, she determined.

She might not know if she could trust Laurince, but she could at least work with him.

Myra took a deep breath and said, "While I wish I could claim to be all those things, I am rarely honest. I care deeply, but I can be incredibly selfish. I try to be kind, but even though I often try to have the best intentions, I often seem to hurt the ones I love, even if they do not know it."

"You can claim to be dishonest, yet that might be the most honest thing I've heard in a long time," Laurince replied, tilting his head in thought.

His gaze stayed on her, but its intensity became too much to bear. Myra dropped her attention to her hands in her lap.

Then, a hand fell atop hers. When Myra flinched, Laurince retracted it immediately. "Apologies, I did not mean to scare you."

"I..." Myra bit her lip, then released it. "I'm fine."

"It is all right not to be fine, you know," he whispered, his voice more gentle than she deserved. "You are a prisoner."

"For the things I have done, I deserve to be."

Laurince reached out again. But this time, when his hand wrapped around the back of hers, Myra did not jump.

When Myra met his gaze, Laurince offered her a sad, knowing smile. "We have all done things that we regret. But our past does not have to define us if we do not give it the power to do so."

Myra did not know what to say. As she looked at him and the silence spread between them, she wished she could conjure the strength to act out against the king. She wished she could refuse him. She wished she did not have to let her fear consume her.

As Laurince's lips parted, another question on his tongue, a clattering sounded in the distance.

His gaze hardened. "I must go. If someone finds me here..." He shook his head, his words trailing off as he stood.

Panic rose in Myra's throat, and she scrambled to her feet. "Wait!"

He spun toward her, raising a brow.

"Don't...don't leave me here. I cannot..." Tears sprung to her eyes.

She hadn't had a conversation that wasn't filled with threats for so long. Gods, how she missed feeling *human.*

"I'm sorry," Laurince whispered, raising his helmet. "I'll be back. I promise."

But as the door shut behind him, the lock clicking into place, Myra feared that if he ever did fulfill that promise, it would be too late.

CHAPTER 33
KALLIE

THE NEXT FEW DAYS WERE MUCH THE SAME. KALLIE LAY IN HER BED in the infirmary, watching dawn rise as the sun lit the room. Medenia would come in the early mornings after Kallie had received a warm breakfast and would force her out of bed to walk the grounds.

The first few times, they came across no one but guards and Nyrri during their stroll, which Kallie didn't entirely mind. She found comfort when she was in the presence of the dragon-wolf.

However, Kallie quickly deduced that Medenia had chosen the enclosed garden for a couple reasons. Privacy was one of them, as civilians were unable to see into the area due to the large hedges that surrounded it. The other was the very *lack* of privacy it offered in actuality. The windows of the infirmary looked over the garden, and guards were stationed throughout the enclosed space and nearby outlooks.

The moment Kallie and Medenia stepped outside, the women standing guard straightened, their hands flexing near their weapons.

"Are all of the queen's guards truly women?" Kallie asked one morning as they sat brushing Nyrri's fur.

"Indeed," Medenia replied with a nod. "It has always been the case since the first leader. Because of her past, she did not trust men easily. When she came to power, she requested an all-female guard for her own comfort.

"Unlike many other territories at the time, and even to this day, my people have never prevented women from training with a blade. Men and women alike are equally trained here. However, the number of women outweighs the number of male guards throughout Tetria. Other kingdoms often underestimate us because of that fact."

"Does that not upset you?" Kallie asked, setting the brush aside.

Medenia shrugged a shoulder. "Honestly, no. They can doubt us all they wish, but when our blade is pressed against their throat, their hesitancy will be their undoing."

"The king once told me how foolish Tetria was for having the queen's guard entirely female. He had said it put her at risk."

Medenia snorted. "If anyone even got within range of my mother, they would be dead within minutes. The queen's guards undergo intense training and must meet several qualifications even to be considered for the position. Even if an enemy *were* to get past one of the guards, my mother is just as deadly as the rest--if not more so."

Kallie didn't doubt that for a second. She had felt the queen's power ripple from her when Kallie had sat chained to the chair. She could only imagine what it would be like to confront her as an enemy.

ON THE FIFTH DAY, Kallie was already up, awaiting the princess when she arrived. While Kallie talked very little, and even the pieces of information Medenia offered Kallie were carefully chosen, she was beginning to enjoy the company. Or at least she found some semblance of peace during their daily strolls.

Everywhere she looked, nature bloomed, weaving over and up buildings like a living entity. All around her, life existed and thrived.

Yet, as Kallie would amble her way through the garden, she couldn't help but notice how the vines and branches wrapped around the spires of the castles, almost as if strangling them. The castle had been built around the ancient oak tree.

While she had learned from Medenia that the choice to build around the tree was meant as a sign of respect, it pained her at the same time. The tree had little room to grow. It was confined, trapped. It tried to find ways to persevere despite its surroundings, to grow in different directions, but the results were mangled limbs twisted at odd angles. There was no way for it to thrive, not with the world pressing in around it.

Kallie had never been surrounded by so much nature before, and yet she couldn't help but see the cage she lived in. The Pontians thought they had freed her. And to an extent, she supposed they had. Her mind was finally hers. Yet...

Yet she still felt *lost* despite their efforts.

The only thing she knew was she had to keep moving forward. No matter how much she wanted to get lost in the past and the world behind her.

But how was she supposed to move forward if she still didn't understand the truth?

Why did Domitius take her? What did he want with her? Why did her mother not come for her sooner? Why wait? Why let Kallie live with a foreign king for so long? They were the same questions that had plagued her mind for the past few months, yet they felt different to her now.

Before, Kallie didn't want to know the truth. She evaded the truth any chance she had. She made excuses for Domitius. But while she now saw through his wicked manipulations, she also struggled to move past them.

Who was she now that she wasn't the Princess of Ardentol? Who was she now that she wasn't his daughter? Who was she now that she wasn't the king's weapon?

She was lost.

Purposeless.

Hopeless.

Before, Kallie at least had an objective, but ever since her mind had been fractured, she was confused about her purpose. Without a purpose, Kallie struggled to keep her eyes forward and set on the future.

"Is something wrong?" Medenia asked, pulling Kallie to a stop.

Nyrri halted beside them, and when Kallie peered up at the castle once more, searching the windows, she could have sworn Nyrri did too.

Medenia held up a hand as she squinted in the direction she was looking. "What is it?"

Kallie, however, found nothing amiss as she searched the castle's walls. Still, the uneasy feeling dwelling within her continued to prickle at the back of her neck, an awareness she couldn't shake.

Finally, Kallie dropped her gaze, confusion twisting her features. "It's probably nothing."

Medenia hummed as she stared a moment longer at the windows, tightening her arm around Kallie's and guiding them forward. "I believe our bodies often know more than our minds do."

Kallie snorted in a very un-princess-like manner. "These days, I am not sure my mind knows my left from my right," she retorted.

Medenia tapped Kallie's arm gently and offered her a small, knowing smile. She assured, "Do not rush it. You will feel normal again soon."

Normal, Kallie thought bitterly. *Such a simple word, and yet...*

Kallie no longer knew what normal was for her. She supposed this was normal: walking through the gardens with a practical stranger with guards at the ready in case she attacked the princess or ran. All the while feeding dead rabbits to the beast that walked with them.

Perhaps Kallie's new normal was a sense that someone was watching, for the feeling never left as she and Medenia continued their stroll around the enclosed garden.

A COUPLE OF DAYS LATER, Kallie sat beside Nyrri, staring up at the cloud-covered sky, when Medenia had been pulled away by a guard named Ophelia.

After the two women whispered to one another for a while, Medenia returned to Kallie and Nyrri, a sad smile gracing the princess's lips. Ophelia stepped beside her, her hands folded behind her back.

"We will have to cut today's walk short," Medenia said apologetically as Kallie sat up. "I am needed back inside."

"Oh," Kallie whispered, then looked to Nyrri. "Is it all right if I stay for a little longer?"

Medenia and Ophelia exchanged glances, an unspoken conversation passing between them. Finally, the princess's shoulders dropped. "I don't think--"

"I can walk her back in a little."

Kallie went rigid as Terin approached from behind them. She cleared her throat and began to rise to her feet. "It's quite all right. I do not want to impose," she said carefully.

"It's no imposition," Terin said, waving off her concerns. When Kallie's lips parted, an objection on her tongue, he smiled. "Really, I don't mind."

"Thank you, Terin," Medenia said with a grin. The princess turned to Kallie. "I'll see you tomorrow, then?"

Before Kallie could say anything, the desire to flee rising in her bones, Nyrri laid her large head across Kallie's lap with a final huff. Kallie narrowed her gaze at the creature. Nyrri squinted an eye open, peering at her before nuzzling against her lap.

Traitor.

Swallowing the lump in her throat, Kallie nodded.

Once Medenia and Ophelia left, Terin shifted uncomfortably on his feet. "Mind if I sit?" he asked.

Kallie shook her head, her voice suddenly stripped from her throat. Terin had visited her often in those first few days when she lay in the infirmary. But since she had joined Medenia, he had not come to see her.

Medenia mentioned that Terin had been pulled away in other discussions with the queen, but Kallie didn't press her for more information.

Until this moment, she hadn't realized just how much she dreaded coming face-to-face with him, but there was no escaping it now. Nyrri made sure of that.

Terin cleared his throat. "How are you?"

Kallie shrugged, feigning a casual air. "Fine, all things considered."

Terin nodded, picking at the grass absentmindedly. "I..." He hesitated, his brows drawing together as he stared at a pile of blades in front of his lap. "I'm sorry."

Kallie snapped her gaze up. "For what?"

"For letting them do that to you," he admitted.

"Do not be sorry for that," she mumbled. "It had to be done. I was a danger to all of you. If I had been in your shoes, I would have done the same thing."

Terin offered her a small smile, though it didn't reach his eyes. "I'm glad you see it that way. Not everyone does."

Kallie wanted to ask who, but for some reason, she couldn't. Instead, she shrugged.

"But if you won't accept my apology for that, I apologize for forcing you unconscious again without your permission," Terin added.

Kallie pursed her lips. "You do seem to have an annoying habit of doing that."

He chuckled softly, but the sound was short-lived as it fell away on the breeze. An uncomfortable silence followed, full of unspoken words neither dared voice.

Kallie swallowed. "The dreams have stopped. That is your doing, I assume?" she asked.

Terin exhaled, but Kallie did not look at him. Her attention remained fixed on Nyrri as she stroked the top of her head.

"Yes, it is," he confirmed.

"Did you...did you see them?"

Terin could have lied to her, but he didn't. "I did. It was a violation, and I am sorry for that, too. I do not take enjoyment out of glimpsing one's memories."

Kallie nodded and bit down on her tongue as she faintly recalled the various dreams that Terin had called forth.

"So you know what he did then?"

"The king?"

Kallie nodded again.

His hand fell on top of hers, and Kallie stared at it. His gentle touch surprised her, but what surprised her even more was that she didn't remove her hand from beneath his.

"If you ever want to talk about it," Terin whispered, "I am here."

"Thank you," she said, though her words were barely audible as her throat grew thick from recalling the years of abuse and torment under the king's care.

She did not wish to talk about it at that moment, but perhaps eventually...when she could make sense of everything. When she could truly feel the weight of her past rather than the emptiness that currently consumed her.

As if knowing this, Terin squeezed her hand once before removing his from hers.

Kallie peered up at him, and another question slipped from her lips. "Was that truly him?"

"Fynn?" he asked, his brother's name a whisper.

Kallie nodded. A cold snout nudged her hand, and Kallie began petting Nyrri again, happy for the small distraction.

"Yes," Terin said with a long exhale. "A version of him, anyway."

Kallie released a heavy breath, her shoulders rising and falling with it. "I'm still confused as to how that is even possible," she admitted.

"It is hard to explain."

"But Dani truly doesn't know?" Kallie asked.

When Terin did not answer immediately, Kallie looked at him.

"She does now," Terin mumbled, scratching the back of his neck.

"How?" she asked, eyes wide.

He weighed his words for a moment. "It's a long story."

"Has she talked to him?"

Terin shook his head. "Fynn does not want her to live in the past."

"So he has said," Kallie sighed. She turned her head toward the sky and watched as the clouds swam across the blue expanse. "Is that really either of your choices?"

"I..." Terin paused. "I am not sure it would help."

Nyrri shifted in Kallie's lap, her snout nudging her calf.

"It might not, but perhaps Dani still has things to say to him. We do not often get a second chance at speaking to those we have lost."

Terin hummed but said nothing more.

The silence that followed, while still thick, was less uncomfortable than it had been moments before. Perhaps the uncomfortable was simply becoming comfortable.

CHAPTER 34
GRAESON

Graeson's leg bounced beneath the table as Medenia and Ophelia entered the dining room.

"Stay, Beau," Medenia ordered as the dog attempted to sneak under the table in search of scraps.

Beau whined, his ears dropping as he retreated to the hallway. He plopped down at the entrance, his big, wide eyes pleading. A small grin tugged at the corner of Graeson's mouth as he watched in amusement.

Medenia shook her head, chuckling.

"You spoil him too much," Ophelia said, pulling out Medenia's chair.

Medenia scoffed. "No more than you do."

"Where is Terin?" Dani asked, gripping a knife tightly.

Tension filled the room immediately, and the smile disappeared from Medenia's face as she sat.

"He is with Kalisandre," the princess said.

Dani snorted. "Why am I not surprised?"

Sylvia touched Dani's wrist and whispered, "He cannot avoid you forever."

Dani's jaw popped as she released the knife in her hand and pushed her plate away, the food untouched.

"How long must we cater to her?" Dani asked, disgust curling her lip.

Graeson's hands gripped the arm of his chair, his temper rising as the beast within stirred. "She needs time to recuperate. Her mind is--"

"Fragile," Dani spat with a roll of her eyes. "I *know*. But we cannot stand to wait here forever. Domitius will come sooner or later. Are we just going to pretend he still does not search for her?"

"Wouldn't we be safer if we returned home?" Emmett pondered over a mouthful of food.

Sylvia rolled their eyes. "You only wish to return home so you can lounge about again."

"Can you blame me?" Emmett drawled, brows raised conspiratorially as his gaze fanned across the room.

"The search parties for the princess have lessened," Ophelia added after taking a bite of her meal.

"Do we know why?" Sylvia asked, peering over the rim of their glass.

Ophelia shook her head, a look of uncertainty falling over her features. "No, our forces have been preventing them from stepping on Tetrian soil, though."

"Won't that only raise their suspicions?" Sylvia asked, taking a sip of tea.

"While the seven kingdoms have been at peace since the Great War, it has been a strained one at best," Medenia said, grabbing the kettle from the middle of the table and pouring the steaming water into a cup. "We are not the only ones who do not want foreign soldiers marching through our lands. After the destruction of the Frenzian temple, paranoia has begun to spread across Vaneria."

"It also seems that the bull king has been calling a good majority of his forces back to Ardentol, which has not helped calm the nerves of the people in the slightest," Ophelia added with a frown.

"Any word about the happenings in Frenzia?" Graeson asked, rapping his fingers on the table in thought.

"King Rian still remains to be seen. According to the whispers, he is still gravely ill and hides away. Some say he lies on his death bed; others say he suffers from a broken heart."

Graeson shifted in his chair. "And the truth?" he pressed.

Ophelia leaned back in her chair, a grave expression stretching across her face. "We do not know. No one has seen him. Prince Sebastian has been acting in his place."

Graeson's jaw cracked at the mention of the Frenzian as images of Sebastian's hands wrapped around Kallie's throat surfaced.

One day, the god promised.

Ellie nudged him with her elbow, and Graeson lifted his gaze. She nodded at his plate, where his fingers tightly gripped a piece of bread, causing it to crumble. He unclenched his hand, and the remaining crumbs fell onto the plate.

"We have received messages about a call for more soldiers in the event of another attack, though I fear that Sebastian's reasoning is only a coverup," Ophelia said, her expression grave.

"This is ridiculous." Dani slammed a fist against the table, rattling the dishes upon it. "While we sit here waiting for Kallie to heal, Ardentol and Frenzia are raising forces. Has there been any word from Esmeray or my father?"

Ophelia shook her head. "No, I am afraid not."

Beside her, Medenia pursed her lips, worry drawing her brows together. "My mother still awaits Esmeray's word as well. She will not raise our banners unless Pontia does first."

Dani stood abruptly, her chair scratching against the floor as she scoffed. "A war is coming, yet those in power wish to live in ignorance."

Her boots pounded against the ground in her departure, Sylvia following close behind.

In their absence, a deafening silence swept over the room that could not dare be ignored.

CHAPTER 35
MYRA

As Myra laid in her cell praying to the gods for sleep to drown her, her eyes snapped open as snarling sounded outside her cell.

As the noises grew closer and louder, Myra held her breath--as if that would do her any good when she was locked in a cage.

Sweat soaked her skin as thrashing and clawing followed. Nails scraped against the walls. A loud crash sounded, followed by someone cursing and muttering, the clamor setting her on edge.

"Let's get him locked up and get the fuck out of here," a muffled voice--a guard, Myra assumed--said.

A struggle sounded outside, followed by a soft *thump*.

Then they were walking again, the wheels of a cart squealing.

And though the snarling had vanished, terror and fear from the hall flooded into the small space. Myra's body shook as the feelings surrounded her, melting into her skin.

CHAPTER 36
KALLIE

AFTER STOPPING TO TALK TO ONE OF THE HEALERS, MEDENIA MADE her way to Kallie.

The princess wore a sage-green dress with fabric that draped at the wrists and swept across the floor as she walked. Her raven-black hair was woven into a single plait that hung over her shoulders. A silver headpiece with crystals embedded in the metal sat upon her head, nestled within the braid.

Meanwhile, her dog, Beau, weaved around her feet, nearly causing her to stumble twice. Medenia didn't even bat an eye. Instead, the princess smiled brightly at Kallie, and Kallie returned the gesture.

Over the past few days, Kallie had begun to feel better, more herself, whoever that was. She was even starting to consider Medenia a friend, or at least a companion.

"You're rather dressed up for a stroll, don't you think?" Kallie mused as she leaned a hip against the foot of the bed.

The princess chuckled. "That is because I will unfortunately not be partaking in today's walk."

"I see," Kallie said, a pang of disappointment filling her breast before she quickly discarded it.

Medenia grabbed her hands. "Come now, do not be sad. I have made other arrangements for you," she beamed.

Kallie rolled her eyes in an attempt to mask the fact that the princess had clocked her so easily. "I am not a child. I do not need to be cared for."

Medenia pursed her lips, her eyes flicking to the guards at the doors before the princess could catch herself.

Kallie sighed. "All right, the necessity of the guards aside, you have no obligation to entertain me. You have your own duties to attend to," she said, her gaze sweeping over the formal ensemble the princess donned.

When a rising spout of jealousy clogged her throat, Kallie forced it down.

"That is indeed true. Court is being held today, and my mother hates when I skip it." Medenia leaned toward Kallie and held up a hand, shielding her lips from the guards as she whispered, "Although, I do loathe it more often than not and would take any excuse to miss it."

Images surfaced of Kallie attending court in Ardentol, where she spent hours listening, hours forced to be silent, seen but unheard. She swatted them away quickly.

Clearing her throat, Kallie forced a smile and asked, "So you have made other arrangements for me then?"

"Right." Medenia turned to the door just as the woman with stark white hair turned round the corner and strolled through the infirmary, a mischievous lilt to her pitch-black eyes.

Kallie slipped her hands free from the princess's and took a harrowing step back, almost tripping over Beau who had snuck behind her. "What--what is she doing here?"

"I--" Medenia paused when she looked at Kallie. Concern

washed over the princess's face before realization struck. "*Oh. Uhm...*" She glanced back and forth between Kallie and the woman who had helped rip her mind apart.

The woman stepped forward, extending a hand, which Kallie merely stared at. "I'm Ellie, by the way. Sorry about what I did to your mind."

Medenia's jaw fell open, and Kallie was left speechless at the woman's frankness.

"Euralys," Medenia hissed.

"What?" Ellie asked with a shrug, dropping her hand. "There's no point in pretending it didn't happen. Right?" She turned to Kallie and stared at her.

Beau nudged Kallie forward with his snout.

"Right," she said hesitantly.

She wasn't quite sure what to make of this woman. To an extent, Kallie should have been angry that Ellie had taken part in torturing her. However, she felt not a single ounce of anger. Only confusion and a hint of admiration and relief.

She was used to everyone tiptoeing around her and avoiding mentioning what had transpired. Ellie was, to an extent, a breath of fresh air.

"See?" Ellie said, turning her attention to Medenia. "We're fine. Let's get on with it."

"Very well," Medenia mumbled. She forced a light, albeit tense, smile back to her face as she turned to Kallie. "Ellie and I believe it would be beneficial for you if you trained."

Kallie's raised brows nearly touched her hairline. She looked towards the guards. "Are you sure the guards would approve?"

Medenia flicked a hand in the air dismissively. "The guards do as I tell them."

Ellie snorted. "The guards do what the *queen* tells them."

The two Tetrians exchanged glances before the women returned their attention to Kallie.

Ellie shrugged. "Anyway, we went through a lot of trouble getting you back, and we cannot let you waste away and become a liability."

"Euralys," Medenia hissed again.

"No, it's fine," Kallie said quietly. "I'm sorry to have caused so much trouble."

Ellie huffed. "Trouble? That was probably the most fun we've had in a while."

Medenia slowly nodded, amusement flickering at her lips. "She's right. It *was* quite fun. Completely reckless, especially the way it all went down at the temple. But we do not regret it in the slightest."

Kallie stared at the two women, unsure what to say in response. Luckily, Ellie spoke for her.

"Now, come on. Let's see exactly how out of practice you are."

VERY. Kallie was *very* out of practice.

After only half an hour of training, her muscles ached. Her steps were clumsy, and her feet felt unsure beneath her. The wooden sword felt odd in her hand despite the callouses that marked her palms.

Ellie stepped back and placed a hand on her hip as she blew a piece of hair out of her face. "You know, Graeson once told me that you could handle yourself in a fight. I'm starting to believe that either he's not as good as he thinks he is at fighting, or he was a little too preoccupied when fighting you."

Kallie groaned and wiped the sweat dripping down her forehead with the back of her hand. "I'm out of practice, all right?

The most physical activity I've done here or even in Frenzia was walking around the castle's grounds."

"Well, that's obvious," Ellie said with a snort.

Kallie blew her hair out of her face and flipped the wooden sword in her hand, inspecting it. "Did Graeson return to Pontia?"

"Huh?" Ellie asked, blinking. "No, why?"

"Oh, no reason," Kallie said with a shrug. "I just haven't seen him around. That's all."

Ellie stepped closer, spinning her wooden sword at her side. She cocked her head, a coy smirk curling the corner of her lips. "Are you concerned about Graeson, Kallie?"

"What?" Kallie's head shot up, wide-eyed. "No. Of course not. Why would I be?" she said, her words coming out faster than intended. Heat rose to her cheeks.

Ellie hummed, amusement crinkling her eyes as she tried to hold back her smile. She spun around, drawing a line in the sand with the tip of her wooden sword. "It's all right if you're concerned about him. I mean, the man *did* burn down a temple for you."

Kallie lowered her gaze. "He didn't do that for me."

"No?" Ellie asked, turning around. "Then why did he do it?"

"He--He--" Kallie swallowed, her words twisting in her mouth. Finally, she shrugged. "I do not know his motives."

"I'm not even sure if *he* knows his motives. But he's been around. He's just been...preoccupied."

"I see," Kallie retorted, pursing her lips as she tried to swallow the rising disappointment within her. The truth was, she had no reason to be disappointed. She had no claim to Graeson. They were not even friends, really. Still, her stomach twisted.

"Hold up your sword," Ellie commanded, shifting into a fighting stance.

Shaking her thoughts away, Kallie obeyed Ellie's command

despite her muscles groaning and focused on not getting side swept again.

An hour or so later, Kallie returned to the infirmary on shaking legs. After the healer checked her over, Opal informed Kallie that she was to be moved to her own room.

There were still guards stationed outside her room, one of whom followed Kallie everywhere she went, but she still appreciated the privacy the new room afforded her. For once, there were no prying eyes as she lay her head down at night.

She hadn't realized just how much she had missed a sense of privacy until she had it again. She reveled in the feeling, for there was finally an escape from the whispers that once slithered their way into the infirmary as strangers passed.

The next few days were more or less the same. After a short walk with Medenia, Ellie would come to drag Kallie out to the training grounds.

Her muscles screamed and bruises covered her body, but the work felt good.

It felt...normal.

Kallie clung to those moments when sweat beaded at the back of her neck and down her back, when her arms were on fire and her calves burned.

Because with the wooden sword in her hand, she felt something more than the emptiness that had until now pervaded her mind and body. And feeling *something*, even if she could not identify that precise thing yet, was better than nothing at all.

Even when Ellie won fight after fight, Kallie was thankful for the distraction and the chance to escape her ever-racing mind.

Until, that is, the consequences of her actions smacked Kallie in the face.

"You're going easy on her."

Kallie froze at the sound of Dani's voice and missed blocking

Ellie's swing. The wooden sword hit her right in the ribcage, causing Kallie to bend over with a loud *oomph*.

"I wish I could say I enjoyed that, but it's honestly just pitiful watching you struggle."

Keeled over, Kallie squinted up at Dani as she pressed a hand to her stomach. Dani stood a few yards away, twisting a small blade within her fingers.

"Danisina," Ellie hissed.

"What?" Dani asked, wide-eyed as she halted the blade, palming it.

Kallie struggled to stand, the dull pain slow to fade as she continued to stare at Dani. She couldn't shake the image of Dani kneeling in the water, a guttural scream pouring from her throat as Fynn's body floated toward her.

Fynn's words from one of the dreams sang in her mind: *Her forgiveness will not be easy to earn.*

Fynn might have thought that Kallie would be able to gain Dani's forgiveness one day, but as Kallie looked upon the woman before her, she did not believe it was possible.

Yet, despite her mind still unraveling itself, Kallie still mourned Fynn's loss. Domitius had tried to construe Fynn's death as a needed sacrifice, but that was a lie. His death had never been necessary. But Kallie could not rewrite the past. She couldn't undo it.

All she could do was live in the mess she had created and face the consequences.

Kallie read the plea in Ellie's gaze as she glared at Dani, but Kallie did not want Ellie to save her from Dani's wrath. No, Kallie deserved all of Dani's anger.

"It's fine, Ellie. She's right. You've been going easy on me."

Dani took a step forward, a fire smoldering within her hazel eyes. "You want a real challenge, Princess?" she drawled, now smiling. But the stretch of her mouth was anything but kind as she raised a brow. "Perhaps a rematch of our first dance together?"

Dani tightened her fingers around the hilt of her dagger, and a memory of Dani in a cloak, taunting Kallie as she and the other Pontians attacked Kallie's carriage surfaced. That was the fight that had started it all, the preface to the destruction and death that would follow.

"Dani, you really shouldn't--" Ellie began, but Kallie cut her off.

"I said it's fine," she snapped, shifting her stance and raising the wooden sword. If Dani wanted to release her anger on her, Kallie would let her. She could at least give her that, even though it was not much at all in the grand scheme of things.

Dani smirked and pocketed the dagger before pulling a short sword from her hip. "Let's play with real weapons, shall we? Make it a true challenge."

"Seriously, Dani?" Ellie asked, hints of anger flushing her cheeks.

Dani's gaze flicked from Ellie to Kallie. "Unless you have an objection, Princess?"

"No objection," Kallie said smoothly, grabbing the proffered sword.

"See, Ellie?" Dani grinned, her attention never leaving Kallie's.

A hungriness illuminated Dani's gaze and flowed through her stance. And Kallie knew before they had even started by the shift in Dani's posture that this was not about pushing Kallie's limits. It was about destroying them.

Ellie reluctantly stepped back, folding her arms over her chest and mumbling something Kallie didn't quite catch as Dani struck and forced Kallie to scramble backward.

Each swing from Dani, each thrust, each dive forward was fueled by an unfiltered rage. And despite Kallie's aching muscles, she dodged each attack as if her survival instincts were kicking in.

Because while Dani was clearly not trying to help Kallie, she had been right. Ellie *was* holding back, which was only doing Kallie a disservice.

All the memories Kallie had tried to push away--all the nights training with Domitius and his guards, the days spent jumping through mazes--came storming back.

Kallie's own anger poured through her veins, stabilizing her and pumping strength into her arms and legs.

Dani was enraged.

But Kallie was, too.

She wasn't mad at Dani, of course. Dani hadn't done anything to deserve Kallie's anger. No, Kallie was mad at herself for believing in a man who only ever cared about his own success. She was mad that the king was able to manipulate her. She was mad that he stole the life she was supposed to live from her. She was mad that he turned her into a *villain*.

But Kallie was even more furious with herself that she let him have that power over her.

So, Kallie did the one thing she could at that moment: she kept her blade high, her movements strong and nimble. She didn't let Dani get the upper hand, didn't let her push her down. But Kallie didn't strike either, and soon enough, Dani realized it and groaned in frustration.

"Fight back, you little bitch!" Dani yelled, her teeth bared.

Sweat dripped down Kallie's forehead, and as she braced her sword against Dani's, she rasped, "I'm not going to hit you."

Dani screamed in rage. She yanked her sword up, and Kallie stumbled from the abrupt change in force.

Dani didn't stop there; she spun around, knocking the back of Kallie's knee.

Kallie's legs buckled, and she sank to the ground, her knees smacking into the soil. With a *thunk*, the sword fell from Kallie's hand as the cold tip of Dani's blade kissed her jugular.

Kallie held up her hands in defeat, swallowing hard.

Yet Dani didn't remove her blade from Kallie's neck. She snarled and hissed, "It would be so easy, you know..."

Dani added more pressure, the point digging into Kallie's skin so hard it hurt.

As Kallie stared at Dani--as she looked at the freckles that covered her nose, the twitch of her lip, and the vein throbbing in the center of her forehead--she felt nothing and everything at once.

Pain.

Grief.

Regret.

Confusion.

It was all too much. The emotions wrapped around her mind. They twisted and pulled, tugging at her, choking her.

And Kallie was helpless to it all.

"Then go ahead," Kallie whispered, tipping her chin up. "Do it."

Dani's jaws flexed, her arm steady despite the flood of emotion coating her eyes. "He never gave up on you," Dani said, her voice no more than a cold whisper. "All of those years he fought for you, begging to be sent to Ardentol to save your spoiled ass. He would have done *anything* for you. You do realize that, don't you?"

Each word Dani spoke was like an icy slice across Kallie's heart. But Kallie remained silent, unable to speak. She rolled her fingers together, her nails biting into the flesh of her palms until her hands begged for release.

"He gave his life away for you, and yet you give yours away so freely?" Dani asked, disgust spilling from her tongue and filling her words. She spat on the ground, missing Kallie's foot only by a couple of inches. "You are a coward and a waste."

Kallie's shoulders sagged. "What do you wish me to say, Dani? An apology will not bring him back."

A layer of water glistened over the raging fire that burned

bright within Dani's hazel eyes. Dani blinked it away and put more pressure on the blade.

"I want you to feel remorse! I want you to feel what I feel. You sit in the castle day and night, walking around as if nothing has happened. Do you not think that I do not see that? How you are completely and utterly unaffected?" she challenged.

"I will not sit here and make excuses for the things that I have done in the past." Kallie broke their eye contact and looked at the sky. "I cannot apologize for Fynn's death, but do not think I do not grieve him."

"You do not *deserve* to mourn him! You didn't know him! You betrayed him."

She scoffed then. "Do you not think I know that? I am the last person who deserves your forgiveness, and am I not asking you for it." Kallie bit down on her lip and forced her tears back. "No one was supposed to get hurt."

"But *he* did."

"I didn't know he was my brother when Domitius set the plan into motion. If I had--"

Dani huffed a rough laugh, cutting Kallie off as she snapped, "It shouldn't have mattered who he was! He was kind to you. He cared about you. And you..."

Dani shook her head. She took a deep breath in, her chest rising.

When she spoke next, her words were as cold as the northern glaciers. "One day, I hope you'll understand what it feels like to have your soul bond ripped from you."

A deep groove marked Kallie's forehead. "A soul bond?" she repeated.

Dani smiled, the stretch of her lips pure ice. "There are many things you still do not know--about our kingdom, your family, yourself. And honestly, I cannot wait to watch it all collapse on top of you."

"Danisinia," Graeson hissed, and Kallie startled as he appeared.

But the warrior didn't flinch at the sound of the low voice, her eyes remaining locked on Kallie. A suffocating grief soaked Dani's gaze, the barest hint of water pooling on her lashes.

"Lower your sword, General," Graeson ordered.

A feral, pained noise vibrated in Dani's throat as the blade remained against Kallie's throat. "You are not my commander nor my queen. You have no power over--"

"Do not test me right now." Graeson's voice turned icy and ominous.

Kallie kept her gaze locked on Dani.

She did not want Graeson's protection.

She was not worth protecting. She was not worth *anything*.

Vengeance darkened within Dani's hate-filled gaze. Yet as Kallie saw Dani's chest rise and fall as she took a breath, the blade finally disappeared from Kallie's throat.

With a snarl curling her lip in disgust, Dani took a step back. Her hand tightened around the hilt of the blade as if she were struggling to release the tension spiking through her. As if she still debated her choice to release Kallie.

Kallie didn't blame her.

As she dropped her gaze to the ground and exhaled, the breath Kallie released wasn't from relief; it was pain.

"Leave, now," Graeson thundered.

Footsteps pounded against the ground as Dani huffed and spun, heading back to the castle.

Twigs and leaves crunched behind her, but Kallie didn't move. She didn't react as the notes of cedar mixed with citrus came closer and a pair of black leather boots stepped into her vision.

A small, infinitesimal part of her wanted to reach out, aching to crawl forward and let the warmth consume her and whisk the torment away.

But that part was too small. A fire unable to spark amidst the coldness that whipped around her core.

Kallie refused to look up. Well, it wasn't that she refused per se; it was that her head was too heavy to raise, and the weight of every word Dani spat at her bore down onto her shoulders.

Every piece of her felt like it was breaking, falling apart, and collapsing before her.

No matter what Kallie did or how much she tried to keep things together, she failed. The pieces wouldn't stick.

They fell.

They crumbled.

They disintegrated.

Even weeks after her mind had been torn apart, Kallie still couldn't identify up from down or left from right.

Graeson crouched down before her. He reached out a hand but then let it fall onto his knees as if thinking otherwise. He said nothing, simply balanced precariously on the toes of his boots.

Kallie averted her gaze. As Graeson observed her silently, she refused to acknowledge whatever feeling was stirring in her core. Still, she couldn't help but notice how his hair had grown a little longer or how the scruff on his chin made him look even more rugged than usual.

Finally, he sighed and whispered, "Dani is hurting. She doesn't know what she's saying."

Kallie scoffed and looked up at him, her sea-storm eyes meeting his blazing silver ones. "She knows *exactly* what she is talking about. I betrayed him. *I* am the reason Fynn is dead."

Graeson's expression shadowed. "Your brother--"

"He may have been my brother by blood, but he does not deserve to have my name tied to his, even in death." Kallie looked away and out toward the surrounding swamp.

Even after a few weeks, the putrid musk of the Tetrian lands was horrid. Someone had said she would get used to it after a few days once she became accustomed to it, but Kallie was beginning to think she never would.

Just like she would never get used to the void in her mind, the emptiness inside of her, or the echo that rang in her ears.

Graeson reached out then. The coarse pads of his fingers, worn by decades of training, were a foreign comfort she did not wish to feel. "That wasn't you, Kalisandre."

Kallie laughed, but the sound came out gravelly and hoarse. Through tear-stained eyes, she glared at him. "Isn't that the worst part? It *was* all me."

"No, it wasn't."

Kallie stabbed a finger into her chest. "I was the one who let you take me to Pontia. I was the one who let you welcome me into your home. I was the one who let Fynn believe he could trust me, who blocked him out at every turn. My mind was a fortress, one even your best mind reader could not break." Her sternum spiked with pain, her finger bruising, yet she pressed on. "That was *my* doing, despite how much you all claim it wasn't. I didn't even see the monster hiding inside me. The lies and deceit sinking into my veins. I am a master manipulator, and yet I didn't even realize that I was being manipulated the entire time. How is that not my fault?"

Graeson's thumb stroked her cheek. When he spoke, his voice was sincere, tender as his breath brushed her skin. "Domitius has tricked many. He has been five steps ahead of us."

Kallie swatted his hand away. "I tried to kill you!" she protested.

"And I doubt that will be the last time," Graeson said with a smirk that soon fell, replaced by an unamused expression. "But it does not dispute the fact that you are not *him.*"

Kallie leaned back, her bottom hitting the ground and her legs collapsing around her.

"You are in control of your mind now, Kalisandre," Graeson whispered. "He will never manipulate you again."

A shiver ran down her spine, sticky and slithering.

Kallie shifted and wrapped her arms around her knees, hugging them tightly to her chest. "I can still feel it, Graeson. I can still--"

He grabbed her shoulders, his grip tightening around her as he stared at her with fear and dread in his eyes. "What do you mean? I thought it...I thought it worked."

"It did," Kallie said. She blinked, and her brows drew together. "At least, I think it did, but that doesn't erase the memories."

Then, as the warmth from his hands pressed into her arms, the heat sinking into her body, panic rose in her throat. She stumbled backward, away from his grasp. Graeson reached for her, but Kallie shook her head.

"Don't...don't touch me," she whispered.

"Kal?" Graeson asked, pain coating his eyes.

"Don't," she said again, her voice quiet but stern. "I don't...I don't trust myself right now, and neither should you."

His head sank, strands of hair cascading in front of his eyes and masking his face in shadows. Then, he stood, his eyes burning silver as he extended a hand to her. "You will not hurt me, Kal."

His words were stone, solid and firm, but even the strongest castles crumbled.

"You do not know that." Kallie ignored his outstretched hand and stood. She spun on her heel and headed back to the castle, refusing to look back.

CHAPTER 37
MYRA

LAURINCE PACED IN FRONT OF MYRA, HIS HELMET NESTLED IN ONE arm as he rubbed his face with the other.

Myra did not have to reach out to feel the stress pooling off every pore. It showed in every movement he made: his feet dragging across the ground, his knuckles blanching as he tightened his hold around the helmet, his eyes darting across the room, looking at everything yet nothing at the same time.

Anxiety was an infestation that seeped its claws into everything. It ate away at one's ability to think properly. And it was present here in scores.

"Getting out of here will not be easy," he mumbled.

Myra nodded in agreement, though she knew Laurince was not paying attention to her.

"More and more guards arrive every day."

"Is the king preparing for something?" Myra asked. She had not seen Domitius since he had delivered Rian.

Laurince halted and looked at her, his brows drawing together as if he had just recalled she was there. "Huh?"

Myra cleared her throat. "You said there are more guards than before. Is the king preparing for something?"

"Oh," Laurince muttered, raking his fingers through his hair. "It seems that way, yes. No one quite knows the reason for the gathering yet, but there's a nervous energy in the castle."

Myra twisted her fingers together, Laurince's words sinking in. Domitius was indeed preparing for something. The only question was what.

"Has there been word about the princess's whereabouts?" she asked.

Laurince shook his head. "We cannot concern ourselves with her right now."

Myra nodded. He was right, but she still hoped for Kallie's safety. The king no doubt had expected her to return by now or at least hear word from her. Myra had twisted Kallie's emotions so much that she would have felt an intense need to return to him immediately.

But if Kallie hadn't returned, perhaps that meant Myra had failed.

She could only hope.

Laurince's voice broke through her thoughts. "I can manage to get the keys and get Rian out of the cell. But then we will need to get out without being seen."

"Have you...have you heard about my brother's whereabouts?" Myra asked lowly.

"No, but I have narrowed it down, for the king only visits a select few cells himself. It has to be one of them."

"Why haven't you confirmed which one yet?"

Laurince scoffed. "I barely trust you as it is. The fewer people who know about our plan, as small a plan as it is, the better. We cannot afford to let your brother know. We do not know where his allegiances lie."

Myra's lips parted, a rebuttal on the tip of her tongue, but Laurince clocked it immediately and spoke before she could.

"Do not feign to be that ignorant. From what you have told me, your brother has been under Domitius's hold for nearly a decade. He may be a prisoner like you, but you have been allowed to form your own opinions. We cannot be certain that your brother feels the same way."

"But you just said so yourself! He is a prisoner. Why would he relay our plans to the king?" she challenged.

He gave her a pointed look. "All your brother knows is this life. Even a dog would hesitate to bite the hand that feeds him."

Laurince's words sat between them, a heavy weight that pressed against Myra's chest. She did not want to admit that he was right, but she also could not admit that he was wrong either.

"Even taking him with us is a risk," he added.

Myra stood, her hands curling angrily at her sides. "I will not leave him."

"Then what assurance can you give me that he will not betray us?"

Myra held her breath as she glared at Laurince. The answer was on the tip of her tongue, but she hesitated to speak it aloud. While Laurince had been kind, she still did not know him well enough to trust him completely, especially with a secret she had guarded for her entire life.

Her parents had told her to keep her ability hidden, for that sort of information could be dangerous in the wrong hands.

Yet Domitius still had discovered the truth, hadn't he?

Perhaps secrets did more harm than good...

She took a deep breath, exhaling slowly. "If it comes down to it, I can change his mind."

"How can you possibly do that? We might not have the time for you to spin some sob story that will--"

Myra shook her head and interrupted Laurince, saying, "I only need a few seconds."

Laurince narrowed his eyes. "What do you mean?"

"It is easier if I show you." She bit her lip.

Myra held out her hand, and Laurince stared at it with distrust.

"You came here for a reason, Laurince," Myra whispered. "Do you trust me?"

"I don't trust anyone anymore."

"Good. You shouldn't," Myra said with a slight smile that didn't reach her eyes. "But if you seek reassurance, this is the only way I can give it to you."

Laurince snorted. "Holding your hand isn't going to magically make me believe you."

"Actually, it might," Myra said, her words a heavy weight between them.

She could sense Laurince's apprehension thicken, and she wiggled her fingers because although Myra did not need to touch someone to transform their emotions, it was easier to do so if she did. And perhaps it would be easier for Laurince to understand.

She added, "I have learned that having too many secrets only makes matters worse in the end, even if the intent in keeping them is to protect the other person."

"What do you mean?" Laurince asked, brows furrowed.

Instead of answering with her words, however, Myra grabbed Laurince's hand. The confusion that once covered Laurince's countenance vanished and was replaced with pure bliss. A smile spread across his face, splitting it into two. His eyes crinkled.

Then, in a flash, Myra snatched her hand from his and cut the connection.

Laurince blinked. When her gift slipped from him, he backed up slightly, shaking his head. "What did you--what did you do?" he stammered.

Myra took a deep breath and said, "There are people in this world who can do things that are not normal."

Laurince stared at her in disbelief. "How? Why? I--I don't understand what just happened." He peered down at his hand before looking back up at her. "Are you...are you a goddess?"

Laurince's fingers twitched over his short sword. When he saw where Myra's attention had gone, he removed his hand immediately.

"I didn't mean--" He brushed a hand through his hair. "I--I'm sorry."

Myra nodded. "I do not blame you for being wary. The unknown is a dangerous place to exist. It is why people like me usually keep their abilities a secret."

His eyes widened. "People? There are more people who can-- who can do whatever it is you did to my emotions?" he exclaimed.

"Yes and no," Myra said, weighing her words. "I have only encountered a handful of people who bore them, but all abilities differ. My mother was gifted in embroidery."

His forehead creased. "That is...a gift?"

"The way she embroidered? It most certainly was," Myra said, her tone lighter than it had been in weeks as she thought of her mother embroidering in the garden.

However, the moment of reprieve was brief, as Myra recalled the last night in her childhood home, when spools of thread were thrown onto the ground and pieces of embroidery were slashed through with a blade as the king's guards ransacked the house.

Myra cleared her throat. "You asked for reassurance. I have given you that. If my brother wishes to run to the king, I can force him not to by changing his emotions."

"And you are sure that will work?" he pressed.

Myra nodded. "It has worked in the past."

She could see the question rise to his face before he even spoke it.

"Who?" Laurince asked, the single syllable wrapping around her and threatening to strangle her.

"Kallie."

CHAPTER 38
KALLIE

Kallie's limbs were frozen as she sat in the deep tub with her arms wrapped around her legs. The once scorching water, now lukewarm after sitting in it for who knows how long, had done little to bring life back into her body.

After the normal training with Ellie and then getting kicked on her ass by Dani, Kallie had returned to her room and immediately had a bath drawn. But it wasn't just her muscles that ached; the moment the handmaiden had left the room and the door clicked shut, Kallie had entered the bathtub and tears immediately erupted.

Kallie didn't know when the tears had stopped streaming down her face in torrents. She could still feel them staining her cheeks, the steam from the water having caused the salt to stick to her skin.

For once in her life, numbness didn't coat her mind. And even though she knew she shouldn't, Kallie almost missed it.

She missed the way the numbness shielded everything. The way it kept the world at bay and allowed her to live ignorantly.

But now that her mind was broken? Now that her insides had shattered into crystal glass shards, the images within them distorted and untouchable with their sharp edges? Kallie felt everything all too much.

It was as if Dani had caused something to snap within Kallie when she had forced her to her knees.

Dani's gaze bled with so much hate and pain. It was the first time Kallie had truly come face-to-face with the consequences of her actions.

It didn't matter what Graeson had said. It didn't matter if Domitius and Myra had altered her mind; Kallie was still to blame.

One thought after another weighed down on her as she sat in the tub.

But she couldn't focus on a singular thought. Not when there were too many holes that had been ripped in the fabric of her life.

For years, Kallie had lived a lie, a fabrication she had been made to believe was the truth. What was she supposed to do now that she knew her reality had only been a simple manipulation?

It was almost laughable.

The manipulator had been manipulated.

The woman who had vowed against love when she was a young girl had been betrayed by the one man she thought would never betray her. And even further, she had been betrayed by her best friend, Myra, whom Domitius had instructed to twist Kallie's mind while snaking her way into her heart.

Kallie shouldn't have been surprised.

She should have seen through the deceptions, the lies, the stained glass.

Yet she had ignored the warning signs. She never questioned Myra's presence or why she always felt better after Myra held her.

She had pretended that the holes in Domitius's story--the lack of paintings of her mother, the dismissal of her brothers' involvement in her initial abduction, the endless assignments furthering his own agenda--didn't exist.

The tears threatened to return, but she had no more to give.

Kallie bit down on her lip, pain spiking as her teeth pierced through her skin. She curled her fingers, balling her hands into tight fists beneath the water.

When she was told Domitius had kidnapped her, she had been made to believe that he had done it to protect her. When confronted, Domitius had said he kidnapped her because her mother wished to use her for her gift, that Kallie had been born simply to be used by the Queen of Pontia.

Then, when she was told Domitius had killed the father whose blood ran in her veins, Domitius had told her that *he* was her father--the one who had raised her, cared for her, and given her everything she needed in life.

He had turned it around on her, as if she was in the wrong for questioning him. As if she was claiming he had not been good enough after everything he had done for her.

When Fynn died, Domitius claimed he was a needed sacrifice, a death that couldn't have been avoided because of Kallie's actions. An unfortunate casualty, but one that shouldn't have been a concern of hers.

Fynn did not care about her, Domitius had said. The prince had only wished for Kallie's demise.

And when Kallie had agreed to marry the King of Frenzia, she'd been told it was to gain her crown, not to give Domitius access to a sea of knowledge.

Domitius had told her he cared for her.

He assured her the crown would be hers.

The *power* would be hers.

He never told her, however, that he loved her. Never once had he uttered those words in all those years she had lived within the marble castle. Not even as a child.

And the worst part? Kallie was led to believe that was normal and was to be *expected* of a parent, of a father, of a king.

Rulers were above love, for love weakened and love destroyed.

That's what he had said to her when she had asked about her mother at seven years old with bright, wide blue eyes and an eager, scared mind.

When seven-year-old Kallie had finally gotten the courage to ask the question that rose in her mind at every turn, at every glance in the mirror, every time she had seen another child's mother in the castle, he had looked at her with such disappointment and resentment.

All Kallie had asked was to see a painting of her mother, to get one glimpse of the woman whose eyes Kallie must have shared because she looked nothing like her father. But when the question had left her lips, Domitius had grabbed Kallie's chin, his grip pinching as he forced Kallie to meet his gaze.

As Kallie stared up at the king, tears rolled down the soft contours of her cheeks. His attention immediately went to them, tracking them with a predatory gaze.

His nose twitched as he hissed, "Queens do not cry over the dead."

"But--" Kallie had begun before snapping her mouth shut as he shook his head.

"Am I not enough for you? Is all of this"--he waved a hand at his office and the castle at large--"Not enough for you, Kalisandre?"

Her lip quivered. "But my mother--" she tried.

Domitius shook his head again. "A mother would not solve your problems for you."

"Then what will?" Kallie asked, her voice just as meek and small as she felt.

A fire had sparked in Domitius's eyes then, and the corner of his mouth twitched up. "You, Kalisandre. *You* will solve all of my--*our* problems."

"Me?" She struggled to understand him.

So much hope had filled his eyes at that moment that Kallie couldn't help but believe him when he said, "Yes, you."

She was too young to see the truth then. Too naive and ignorant to see the hunger and greed stewing beneath the falsified hope he portrayed.

That was the night her training had begun.

When the King of Ardentol had begun to shape and mold Kallie into his weapon. Kallie, a child then, had thought it was to better her, to make her stronger and more capable. She thought it was for *her* benefit.

She never saw the truth, though.

She never saw through his endless lies, the falsehoods that slipped so easily from his tongue.

She never questioned why she couldn't manipulate him. Why, every time she got mad or angry at him for sending her off on another assignment or locking her in the room after she had been out past curfew, she couldn't manipulate him like she was learning to do to others.

But whenever she thought to do it, *something* would pull the rage back. A little voice in her mind would whisper into her bloodstream that he was doing it for her, that these punishments were only to make her stronger, better, *more*.

But now, as the water of the tub lapped at her skin, as the sweltering heat in the air stuck to her neck, as sweat beaded on her flesh, she saw the truth at last.

Finally, she saw the bull king for the bastard he was, and her best friend for the traitor she had always been.

Domitius and Myra would pay.

They would pay for every assignment, every betrayal, every life they had forced Kallie to take.

Even if it was the last thing she did.

Even if it meant she had nowhere to run to, no castle to her name.

She would destroy them.

She would destroy everything the king cared about by becoming the blade that would pierce his very heart.

One day, anyway.

Because right now, despite this newfound resolve, all she could do was lie in her filth, her head resting atop her knees as she held herself as if she might fall apart.

She tried to stuff all the feelings back inside and stitch herself back together. She tried to hide away everything she had been ignoring, but she couldn't.

Without the block that Myra had placed in her mind, Kallie was drowning in her thoughts and emotions: her dead brother, her pretend father who had never cared, the fire in the temple, the fire all those years ago that had started it all.

Her life had become a series of fires and lies, and she couldn't find her way out.

It was an endless cycle, an endless torrent that kept repeating and repeating. But she needed it to stop. She needed it to stop like she needed air.

Kallie tried counting.

One.

Breathe in.

Two.

Hold.

Three.

Breathe out.

A knock came at the door, but she ignored it. She started counting again.

One.

Two.

Three.

Shoes clapped against the ground, and her eyes sprung open. Soaked tendrils of her hair had fallen in front of her face, but she didn't dare move. She pretended he wasn't there. She tried counting again, trying to focus on the numbers, her breathing, and most definitely not on Graeson's presence.

One--

"Kalisandre," Graeson said. But based on his voice, he was still several feet away. Near the threshold of the bathing chambers, if Kallie had to guess.

So she ignored him, hoping he would leave.

She squeezed her eyes closed and *willed* him to go away.

If the gods wished to show her any mercy, they would make him leave.

But did she deserve their mercy? She had brought this on herself after all, hadn't she?

Deep breath in.

One. Two--

Steps lightly rapped against the bathroom tile.

What number was she at? Her brows furrowed.

No matter. She started over.

One.

Exhale.

She could feel his approach, and something within her stirred. She quickly shook it away. But as she tried to count again, fingers brushed a strand of hair behind her ear, the pads of them rough.

Kallie didn't dare breathe as Graeson's hand remained on her face a moment longer, cupping her cheek. His thumb circled the space beneath her ear, but she didn't raise her gaze to meet the silver eyes she knew she would find.

"Kalisandre," he whispered.

Kallie took in a sharp inhale as the sound of her name repeated on his tongue. Her brows drew together, and her eyes cracked open slightly.

Graeson knelt beside the tub, an arm resting on the edge.

Staring at the top button of his black blouse, Kallie at last asked, "Why do you call me that?"

Graeson's fingers danced across the tub's ledge, the gold rings on them sparkling in the candlelight of the bathing chambers. "It is your name, is it not?"

Kallie could almost hear the smirk that was no doubt on his face.

"No one calls me that, though," she mumbled.

Besides Domitius, she thought.

She squeezed her arms tighter around her knees.

"Would you prefer that I call you something else?" he asked thoughtfully.

"I--" Kallie's mouth grew dry, and she tried to swallow. "I don't know. I just..."

Graeson sighed and shifted, getting more comfortable. "I call you Kalisandre not only because it is your name but because you asked me to when we were children."

"I did?" Kallie asked, taken aback. She recalled him calling her *little mouse* but not asking him to call her by her full name.

"You said it made you feel older." Graeson chuckled as if recalling the memory and scratched the back of his head, the fabric stretching across his arm. "You actually tried saying it made you feel respected, but back then S's and P's were kind of hard for you to say."

The corner of Kallie's lip twitched, but the smile quickly fell. Too much was on her mind.

Graeson sighed, his fingers tapping on the porcelain. "Will you please look at me, Kalisandre?" he murmured. He slipped his hand beneath her chin, coaxing her to raise her head. "A queen does not bow her head."

Kallie wanted to laugh, but she refrained from doing so. "I am no queen," she said, the words sour on her lips.

"You are right," he agreed after a moment.

Despite the truth of the words, pain still pierced her heart. She never would be a queen, and perhaps that was for the best.

But did Graeson think those words would help her? That they would clear the troubles from her mind? They might have been the truth, but they were a truth she had yet to come to terms with.

Without Frenzia's crown, or any crown for that matter, what was there for her in this world? When her mind broke, so too did her desire for that hunk of metal. It was as if the two were tied together so inextricably they could not dare part.

Kallie didn't know what to make of that.

She didn't know if she wanted to.

He quirked a brow. "You are so much more than that. You *could* be so much more than that if you just let yourself."

Kallie dropped her gaze. She had said it too many times to count, so she didn't need to waste her breath to repeat it. Graeson knew nothing. Gods, none of them did.

He sighed. "Come on, get up," Graeson said softly.

Kallie made some noncommittal noise in disagreement, for she still needed to wash herself.

His gaze scanned over her face, looking for an answer she didn't have.

She was so tired of the pitying eyes. She was tired of the silence that permeated any room she walked into, as if her mere presence was a storm that sent even the most skilled sailors scurrying away and hiding on land.

She was tired of feeling as if she had been buried alive with no way out.

She was tired of people taking a step back when she took a step forward.

Kallie tilted her head to the side as she looked at Graeson.

Unlike the others, Graeson never stepped away from her.

She lifted a hand, splaying it across his chest. She may have been in pieces, broken and discarded, but right now, she didn't care. She didn't care if she never felt whole again.

Because right now, as she ran her fingers over the polished buttons of his cotton shirt, all she wanted was to feel *something*.

Anything other than this grief that crawled over her skin and soaked into her veins.

But as Kallie made to speak, Graeson stood and disappeared out of the bathing chambers. Her hand hung in the air, quickly growing cold and limp without Graeson's warmth.

She shook her head, shooing away the thoughts inching to the surface.

Part of Kallie was thankful for the peace his leave brought, but another part of her crumbled as she watched him turn his back on her. The least he could have done was shut the door.

She closed her eyes again.

She would get up, she told herself.

Soon.

In a moment, she would wash her hair, rinse the scum from her skin, then get out of the tub. That was only three things; how hard could it be?

Seconds went by, yet she did none of that.

Then footsteps sounded outside once again.

Her eyes sprung open as Graeson reentered her bathing chambers carrying an iron bucket.

"If you insist on staying in there, you can at least do so with fresh, warm water," he said, sitting the bucket on the ground. "Do you need anything else?"

Kallie shook her head, a flush climbing up her neck. Only the sound of the water lightly hitting the sides of the tub and their breaths filled the room.

Then he turned to leave again.

"Wait," she breathed.

Graeson's steps stopped.

Silence filled the air as Kallie cursed herself for speaking. She hadn't meant to, yet the word slipped free, nevertheless.

He stared at a spot on his shoulder as if he couldn't bring himself to look at her fully. She wished he would.

"Do you want me to leave?" Graeson asked carefully.

Did she want that? Was being alone better than being in his company? For some reason, Kallie did not think so.

"Kalisandre, I need you to tell me." His voice was soft yet stern.

Still, Kallie said nothing.

But then, when she heard him begin to shift his weight as if to leave once more, she whispered, barely audible, "Stay."

His hesitation lasted less than a second. "All right."

He sat on the stool behind her head, his knees brushing against the porcelain tub. Somewhere behind her, in the bucket perhaps, she heard the sound of water sloshing.

"May I?" he asked.

She glanced up. "Hmm?"

Graeson cleared his throat. "May I help you? If you wish for privacy, I'm sure we could lay a--"

Kallie closed her eyes. "It's fine." She scooted forward a couple of inches away from the back of the tub, her movements slow and uncoordinated from having been sedentary for so long. Then, she tipped her head back.

"I--okay," Graeson stammered, almost as if unsure of himself.

A stream of water flowed down the back of her head moments later. He held his other hand at the edge of her hair, preventing water from spilling down her face.

Then, Graeson cursed.

"What is it?" Kallie asked, beginning to sit up.

"Nothing. It's fine," he mumbled. "Just a little water."

A second later, a swatch of black fabric was tossed onto the ground. Heat rose to her cheeks as she glimpsed his black shirt from the corner of her eye, but she said nothing.

Soon, the smell of citrus filled the room. She took a deep, shaky inhale before shutting her eyes again. He placed one hand on her forehead as he dripped the soap onto her hair.

Graeson worked quietly as if washing her hair was a job that required his sole attention. He scrubbed from the front of her hairline to the base of her neck. His fingers wove into her hair, scratching her skull and spreading the soap into a lather.

She would never have guessed they were the hands of a man who fought with the strength of ten men as they ran through her tangled waves, massaging her scalp with a careful touch.

Then his hands traveled to the divots between her shoulders, his thumbs circling. The proper thing would have been to tell him to stop, that she did not deserve this kind of treatment, but as he continued to apply pressure, the release felt too good to deny it.

"I wish...I wish I could take it all back," Kallie whispered finally.

"It does not do anyone any good living in the past," Graeson scolded.

She smiled sadly. "Dani hates me."

"Dani does not--"

Kallie arched a brow and snorted.

"She doesn't hate you," Graeson said, though his words were less convincing. "She is still grieving. She just needs time."

"There is not enough time in the world that would make her forgive me."

Silence fell between them then, and Kallie couldn't blame Graeson for hesitating. And perhaps it was wrong of her to express her feelings to him when Fynn was his best friend, too. A part of Graeson must have hated her too, yet he never showed it.

"Dani is mad at all of us right now," he said at last.

Her eyes widened in surprise. "Why is she mad at you?"

He chuckled. "She's always mad at me for one reason or another. This time it might be because I am the one who dragged her here and let Domitius slip through our hands."

Kallie recalled the events Terin had relayed to her in the infirmary, and her brows drew together. "But from what Terin told me, that is not your fault. You saved her."

"Sure, but she does not see it that way." He shrugged.

"And Terin? Why is she mad at him?"

Graeson sighed. "She knows that he still has a connection to Fynn."

Kallie bit her lip. She had hoped that Terin had listened to her suggestion of letting Dani speak to him, but it seemed he hadn't.

"Fynn didn't want her to know," she murmured.

"Terin told her and I as much, but that does not lessen the pain. When he refused to let her talk to him, she was enraged. She still is."

"And Terin hasn't given in?"

Graeson shook his head.

"Maybe he should," Kallie said.

"Maybe."

Graeson's palms rolled over her shoulders, and the tension in her body lessened. She focused on her breathing, taking deep, slow breaths.

Then she sunk back into his hands, stretching out her legs, her arms resting over the sides of the tubs. After a moment, Graeson's hands stopped, and Kallie's eyelids fluttered open. Although she couldn't see him, she didn't need to in order to realize why he had stopped.

When he had entered the room, she had been covering herself with her limbs. But now, with her legs stretched out, her arms hanging on the side of the tub, she was laid bare before him. The peaks of her breasts lay above the water.

"I thought you said you wouldn't look?" Kallie asked, unable not to poke fun at him and break the tension.

Graeson cleared his throat. Once. Twice. Three times. "I--I wasn't."

"Mhm," Kallie hummed. "Don't worry. If there was someone else in this tub instead of me, I would probably have a hard time looking away, too." She forced her tone to be nonchalant, smug. Unfazed.

This was normal, she told herself. But another part of her said that it was a distraction, a way to divert the wayward thoughts that had consumed her earlier.

But she didn't care.

She inhaled, holding her breath, and submerged herself under the water, fully realizing that it only made her more vulnerable to prying eyes. But also fully knowing she did not care if he looked at her.

She was never one to be self-conscious of her body. To her, it was another tool. However, there was no longer a need for her to use her body against Graeson, was there?

She stayed under the water, scratching her scalp to remove the soap from her hair.

And perhaps she stayed under the water for a little longer than she needed to because she didn't know how to face him now.

After drowning out the intrusive thoughts, she resurfaced, but Graeson was gone when she opened her eyes. His black shirt, discarded on the ground, was the only proof that he had even been there at all.

CHAPTER 39
GRAESON

Brilliant flames surrounded him everywhere he looked. The heat of the fire licked his skin, and sweat poured down his face and back. His muscles ached, but he couldn't stop. He had to keep going. No matter how much she clawed at him or how much she kicked.

He had to save her.

He had to get her out.

But when Graeson burst through the doors, windows shattering in his wake, she disappeared from his arms.

A maniacal laugh echoed all around him, making his stomach turn with dread.

The bull king flashed before his eyes, but before Graeson could grab him, he, too, vanished.

Yet the laughter continued to rain down on Graeson.

He spun, round and round, but he could not tell where the sound was coming from.

"You think you can save her? You can't even save yourself!"

Graeson fell to his knees. He pressed his palms against his eye sockets, willing the voice to go away--to leave him alone. But no matter what he did, the voice continued to berate him.

Soon enough, though, it transformed. Despite the heat that coated his skin, an ice-cold breeze swept over him.

"You continue to hold back, son," Barinthian whispered.

Graeson slammed his hands against the ground, and the earth trembled beneath his palms. "I am not your son!" he roared to the god.

Barinthian laughed. "Still telling yourself that, I see."

The air shifted around him, the flames growing taller and taller. When Barinthian spoke again, Graeson could feel his breath against his throat. "Why do you stop yourself from becoming who you were meant to be? Wouldn't it be easier to just let go? To free yourself from this cage you have built?"

Graeson dug his fingers into the dirt, the ground peeling his nails back. "I will not be like you. I will not destroy worlds and families. I will not--"

"Be a monster?" Barinthian taunted, cutting Graeson off.

The god laughed again, the sound wrapping around Graeson's throat and strangling him. He fought to break free, but it was no use.

"You already are."

GRAESON JERKED AWAKE, his entire body feeling as if it were on fire. A rumbling roared inside him. And before he could think twice, he ran.

CHAPTER 40
KALLIE

While Kallie braced against Ellie's swing, Graeson burst from the castle, his eyes blazing silver.

As she followed him with her eyes, distracted, Ellie shoved her and then knocked her legs out from under her.

Kallie barely registered the fall, only momentarily feeling its sting as she fixed her attention on Graeson. "Where is he going?"

"Huh?" Ellie asked, turning towards where she was looking.

Even yards away, Kallie could practically sense Graeson's entire body vibrating with an untamed energy.

"Should someone go after him?" Kallie urged.

Terin, who had been observing Kallie's training, extended a hand, and Kallie took it. As he helped her up, he said, "I don't know. I don't think it'll help."

Mouth agape, Kallie snapped her attention to him. "You're just going to let him run off?" she exclaimed.

Terin scratched his head and shrugged.

"Trust me," Ellie said, her tone weary, "whatever is going on, he does not want company right now."

Kallie's lips parted, but she was at a loss for words.

Were these not Graeson's friends? Were these not the people who should care about him? The ones who should run after him and make sure he was okay?

Kallie shook her head in disappointment. "I didn't want company either, yet that never stopped any of you from barging into the infirmary and talking my ear off."

"Graeson is...different," Terin said, as if that explained everything. "You have to tread lightly when he's like this." He frowned.

"Tread *lightly*?" Kallie repeated, her voice raising in disbelief. "He is your friend!"

"And as his friends, we know him best," Ellie said, folding her arms over her chest.

"Bullshit," Kallie spat.

And then she was off, chasing after the one man who had always come running after her.

Boom.

A thunderous clap ricocheted through the trees, and Kallie halted, her breath catching in her throat. Graeson had managed to go deeper into the woods than Kallie had initially thought. Cautiously, she turned toward the sound and peered through the never-ending brush.

"Graeson?" Kallie asked, his name no more than a whisper on her tongue.

Graeson stood with hands pressed against the beaten bark of a tree, his head slumped, and his hair falling, shielding him. His shoulders were tense as he mumbled something unintelligible under his breath.

Kallie took a hesitant step forward. "Are you...are you all right?"

Graeson still did not respond, and before she knew what she was doing, she was only a few feet away when she slapped a hand across her mouth, covering a gasp.

Blood was smeared across the bark of the tree, and his knuckles were stained red, raw and ghastly.

Without thinking, she ran forward.

Body trembling, she placed a hand on the back of his head.

"We need to take you to a healer." Concern creased her forehead as the blood continued to drip down his fingers and fall onto the roots of the tree.

Kallie looked around them, but there was no one within shouting distance.

She looked back at Graeson and bit her lip. "Stay here. I'm going to go get help."

Kallie began to pull away, but as her hand slipped from his shoulder, Graeson grabbed her wrist.

"Stay," Graeson whispered, the word almost inaudible. Kallie would have questioned if she had heard him correctly if it wasn't soon followed with a gut-wrenching, "Please."

Kallie hesitated, her heart a loud echo in her chest. "You need help."

"No," he gritted out. "I'll be fine."

"Fine? Graeson, you're bleeding," she protested.

"*Was.*"

Kallie blinked, her brows furrowing. "What?"

"I *was* bleeding, little mouse. I am no longer."

"But there's--" Kallie's words disappeared into the air as she inspected his hand once more. It had just been dripping blood, yet the raw skin only appeared to be scratched, the wounds already congealing. "How--" She shook her head, taking a deep breath. "You still should see a healer. By the looks of it, you've lost plenty of blood, and you could get an infection if not properly treated."

Graeson released her wrist and chuckled as he turned and leaned against the tree as if he needed it to stay upright. His eyes were shut, and his expression was pained. Yet there was a flicker of a smirk on his face.

"Funny how things can change so quickly, isn't it? One day you're trying to kill me with your own two hands, and now you worry over a few scratches," he mused.

"That's not--" Kallie swallowed as she brushed her fingers across her wrist, still tingling from his lingering touch. "That's not funny."

Graeson let loose a heavy sigh and pushed his hair back with his hand, smearing blood across his forehead. "I suppose it is a little early for those jokes, huh?"

"A little," Kallie mumbled, though she knew he said it with no malice. "Either way, a healer surely should take a look at you."

With a rough snort, Graeson shook his head. "A healer will find nothing." He finally met Kallie's gaze then, and Kallie stumbled backward.

The hue of Graeson's eyes was nearly as white as snow. Their normal smokey gray color had nearly vanished. And despite the shadows cast by the foliage of the trees, they pierced through her very soul as they glowed.

Her heart pounded, and she could not decide whether it was from worry or fear. Part of her wanted to run, but another part of her urged her to reach out.

Kallie gulped. And after a moment that seemed to span time, she finally asked, "What happened?"

"It's complicated," he shrugged, the picture of ease.

Kallie blinked, her mouth falling open. "*Complicated*? What is so complicated about this?"

Graeson chuckled as if the entire situation was comical. "Nothing is ever simple."

She tried to protest, "But--"

Graeson groaned out in pain, his eyes squeezing shut. He pressed his head back against the trunk of the tree and hissed.

"Graeson!" she gasped.

He leaned away from her, but there was nowhere for him to go. "Go," he gritted out through clenched teeth.

"Excuse me?" Kallie's eyes widened.

"Leave." His fingers dug into the tree's bark as veins protruded from his neck, and his complexion reddened.

Kallie scoffed and folded her arms over her chest. He would not push her away. Not that easily.

She raised her chin. "No."

"Please, Kalisandre," Graeson begged, but the tone of his voice had shifted. Kallie could no longer tell if he was pleading for her to leave, to listen to him, or if he was begging for her to stay. Either way, she would not leave him.

Kallie didn't know who Graeson was to her; she didn't know if he was her enemy or friend. Truthfully, she barely knew him at all, yet she felt like she understood him. Whatever was happening to him was coming from *inside* him. That much was clear as he clawed at the bark, and his brows twisted together in pain, deep wrinkles creasing his forehead.

Kallie stepped closer and grabbed his arm. His skin was cold to the touch, yet she didn't let go.

"Tell me what to do," she whispered. "Tell me how to help you."

Graeson grimaced. "You can't," he rasped.

"Then tell me what's happening."

"I told you," Graeson said, groaning as if merely speaking was painful. "It's complicated."

The bark cracked as he pressed the back of his head further into the tree.

"Graeson," Kallie said, gasping, "you're hurting yourself."

"I'll heal," he mumbled, a noncommittal sound.

"You do not know that!"

"I do!" Graeson shouted, startling her. Black strands of hair fell in front of his face, and sweat coated his forehead. His breaths were ragged, his chest rising and falling hard with every intake.

"Graeson," she whispered.

Graeson turned his head away from her. "You need to leave."

"I already told you. I'm not going anywhere."

"I don't want--" Graeson swallowed, the lump in his throat dipping as Kallie caressed his cheek and gently turned him toward her. He looked at her, his eyes burning silver and twisting with pain. "I don't want to hurt you, Kalisandre."

"You won't hurt me."

"You don't...you don't understand." He shook his head, shaking his hair. "In this state, I'm--I--I don't have control."

"What state?" she pressed.

Graeson stared at her with such intensity that something broke within her. At that moment, she couldn't help but wonder if anyone had ever come for him. If anyone had ever fought to stay with him.

"Am I supposed to be afraid of you?" she asked.

Graeson's gaze bounced across her face. "You should be."

"Why?" Kallie's head tilted to the side. She recalled all the fights they had been in and knew, without a doubt, that Graeson had always held back when it came to fighting her. She had seen him take on multiple soldiers without breaking a sweat. But with her, he was always careful.

"In this state, logic and reasoning vanishes. I...I could hurt you. I'm a monster, Kalisandre."

But before Kallie could say a word, Graeson screamed out. His head slammed against the tree again, and the birds sitting among the branches scattered, the leaves rustling as they flew away.

"*Run*," he said through clenched teeth.

But Kallie didn't move.

She was not afraid of him. Not now, not ever. For once in her life, despite the past that divided them and begged to force them apart, she knew that she was safe with him.

Kallie wrapped her hands tightly around his, squeezing them, and stayed right where she was, her feet firmly planted on the ground.

Because while Graeson might have thought he was a monster, so was she. He hadn't abandoned her when she told him to. Instead, he always came back for her even when he shouldn't have. Even when she gave him no reason to.

And for that, if nothing else, Kallie wouldn't abandon him either.

CHAPTER 41
GRAESON

G RAESON WAS LOSING THE BATTLE THAT RAGED WITHIN HIM, AND IT was only a matter of time before he lost completely.

Yet as Kalisandre stood with him, her hand caressing his cheek and her presence engulfing him, he somehow managed to keep the beast within from ripping apart his body.

Still, even as his breathing steadied and his body stopped trembling, he knew he was only delaying the inevitable. With every passing moment, he could feel the internal clock clicking, the fight nearing its climax.

But Graeson would fight off the god as long as he could. For Kalisandre.

Until she was safe, until whatever was brewing in the East settled.

Until then, he would keep fighting, no matter how much strain it put on his body.

"ARE you going to explain to me what happened?" Kalisandre asked as they sat side-by-side against the trunk of the tree.

After an hour of fighting to hold onto the little strength he still possessed, Graeson's heart rate had finally settled. Still, he had no energy to return to the castle. Thankfully, it seemed he didn't need to.

When the screams had finally stopped and he could finally peel his fingers, raw and bloodied, from the bark, Kalisandre had said nothing as she guided him to sit on the ground.

He'd expected her to leave then, but she hadn't.

Graeson didn't want to think about what that may or may not have meant, for he couldn't afford to when his hands still trembled slightly. Graeson was merely glad he hadn't hurt her. Even though he knew that the god had never tried to harm Kalisandre in the past, he still did not trust himself.

"Graeson?" Kalisandre called, bringing his attention back to her.

"We should go back. I should wash up," he said softly, flexing his fingers, the dried blood cracking from the movement.

Nodding, she stood and held out a hand.

Hesitantly, he took it, and the instant his hand wrapped around hers, a small flame spiraled up his arm.

Standing inches apart, he could feel the warmth of her breath against his chest. He spotted the faint freckles adorning the bridge of her nose from the sun's kiss. Her cheeks were no longer hollow like they were in Frenzia. He could see that life was slowly returning back to her.

There was so much he wanted to say to her. So many things he *should* say to her. Yet he was unable to speak.

A soft breeze tousled her hair. He lifted his hand and curled her hair behind her ear. His lips parted, but Kalisandre cleared her throat.

She delicately swiped the hair behind her ear, turning. "Come on," she said as she turned and tugged him behind her.

However, when Graeson registered the direction they were going, his heels dug into the ground. "The castle is that way," he stated.

She looked over her shoulder with a coy smile. "I know."

"Then where are we going?"

"Some place Medenia told me about," Kalisandre said. The left corner of her lip turned upward, forming a half smile that almost met her eyes. "The last thing you need is to be around everyone else."

THEY STROLLED THROUGH THE WOODS, their pace leisurely as if they had all the time in the world. Notes of sulfur grew stronger with every step. But the farther they walked, the more Graeson was unsure of where they were going. When he tried to ask Kalisandre for more details, she ignored his questions.

Then, as he held a batch of low branches out of Kalisandre's way when they hiked a steep hill, she glanced over her shoulder and nodded. "It's just past these trees," she explained.

Kallie waved him forward, and when the trees parted, he looked out and inhaled.

Massive evergreens encompassed three large craters, each the size of three porcelain tubs, which overlapped one another. A narrow river flowed through the hollow cavities in the earth, filling them to the brim and creating a constant flow of water.

"Medenia brought you here?" Graeson asked in wonder.

"During that first week, Medenia had tried her best to make me feel welcome and safe. She kept me company and forced me outside. While the fresh air helped, I still felt...trapped," she said, making a face. "I think Medenia noticed how lost I felt, so one day, she took me out here instead of the gardens. I haven't been back since, but..."

Kalisandre scratched the back of her neck and peered at him from the corner of her eye. With a soft, nervous chuckle, she shrugged.

"I almost thought I had gotten us lost for a moment, but I found my way in the end," she remarked.

"You did," he said as he watched her tilt her head toward the sun.

Then, Kalisandre headed for one of the craters. Stepping on the heel of her shoe with one foot, she slipped off one shoe, then the other, her bare feet on the ground. Dipping her toes into the water, she released a heavy sigh.

"I find the water and the trees relaxing. It...well, it reminds me of..." Her words trailed off as she stared at the scenery before them, biting her lip.

"The Whispering Springs?" Graeson supplied.

Kalisandre nodded. "When I was knocked out, I often found myself back there. Initially, I thought it strange, but then I began to yearn for its familiarity as if a part of me belonged there. I don't know if I've ever felt like that before."

"Not even in Ardentol?" Graeson asked, raising a curious brow.

"Ardentol was always *his* kingdom, his people, his plans. While I do care deeply for the kingdom and want to see the people happy, it has never been *mine*." She stared at the water.

Something akin to longing passed over her expression, but it was also mixed with grief and regret, contorting her features.

She went on, "Frenzia was supposed to be mine--at least, that's what he told me. But it was never going to be. The people...they would not have accepted a queen as their ruler."

"Change can be hard," Graeson said as he stepped forward and stood beside her, leaving a few feet between them.

"Indeed." Kalisandre gazed out over the small ripples. "But water is constantly changing, is it not? As the river flows and the seasons shift, the water changes as new things and elements are introduced. Change can be hard, but it is also inevitable."

Graeson squatted and reached out, dipping the tips of his fingers into the water. Steam came off its surface, yet its heat did not burn his hand. When he pulled his hand out of the crater, some of the grime that had once covered his fingers had washed off.

"Do you really think people can change?" Graeson asked after a few seconds passed.

"I hope so," Kalisandre said with a nervous chuckle. "If not, what was the reason for all of this?"

Graeson looked up at her and found a hint of sadness there. But beneath the melancholy within the deep blue depths of her irises, he also spotted a glimpse of hope.

Clearing her throat, she rolled her shoulders back and nodded toward the pool. "Are you going to get in?"

"It's getting late," he said, standing up. "We should probably get back."

"You could go back if that is what you want," Kalisandre said as she ran her fingers across the hem of her blouse.

His heart hammered in his chest, and he swallowed the rising lump in his throat.

"Is that what you want?" he asked, though the question did not come out as smoothly as he intended.

Kalisandre arched a brow and reached for the ties at the top of her blouse. "I didn't come all this way just to turn around before even enjoying the springs." She pulled the end of the bow, loosening the top.

Graeson immediately spun around, the collar of his shirt suddenly feeling too tight as heat flushed his cheeks.

Behind him, fabric hit the ground with a soft *thump* as Kalisandre giggled.

Graeson tipped his head back, willing his restraint to remain firm. But by the gods, whenever Kalisandre laughed, the sound did something to him. It was as if he could feel the sound crawl across his body and break away every wall he had built.

He heard a small sigh of relief escape her lips.

Shit.

Graeson rolled his hands in tight fists at his sides before releasing them. He undid the buttons running down his shirt, each one more torturous than the last as he waited to turn around. Once he tossed his shirt and trousers on the ground, he faced the springs again.

Kalisandre was already seated inside the nearest crater, her elbows propped on the edge as she tipped her head toward the setting sun. She pushed her hair back behind her shoulders, allowing the steam to kiss her face.

She peered at him, her lashes fluttering. She arched a brow, a smug grin stretching across her features.

"Are you going to stand there all day and gawk, or are you going to get in?" she teased.

Graeson ran a hand through his hair and took a deep breath before approaching the crater's edge. Despite his desire to be near her, he opted for the opposite side of the small pool.

He stepped into the water, and the steam wrapped his body in a warm embrace, cloaking him. Once he submerged his lower half in the water, he finally understood why she had taken him here. The heat of the water was absolutely delectable. It soothed his muscles, and for once, he felt the tension in his body dissipate.

Graeson shifted backward, his back touching the wall, and

sighed as he sat down on a bench that looked to be carved out of the pool itself.

"See?" Kalisandre asked from the other side, calling his attention toward her as she grinned. "I told you this would help you relax."

Graeson swallowed as his gaze dipped to her collarbone, already speckled with water droplets.

He forced his attention up and cleared his throat as he shifted. "You were right."

Kalisandre gasped and pressed a hand against her chest. "You, saying that I am right for once? Now, that has to be a first."

Graeson snorted. "Surely not. You have been right about many things."

"Oh? Like what?"

Graeson hummed his eyes fixed upon her. But as he struggled to keep his gaze from slipping to where the water sat at the curves of the top of her breasts, he had a hard time recalling the question.

"See?" Kalisandre mused. "Getting you to admit that I, or anyone else for that matter, is right is a hard feat, indeed."

Graeson rubbed a hand across his face. "People are sometimes right. It's just that they're usually wrong more often."

She snorted. "No, you're just a cocky bastard."

A small, genuine smile rose as Graeson recalled her having made the same statement at the fire that first night months ago.

They fell into a comfortable silence for a while after that. Soon, however, Kalisandre shifted, her brows twisting together as concern blanketed her countenance. "Will you tell me what happened back there?" she asked quietly.

Graeson brushed a hand through his hair, causing water droplets to drip down the sides of his face. "I do not wish to burden you."

"As if I have not burdened you?" she scoffed.

His gaze snapped to hers. "You are not a burden, Kalisandre."

She rolled her eyes, but Graeson still caught the doubt creeping in behind those sea-blue eyes. He couldn't bear another moment of witnessing it.

"Do not roll your eyes at that," Graeson grated out across the pool.

Kalisandre quirked a brow. "I will do whatever I please, Graeson."

"True, but I cannot let you carry on thinking you are a burden to me. It wouldn't be right."

"Aren't I, though? How many times did you try to tell me the truth, but I wouldn't listen? How far did you and the others have to carry me while I was unconscious? You all have risked so much for me despite never having deserved it." She shrugged.

"I did those things because I wanted to and because it was the right thing to do."

She shook her head in disbelief. "That does not mean it was not burdensome; surely you had a life in Pontia that you have uprooted to come here."

Graeson huffed. "It's ironic that you wish me to tell you the truth, yet you sit there avoiding it."

"I do not." She bristled.

Graeson could hear how she tried to force her words to sound steady, yet the way she dropped his gaze proved otherwise.

"I will say it as many times as I need to: you have never been a burden, Kalisandre. You never asked me to cross the sea or the mountains, yet I would do so gladly, even if it meant I only got to be in your presence." When Graeson spoke next, he held her gaze, lest she think he was lying again. "I told you once before that you consume me, and that has not changed."

Her face flushed. "Then why won't you tell me the truth about what happened earlier in the woods?" Her gaze fell to the space between them, and when she met his eyes a second later, she arched a brow in challenge. "Why do you continue to maintain your distance?"

"Because it is safer for you," he murmured, voice thick.

"Safer for me?" Kalisandre asked, her tone taking on an edge. "Or easier for you?"

Graeson laughed, the sound quickly disappearing into the steam. "Nothing about this is easy for me." He curled his fingers inwards, his nails driving into his palms as he forced himself to remain where he was and ignore the pull toward her. "Everything I do, I do for you. It pains me not to be near you, to touch you."

"If it pains you, then why do it? Why stay back?" she asked quietly.

"Because Kalisandre--" he began but swallowed as the words became stuck in his throat. He was riding a fine edge of needing to wipe the smug look off her face and being a decent man by staying put.

With an agitated groan, Graeson brushed his hair back. Water fell down the sides of his face, but the steam from the springs only increased the rising heat in his chest.

"Because...?" she pressed, her head tilting.

Graeson squeezed the bridge of his nose, then sighed. "You want to know what happened back there?"

She nodded.

"I'm not...I'm not in control of myself half of the time. I told you before that my mother passed when I was born, and the one who claims the title of *father* was no father to me. He abandoned my mother the moment he was done with her, tossing her to the side as if she was no more than last week's bread. He's not someone I look up to, nor someone I ever wish to be. However, the world never listens to the things we want, does it?"

Graeson twisted the rings on his hands. Each one was a reminder of who he was and who he wished to remain.

He sighed. "The more time that has passed, the more I become just like him."

"But I thought you didn't know your father?" she asked.

"I do not claim to know him, for I do not think he truly lets anyone *know* him. But I have met him. And every time I have the misfortune of interacting with him, the anger that has lived within me only grows worse," Graeson gritted out. "I didn't realize it until a few years ago, but that's what his objective has been the entire time.

"He only wishes to push me to my limits, to enrage me, and to force me to turn into him. My mother was a seer, yet somehow my mother never saw my father for who he was."

"Which was?"

"A god."

The two words sat heavy between them as the steam surrounded them, the hot air wrapping its tendrils around their bodies.

Graeson had thought that when he spoke the words aloud, the truth would have a way of destroying the world. That it would shatter his life and change how Kalisandre looked at him. But when Graeson met Kalisandre's gaze, he did not see an ounce of fear in her blue eyes.

As if she knew he was searching for it, Kalisandre said, "You say that as if it changes anything."

"It should change everything," he scoffed.

"Why? Because you are half god?" she chuckled, as if they were discussing the weather or something humorous Nyrri had done.

But perhaps she did not understand the ramifications of the statement.

"I am dangerous, Kalisandre. When the god side comes out, reason goes out the window. I am unable to see logic or sense. I am unable to do anything but let the rage control me."

"Is this what you were so nervous about telling me?"

Graeson blinked.

Her brows furrowed in utter seriousness. "Graeson, I am not scared of you."

"That is your mistake then," he whispered, his gaze falling to the water between them.

"Were you ever scared of me?" she asked after a moment.

Graeson snapped his attention back to her, his mouth falling open. "No, I could never be scared of you."

She tapped her fingers on the edge of the pool. "How many times did I try to kill you, though?"

"Do nightmares count?" Graeson asked with amusement.

Kalisandre shook her head, but a small smile formed before she sighed. "I am being serious, Graeson. I have done terrible things in my lifetime. I was a weapon for a king who lied to me my entire life. You have never been afraid of me, so why is it so odd that I would not be scared of you?"

His hands fell into the water with a small splash. "Because most are," he said with a shrug. "Even those who do not understand my background are scared of me."

"Well, I am not most people." She shrugged.

Kalisandre pushed off the bench and stood, the water sloshing around her. The tips of her hair were soaked and fell over her chest, covering her breasts.

Graeson quickly turned his attention back to her face.

She smirked and walked forward as she spoke. "I have always known that you can be a dangerous person."

As she strutted forward, her hips sashaying with each step, Graeson could do nothing but watch her. His breathing grew uneven, heat flushed his cheeks, and his entire being beckoned to meet her in the middle. Yet he could not move as if each word she spoke put him more and more under her spell.

"I have seen you fight as if you were ten men. I have known since the beginning that you are not an ordinary man. You think you are a monster, but I am too."

She was only a couple of feet away from him now. If he reached out, he would be able to touch her. But if he touched her, if he placed his palm on her hip that was now hidden beneath the water, the little control he had left would slip through his fingertips.

"Kalisandre," he said in warning.

But she only chuckled as she edged closer, her knees brushing against his and sending a chill up his body. "I recall you saying my name that exact way in Pontia that first night. You know what I thought when you said it then?"

"What?" Graeson rasped, the question no more than a whisper in the air as he stared up at her. His gaze was fixed on her as if she had pulled him into the sea that existed within her eyes with no way to escape.

"That I did not care for those sorts of warnings."

Kalisandre reached out, her hands caressing each side of his face. She tipped his head up, and her gaze skimmed over his features.

Graeson didn't realize he was holding his breath until he inhaled sharply, the citrus scent of her bath oils spilling off her. As if he had no control of them, his hands finally found their way to her hips, his fingers gently dancing across her skin.

"And now?" he asked, his voice low.

"I still don't."

Then, her lips were on his, hard and bruising, and everything he needed at that moment.

The world around them vanished, and Graeson pulled her closer, bringing her thighs between his. She leaned against him, her hands gripping the back of his head, digging into his hair as their kiss hardened. Her lips were sweet, though the intensity with which she kissed him back was anything but.

She was a wild sea storm, and he was a reckless sailor yearning for a tempest to threaten to engulf him.

He nipped at her lip, and she groaned against him. He squeezed her hips, the skin soft beneath his palms.

Then, despite every bone in his body telling him not to, Graeson broke the connection, pulling away. Their chests rose in synchronicity, their breaths heavy. Kalisandre's lips were swollen, and tiny fires were aflame in her stormy eyes.

He pressed his forehead against hers and sighed.

"Don't," she whispered, trying to pull his mouth back to her.

"Don't what?" Graeson asked, his mouth brushing the corner of her lips.

"Don't ruin this," she muttered as she shifted and kissed the side of his face right by his ear. She shook her head, her nose brushing his cheek and tickling him. "Don't tell me we should go back." Another kiss, this one closer to his mouth. "I do not wish to go back."

"Then tell me what you are truly thinking."

Kalisandre leaned back and locked her hands behind his neck. Her teeth scraped across her bottom lip.

While they may have broken Myra's hold on Kalisandre's mind, Graeson could only imagine that there were still broken remnants in its wake. What was once black and white was now too many shades of gray. And more than anything, he wanted her to trust him. He wanted her to let him in.

"I'm still trying to work through a lot right now," she said at last.

"Then perhaps we should take a breath."

"We are taking a breath. Is that not what this is?" She took a deep breath for emphasis, her chest and shoulders rising.

Graeson rolled his eyes and chuckled softly. "That is not what I meant, and you know it."

Kalisandre grabbed his shoulder, pulling him toward her. "Gray, listen to me carefully: there may be many things I am confused about, but one thing remains perfectly clear."

"And what is that, Kalisandre?"

"I need this."

When Graeson cocked a brow, she kept her gaze steady, even.

Graeson, however, knew the truth. "You mean you need me to be your release?"

Her hand slipped across his neck. With a dangerous smile, she said with a shrug, "Semantics."

Closing his eyes, Graeson inhaled, his body tense beneath her touch. He was on thin ice, but these days, Graeson always was.

He knew what she wanted. But right now, she couldn't give him what he desired. Not fully. And while he would be happy with any piece she could give him, he didn't know if he should. Especially when going any further would not help her.

"Gray."

He shook his head, and her hand fell.

"So that's a no?" Kalisandre asked, her hands loosening and rejection flashing across her face.

"It's a no for now."

"For now?" Kalisandre repeated, her brows drawing together. "What is that supposed to mean?"

"You have been through a lot over the past few weeks--"

Kalisandre flinched, taking a step back, and he knew he had made a mistake. But he didn't have a chance to explain before she was speaking over him.

"I've been through a lot over the past few *weeks?* My whole life has been a lie, Graeson! I have been tricked and deceived. My mind has been warped and torn to pieces. I barely even know who I am anymore!"

"And that is precisely why we can't do this," he explained. He tried to grab her hand, but she snatched it away, turning around and splashing water around her. "Kal."

She spun around, pointing a finger at him. "Don't do that. Don't *Kal* me. I ask for one thing, one, and you can't even give me that? I just want a distraction--a distraction from all of this." Kalisandre rubbed her hands across her face, the heels of her palms grinding against her eyes. "I just want to feel in control for once!"

His jaw ticked. "I'm going to try not to take offense to what you just said."

"Offense?" she hissed. "*Your* life hasn't fallen apart. You haven't lost a crown or your family. You haven't lost your whole identity. Yet you're offended?"

He cracked his neck and stood. "I am not a distraction for you to use."

She huffed, folding her arms over her chest. "Really, Graeson? You're going to play that card right now? Why are we even here then?" she demanded.

Graeson raked his fingers through his hair. "Do not play this game with me right now, little mouse."

Kalisandre lifted her chin, and the god within marveled at her confidence. In the reflection of her eyes, he could see the god rearing its head as his eyes illuminated beneath the night sky. It was supposed to strike fear in the mortals beholden to that stare, but Kalisandre did not fear the man who stood before her.

More than anything else, she feared herself.

"And what if that's exactly what I want to do?" she asked with a dangerous smirk.

His gaze dipped down her body, and as it lingered over her skin, scanning every inch of her, Graeson could almost hear her heartbeat pick up.

When he locked gazes with her once more, he scoffed. "You don't even know what you want."

He turned and lifted himself out of the water, his biceps straining.

"We need to go back," he said as he swiped his clothes from the ground. "The others will get worried."

While Graeson could have stayed there for hours, he knew they were both only hiding from their responsibilities and the world.

They couldn't hide forever, though.

CHAPTER 42
KALLIE

Even hours after returning from the springs, Kallie couldn't erase the memory of Graeson's kiss from her lips. She lay in her bed, twisting and turning, as the midnight air swept inside the room.

If she was honest with herself, she had been restless for a long time, but Graeson's rejection had increased it ten-fold.

She didn't know what had come over her when they were at the springs. Perhaps it was the heat from the water. Maybe it was the vulnerability that Graeson had shown her. Or maybe it was the confirmation that they were both monsters, that Kallie didn't have to pretend when she was with him.

Or maybe it was the constant pull she always felt around him. An inexplicable force that beckoned her to step closer, to push the limits of their budding friendship.

No matter the reason, however, she was foolish to have thrown herself at him.

And yet...

Kallie brushed the tips of her fingers across her lips. When he had kissed her...

Kallie sighed, pressing her head back against the pillow as she recalled his lips on hers, his hands on her hips. Sighing, she pulled the forgotten black cotton shirt closer to her face, the faint notes of cedar and citrus surrounding her.

And as the night breeze caressed her hot skin, Kallie did not regret a single thing.

CHAPTER 43
MYRA

THE SYRINGE SHATTERED ON THE FLOOR. THE MURKY LIQUID SPREAD across the concrete, soaking into the stone.

With a thump, Rian laid his head back against the metal bed. A small, satisfied smirk pressed past the gag within his mouth.

"Shit," Dr. Thorne hissed as he squatted and inspected the broken syringe. Picking up the needle, he glared at Myra over his glasses.

Myra sunk back within herself, her hands shaking in her lap.

She was trying to delay Rian's progress as much as she could. Laurince had yet to return with a plan. He delivered food but never said anything more than an obtuse *soon*. But soon might not be soon enough at this rate.

She could feel Rian's strength draining, the hope for an escape disintegrating with each passing day.

Dr. Thorne shouted, "Guards!"

Myra gripped her hands tightly, willing them to still as her attention flicked to the door.

Only silence answered the healer's call. The iron door was too thick for any guard to hear his shouts.

"Imbeciles," Dr. Thorne muttered, slamming the useless syringe onto the table. He wiped his hands on the blood-stained apron. "No one can do anything right." He headed for the door. With his hand wrapped around the handle, he looked over his shoulder. "You'd better hope His Majesty does not hear about this misstep, or else he will have all our heads."

Then with a final sneer, he slammed the door shut behind him.

Myra's heart raced as she stared after his retreating form, fear wrapping its limbs around her throat.

This was her chance, she realized. She could run. She could--

A hand wrapped around her wrist, and Myra's attention snapped toward the metal table. Rian's green eyes stared at her, the whites of his eyes stained red.

He groaned, but the rod in his mouth muffled his words, making them unintelligible.

With trembling hands and a quick glance back, Myra reached over and loosened the gag.

Rian took in a deep breath and whispered, his voice hoarse from the screams that had previously ripped through his lungs. "Please. I do not wish--I do not want--"

He coughed, his entire body shaking with the motion and pulling taut against the restraints.

Myra pressed a light hand atop his chest. "Don't speak," she whispered, her forehead creasing in concern. "It'll only make it worse."

He shook his head. "No. Please, just"--more coughing--"please end this."

Myra bit her lip. "You don't understand. If I help them..."

His fingers squeezed around her wrist. "*End* this," he begged.

The hopeless gaze in Rian's eyes pierced Myra's heart. The young king looked away from her, and she followed his gaze toward Dr. Thorne's table.

A scalpel lay among the various instruments.

Myra looked back at him. "I I can't. I--" Her voice trembled as water rimmed her bottom lash line.

Death may have been a better end than being turned into one of those creatures, but they were supposed to get out of here. *Alive.*

Laurince promised. He gave his word.

But what if they couldn't?

"Please," Rian repeated, calling her attention back to him. "I do not want to be one of them."

The breath Myra took did anything but calm her trembling hands. She bit her bottom lip and glanced at the scalpel again, the razor-sharp edge shining in the flickering light of the torch.

Pure hopelessness and despair poured from Rian in droves. The sickening emotions wrapped around her hands, her throat, choking her.

She had never taken a life before. Would she even be able to?

Her entire body trembled at the thought.

Frustration seeped into the room, startling her.

Myra reached over and tightened the gag around Rian's mouth. He groaned and pleaded with her.

She brushed a light hand across his face and leaned down. "Keep faith. We're going to get out of here," Myra whispered. "I promise."

She removed her hand from the king's face. A thin layer of water coated his fear-stained eyes. He did not believe her, and Myra did not blame him.

She had made the same promises before and failed to fulfill them.

But she had to hold on to the hope that this would not be their end, even as Dr. Thorne reentered with the guard and spoke, his words threatening to destroy the hope Myra held onto.

"Be ready tomorrow. His mind is fragile. I can see him breaking."

BOOTS POUNDED outside Myra's cell, the metal armor creaking with every movement.

Myra threw herself at the slot as the guard opened it and pushed her meal toward her.

"Soon," the familiar voice said, the repeated phrase grating against her bones, her very mind and threatening to break both apart.

Myra grabbed the edge of the slot before Laurince could close it and hissed, "It has to be tonight."

On the other side of the door, Laurince stilled. Apprehension spilled from him.

"What?" he spat. "Are you crazy? We're not prepared. We--"

"We do not have time to prepare," she quickly countered, voice urgent. "The king will not deal with any further delays. If you wish to save him, we must act now. He is weakening by the minute. I--I fear for his safety."

Fear dripped from Laurince like a living thing. She could sense his hesitancy, taste it even. The king's captain, Myra already knew, was not a man who wished to act without a plan.

But Myra was tired of waiting. Waiting had only ever made things worse.

"Fine," Laurince whispered. His armor creaked as he made to stand, but Myra called out.

"Wait," she whispered.

Laurince paused his retreat.

"What about my brother?"

"I will see what I can do."

CHAPTER 44
KALLIE

KALLIE WIPED THE SWEAT FROM HER FOREHEAD WITH THE BACK OF her hand as Ellie and Terin sheathed their weapons. They had been training in the gardens for a little over an hour. The warm rays of the autumn sun poured down on them, casting a golden glow over the orange and yellow mums surrounding them.

"You're getting better," Terin said with a small smile.

"Yeah, we only knocked you on your ass, what? Five times?" Ellie remarked with a snort.

Terin's eyes widened, a rebuke forming on his lips, but Kallie only laughed.

"That's only because it was one versus two," she said. "If it was just you and me, Ellie, you would have been the one hitting the ground."

"Ha! Only because I would feel sorry if I kicked your ass too many times."

Kallie rolled her eyes.

When the laughter died down, Terin cocked his head to the side, his brows furrowing. "But you're still holding back," he noted.

Kallie snapped her head in his direction. "I am not."

"Really? Then why have you not manipulated us?" Terin retorted wryly, folding his arms over his chest. "You could have easily won numerous times and saved yourself from a couple of bruises."

Mouth agape, Kallie averted her gaze as her tongue grew heavy. She cleared her throat, trying to find the words.

"That would uneven the playing field," she muttered at last.

Terin snorted as Ellie asked, "Uneven the playing field? And what happens if you were to come across an enemy? Someone who wishes to take you?"

"Oh, like all of you?" Kallie retorted, her comment sounding more snarky than intended.

"Fair point," Terin mumbled, scratching his head with a frown.

"But it still does not warrant you holding back," Ellie argued, the tip of her sword digging into the dirt as she leaned on it. "We're not only taking the time to re-train you to help your recovery, but we also must prepare you for what is to come."

"Oh, and here I thought this was all just a fun distraction," Kallie said, trying to change the topic. Her efforts were futile, however, for Terin pressed forward.

"Ellie is right. Domitius will not give up his search for you."

"I think you all overestimate my worth to him," Kallie countered, rolling her eyes.

"And you *under*estimate it," Ellie said. She took a step forward, and the tension between them increased ten-fold. "There was a reason he took you, remember?"

Kallie pursed her lips. "He hasn't come for me yet, has he?"

Almost two months had passed since her wedding had gone up in flames. Other than Terin and the others running into a group soon after they had left Frenzia, they had not encountered any further issues. Although Kallie had heard rumblings of search parties wandering Vaneria, there was no immediate threat of danger.

Perhaps Domitius had finally given up on her or found another way for his plans to come to fruition. The king was not a patient man. He would find a way. After all, he had made it clear that she was only a tool to be used. He would craft another, and perhaps he already had, Kallie thought as her mind wandered to Myra.

Terin shook his head. "While it has been quiet in recent weeks, we should not take the bull king's silence for complacency. He took you once. He will take you again."

Kallie tossed her head back, and frustration colored her voice when she asked, "What need does he have of me?"

Terin and Ellie exchanged wary glances, but it was Ellie who spoke. "That remains to be determined, but I hope for all our sakes that we never find out. Still, we would be foolish to think that this game of his is over so easily. He told you he wanted to control the seven kingdoms. As far as we know, his goal has not changed."

Terin nodded and added, "He gave you up to us with little to no fight. There has to be a reason. Something we are missing."

Kallie huffed, for she already knew why. "The reason was he believed I would kill you all in anger."

"Would you have?" Terin asked, brow arched.

Kallie pursed her lips, but she could not lie to him. "I--I do not know. I cannot say for certain. When I awoke in the woods, I was angrier than I had ever been before when I saw Graeson. It was as if something had come over me. I didn't realize at the time that was exactly what was happening, that Myra had manipulated my feelings toward you all and increased my rage and anger. I almost killed him then."

Kallie turned away from Terin, unable to bear his gaze any longer.

If she had been successful, it would not have been only her hands that would have been covered in Graeson's blood, but Terin's, too, as her command filled his veins.

Kallie cleared her throat and turned to Ellie. "But you and the queen fixed that, did you not?" she asked.

She didn't know why she needed to ask, but perhaps she feared Domitius still held her in his trap, as if she were still running through one of his mazes, lost with no trace of an exit.

Ellie nodded. "We did," she said softly.

"So what are you afraid of?" Terin asked.

"I am not afraid," Kallie corrected, squeezing her clammy fists together.

"*Yet*," Terin said, the word drawn out as his stare bore into her, "you hold yourself back."

Kallie rolled her eyes. "I see no reason to manipulate Ellie. I shouldn't rely on my gift in a fight in case it fails me."

"Have you tried?" Terin pressed.

Kallie's tongue became lead in her mouth as her gaze bounced from Terin to Ellie. She cleared her throat. "It's a violation. It would be wrong."

"It would be good practice," Ellie piped up.

Kallie's entire body burned as they stared at her, waiting for her to admit they were right. But Kallie wouldn't; she couldn't.

"I really shouldn't," she said after a moment. "It's--"

"Have you tried at all since you woke?" Terin interrupted.

Kallie rubbed a slick hand across her throat. She felt as if the air was swept away, as if the world had been stripped of all the oxygen.

"Kallie?" Terin urged.

Unwillingly, she looked at her brother.

"You haven't, have you?" Terin asked as if he could see the truth behind her gaze.

Kallie bit down on her tongue as she squeezed her throat slightly with her hand. She hesitated in answering him, for she found it hard to find the words.

When the intensity of his stare did not lessen, she relented, forcing a weak explanation out. "I just--I do not wish to use it."

"Why not?" Ellie asked, frowning.

Kallie stared at the sky. A light hand touched her shoulder. When she looked at Terin, he was watching her carefully with only empathy shining in his brown eyes. He squeezed her shoulder, and Kallie sighed.

"You do not understand. I've done horrible things. For as long as I can remember, I was the king's puppet. He used me; he used my gift, forcing me to manipulate anyone who spoke out against him. He didn't just wish for their obedience, though." Kallie took several steps away from the other two when she grew silent as the memories of past assignments surfaced.

"What did he make you do?" Ellie asked softly.

Kallie rubbed her throat, and she could feel her skin becoming raw beneath her palm. She dropped her hand but kept her back turned toward them, unable to look at either of them as she relayed what the king had forced her to become.

Domitius may not have had his claws in her mind, but his shadow still loomed over her past. And while Terin, no doubt, knew some of what the king had done, she didn't know how much he truly knew.

Certainly, if he knew everything, he would no longer look at her with empathy.

"Manipulating them to obey, while still immoral, would have been one thing," Kallie said, her voice shaking slightly. "It would have been easy, but nothing with Domitius is easy. He did not wish his opposers to get away with disagreeing with him. He wanted them to suffer. And...I think he wanted me to suffer a little bit, too.

"When I was younger, I argued with him constantly, trying to find logic and reasoning in his actions. Sometimes, I argued with him when he denied a citizen more food rations after court. He would say I was too emotional, too easily swayed to feel sympathy for others who did not deserve it. Then, he would send me on an assignment. Sometimes, he'd force me to manipulate a man into entering a brawl."

"Well, that doesn't sound too bad," Ellie said hesitantly.

Kallie shook her head with a huff and turned, facing her. "I would command them to lose the fight, to get injured purposely. Other times..." She paused, the memories choking her. She pressed forward. "Other times were much worse. My hands may not have ever driven a sword through someone's heart, but I might as well have. Death has been a shadow that has followed me far longer than I care to admit."

When Kallie met their gazes with hesitancy, horror blanketed Ellie's and Terin's faces.

Kallie took a step back. Then another.

She shouldn't have told them.

The urge to flee thumped in her chest.

Yet she forced her feet to remain plastered to the ground because, if nothing else, they deserved to know the monster they had welcomed into their home, the monster they rescued.

"So you see," Kallie said, her voice hoarse, "I do not deserve your kindness or your trust. My gift is no more than a curse, and it is not one that I wish to use."

Terin stepped forward, his brows knitting together and deep grooves creasing the center of his forehead. "What Domitius made you do is horrendous, Kallie. No one should ever be forced to use their gift, especially in such a wicked way as he made you use it. But..." Terin hesitated, twisting his hands together. After thinking about his words briefly, he straightened and held his fists at his sides. "Our abilities need to be nurtured, Kallie. If they are not--"

Kallie shook her head and cut him off. "I will not manipulate anyone again," she breathed.

"But you must," Ellie said, taking a step forward, her eyes wide. "If a war is coming, your gift will be more useful than you can imagine."

"I said no!" Kallie dug her heels into the ground, fury quickly rising in her throat and forcing the words to come harsher than she had intended. "I will not be used again. Because it is not just my gift you wish to use, it is me."

"And if war comes?" Ellie pressed, brows raised and her hand tensing around the hilt of her blade. "If Domitius marches his troops across the seven kingdoms? If he spreads the destruction he has already caused in Pontia? What will you do when the Frenizians give the bull king their grenades to use? What will you do when more creatures like Nyrri, but more feral and ravaged, take to the skies? What will you do then, Kalisandre?"

Ellie was toe-to-toe with Kallie now, her chest rising quickly.

But she wasn't the only one angry. Every muscle in Kallie's body vibrated. As Ellie continued to stare down at Kallie, Kallie tipped her chin up and spoke past the tears burning the back of her eyes. "I will not be a weapon for another kingdom. I cannot. I refuse to do so."

"Ellie has overstepped," Terin said, stepping between them, forcing Ellie backward. "No one will force you to do anything."

Despite the sincerity within Terin's words, Kallie did not miss the shock across Ellie's features, the way her lips parted and the whites of her eyes enlarged.

Terin continued, "I only asked about your gift because it can be dangerous to keep it bottled up."

"Dangerous how?" Kallie asked, her stomach twisting.

He grimaced. "Your emotions can be hard to control."

"That doesn't sound too bad," Kallie mumbled.

Terin's grim expression, however, suggested otherwise. "I have never experienced it myself, but from what I've read, it is not pleasant. I would be careful if I were you."

His warning turned over and over in her mind. There was much Kallie still did not understand about her gift, but she meant what she said. She would not manipulate someone again. To manipulate someone was to control their will.

No one deserved to have that kind of power over another.

At night, memories of Domitius's assignments would infiltrate her dreams. Somehow, she knew instinctively that Terin hadn't put them there. They felt different, more haunted.

Kallie never recalled fearing her gift before. The headaches were unbearable after extraneous use, but she had always felt strong and powerful when she used her gift and felt its honeyed tendrils wrapping around her.

As Kallie looked inwards, she instantly recoiled, unable to even reach for her power.

"I think that's enough training for today," Terin said after tense silence permeated the air. He nodded toward the castle as he tossed his jacket over his shoulder. "Are you joining us for lunch this afternoon?"

Kallie bit down on the inside of her cheek as the previous conversation still hung in the air uncomfortably. She had only taken Terin up on his offer to join him and the others for lunch twice. Both times, she had sat there in silence, her attention bouncing between Terin and the others. Their conversations were so easy, and Kallie felt a foreign longing to partake.

But she wasn't one of them. She didn't share their inside jokes or know the places Emmett and Sylvia spoke of back in Pontia.

The recent argument aside, training with Terin was one thing, for there was never a need for small talk. But sharing a meal with him? With all of them? Kallie couldn't quite stomach it, especially today.

While she may have wanted to dismantle the wall that still existed between them, she couldn't quite get herself to remove the first brick.

Kallie looked toward the tree line that bordered the castle's property, and something beckoned her toward the woods, as if telling her today was not the day.

Finally, she shook her head. "Not today."

Terin nodded before turning on his heel. Although guilt rose in her throat, Kallie could not call Terin back as he and Ellie walked away.

Kallie sighed and headed toward the forest, listening to the pull of the wind.

THE BREEZE BRUSHED through Kallie's hair, pushing through the long chestnut locks and sweeping them off her shoulders.

She could feel the guards watching her as she made her way to the forest. And for a moment, she hesitated. She shouldn't wander too far from the castle. Everyone still mistrusted her, yet her feet propelled her forward as if a rope was tied around her waist tugging her deeper and deeper into the woods.

When she glanced over her shoulder, she could barely make out the castle within the spaces between the trees.

The guards had shifted closer, but none made to follow her. Her brows furrowed, but she did not stop to think on it long as the wind ruffled the leaves and swept a caress across her face.

She curled the stray pieces behind her ear and continued.

Then, as the woods swallowed her, she froze as light, unfiltered laughter filled the air.

Kallie squinted.

There, through the trees, she spotted Nyrri in a small opening, her tail whipping back and forth. The dragon-wolf jumped, her large wings beating and lifting her higher as she snapped her large jaw.

Nyrri landed with a loud thud, sending a dust cloud into the air.

"That's a good girl."

Kallie's heart thumped in her chest as Graeson came into view and scratched Nyrri beneath her chin. Nyrri tipped her chin up, her tail beating against the ground as she received his praise.

Out in the woods, he looked a little unruly, wilder, less contained. But the fear that existed when she found him bleeding and trembling before was nowhere to be seen.

He looked...good.

A blush heated Kallie's cheeks, and she stepped backward.

A twig snapped beneath her foot.

"Shit," Kallie hissed under her breath.

Graeson's gaze immediately found hers, and his hand fell from Nyrri's chin, which caused the creature to whine and push at his hand, which was now limp at his side. Surrendering to her pleas, Graeson lazily patted Nyrri's snout, but his attention was fixed on Kallie.

"Sorry," Kallie mumbled, scratching the back of her head. "I didn't mean to interrupt."

"You're not interrupting," Graeson said perhaps a little too quickly. "We were only training."

"Training?" Kallie asked as she walked over.

Graeson hummed. "The Tetrians are still a little nervous around her, but she needs to be stimulated. If she sits in the garden for too long, she'll grow restless. It's the same thing for horses or dogs. You have to entertain them and exercise with them. Restlessness and boredom aren't good for an animal."

"Is that what Ellie, Medenia, and Terin are doing with me?" Kallie mused darkly as she began petting Nyrri.

"That's not--" Graeson sighed, raking his hand through his hair. "They're only trying to help, but if it is a bother--"

She waved him off. "I'm only joking. I don't mind them dragging me out of the castle."

"Are they treating you well?"

Kallie could feel his gaze on her, but she did not look at him. "Yes. Ellie has knocked me on my ass several times, but it at least gives me something to do. I feel...well, useless," Kallie said.

"You're not useless," Graeson said, his tone serious.

"Ever since I woke up, I have felt lost. It's strange." Kallie peered up at him and shrugged. She wasn't sure why she was telling him this, yet it felt good to say it aloud. "I don't know. For so long, my objective has been showing Domitius that I was capable of more, that I was worthy of him."

"You've always been worthy, Kalisandre," Graeson assured her. "You never needed anyone to tell you that, especially not him."

Kallie could hear the conviction in Graeson's voice, but she couldn't quite bring herself to believe him. While she no longer sought Domitius's approval or validation, his words still felt wrong.

"You may not believe it now," Graeson said as if he could read her mind, "but one day, you will."

Kallie offered him a sad smile but remained silent.

Graeson tipped his head toward Nyrri. "Do you want to see what we've been working on?"

Kallie smiled and nodded, thankful for a change of subject.

"Sit over there," he said, pointing to one of the nearby trees.

Kallie did as he instructed, and then he was commanding Nyrri.

ONCE GRAESON HAD EXHAUSTED the dragon-wolf with his commands, Nyrri curled into a large ball between Kallie and

Graeson. And for a time, a comfortable silence befell them, punctuated only by birds chirping.

As Kallie sat there, her mind began to replay the conversations that occurred recently, and one thing Dani had said kept repeating over and over until Kallie couldn't take it anymore.

"Graeson, can I ask you something?" she asked, sparing him a glance.

"Hmm?" Graeson hummed, his eyes still closed as he rested his head against the trunk of one of the trees. His black hair was a stark contrast against the white bark of the trees.

When Kallie hesitated, the question stuck in her throat as she watched him. He arched a brow, waiting.

Kallie finally forced the words out. "What is a soul bond?"

Graeson's eyes snapped open. "I'm sorry?" he stammered.

"A soul bond, what is it?"

Nyrri, as if sensing the tension, stood and trotted away. She curled into a ball in a spot in the sun. As she laid her head atop a paw, a red eye peered at them.

"Dani mentioned it a few weeks ago when she and I were fighting," Kallie added, plucking petals from a flower with a shrug.

"Why are you bringing it up now?" Graeson swallowed.

"Why are you avoiding the question?" she retorted with a playful smirk.

Graeson shifted and sat up straighter. He twisted one of the gold rings on his fingers. "Soul bonds are a type of connection between two people. Your mother and father were soul bonds."

"But what does that *mean*?"

"For some people, there is a thread that connects them to others. According to the stories, Pontanius had created bonds to help strengthen people's abilities. But it's more than that; it's a deep connection between a couple, stronger than a mere marriage. It does not always exist, but when it does, it is a powerful connection that is hard to ignore once realized. "

Kallie weighed his words, then asked, "Were Fynn and Dani soul bonds?"

Graeson nodded. "They were."

"When did they discover the connection?"

A small smile flicked over his mouth. "Your brother, being his arrogant, egotistical self, did not realize it for a long time, actually." He chuckled and scratched his chin. "Dani has never said as much, but I believe she discovered they were soul bonds much sooner, probably when we were all children."

"What happens when you lose a soul bond?" Kallie asked.

Graeson stopped twisting the ring, his fingers freezing on it. He swallowed, the bump in his throat dipping. "It destroys a part of you."

"Forever?" she prompted.

"After your father was killed, your mother wasn't quite the same, and she still isn't, not really. For years, she was a walking shell of herself. The grief from losing a soul bond can be overwhelming." Graeson began twisting the same ring, his browns bunching and expression twisting with worry. "It is a tradition that soul bonds exchange rings crafted by their families and made from a rare metal found on an island off the coast of Pontia. The rings solidify the bond. When one's partner passes, the connection becomes something different and can drive the survivor mad."

Kallie stared at the ring he twisted. Had Graeson lost his soul bond? Was that why he was so tormented? A feeling Kallie did not wish to identify nor admit existed twisted in her gut. She quickly shook it away, forcing her gaze away from the ring.

"Doesn't Dani still wear hers?"

"She does," Graeson said.

"Does she know the consequences?"

He nodded. "I think she is waiting to take it off."

"Until when?"

"Until she can avenge Fynn."

Kalisandre swallowed as Graeson's gray eyes met her.

"She will not harm you. Despite how mad she may be at you, she knows Domitius is the true person to blame. He is the one she is truly after."

Kallie rubbed a hand across her throat. "It's not his fault."

Graeson's lip parted as he stared at her, blinking. Something akin to shock flushed his face. "You still defend him, after everything?"

"No," Kallie said, shaking her head, her hand falling from her throat. "Domitius is a monster. I am not defending that. But he did not drive the final blade through Fynn's heart."

"Then who did?"

"Sebastian."

CHAPTER 45
KALLIE

LAUGHTER FILLED THE ROOM AS EMMETT AND SYLVIA WENT BACK and forth. But the joy ceased when Kallie and Graeson stepped inside the room, and the attention of those sitting at the table turned to them. Tension ripped through the air as eyes bounced from Kallie to Dani.

Dani stood, her chair screeching as it scratched the floor. "What is *she* doing here?"

Kallie went rigid as Dani's gaze bore into her. Since the two of them had sparred, they had managed to evade each other. Any time Kallie had turned down a hall and heard Dani's voice, she had turned the other way, even if it meant taking a longer path to her destination.

Kallie was a walking reminder of Fynn's passing, and Kallie did not wish to cause Dani any more stress than she already had.

Yet, when she had told Graeson that it was Sebastian who had been the one to take Fynn's life, he had asked if she would come with him to talk to the others. She had initially denied him despite his reassurance that it would be all right. However, when he looked at her, a plea on his lips, she had relented.

She was wondering if she should have held her ground, though.

"She has a right to eat with us," Graeson argued, placing a gentle hand on Kallie's back, and some of the existing stiffness dissipated. Marginally, anyway.

Dani scoffed. "Fine, but that does not mean I have to sit here, too," she said, scooting her chair further back.

"Sit, Dani," Graeson ordered.

Dani pursed her lips, her nose twitching as she glared at him. "You do not command me."

"We all cannot avoid each other forever," Graeson said, his voice surprisingly even. "We have matters to discuss."

She arched an eyebrow. "What matters?"

A smirk pushed at the corner of Graeson's lips. "Such as what we should do about Domitius and those he has been colluding with. And considering you are a general, I had thought you would like to be a part of that discussion."

Dani's hands curled around the back of her chair, her knuckles draining of color. Everything about her stance gave the impression that she wanted to flee, yet Dani hesitated as her gaze flicked from the door to the table.

"And it would behoove any general to point out that *she* is not one of us. Whatever plans we need to discuss should not be done within her earshot," she finally said, pointing directly at Kallie.

"You're letting your feelings blindside you, Dani," Graeson snapped, his hand falling from Kallie's back as he stepped toward the general.

"And you're not? She was fucking raised by Domitius!" Dani shouted, her hand pounding against the table. "Or have you forgotten because you two are--"

"Mind your tongue, Danisinia," Graeson hissed.

Dani cackled and began again, "She--"

But before Dani could say anything else and push Graeson even closer to the edge he was already teetering on, Kallie stepped forward. "*She* is standing right here."

Dani snorted, a sneer curling her lips. "I see you have finally regained your backbone."

Kallie tipped up her chin and squeezed Graeson's arm, gently tugging him back. While she was grateful for his desire to defend her, this was not his battle.

"You are right to be leery of my presence. Domitius did raise me. He taught me almost everything I know. He taught me how to lie and deceive; he gave me the skills to wield a sword; he made me into his perfect weapon. But you are not the only one who wishes to put Domitius in his place once and for all. And with or without you, I will be his undoing."

Dani pursued her lips, and Kallie thought she was still going to leave. Even in their pursuit of vengeance, there would be no common ground between them.

But then Terin spoke for the opposite end of the table, brows drawn together, "Dani."

It was only one word. His tone was not commanding, even though Terin had the authority to demand that Dani sit. He hadn't even begged. But there was something else in his voice, in the unsaid words perhaps, that made Dani unfurl her fingers from the chair and finally sit.

She said nothing, her mouth drawn in a flat line, her ire still swimming on the surface of her irises and spread plainly across her features.

Kallie did not think it was progress, but it was something. A momentary truce, perhaps.

Graeson pulled out a seat and nodded to Kallie. Once she took it, he sat in the chair beside her. He placed his elbows on the table and folded his hands tightly together.

Terin nodded to them, offering them a small smile.

"Domitius has been left unchecked for too long," Graeson said. "We cannot delay any longer. We already know King Rian has fallen ill and Sebastian has taken his place."

"Sebastian is acting as regent?" Kallie asked in surprise.

Graeson looked at her, his attention dropping to her throat. Kallie's hand froze. She hadn't even realized she had placed her hand there. But as Graeson's jaw popped and Kallie recalled Sebastian's hands wrapped around her neck, she could feel his hands burning her skin, her lungs depleting.

Graeson took a deep breath and placed a gentle hand on her thigh. "Yes," he said softly before returning his attention to the rest of the table. "Sebastian is not a man we can dismiss. He's rash and hotheaded."

Kallie nodded beside him, her brows furrowing.

"And he's the one who killed Fynn."

Graeson's words swept across the room, and Kallie peered at Dani from the corner of her eye. The general sat back in her chair, her lips pursed and hands gripping the table's edge as if to steady her.

"He was right there," she whispered. "I could have--" She shook her head as Sylvia lay a hand atop Dani's. But it was as if Dani did not even feel her friend's touch, as if her mind was lost to the past.

Graeson scooted closer to the table. "We must act before it is too late--"

But before Graeson could continue, a loud commotion sounded outside the dining room. Not a second later, Ophelia stormed through the entrance, her gaze quickly flicking across the room.

Her cheeks were flushed as if she had run the entire way to the dining room, and her chest rose rapidly. Wisps of blonde hair had fallen across the warrior's face, but she ignored them as she stepped further into the room.

"Good," Ophelia said, her voice no more than a huff as she tried to regain her breath. "You're all here."

"What is it?" Medenia asked, her hip bumping into the table as she stood. The dishes rattled atop it.

Coming to Medenia's side, Ophelia held out a piece of folded parchment, the wax seal broken. With furrowed brows, Medenia took the letter from her and unfolded it.

"We've received a letter," Ophelia explained. "The queen has already been made aware of it, and I came here right away to deliver it to you all."

"A simple letter has put you in this state?" Emmett asked with an amused snort.

Turning toward Emmett, Ophelia glared at him, her eyes blazing and a sneer curling at her mouth. "Now is not the time for jokes."

"Who is the letter from?" Dani asked hesitantly.

Ophelia glanced at Medenia, who scanned the words. Her eyes darted across the parchment, and her fingers tightened around the letter, crinkling it as the blood rushed from her face.

Ophelia shifted on her feet. "We finally have received a response from Pontia."

Kallie went rigid at the mention of the island. She looked at Graeson, a question she did not dare ask aloud on her lips, but he only offered her a grimace in response as his hand found hers beneath the table.

"And?" Dani pressed, scooting closer to the table.

"She has declined," Ophelia said carefully.

"What do you mean she has *declined*?" Dani spat at the same time as Kallie asked, "Declined what?"

Medenia's gaze was far away when she answered, the letter crumpling in her hand. "Esmeray has declined to declare war against Ardentol. She claims that it is not in the kingdom's best interest and that the people must rebuild first."

The blood drained from Kallie's face as the words settled in her stomach. She had known war was coming. By the gods, she had been on the other side before, forcing the pieces to fall into place by order of Domitius. Yet somehow, the true weight of her actions, of everything she had done, did not settle until she had heard those words.

All around her people moved, words were spat, but Kallie barely heard them as her ears rang.

"Typical," Kallie heard Dani say. "This is the exact bullshit Esmeray preached before we left."

"What else has she said?" someone else--Terin, Kallie thought numbly--asked.

"She has demanded your return home," Medenia said, looking at each of them. "Immediately."

Kallie absently felt Graeson squeeze her hand, but she barely registered it. Her pulse was thumping in her ears, louder and louder.

She wasn't ready.

She wasn't--

"And?" Graeson asked, his voice cutting through the noise of her heart ricocheting beneath her ribcage.

"And that upon your return, you shall face the court on the grounds of possible treason."

Kallie didn't know when she had stood, but her legs shook beneath her as she stared at Medenia, her mouth agape as she struggled to understand what was happening. She jumped as Dani's hands smacked against the table.

"*Treason?*" Dani shouted. "You have got to be kidding."

Kallie heard a noise beside her, but she didn't turn to look. She felt someone's hand brush her own, but she could not take her eyes off the letter that Medenia held out to Dani.

"I am not," Medenia said as Dani took the letter from her. "According to the queen, you all went against her orders, and as a result, a war is on the cusp of breaking out because of your actions."

Before Kallie knew what she was doing, she ran from the room, her heart in her lungs as shouts erupted behind her. But Kallie did not stay to hear what they said, not even when someone called her name.

As the tears ran down her face, she already knew.

CHAPTER 46
GRAESON

Graeson couldn't tear his focus away from Kalisandre's retreating figure. Just as he began to follow her, Dani's sharp voice stopped him in his tracks.

"This is all her fault," Dani spat.

Graeson turned toward her, his hands clenched into tight fists at his sides. "Do not blame Kalisandre for this," he said, rage boiling in his veins.

Dani huffed, shaking her head in disbelief. "All the destruction, all the lives lost over the past few months are *because* of her. We know it, and she knows it. It does us no good to lie about it. A few meals, some trivial conversations, and simple training sessions do not erase the past."

"Dani," Terin growled, his gaze flicking to Graeson as he scooted back his chair. "This is not--"

"Not the time?" Dani asked, fury rising to her face. "It is *never* the time!"

"You cannot put this all on Kallie," Terin snapped, his voice taking on a foreign edge. "You wanted to come here, as well. You wanted your revenge just as much as we wanted to save her. One person is not to blame for the fate of the seven kingdoms!"

"One person can make all the difference, though," Dani countered, her lip curling in disgust. "One *person* can set things into motion. Did you not hear your mother? We are being charged with *treason.*"

"Perhaps we should--" Sylvia carefully started, standing as well, but Dani talked over them as if Sylvia hadn't even spoken at all.

"All it takes is one person to slither their way into your home and take everything you know and love away from you! Hasn't she caused enough harm?" she demanded.

Fury propelled Graeson forward, his feet carrying him around the table toward where Dani stood.

But Dani did not retreat. She did not take back her words. She only dug her heels further into the ground. "Coming to protect your precious little soul bond?" Dani challenged, quirking a brow.

A feral noise vibrated in his throat as the blinding rage of the beast rose even higher. Graeson stepped forward before Ellie pressed a firm hand against his chest, stepping between them. He scowled at her hand, glaring.

She dares stand in our way? the god within roared, furious.

He heard someone--Sylvia, perhaps--whisper, "Soul bond?"

But he ignored her, just as Dani did.

"Does she know yet?" Dani asked, a slight smirk twitching at the corner of her lip. "Based on how she acted when I mentioned soul bonds several weeks ago, my guess is no. She had no idea what they even were." She chuckled darkly. "I wonder how that conversation is going to go."

"You have no right," Graeson roared, his vision blurring with rage as Dani stood at the epicenter.

"No *right?*" Dani retorted as Sylvia shifted beside her. "That's hilarious, Graeson. I wonder what will be more painful: losing a soul bond or being denied by one. I, of course, can only speak for the former, but I have heard the latter is just as painful, if not worse."

As if sensing his anger toppling over, Ellie wrapped her arms around him, holding him back.

"Graeson," Terin beckoned. Graeson didn't know when the prince had gotten up, but now Terin was standing beside him, gripping his shoulder. "Kallie needs you right now."

Graeson felt Terin prod at his mind as if an ice-cold bucket of water had been doused over his head. He took a strained step back, and with a final glare in Dani's direction, he left the room, chasing after Kalisandre.

GRAESON, however, did not get far.

The moment he stepped out of the dining room and turned, Kalisandre was there, her back pressed against the wall. Her cheeks were stained with tears, and her wide eyes were streaked with red.

And as Graeson made to approach her, she held up a shaking hand and croaked, "What did Dani mean?"

"What?" Graeson asked, his brows furrowing together and gut twisting. His breaths were still unsteady, his previous rage slowly dwindling as he stared at Kalisandre, speechless.

She pushed herself off the wall and took a step backward. "She asked you, 'Does she know yet?' Who was she referring to?"

Graeson squeezed his eyes shut and pressed his fingers along the bridge of his nose.

He hadn't known she was still there. He didn't know Kalisandre had heard them. In his rage, he had assumed she was long gone, racing down the hall.

Graeson took a deep breath and opened his eyes. Tears

continued to fall down the contours of her face. This was not how she was supposed to find out.

A small movement near Kalisandre's hands caught his attention. She twisted the ring around her finger, an anxious habit she still had not done away with.

Graeson swallowed and whispered, "I think you already know the answer."

"I want to hear you say it," Kalisandre said, her voice clipped.

Graeson took a step forward, and this time, to his surprise, Kalisandre did not take another step back. She stared up at him, her expression unreadable.

"You," he said firmly but gently. "She was referring to you."

"No," she rasped, shaking her head.

Fear laced Kalisandre's eyes, and it was as if she had stabbed him with a knife and twisted it.

For a moment, Graeson had believed that the monster residing in him didn't matter to her, that it, in fact, only brought them closer. It seemed he was wrong.

Despite what she had told him, she was afraid of him.

He could see the fear written all over her face.

"That's not--that's not possible. I don't--I can't be your soul bond."

"Why not?"

"Because!" Kallie shouted, the sound echoing in the hall, causing Graeson to flinch.

He glanced at the door and knew that the others in the room could all hear them. "Can we talk about this somewhere else?"

"What is there to talk about? I am not yours, Graeson. I refuse to be another man's tool."

"It doesn't--" Graeson shook his head, struggling to find the right words. "It doesn't work like that."

A shadow fell over her features. "Oh, really? Then please explain how a bond that ties our souls together would not tether me to you."

He rubbed his hands across his face.

He didn't know how to explain something that was natural to him. It wasn't that Kalisandre would be tethered to him, but rather that their souls connected on a deeper level. The connection was said to fill a void that lived within.

"When were you going to tell me, Graeson?" Kalisandre asked when he still hadn't formulated a response.

He dug his fingers into his hair, tugging on the strands.

"When it was the right time," he muttered.

She scoffed and threw up her hands. "When is any time the right time? You know what? I can't deal with this right now." Kalisandre spun and without looking back, she spat, "And do not even think about following me."

Graeson jolted to a stop as he made to take a step forward. He stared at her, unsure what to do, as she disappeared down the hall.

A hand landed on his shoulder. "I'll see if I can talk to her," Terin murmured.

Graeson's relationship with Kalisandre was not something Terin could solve. However, before Graeson could argue with him, the prince was already jogging after her.

CHAPTER 47
MYRA

MYRA PACED BACK AND FORTH IN THE CELL, HER HEART POUNDING and palms slick with sweat. Soon, her steps would likely form grooves along the ground as her anxiety rose if she had to wait much longer.

Laurince had said he would see what he could do, but what if he was pulled away? What if he was discovered?

With each passing minute, another worry surfaced. Unable to take it anymore, she pressed her back against the wall and slid down to the floor.

She could only hope that time and the gods were on her side for once.

CHAPTER 48
KALLIE

"THERE IS NOTHING FOR YOU TO EXPLAIN, TERIN! I DO NOT WISH TO speak about this," Kallie snapped, pacing inside her room.

Despite her attempts to ignore him, Terin had followed her, pushing past her before she could lock him out.

"By the gods, you are more like Graeson than you even realize. Neither of you ever wish to speak about your problems. But have you ever thought that maybe if you did, you would have less of them?" he retorted, his frustration evident in the way he repeatedly ran his hands through his hair.

Kallie stared at Terin, her mouth agape. She snapped her mouth shut. "When will we return?" she gritted.

Terin blinked.

"To Pontia," Kallie clarified.

His hands fell to his sides. "I...I do not know. I am sure we will need to return sooner rather than later."

Kallie nodded, her mind reeling as she thought of coming face-to-face with Esmeray again. But Kallie could only deal with one thing at a time.

"And we are just going to let Domitius carry on?" Kallie asked.

"What choice do we have? Our mother is still queen. If she demands our return, who are we to refuse her?"

Kallie scoffed and spun away from him.

"Kallie," he beckoned, but she did not turn around. "Everything will be all right."

It was the biggest lie she had heard all day. Nothing was all right, and she felt helpless to do anything to fix it.

Her eyes darted across the room as she searched for a solution, but she knew she would find no answers there.

Spinning to face her brother, Kallie folded her hands over her chest. "I want to speak to him."

Terin looked to the door and back at her, confusion twisting across his features. "Graeson? I can go get him."

Kallie snatched Terin's arm as he made to leave. "Not Graeson. I want to speak to Fynn."

Terin scratched the back of his head. "Why?" he asked.

She rolled her eyes. "Does there have to be a reason?"

"No, but like I told Dani, speaking to the dead is no way to move forward."

"Terin, your mother is on the verge of charging everyone with treason. I need to speak to someone who will tell me the truth, not just what I wish to hear!" Kallie's hand loosened around his arm, but she did not let go. She couldn't get herself to.

She didn't know if Terin would let her speak to Fynn, but she needed to try.

Terin ground his teeth together, his jaw flexing as he stared at her, debating. He squeezed his eyes shut, wrinkles creasing his forehead.

Kallie knew the moment he had made his decision, for his shoulders relaxed and he released a heavy sigh.

"Fine," he said, giving in. "But this is the last time. The dead need to rest, too."

CHAPTER 49

MYRA

THE HINGES OF THE CELL DOOR GROUND TOGETHER, STIRRING MYRA from her sleep.

She didn't know when she had fallen asleep nor how she could, but none of that mattered now. Although Laurince's helmet was still on, she didn't need to see his face nor hear his voice to recognize whom the emotions filtering into her cell belonged to.

She stumbled to her feet, her legs only slightly trembling once she stood.

"What took you so long?" she hissed as she rushed over.

Myra's brows furrowed as she quickly spotted a smear of blood on his breastplate. She gasped, her hand flying to her mouth. "What happened?"

She began to reach out but thought better of it, dropping her hand.

"I'm fine," Laurince assured her. Then he peered behind him and down the hall. "Move."

She took a step back, and Laurince entered, dragging an unconscious body behind him. Her mouth fell agape as he propped the Frenzian King against one of the cold, stone walls.

Like Laurince, a smattering of blood was spread across his clothes.

"Is he all right?" Myra asked, falling on her knees before the king.

She pressed her palms against his face and swiped away the fallen strands of wine-red hair stuck to his forehead from sweat.

Rian groaned, but his eyes remained closed.

"Yes," Laurince said, and she breathed out in relief. "Though, I can't say the same for the healer."

Myra's eyes widened. "Did you--"

"If you do not want the answer," he said, cutting her off, "do not ask the question."

Myra bit the bottom of her lip but remained silent. He was right; she did not wish to know.

"I hadn't expected the healer to be there, so I did what had to be done, " Laurince said. He rubbed the back of his neck. "Especially when the asshole threatened me with a scalpel and bone saw."

"You didn't have to go alone. I could have helped," Myra said, shifting on her feet uncomfortably.

Eyeing her, Laurence grunted. "It was easier this way."

Myra nodded. While a part of her felt guilty for not helping him, she was also relieved not to have witnessed Dr. Thorne's death. Whether or not the healer deserved it did not matter. Death was still death.

"We need to go now. Domitius is asleep in his room, but if word gets to him--"

"I know the consequences," Myra cut him off, swallowing hard. She straightened, wiping her hands on her tattered blouse. "We need to find my brother first."

Laurence shook his head. "This is our only chance at escaping. We shouldn't risk our own safety. It's going to be hard enough as it is."

Myra stepped forward. She had failed Mynhos once already. She would not fail him again.

"I will not leave him," she said, her voice firmer than she felt.

On the other side of Laurince, Rian murmured something unintelligible, no doubt an effect of whatever drugs Dr. Thorne had pumped through him. He could barely keep himself upright.

Laurince squatted down beside the king. "What was that?"

Rian slapped Laurince in the chest, his nails digging into his shirt.

"What?" Laurince snapped, louder than he probably intended based on the instant regret Myra noted flashing across his features.

Rian tried to right himself, but his body was still too weak. He fell forward, and Laurince caught him.

"Save the boy," Rian said finally, his voice rough.

"But, Rian, we--"

"Save. Him," the king rasped.

The fear and worry wafting off him smacked Myra in the jaw. But Laurince did not need Myra's ability to feel it, for so much pain bled from Rian's green eyes as he fixed his gaze upon the captain that it was impossible to ignore.

Laurince tipped his head to the ceiling, his eyes fluttering shut as he whispered a prayer to the gods.

Then, he shifted, wrapping his arm around Rian and hoisting him up. "Fine. But if I die, I will come back and haunt you, little goddess."

LAURINCE GUIDED them through the dim, grimy dungeons. With each step, Rian groaned and muttered a curse under his breath, his royal vocabulary long since forgotten.

The further they ventured, the colder the corridor became and the thicker the cell doors were. Yet, even the heavy iron could not muffle the low, blood-curling growls seeping through the cracks. Myra and Laurince exchanged uneasy glances as they passed, both too afraid to admit the unsettling truth: the monsters no longer resided only in Frenzia.

An unspoken question hung in the air between them. What exactly was Domitius planning?

She held her breath as they reached one of the two cells Laurince believed Mynhos to be in.

"Are you sure it's this one?" Myra asked with a frown. Something within her gut told her he was wrong, but she didn't know why.

Laurince shifted his arm beneath Rian's shoulder. "No," he admitted. "But it's the best shot we have. I heard another guard talk about how important the prisoner inside was to the king. If it's not your brother, then who else could it be?"

Quickly digging through his pocket, Laurince pulled out a set of keys.

"If it's not him, are you ready to...do whatever it is you do?" he asked uncomfortably.

A chill crept down her back as she searched for the emotions on the other side of the door. All she could feel was an eerie calmness seeping from the room.

Myra straightened and forced her voice steady despite her trembling hands. "I'll do whatever needs to be done," she declared.

Laurince nodded briskly and inserted the key into the lock.

With a resounding click, he pushed the cell door open.

The shadows in the cell retreated as the flickering light from the torch in Myra's hands spilled across the floors, illuminating the prisoner within.

"Right on time."

CHAPTER 50
KALLIE

"I WAS WONDERING WHEN YOU WOULD RETURN, SISTER," FYNN CALLED out, stirring Kallie awake.

Her eyes fluttered open, and the familiar bright blue sky stared down at her in its unnatural beauty. Pressing her palms into the dirt, she pushed herself up. And there Fynn was, sitting upon the same rock as always.

This time, however, one of his legs hung over the edge, sweeping lazily in the air. He wore a coy smirk, the dimple at the corner of his mouth prominent.

He observed her, his gaze quickly sweeping over her. "Congratulations are in order, I believe."

"For what?" Kallie asked, her forehead creasing in confusion.

"For finally being free."

Kallie scoffed and stood, brushing off the sand from her hands. "Am I though?" she asked, the question barely audible, yet somehow Fynn still heard her.

"Is there reason to believe that it didn't work?" he questioned.

Kallie shrugged and looked at Fynn. "Can't you tell me?"

Fynn stared at her, his brown eyes narrowing slightly. "Is this why you wished to speak to me? For reassurance?"

"Perhaps," Kallie mumbled.

Folding his arms over his chest, he clicked his tongue. "Only you can know the true workings of your mind, sister."

Kallie scoffed. "If that was true, wouldn't I have known Myra was manipulating my emotions to begin with?" she hedged.

"Maybe you just did not want to admit it then," Fynn replied with a slight shrug. "I think some part of you always knew something was wrong. If Myra had been truly successful to begin with, she would not have needed to mess with your mind constantly. However, from what I can tell, you fought her. Perhaps you did not know it then, but subconsciously, you were fighting her the entire time." He smiled.

Kallie pursed her lips. "So...what? I just wasn't strong enough on my own?"

"Needing the help of others does not mean you are not strong enough on your own." Fynn sighed and jumped off the rock, his feet landing with a soft thud. "Tell me what is truly bothering you."

Kallie bit the inside of her cheek, then released it. Brushing back her hair, she said, "It seems I might have only exchanged one cage for another."

"How so?" Fynn mused, folding his hands behind his back.

"Where to begin?" She tilted her head up to the sky and laughed, the sound cold. "Ever since we've arrived in Tetria, I've been followed by guards. When the guards are not around, someone else is. I'm always being watched and am rarely left alone besides when I sleep. And trust me, I understand why, but it still does not make the collar around my neck feel any looser." Kallie pressed her palms against her temples. "And now, when I finally feel like I'm becoming comfortable with this new normal, Esmeray sends a letter stating she has grounds to charge everyone with treason."

Fynn dug his hands into his pockets and shrugged. "Well, in her defense, they did not seek her approval before rescuing you."

Kallie dropped her hands from her head and looked at Fynn. "Does that matter when it is my fault to begin with?" she snapped.

Arching a brow, Fynn cocked his head to the side and asked, "How long are you going to take the blame for the wrongdoings of others, Kallie? You were manipulated. You didn't know any better."

Kallie groaned. This was the same conversation she had with so many others already. Yet their response never changed.

"Our mother is not an unreasonable woman. While she often follows the natural order of things, she will come around. Ultimately, all she wants is peace and for the kingdom to be safe."

"And naming Terin a traitor will keep him safe?"

"If it means he will return home, yes. It does," Fynn said, running a hand through his hair. "At least in her mind."

"Do you mean to suggest this is just a rouse to get everyone to return to Pontia?"

Rocking back on his heels, Fynn pursed his lips in thought, then shrugged. "I cannot be certain, but I would not put it past her."

Kallie hummed in acknowledgment. Then, sensing another question coming from him, she asked, "What?"

"Is that all you wish to ask me? What my mother's motivations are?"

She dropped her gaze and dug her toes into the sand. "Did you know?" Kallie asked lowly.

"Did I know what exactly?" Fynn asked with the faintest trace of an amused smile.

Kallie rolled her eyes. "You can read my mind, can't you?"

He half shrugged, the grin only growing. "Sure, but then I wouldn't get to hear you ask, and that ruins the fun."

"By the gods, you are even more tiresome than I recalled," Kallie grumbled.

Fynn simply stared at her, patiently waiting.

But this was one of the reasons she came here, wasn't it? To learn the truth?

She groaned and rubbed her hands across her face in frustration. "Did you know Graeson and I were soul bonds?"

Fynn laughed, the corners of his eyes crinkling. "Yes, sister. We all knew."

"Everyone?" she balked.

He shrugged. "Pretty much."

"Then why didn't he tell me sooner?"

He quirked a brow. "You mean when you just had your mind ripped apart or before that when you were trying to kill him?"

Kallie's lips parted, but she had no answer to give. Fynn had a point. She supposed there hadn't been an appropriate time for Graeson to tell her, yet it still did not sit right with her.

"Graeson has known you were his soul bond since he was a child. His mother had a premonition that only one path would lead you together."

"What do you mean only one path?"

"Our futures are ever changing, and Lysanthia, Graeson's mother, had seen various futures, most of which resulted in the two of you being torn apart, one way or another. Graeson has hung onto the small hope that he could prevent that future from happening. He has known there was always a risk that you would either not accept the bond, or..."

"Or Domitius's hold on me would get in the way?" Kallie guessed.

Fynn nodded in response. "He never gave up on you. However, I understand your hesitancy towards accepting the bond. But if I know Graeson, I know he won't force you to make a decision. He will let you decide when you're ready."

Frowning, Kallie twisted her mother's ring around her finger. "What if I'm never ready?"

A pained expression passed across Fynn's face as he said, "Take as much time as you need, but sometimes, we do not have all the time in the world. I do not regret much, but I do regret not realizing that Dani was my soul bond sooner. Because if I had..." Fynn's words trailed off, grief shadowing his features.

He sighed and raked his fingers through his hair.

"I cannot change my past, and I cannot force you to accept the bond. No one can. But perhaps you shouldn't dismiss it so quickly," he said softly.

WHEN KALLIE AWOKE, Terin had since vanished, perhaps knowing she would need space once she woke up. But as she sat alone with Fynn's words circling in her mind, she was left more confused than before she talked to him.

She thought he would give her the answers she needed, but instead, she was left with only more questions.

As Kallie sat there, her mind spinning, she knew there was only one person who would be able to quiet her tumultuous thoughts.

CHAPTER 51
MYRA

"WHO THE FUCK ARE YOU?" LAURINCE ASKED THE WOMAN CHAINED to the wall.

The woman did not flinch. She only stared at Myra, her dull, gray eyes fixed on her.

"You knew we were coming?" Myra asked.

"I always know," the seer said. Her black hair fell across her face in thick, greasy strands.

"Do you *know* her?" Laurince asked Myra in shock.

"It's...complicated," Myra said to Laurince, recalling the first time she had met the woman. If she stared at the ground long enough, she could almost make out the stain where the guard had cut off Mynhos's hand by order of the king.

Shivering, she returned her attention to the woman. "Do you know where my brother is?" she asked.

The woman chained to the wall nodded. "Close the door. We do not have much time," the seer said, glancing behind them.

Myra stepped forward, but Laurince snatched her wrist, pulling her back.

"What are you doing?" Laurince demanded, his eyes wide. "We don't have time to chat."

"She knows where he is," Myra urged, tugging her arm free from Laurince's grasp. "Stay outside if you wish, but I want answers."

She passed the threshold of the woman's cell. When Myra turned to shut the door, Laurince slapped it away with his hand.

"Fine," Laurince whispered, though his reluctance was apparent as he helped the king inside.

Rian sat against the wall with a groan in relief, and the cell door clicked shut behind them.

"Care to explain now," Laurince demanded.

"I am the very reason you are here," the woman said ominously.

"Excuse me?" Laurince's eyes widened. He reached for his sword.

"She is the reason Domitius knew to take Kallie, the reason I was taken," Myra said. "She has been providing the king with his information."

"So she's a fucking traitor," Laurince hissed, pulling out his sword, the metal sliding against the leather sheath, shattering the silence.

The woman chuckled. "Put the sword away, you fool."

"You're a traitor," Laurince spat.

"Today is not the day I will die," the seer said, unfazed by Laurince's anger

"No? Are you sure about that," Laurince challenged. He made to step forward, but before he could, Myra placed her hand atop his.

With a sneer, Laurince met her gaze. Myra felt for the invisible strings connecting to his emotions, but she didn't pull or transform them.

She waited.

After a moment that seemed to span time, Laurince's hand

finally relaxed beneath hers. Although a deep-rooted wariness still sparkled in his eyes, he sheathed his sword.

He turned to the seer. "You have one minute to explain."

"Hush," she hissed, holding up a finger to her lips, her chains rattling.

"What--" Laurince began before Myra shushed him, too.

Loud footsteps sounded down the hall, rushing past the cell.

Laurince straightened, and Myra could sense the panic rising within him as he realized how close they had been to being seen.

When the sound of the boots disappeared, Laurince turned to the woman. But before he could ask her the question that was no doubt sitting on his tongue, the seer spoke, "Do not fret. They do not know that the handmaiden and the king have slipped free from their cells. The beasts held captive deeper in the dungeon have grown increasingly restless and will serve as a distraction for the time you require to escape."

"The beasts? What beasts?" Laurince pressed.

"The king has been raising an army thanks to the woman standing beside you."

Myra straightened as everyone turned to her, but she had no defense to offer. She knew what she had done, but it wasn't until now that she felt the true weight of those actions.

"Do not blame yourself, child. You had no choice. If you hadn't assisted, he would have found another way," the woman said, calling their attention back to her. "Kage always does."

"Who is Kage?" Laurince asked, confused.

The woman released a heavy sigh, a strand of hair fluttering in front of her face. "King Domitius. His first name is one that he wishes to wipe from existence, though our past has a way of following us no matter how much we try to escape it." The woman shifted, her chains rattling slightly. "But it is not names you wish to discuss. Unfortunately, the answer you seek is not the one you wish to gain."

"What do you mean?" Myra asked, stepping further into the room.

"The boy is out of reach," the seer said with a flick of her wrist.

Myra gasped. "My brother is gone?"

The woman cocked her head to the side, her eyes narrowing slightly and growing unfocused. Then, she straightened. "In a manner of speaking, yes."

"Where?" Myra asked, rushing forward and falling to her knees before the seer. She snatched the woman's hands as panic rose in her throat. The seer's fingers were frail in her palms, and Myra quickly softened her hold on them, afraid of breaking them.

"Where is he?" she demanded.

The seer shook her head. "It does not matter where he is, for his mind is the thing that is truly gone."

"What? What are you saying?" Myra demanded. "He's alive. He's--"

"Gone, my dear," the seer interrupted. Pity soaked her countenance. "He's been gone far longer than you think. If you would only open your eyes and let yourself see, you would know this already."

"Speak sense!" Myra shouted.

She faintly heard Laurince hiss her name, begging her to be quiet, but Myra did not care. She needed to know where Mynhos was.

"The king promised to keep him alive if I did what he asked," Myra said.

"Being alive and *living* are two different things," the seer replied, her voice sounding far away. "You were not the only gift Kage received that fateful day your parents died."

"What are you saying?"

The seer offered a sad smile, one that struck Myra in the chest. "Kage does not keep people alive for no reason."

"What are you talking about? This has nothing to do with--"

Myra's words were cut off, though, as the seer gripped her hand with surprising strength, a look of horror brandishing her eyes nearly stripped of their gray hue.

"He kept you alive because you served a purpose," the woman hissed. "For years, you have kept the princess loyal to him. But why is your brother still alive? *That* is the question you should be asking."

"What is she talking about?" Laurince asked, still standing near the door. "We did not come here for this."

Myra shook her head and ignored Laurince, her attention solely on the seer. "I--I don't know. He never had a gift. He was just a boy."

"There is always a reason for why he takes someone. He took Kalisandre because of her gift of manipulation in the hopes of weaponizing her. He took me to guide him down the path. But why did he seek out your family?" the seer demanded.

"He took us because of me," Myra said firmly. "He used me to manipulate Kallie. I...I already know this."

The woman shook her head. "No, my dear. You were only a bonus gift."

I was going to just take the one child, but I suppose I can make use of both.

The king's voice sifted into her mind, the words he spoke before he killed her parents. Myra had given those words little thought over the years, but now she couldn't help but wonder if she had been wrong to ignore them.

Myra's brows drew together. "But my brother is giftless. He's just a normal human."

"No one is normal. Everyone serves a purpose in this world, and your brother is more powerful than you think."

Myra didn't understand. Her brother did not have a gift. But if what the seer said was true...

Myra scooted closer, her knees scraping against the grime on the floor. "We have to save him! You have to tell us where he is! We have to make sure the king cannot use him too."

"Myra," Laurince warned.

Time was ticking, yet Myra would not leave until she got her answers.

She shook her head, tears burning the back of her eyes. "We can't. Not until she tells us where he is," she pleaded.

"He is gone. I have told you this. Listen to the guard. You must not waste your time, for you will not find him within a cell. You will see him, but you will not be able to reach him," the seer said.

Tears began to fall. Myra would not leave without Mynhos. She made him a promise.

"I have to try at least," Myra whispered, her entire body trembling.

"Try you will, but you will fail. The king has had his claws in him for far too long. Not even your gift can free him."

"But--"

"You and your brother are not the same," the seer said with a shake of her head. "Your brother has already been made into a weapon."

"He cannot just keep my brother! I made a promise," she cried.

"Some promises are not meant to be kept." The seer wrapped her fingers around Myra's hand, pulling Mrya closer. Her words grew harsher, sharper, the previously gentle tone gone. "If you do not grab the blade, you all will die."

"Blade? What blade?" Myra asked, voice panicked as her gaze flitted across the woman's face.

The woman dropped Myra's hands and sunk back against the

wall. "That is all I can say. If I say more, the future will shift, and there is no telling the outcome if that happens."

Tears laced the bottom of Myra's eyes, threatening to spill over.

"Go now," the seer ordered. "Do not go searching the dungeons. You will not find anything but death there."

Myra stared at the seer, and her vision began to blur. "Come with us," Myra begged.

The seer shook her head.

"But you've been helping him! You've been telling him the future."

The woman smiled, but it did not reach her eyes. "The future is not something he can control. The future is constantly moving, shifting. To many, knowing what is to come is seen as a gift, a blessing even. People view it as a way to prevent the inevitable. But in truth, it is a curse. I am too weak. I haven't left this castle for over twenty years. If you take me, I will slow you down. The captain is strong but not strong enough to carry more than the king."

"Myra," Laurince said from behind her, "she's right. We need to go."

Myra looked over her shoulder at Laurince hovering inside the door. He was already picking Rian back up, preparing to move. But Myra remained seated in front of the seer.

"You will need to move fast. You cannot do that with me," the seer explained, her expression neutral.

"But we can't just leave you here," Myra said, unwilling to face the truth.

"I can do more here than I can if I leave. If things follow fate's path, we may see each other again. Leave now," the seer commanded, her eyes a sea of emotions that Myra could barely begin to parse. "Leave so that hope lives on."

Myra's lips parted, another protest forming, but the woman shook her head, the chains around her neck rattling.

Myra's shoulders dropped, guilt already filling her body and dragging her down as she was forced to face the woman's dreaded fate.

Even if they wanted to take her, the woman was chained to the wall, and Myra had a strange feeling that the keys Laurince had procured did not include the key to the seer. The king would not have been so foolish as to let someone other than himself hold onto the key that kept the future captive.

The seer offered her a small smile as if she knew Myra was finally realizing the truth. The corner of her lip twitched, and her eyes glistened with acceptance of her fate.

"You can do me one favor, though," she whispered.

"Anything," Myra said, scooting closer.

The woman smiled softly. "Tell my son I love him. Tell him he shouldn't fear his true self. He must embrace it."

Laurince had reached for Myra and was pulling her up by the elbow. "We have to go now."

But Myra wasn't done. She fought him, pulling away. "But who's your son?"

Her lips moved, her voice not even a whisper as Laurince dragged Myra out of the cell room. But Myra heard the name as if she had screamed it.

CHAPTER 52
KALLIE

KALLIE'S HAND FROZE AN INCH FROM THE DOOR. IT WAS NEARLY midnight, yet she had stormed down the halls of the castle with little care about waking up anyone who might be sleeping. However, the second she stepped in front of the door and lifted her fist to knock, the determination with which she had strutted through the halls vanished.

What *was* she doing? Did she truly think that--

The door flew open, and Graeson's eyes widened as he spotted her.

Her hand dropped to her side.

"Kalisandre," he said with a gasp. "What are you...what are you doing here?"

Kallie should have turned around when she had the chance, but now that he was here, standing in front of her, Kallie couldn't get herself to move. Her breathing was unsteady, her chest noticeably rising as she bit her bottom lip.

"Is there something I can help you with?" Graeson asked when she still had not answered.

Kallie swallowed, looking past him into his room and tugging the silk robe tighter across her body. "Can I come in?"

"Uhm." Graeson looked over his shoulder, his fingers tapping along the doorframe.

As Graeson hesitated, Kallie she questioned why she had come. She felt so silly for storming over here. What had she expected? She had practically run away from him only hours ago, so why would he open his door to her?

Kallie took a step backward, curling a loose strand of hair behind her ear. "I'm sorry," she mumbled. "It's late. You were probably heading somewhere."

"What?" Graeson asked, blinking down at her as if he hadn't quite heard her.

Kallie tilted her head and pointed. "You opened before I knocked. I'm sure there was somewhere--"

"No," Graeson said, interrupting her.

Her eyes widened. "No?"

"I wasn't going anywhere."

"Then why did you open the door?"

"I..." Graeson began but quickly stopped, his gaze roving over her features. His hand dropped from the door frame, then he stepped back and gestured for her to enter. "Please, come in."

With a tight smile and a knot in her stomach, Kallie headed inside before she could sprint down the hall.

As the door clicked shut behind them, Kallie scanned his guest room. While she knew it wasn't truly his, she could see his presence everywhere she looked.

His jacket was thrown over the back of the chair in a corner. The blankets on the bed were tossed across the bed, and there was an indent on the right side where he must have been laying moments before. A blush began to creep across her cheeks as she imagined him lying in bed, staring at the ceiling.

She quickly averted her gaze and stepped toward the desk where his scimitars lay across the table, unsheathed and gleaming in the moonlight. A whetstone sat beside them.

As she ran a finger across the freshly sharpened blade, she whispered, "They're beautiful weapons."

"Thank you. Dani's brother, Xander, made them for me years ago."

"He is very talented. They almost remind me of my own dagger," Kallie said as she inspected the intricate design carved within the metal. Her brows twisted together. "Do you know where--"

Kallie didn't have to finish the question, however, because when she turned, Graeson was already holding her dagger out, hilt toward her.

"You've had it this entire time?" she breathed in surprise.

Graeson shrugged. "I knew you'd come looking for it at some point."

Kallie took the ornate dagger from him and flipped it in her hands. The ancient script on the blade stared back at her. "It's ironic," Kallie mused as she read the words scrawled on the metal.

"What is?" he asked, leaning closer to look at the dagger.

"It says, 'You are the holder of your own fate.' Myra had worked with the blacksmith back in Ardentol to craft this. She had him write these words on the blade for me, yet she was the one who was controlling my fate the entire time."

He frowned slightly. "She may have played a role, but she was never in control of it. You broke free, did you not?"

Fynn had said something similar when she visited him. While she still found herself to be in a cage, perhaps she didn't have to exist in one forever if she didn't wish to.

Kallie ran her finger across the words, the grooves rough beneath her skin. She grabbed the blade by the hilt. The wrapping was perfectly formed for her hand.

"I suppose," she said at last.

"Did you come here only on the off chance I had your dagger?" Graeson asked, pulling her attention back to him.

She adjusted her grip on the hilt, her fingers flexing over it. When his gaze flicked to it, she set it down on the table beside his scimitars. "No, I did not."

Graeson cocked his head. "Then why did you come here, Kalisandre?"

"I am still trying to figure that out," Kallie said as she leaned her hip against the table, placing her palms flat atop it. "All I know is that when I'm with you, things are less loud. For once, it feels like I can breathe. I do not know if that is because we are soul bonds or not."

Kallie quickly held up a hand the moment a flicker of hope coated his gray eyes.

"I do not know if I even want to be soul bonds," she hurried to say.

"Then what do you wish to speak about?" Graeson asked, his expression falling once more.

Kallie took a step closer to him. "I do not want to speak at all."

"Then what do you want?"

For the first time since she walked into his room, Kallie finally let herself truly observe Graeson. He wore a pair of simple black trousers that hung low on his hips. His cotton shirt was half-untucked as if he had tossed it on before opening the door. His black hair was a little more unkempt than usual, like he had been running his fingers through it nonstop, tugging on the ends as his mind stewed. The scar that ran across the left side of his face was even more visible than normal as a result.

Tonight, there was a wildness to him that intrigued her more than she probably cared to admit aloud.

For her entire life, she had been told every strand of hair had to be perfectly in place and every wrinkle flattened. But Graeson never seemed to care about that.

While Kallie did not know what he was to her, she certainly could not deny that she was attracted to him. She always had been.

"I want to feel as if the world does not exist for at least one moment. I want..." Kallie swallowed, the words getting stuck in her throat.

"Yes?" Graeson prompted, his fingers curling around the back of the chair that sat between them, almost as if it was some sort of shield. But Kallie didn't know if it was a shield protecting him or one meant to protect her.

She took a deep breath as her heart thumped louder and louder.

"I want to feel like I have some choice in what happens next. I want to forget the rest of the world for just one night." Kallie stepped closer and placed her hand atop his, the chair still separating them. "Can you make me forget?"

She could sense Graeson debating as he processed what she was truly asking him. The bump in his throat dipped, and she felt his fingers tighten around the chair.

Kallie had to give it to him, his restraint was admirable.

He was trying to do the right thing--the respectful thing.

"You've been through a lot today," he said, voice thick. "We shouldn't--"

Her fingers danced atop his hand. "I have told you once before: you do not get to tell me what I should or shouldn't do."

Graeson arched a brow, concern filling his expression. "This is a dangerous game, Kalisandre. Terin told me you have yet to use your gift since you awoke. Your emotions--"

"My emotions are *fine*," Kallie interrupted. "They are messy, but they're my *own*, and that is all that matters to me right now."

For over half of her life, Kallie's emotions had been twisted and manipulated. When she woke up after Cetia and Ellie had ripped her mind apart, she could still feel the remnants of Myra's manipulations, as if the fabric of her mind was still being unwound.

And then afterward, she had been dull, empty, and lifeless.

But whenever she was with Graeson, she *felt*. She couldn't quite identify what the exact feelings she experienced were, but she realized she no longer cared.

Graeson didn't look at her as if she had destroyed the world.

He never retreated out of fear of what she would or wouldn't do.

And maybe she should have been more concerned that she hadn't used her gift yet, that she still feared it. However, it was one of the many things that she did not wish to think about right now.

She had once despised the fact that she couldn't accidentally manipulate him. But now, she was seeing it for the gift it could be because she did not wish to muddy whatever she and Graeson had.

With Graeson, everything was *real*. With him, she didn't have to question whether she had forced him to look at her with those searing eyes. She did not have to question what he wanted from her or why. He had never been after her power or her title.

Kallie did not care that their past, present, and future were messy. It was theirs and it was real. It was not something she had conjured up or manipulated into existence.

"Graeson, if you do not want this," Kallie said, taking another step forward, "if I have misread your feelings toward me, then tell me."

She looked past his shoulder toward the entrance to his room. When she lifted her hand as she made to point toward the door, Graeson snatched her wrist. He stepped around the chair and closer to her.

"You have not misread anything, Kalisandre," Graeson said, his silver eyes darkening.

"But?" she breathed.

The corner of his lip twitched, and he drew circles along the inside of her wrist with his thumb. The small movement sent a spiral of chills running up her arm. "*But* we haven't even talked about what this is between us."

"It doesn't have to be anything," she whispered, her free hand falling onto his chest and crawling up to the base of his collar.

"But do you want it to be?" Graeson asked, his eyes searching her face for an answer she did not have.

Only a couple of months ago, she had been standing in the Frenzian temple about to marry a man she barely knew. And while Kallie felt like she *knew* Graeson, she did not wish to be tied down. She did not wish to be paraded around at another man's side.

Kallie had just gained her freedom; a freedom that may or may be taken away once they arrived in Pontia. But she still wasn't willing to give that up.

Even if she didn't think Graeson was like the others.

He lifted a hand to her face, and with his knuckles, he gently brushed the side of her cheek. Without intending to, Kallie leaned into the soft touch. She closed her eyes and inhaled.

This. This was what she wanted.

To forget and get lost in something other than her own mind.

She loosened the knot securing her robe, letting it fall open and revealing the short, silk slip underneath.

His gaze dipped down, his eyes catching on the thin ribbon of black lace on the top hem. He swallowed, hard.

"I do not know if I can only give a piece of myself to you, Kalisandre."

Kallie dug her fingers into the hair at the back of his neck. "Please, Graeson."

He placed his hands on either side of her face, his thumbs running across her cheeks. Back and forth, back and forth. His gaze was heavy, and his eyes bounced between hers.

Then, sighing, he pressed his forehead against hers and whispered, "You never need to beg me."

He stepped closer, his chest against hers. Until finally, he gave her what she wanted.

He kissed her.

At first, his touch was soft, a mere whisper. A gentle embrace as if he did not trust himself, as if he still questioned whether he should be giving in to her pleas.

But Kallie had never been more sure of anything. Because for the first time in a long time, Kallie was not thinking about the strife between the kingdoms or the lies she had been fed her entire life. She didn't think about what was going to happen to her when they inevitably arrived in Pontia. Nor did she think about the ramifications that would come from this night.

All she could think about was how intoxicating Graeson's presence was. How everywhere he touched, an untamable fire followed in its wake that only urged her to step closer.

She let the robe fall to the floor in a puddle. She gripped the back of his head, pressing his lips closer to hers.

She felt the ground disappear beneath her feet, but she didn't check to confirm because she trusted him not to drop her. She tightened her legs around Graeson's waist and kissed him as if this would be her last chance to do so.

Kallie didn't just want this, she *needed* this. She needed *him*.

Her back hit the bed, her body jostling as she bounced slightly atop the mattress.

When she looked up at Graeson standing before her, the flame of the candle sitting on his nightstand cast dancing shadows across his face. She could see the monster within peering out from whatever cage Graeson kept him locked up in.

But Kallie did not want him to be gentle. She did not want him to be kind.

She wanted everything he was--monster and all.

"I need you, Graeson," she whispered.

The moment she uttered those four words, it was as if a spark had been ignited. His gray eyes brightened, becoming luminescent in the dim room. His knees sunk into the bed, and he crawled toward her.

Kallie swallowed as he hovered above her. His features were masked in shadows, yet his eyes still glowed, like a beacon in the darkness.

He shifted his weight onto one arm and tucked a loose strand of hair away from her face. His hand moved to the nape of her neck, and his fingers dug into her hair, his touch strong yet tender.

"Mine," he whispered, his voice husky and low. His eyes widened almost immediately, and Kallie wondered if he had meant to say it aloud.

Tugging his head down to hers, she whispered against his lips, "I am no one's." And though she said the words aloud, they felt like they were a lie, at least in part.

A laugh escaped Graeson's lips, and it made Kallie's stomach flip, heat rising through her body.

"Right now, Kalisandre, you are mine."

"Oh?" Kallie mumbled. She tried to hide the smirk twitching at her lips, but she knew she had failed when his attention immediately flicked to it.

Graeson brushed his knuckles down the side of her neck and over her collarbone. As his fingers skimmed over the tops of her breasts, a trail of goosebumps followed in his wake.

Kallie pressed her head against the pillow, squeezing her eyes shut. As he palmed her breast, she had the passing thought that maybe being his, at least for tonight, wouldn't be so bad.

Then, his hand disappeared, and she had to swallow her protest.

He tipped her chin up. "Look at me, Kalisandre."

Her eyes snapped open at his command, and a devilish smile crept across his face. He ran a finger over her already swollen lips.

"By the end of the night, I'll have you begging to be mine, little mouse."

As Graeson looked down at her, his hair falling around his face, a stark contrast to the silver hue of his eyes, Kallie knew he meant it.

Then he sunk lower, his eyes remaining on her as he kissed the top of her breast. He tugged the silk dress down, freeing her. When his mouth wrapped around her hard nipple, her eyes almost fluttered shut. Somehow, however, she managed to keep them open, as if there was a magnetic pull forcing her to hold his gaze.

Heat blossomed in her core, and she dug her fingers into the pillow behind her head. She shifted, the heat becoming too much as his teeth scraped against her sensitive skin.

Graeson released her, but his torment wasn't over, far from it. He gently blew on her wet skin, the cool air causing her to gasp and squirm as it tickled her breast.

"Tell me what you want, Kal," he whispered. "Command me."

Her heart raced as she peered down at him, her mind spinning. Not only did Kallie not wish to use her gift, she couldn't, not on him. Not on anyone.

"I can't," she said, her words barely audible.

Raising a brow, he ran his finger down her sternum and over her hips. His finger trailed down her body, and she wished the silk fabric wasn't between them, as thin as it might have been.

"You're more capable than you think, little mouse. Now, tell me," he said, his voice low. "If you could command me, what would you wish me to do?"

He stopped his exploration, his hand wrapping around her hip, patiently waiting for her command. And Kallie knew without a doubt that he would wait forever if she made him.

"Touch me," she pleaded finally.

"Where?"

Kallie groaned, shifting in frustration as his fingers languidly moved over the curve of her hip.

"Show me, Kalisandre," he said, tapping his fingers along her hip bone.

With flushed cheeks, she slowly moved. Her hand landed atop his, and she pushed his hand down, stopping right below her belly. Her dress had risen when he had picked her up and tossed her on the bed. Now, it sat dangerously high on her thigh. Still, the thin fabric was too much.

"Here," she whispered. "Touch me here."

"See? That wasn't so hard, now was it?" Graeson smiled at her, and an insatiable hunger lit his eyes, sending a delicious shiver running down her spine.

Kallie shook her head shyly, a grin pushing at the corners of her lips.

"I have this theory," he said, trailing a finger across her skin teasingly.

"Oh?" Kallie said, unable to form a coherent sentence.

"Mhm," Graeson hummed, his hands dipping lower. His fingers danced across her inner thigh, so close yet so far. "I believe that our gifts are often a reflection of what we desire the most. Take you, for instance; you can manipulate minds because you like to be in control--you *crave* it. But have you ever let someone else be in control when it comes to fulfilling your needs?"

Kallie bit her lip and shook her head.

"That's what I thought." He smiled wider, and Kallie could have melted because of it. "Remember, keep your eyes on me."

His hands wrapped beneath her legs, and he tossed her legs over his shoulder. A small yelp escaped her lips as he tugged her toward him in one smooth, fluid movement.

Then, Graeson devoured her, completely and utterly, as if he was a man starved.

She had said that she was no man's to claim. But as he lapped at her center and forced her back to arch, she could do nothing but moan his name aloud.

Control was her vice, and Graeson was her savior.

She had waited for years for someone who would take control, but her gift had prevented her from finding them. Whenever she needed something before, all Kallie had to do was command it. But she couldn't command Graeson.

She couldn't make him touch her in the ways she wanted.

She couldn't make him give her what she wanted.

She was entirely at his mercy.

And there was some relief in not having to dictate every move someone made. Not that he even needed her to as he drove her closer and closer to the edge with his tongue.

Graeson needed no direction because he could read her reactions, even the smallest ones, without her explaining them. Like he always had been able to do.

So Kallie did not care to fight him as her control was relinquished from her. As his every touch, every lick, every bite, set her entire body aflame.

She let him wipe her concerns and worries away. She didn't think about what tomorrow would bring. She let Graeson erase the entire world for her. Because at that moment, there was only him and her.

As his tongue danced across her sensitive skin, her fingers dug into his hair. Her hips bucked, needing more of him, craving more. As he eagerly answered her plea, Kallie knew it was too much yet not nearly enough all at once.

His fingers pressed against her thighs. He hummed, and the vibration sent a wave of sensation crawling up her body. Her toes curled, and her head slammed into the pillow despite his command to watch him.

Kallie was rendered helpless as he brought her over the edge. And with him, she gladly jumped over it.

She didn't care how loud she was as she screamed out in pleasure. Nor did she care that it was Graeson's name on her lips. Nor that it felt as if she was staking a claim she did not deserve.

She cared about none of the consequences that awaited her as her vision blurred and a myriad of stars danced across the ceiling, twirling and spinning.

All she cared about was the satisfied grin on his face when he lifted his head and said, "*That* is how a goddess should be worshiped."

CHAPTER 53
MYRA

"Who was that woman?" Laurince asked in a hushed tone as they hurried through the dungeon as fast as they could.

"A seer," Myra said, swallowing down the tears that threatened to spill.

"A *what*?" he sputtered.

"She can see bits of the future."

"How is that even possible?" Laurince hissed.

"Come on. We have to hurry, right?" Myra asked, unable to offer him a sufficient explanation that he would be able to understand. If they escaped this godsforsaken castle alive, she would explain everything.

With every step, Rian moaned in agony, but he was still unable to walk without at least Laurince or Myra's help. So when they hit the stairs, they ascended the steps much slower than either of them wanted.

"You know, you could be a little"--Laurince grunted as he lifted Rian--"more helpful."

"Sorry," the king mumbled as he held onto the iron railing with a white-knuckled grip.

When they finally reached the top of the steps, Laurince looked over at Myra. "Keep him steady, all right? I really do not want to do that again if he goes tumbling."

Myra nodded and wrapped an arm tightly around the king as Laurince pressed an ear to the door. Rian leaned against her, groaning in pain, and Myra prayed to the gods that the medicine would soon wear off.

Laurince twisted the handle and pushed the door open an inch, peering through the crack. Then, glancing at Myra and holding up a hand, he stepped out and shut the door behind him.

As Myra and Rian waited, a thick silence filled the space. The only noise that cut through was their ragged breaths.

The seer's words echoed in her mind.

Gone.

Gone.

Gone.

But how could her brother be gone?

The woman didn't say he was dead, but the way she spoke and the haunted look in her eyes made Myra worry that whatever happened to Mynhos was much worse.

She only had herself to blame.

She had believed King Domitius when she knew she shouldn't have. Why did she think that Mynhos was safe from him?

The seer told her not to go looking for him, but was her brother truly better off here?

Myra looked down the stairway soaked in shadows.

Perhaps she could help him. She had seen the creatures within the tunnels beneath the temple. They were feral and wild, but maybe her brother could still be saved. Surely, there was something she could do...

"Everything will be fine," Myra whispered.

"Are you telling me that or yourself?" Rian asked, looking down at her with a raised brow.

Even in the shadows, Myra noted how his brown skin was pale with a slightly green hue and red veins were stretched across the whites of his eyes.

Myra knew she should lie to the king. She knew she should keep a smile on her face and pretend that everything would be okay. But as the minutes ticked by, she was losing the little hope she had left.

Pretending hadn't helped Kallie. Not in the end, anyway.

"Both," Myra admitted.

As Rian's lips parted, the door was thrust open. "Let's move," Laurince whispered.

In the castle's silence, their footsteps were thunderous claps that echoed off the marble walls and tall ceilings.

They just had to get out of the castle, Myra reminded herself. Laurince had already prepared horses for them. They only had to make it to them.

Myra didn't want to think about where they would go next. They hadn't discussed it in detail, but she did not believe Frenzia was the safest place to go despite Rian being the king. With Sebastian working with Domitius, neither Ardentol nor Frenzia would be safe.

They would have to leave their homes, leave everything they knew.

But what choice did they have--

"Leaving me again, sister?"

Myra skirted to a halt, forcing Laurince and Rian to stumble as she pulled them with her. Her lungs dropped to her stomach as she turned and looked to where she had heard the voice.

Sitting on the arm of the throne, Mynhos peered down at her.

Shadows blanketed him as he picked at his teeth, his legs dangling off the large, extravagant chair.

"Mynhos," Myra said, her voice cracking, "we...we looked for you."

"Did you?" Mynhos asked, cocking his head. Shadows moved behind him, but they stilled before she could register them.

"Myra," Laurince said, reaching for her as she took a hesitant step toward the throne.

She shrugged off his hand and pleaded, ignoring the warning in Laurince's voice. "Come with us, Mynhos."

"*Now* you wish to rescue me? After all these years?" Mynhos asked, his voice growing colder by the second. "You have lived inside this castle for nine years, yet you never tried to find me."

"I didn't...I didn't want to make things worse," Myra whispered, her voice shaking.

"But you didn't even try, did you?" he taunted.

Myra was silent, the guilt strangling her.

"You grew complacent, content to do His Majesty's bidding as long you remained alive."

Laurince shifted closer, the command on his lips.

The seer was wrong. Mynhos was not gone. He was right here, and Myra would not leave her brother. Not again.

"Mynhos, please," she begged, reaching out a hand. "We can finally leave this place."

The back of Myra's neck grew cold as her brother stood atop the arm of the throne, balancing precariously on it. "You actually think you can leave?" her brother asked. He laughed, the sound echoing in the large throne room. "You can never leave. You will never escape him, and if you believe you can, you are more foolish than I thought."

"Something's not right," Laurince whispered, but Myra barely registered his words, her attention too focused on Mynhos. "Myra," he beckoned, this time more urgently.

But Myra shook her head. "He's been under the king's influence for too long. He just needs to be shown there is a way out."

She reached for the threads connecting to her brother. She grabbed a hold of them, the anger and fury scorching. But she would not give up on him.

Her little brother was in there somewhere. He had to be.

"A way out?" Mynhos cackled, the sound a cacophony of noise that scraped against Myra's skin as it ricocheted off the walls. "You've always been the hopeful one, sister. Ever since we were little kids. But hope gets you nowhere. Hope only forces you to claw at the cage, waiting for someone to rescue you. I had hoped you would save me once upon a time."

With a huff, he shook his head. "But guess what? You never came. I waited for you. *For years*, I waited for you. During that time, I was poked and prodded. And soon, as the pain became blinding and all-consuming, I realized you would never come for me."

"Mynhos, please," Myra begged, the tears burning the backs of her eyes.

"I did what I needed to do to save myself. And honestly, once I stopped fighting it, I finally felt free." He smiled.

Myra stepped forward, and Rian's hand wrapped around her wrist. Without looking at it, she shook it off. "Whatever has happened, whatever you have done, it will be fine. We will get through this together."

"Oh, I know it will be fine. I've made sure of that," Mynhos said.

"Mynhos?" Myra called to her brother just as Laurince said her name. She continued to ignore him. She tried to tame the rage, but it was a torrent, fueled by so much hate. "Please, come with us."

Mynhos chuckled. "Your gift always failed you when you needed it the most, didn't it?"

He jumped down from the throne, and Myra gasped, jolting back a step. His blond hair was long and shaggy. The strands fell over his eyes, which were cast to the ground. He lifted a hand--

"Your hand!" Myra shrieked. "I thought..."

Mynhos twisted the hand in the air as he chuckled. "Oh, right. I nearly forgot that it had been chopped off. It has healed quite magnificently."

"How is that even possible?" Myra gasped, more to herself than her brother or anyone else.

She had witnessed the guard chop off Mynhos's hand in that cell. Those screams that erupted from his lungs echoed in her nightmares every night. She had seen the blood. And yet...

Myra stepped backward, horror flooding her entire body as she looked up at her brother. "That's--that's not possible," Myra said, her voice shaking.

He clicked his tongue. "You never did pay attention to anyone but yourself, did you? Always too caught up in the emotions of the world to see what was happening directly in front of you."

"What are you talking about?" Myra demanded. Out of the corner of her eye, she saw Laurince maneuvering slowly toward the door, dragging Rian with him.

"You are not that special, Myra. The king didn't want *you*. By the gods, he didn't even know you bore a gift! You were merely a bonus prize that fell into his lap, a helpful tool to manipulate the princess and increase his progress." Mynhos huffed a laugh. "*I* was the true prize. And now because of me, he is one step closer to his goal."

Myra's lips parted, her breathing growing shallow, yet she forced herself to ask, "What did you do?"

"Myra," Laurince whispered, his voice taking on a sharp edge, "we really need to--"

"Oh, you're not going anywhere," Mynhos interrupted, clicking his tongue against the roof of his mouth, tsking as he shook his head. "You should have never betrayed our king. You could have joined me. We could have been at his side together. The king rewards loyalty, and he has rewarded me well."

Mynhos took a step away from the shadows, allowing the light of the flames to pour down upon him.

Laurince called her name, but Myra was frozen to the ground as her brother lifted his head and removed his shirt. But it was his eyes that Myra was paralyzed by.

Once, the two siblings shared their mother's soft, hazel eyes. But now? Now, the softness in Mynhos's was long gone, replaced with something monstrous and cold as his irises glowed as bright and red as rubies, the flames of the torches dancing within them.

Myra didn't realize what was happening until her brother was in front of her, and a gust of wind struck her face. Myra fell back onto her hands as her brother hovered above her, a sneer plastered across his lips as he glared at her.

"What the fuck are those!" Laurince shouted as he placed the king behind him.

Myra was too struck to move or do anything as she spotted large wings protruding from Mynhos's back. She couldn't understand what she was seeing. Her brother had become one of *them*--the rabid creatures from the tunnels under the temple.

This was what they were working toward.

This was what *she* had helped the king create.

"You like them?" Mynhos asked, a hunger filling his gaze. "They're new, courtesy of Frenzia. You should see some of the other men you have assisted the true king with. Some of them are truly impeccable. Though, I am partial to mine, of course."

"Oh, fuck no," Laurince spat.

The sound of metal sliding through its sheath rang in Myra's ear, but she was unable to look at Laurince as her brother continued hovering over her, his head cocking to the side as his wings flapped. The air coming off them kept her plastered to the ground, her hair flying across her face.

He clicked his tongue. "The king should have taken the chance to harvest more of your gift when he had the chance. But of course, he thought he had more time, and who am I to question His Majesty?"

Myra gasped as she recalled those first few weeks in cells. The guards had often taken her blood, claiming to be checking her vitals. How had she not realized it before? How had she been so naive?

Seeing the realization and horror flood her expression, Mynhos smiled wider, the stretch of his mouth twisting Myra's stomach as an eagerness poured from him.

She was going to be sick.

She was going to--

Mynhos screamed and spun around in a flurry. He ripped a throwing knife from his side with a long hiss. As blood seeped from the open wound, he spat, "You're going to regret that."

"Doubt it," Laurince retorted, already lifting his sword high.

Her brother tossed the blade to the side, and it hit the floor with a sharp clang. Then, Mynhos charged.

But Laurince was ready. The moment Mynhos closed in, the captain swiftly swung his weapon, and Myra could barely keep up with them as fear overrode her body.

Mynhos deftly evaded Laurince's attack, his wings beating hard as he changed course. With a roar, he lunged, but Laurince managed to dodge the blow, narrowly escaping as he rolled.

The near miss jolted Myra out of her stupor at last.

She ran to Rian, who was pressing himself up to a sitting position, his eyes fluttering open. Shock and horror immediately spread across his face as his eyes fell upon Mynhos and the wings protruding from his back.

The muscles in her brother's back had since been distorted, and the skin around the spots where the wings sprouted from was raw, as if they had not fully healed yet.

Mynhos slashed at Laurince with an untamed vigor. Laurince, however, managed to dodge or block every attack that came his way.

"Take the king and run!" Laurince shouted as he blocked another swing of Mynhos's sword.

Myra looked at the door. They were only a few yards away. She could take Rian and leave while Mynhos was distracted. But how far would they get? How long could Laurince hold her brother off? How long would it take for Rian to regain full control of his body?

Myra wasn't strong enough to carry him for long.

Laurince struck, but Mynhos was quick. Their swords clashed together as they fought.

Silver flashed in the corner of her vision.

Myra gulped as her attention flicked to the throwing knife her brother had tossed to the side.

The seer's warning echoed in Myra's mind: *If you do not grab the blade, you all will die.*

Laurince hissed in pain as Mynhos nicked him in the arm. As Mynhos snarled and his mouth foamed, she knew what the seer had meant: her brother was truly gone.

Whatever Domitius had done to him, it had transformed him completely, stripping him of the sweet boy she used to run and play pretend with in their mother's gardens.

As she felt the rise of tears in her throat, she pushed herself up and ran for the blade. She swiped it from the floor and spun, swallowing the guilt already flooding her system.

Her aim may have been nonexistent, but a blade was still a blade.

Tears streaming down her face, Myra ran as fast as she could.

Her arms and legs burned as she pumped them faster and faster. The tears blurred her vision, but she did not let them stop her.

They would not die here.

They would not let Domitius win.

She screamed, the sound full of all her pent-up rage and anger and pain. She drove the knife through the bright red spot that seared Mynhos's skin, right between the two black wings.

A guttural scream ripped through her brother as his sword dropped from his hand. He arched his back in pain, his wings spreading out wide.

Mynhos looked over his shoulder at her, agony ripping across his features. Then, before he could turn all the way, Laurince drove his sword through Mynhos's heart.

And Myra stood helpless as she watched the blood spurt from her brother's mouth.

Mynhos glared at his sister, anger and hate bleeding from his ruby eyes. Coughing, Mynhos said, his words barely audible and filled with vitriol, "He'll kill you. He'll kill you all."

Myra stumbled back, her vision blurring as her brother crumbled to the ground, his wings spreading around him.

The tears continued to pour down her face as Laurince snatched Myra's hand and tugged her toward Rian. And despite knowing she shouldn't, Myra looked back at her brother.

Blood pooled around him in a puddle, soaking his wings. His entire body trembled as he tried and failed to stand.

As the fire extinguished from his eyes, Myra whispered through barely contained sobs, "I'm sorry."

She didn't know if he heard her, and she knew it would not fix anything or change the past. Yet she said them, nevertheless.

Then, they were running. Their feet pounding against the ground, with no end in sight.

CHAPTER 54
GRAESON

Graeson felt like he was floating but heavy at the same time as he looked down at Kalisandre, who lay asleep next to him. After he had finally gotten a taste of her, he was too wound up to sleep.

Kalisandre, on the other hand, had no issues falling asleep once Graeson had his way with her. But before she had succumbed to sleep's pull, she attempted to touch him, too. Graeson, however, only shook his head and pulled her close to his chest.

Tonight wasn't about him; it was about her.

She had made it very clear that she wasn't ready to accept the bond--if she ever was. And he could only torture himself so much without her being entirely his.

So that was that.

He didn't know how much time had passed since sleep had overtaken her, but he was perfectly content lying beside her.

Her chestnut-brown hair was spread across the pillow in waves. One long strand was strewn across her face, falling across her still swollen lips. With one hand bearing his weight, he gently brushed the strand away, unable to help himself, and pushed it behind her ear.

Her eyelashes fluttered across her sun-kissed cheeks as his thumb swept across her skin, but she did not wake. She only nestled closer, deeper beneath the blankets, with a small smile.

It was a stolen touch, but one Graeson would cherish. He knew this moment of bliss was fleeting, whether because of her imminent refusal of their bond or their inevitable return to Pontia. Across Vaneria, tensions were rising to extreme heights, and he doubted they would experience such serenity again.

So, like Kalisandre, he put off the concern about the future and focused entirely on the present.

He wanted to carve tonight into his memory, for he would never get over how she reacted to his touch. He was addicted to it. The little movements, the way her breath jumped, and the way she had bitten her plump bottom lip.

When his thumb hovered over her lips as he recalled the image of her biting them with her back arched, he saw red, the god within him begging to come out to play.

But for once, he didn't want to run away from it. He wasn't afraid of the god inside him, not with her. *Never* with her. Because with her, red was his favorite color.

Her passion matched his just as fervently.

As he laid back down and scooted closer to her, Graeson finally allowed himself to rest.

And maybe, just maybe, he could be fine with having this small piece of her. For however long they had. Because whatever this thing was between them, it was something he wanted to get lost in, something he would be happy to drown under.

A BANGING at the door woke Graeson up, and Kalisandre stirred beside him, mumbling something unintelligible as sleep still fogged her mind.

"Go back to sleep," Graeson whispered, tucking her back in. "I've got it."

He placed a soft kiss on her forehead, and the moment he did it, he almost regretted it. She had been very clear earlier.

Tonight was supposed to mean nothing. Yet as he untangled himself from her limbs and she turned into his pillow, tucking it beneath her chin, he yearned to be right next to her.

But if another knock sounded before he could answer, there was no question she would wake up and run off the moment she had a chance. So, on soft feet, Graeson headed toward the door and cracked it open just enough to peer out.

A female guard stood outside, tapping her foot impatiently.

"Sir," the Tetrian guard said with a nod, "we have visitors."

"And?" Graeson asked, annoyed he had been woken up for this.

"Your presence has been requested in the throne room."

Graeson looked over his shoulder, where Kalisandre was still peacefully asleep.

"Whoever it is can wait until the morning," he said, closing the door.

The guard pressed a hand against the door, stopping it. "Sorry, sir, but this cannot wait until morning."

Graeson's jaw flexed. "I--"

"Kalisandre's presence has been requested as well," the woman said, cutting him off.

Graeson arched a brow. "How did you--" He began but was unable to finish the question.

The guard rolled her eyes. "The walls speak."

"The walls?"

The woman hummed, her cheeks flushing bright red in the

torch's flickering light in her hand. "One of the guards saw her leave her room and come here."

Graeson rolled his eyes at the lack of privacy. "And this cannot wait?"

"No, sir."

He brushed a hand through his hair and sighed. "Very well. We'll be there in a moment."

With that, Graeson shut the door. As he padded back over to the bed, Kalisandre's eyes fluttered open.

Through a sleepy gaze, she asked, "Who was it?"

"A guard," he said as the bed sank beneath him slightly.

"What did they want?" Her voice was so soft and light that he did not wish to ruin it and admit that this bubble of theirs had officially burst.

"Our presence has been requested," Graeson said. "Apparently, we have visitors."

The sleep evaporated from Kalisandre's eyes in an instant as she stared up at him, processing his words.

"Did they say who?"

Graeson shook his head.

As the two looked at each other, an unspoken question hung between them. Because if they had not been expecting anyone but their presence had been requested, only a few options were feasible.

CHAPTER 55
KALLIE

Kallie stood beside Graeson, her gaze scanning the faces in the throne room. When the two of them arrived, everyone had already been waiting, including the queen.

Wearing a black satin robe tied around her waist, Cetia sat on her throne. Thin feathers lined the collar and cuffs of the elegant robe. Every time she made even the slightest movement, the feathers danced in the air. Her straight, raven-black hair flowed over her shoulders. Despite the late hour, the queen looked as regal as ever. The tension was taut as the queen tapped her sharp nails along the right arm of the throne.

The guard standing to the queen's right took a step forward and announced, "Graeson Osiros and Kalisandre Nadarean, Your Majesty."

Kallie stumbled as the guard said her name, a name she had no right to bear.

An awkward silence slipped through the room as everyone else registered it as well. Dani, who stood beside Terin, rolled her hands into tightly clenched fists as her jaw muscles popped.

Sensing the change in the room, Graeson squeezed Kallie's hand, and she let his presence ground her.

"Nice of the two of you to join us finally," Cetia remarked.

"Your Majesty," Graeson said, tipping his head before leading Kallie to stand beside Terin.

When they approached, Kallie heard Dani say, "You are no Nadarean."

"Danisinia," Terin hissed. "Now is not the time."

Dani huffed but returned her focus to the queen.

Terin peered at Kallie, a question sitting within his gaze.

Kallie offered him a tight smile. As she was about to reassure him she was all right, the doors opened, and everyone turned their attention to the group of warriors marching into the throne room.

The Tetrians wore their fighting leathers with dozens of throwing knives strapped across their chests. As the group marched down the center aisle, their hands rested on the hilts of the swords hanging on their hips.

Kallie tried to peer past the warriors in the front to see who they were guarding, but she could not glimpse the visitors.

Still, her heart hammered in her chest, an uneasiness crawling over her skin as they waited.

At the end of the aisle, one guard stepped forward and tipped her head to the queen. "Your Majesty, we found these three near the border. They claim to be seeking refuge."

"Bring them forward," Cetia said with an impatient wave.

Three other guards shifted at the command and pushed the refugees forward.

A chill crept over Kallie's arms as she observed the three prisoners. Even though their heads were covered with brown sacks, there was a strange air of familiarity to them.

They stood slightly hunched as exhaustion weighed their limbs down. They wore tattered clothing that reeked of the swamp and woods, the scent so poignant it even reached Kallie, who stood yards away. Two of the refugees were over a foot taller than the third. Long blond hair peeked beneath the hem of the sack top the woman's head. She twisted her fingers together, her wrists chained.

A sickening feeling twisted in her gut. But before Kallie could identify it, the guards pressed down on the three refugees' shoulders, forcing them to kneel. One of the larger individuals fought the guard behind him, but he quickly lost the fight. His knees hit the ground with a *thump*.

Once all three were finally kneeling, the guards behind them ripped the sacks off their heads.

Kallie barely gave the two men any attention, her attention immediately snapping to the woman kneeling on the floor. Her blonde hair was strewn across her face, and her hazel eyes squinted at the change of light.

Before she could think otherwise, rage propelled Kallie forward.

Shouts filled the air, but she didn't give them attention; they were a blur in her ears, nonsensical white noise.

Someone reached for her, but Kallie didn't stop--she couldn't. She slipped through every hand that tried to pull her back, that threatened to stop her. The world around her blurred. She could only see one thing at the epicenter.

"You traitorous bitch!" Kallie screamed as she tackled Myra to the ground. Her hands wrapped around her former best friend's throat.

Myra gasped, inhaling a sharp breath as Kallie stripped the oxygen from her throat.

With wide, fear-filled eyes, Myra tried to scramble away. She attempted to force her chained hands up and push Kallie back.

She tried to speak, but Kallie didn't care to hear the poisonous words spill from Myra's mouth.

Tears spilled from Myra's hazel eyes, wet streaks cutting through the layer of dirt covering her face. But Kallie had no sympathy for the woman who had lied to her for as long as they had known each other.

She tightened her grip, and her vision blurred.

For years, Kallie had been blinded by Myra's feigned compassion and kindness. For years, she had taken solace in the friendship Myra had offered her. Kallie had confided in her and trusted her. She would have done anything for the woman beneath her.

But now Kallie knew the truth.

It had all been a ruse, a trap.

A way to weave a false story and further the king's endeavors.

It wasn't until water droplets splashed upon Myra's face that Kallie realized she was crying. Still, she didn't stop.

She was hurting, and she wanted Myra not only to feel the emotions consuming her because of the gift that nearly destroyed Kallie but also because Kallie wished it so. And more than anything, Kallie wanted Myra to hurt, too. To feel the same pain she had every time Domitius had pushed her beyond her body's limits, when he had bruised her wrists and broken her ribs.

She felt someone's arm wrap around her stomach, and she struggled against them. But even though she fought against them, Kallie was lifted into the air as someone else pried her hands from Myra's neck.

Someone said Kallie's name.

Again and again as they tried to slip through the fury overtaking her.

Her gift stirred within the pit of her stomach, beckoning her. Its honeyed taste coated her tongue, begging her to use the power the gods granted her.

Begging her to succumb to its pull.

Kallie struggled against the person as the tears rolled down her face with no sign of stopping.

The threads of her gift danced, rising higher and higher.

Through her tear-stained vision, she saw someone assisting Myra to sit up. The handmaiden took a deep breath. Her pale, shaking hand rubbed her throat, which was now a vibrant shade of red where Kallie's hands had been.

"Kalisandre," the person holding her repeated, more urgently this time.

Her feet hit the ground, and she was immediately spun around, the person's grip on her firm as her entire body shook with rage.

Silver eyes peered down at her, a beacon.

"Breathe, Kal," Graeson whispered.

"She--she did this," Kallie hissed through the tears still streaming down her face.

His thumb ran across her left wrist as he held her steady. "She is a victim just like you are." Graeson pressed his palm to her face and gently swiped away the tears with his thumb. "You are better than this. You are better than him."

Kallie shook her head, the ghost of tears sticking to her skin. "No, I am not."

"Yes, you are," Graeson whispered as the chaos surrounding them slowly died down. "We need to hear them out. Then the queen will decide what to do with them." He wiped away more tears, his gaze never leaving hers.

Kallie bit down on her tongue and took a deep breath.

"We can leave if you wish," he offered quietly.

She only shook her head. She wanted--no, *needed* to hear what they had to say. She would not run from this.

Myra would not touch her again.

She would never give anyone that kind of power.

Graeson nodded and weaved his fingers between hers. He

squeezed her hand once, and Kallie exhaled, straightening as she turned to face Myra. Only then did she process who the two men with Myra were.

Rian and his guard, Laurince, sat beside her. They all looked like they were dragged to the Beneath and had crawled their way out.

In the time that passed since the wedding, Laurince had gained a new, gnarly scar, which spread across his neck as if an animal had attacked him. Rian was nearly unrecognizable kneeling between Myra and Laurince. His red hair was muted and covered in dirt and grime. His brown skin was dull as were his soft green eyes. He wore a stained, tattered cotton shirt.

Rian's attention flicked to where Graeson and Kallie's hands were intertwined, and guilt twisted in Kallie's stomach.

Sensing her tension as her fingers twitched, Graeson loosened his hand. Kallie only held on tighter, though, and she could have sworn she heard Graeson release a soft exhale, his shoulders dropping slightly as she did.

"Let's be civil, shall we?" Cetia said, calling their attention to her. Her chin rested atop her fist, her features unfazed. She waved a nonchalant hand in the air. "King Rian, please do explain why the entire world thinks you are deathly ill."

"When my home was attacked," Rian began, a cold gaze slipping across his face as he glared at the Pontians standing on either side of Kallie, "I was injured. I had taken a blade to my side and was rushed to the infirmary during the chaos that befell my kingdom."

Graeson shifted beside Kallie, and she looked at him quizzically from the corner of her eye. He offered her only a small shrug that was otherwise unnoticeable. Although she swore she saw a hint of a smirk twitching at the corner of his mouth.

"Mayhem was already filling the streets by then, and I had lost so much blood. The pain was so great that it was hard for me to process what was happening around me. I recognized my brother, though, as his guards carried me out of the temple before I blacked out.

"But when I awoke, I wasn't in the infirmary, at least not the one inside the castle. This place was much darker, colder. One moment, a healer and Sebastian were peering down at me, and then the next, I could hear the creak of a carriage's wheels. I tried to ask someone where we were going, but no one would tell me anything. The next thing I knew, I was strapped to a table."

Myra squirmed beside him, her shoulders trembling.

Beside Rian, Laurince cleared his throat and continued for him.

"I had searched the temple for the king, but I couldn't find him in the chaos of the fire and the panic. Rumors quickly spread around the castle that my king had suffered a grave injury. Some had seen him brought in by a couple of guards, unconscious and half-dead. I scoured the castle, searching for him despite his brother's assurances that he was being cared for.

"Something had felt off, though. I didn't know what at the time, of course. All I knew was that I needed to find Rian. A couple of days later, an unmarked carriage was leaving the castle, and before the curtain fell, I spotted Sebastian. Without thinking, I followed after him--all the way to Ardentol."

Kallie shifted on her feet, nausea filling her stomach at the mention of her former home.

"I impersonated one of the Ardentolian guards and found my way into the castle. That's when I discovered the truth." Laurince paused, his gaze dropping to the floor, unfocused and haunted.

"Which is?" Cetia prompted after a moment passed.

"Beneath the king's nose, Sebastian has been leading an experiment."

Medenia stepped forward, her hand on her stomach. "Do you speak of the creatures in the tunnels beneath the temple?" she pressed.

Laurince nodded.

"And you had no idea this was happening in your own kingdom?" Medenia asked, her gaze falling upon Rian next.

Rian's features contorted in shame, but he quickly steeled his expression. "Do you know everything that happens in *your* kingdom?" he shot back.

Medenia's lips parted, but then she snapped her mouth shut. Everyone knew it was nearly impossible to know all the happenings in one's kingdom, despite how much one paid attention.

Rian shifted and continued, "I wish I could say I was completely ignorant of the experiments, but that would be a lie."

Medenia scoffed in disgust, her lip curling.

"Yet you come here seeking refuge despite knowing these atrocities?" Cetia asked.

"It is not that simple, Your Majesty," Rian said with a shake of his head. "Ever since I was little, I have been fascinated with dragons." He paused and glanced at Kallie; pain soaked his expression. After a second, he looked away and pressed forward. "A week or so before my wedding, my brother said he had a wedding gift for me near the Borganian border. I thought nothing of it at the time and rode out with him and a group of guards. When we arrived, he revealed he was leading a project to recreate the legendary beasts.

"At first, I laughed at him, for how could one create a dragon? But then he showed me his gift: their first semi-successful prototype, a drakonis. A creature created from wolves bearing some of the characteristics of a dragon. But as he was showing the drakonis to me, we were attacked. My brother and I ran as the guards held the invaders off."

Rian's gaze grew distant as he stared at a spot on the ground.

He shook his head. "I do not know what happened to the monster."

"The *monster* is doing quite well, actually," Medenia said, tipping her chin up.

"You--you've seen it?" Rian sputtered.

"We freed her," Graeson said, his cold voice ripping through the throne room.

The two men glared at each other, and a ripe tension riffled through the room. Only when the queen spoke did Graeson and Rian finally release each other.

"So, you discovered this was happening, and you did what? Nothing?" Cetia asked.

Rian blanched at the queen's straightforwardness. "There--there wasn't time. I promised to deal with it after the wedding, but..." He lifted his bound hands.

"What brings you here, then? Why were you in Ardentol?" Medenia asked.

"We came here in search of asylum. My kingdom has been overtaken by my brother, and the experiments he and Domitius have been working on have evolved," Rian said, grimacing.

"Domitius has been working on his own project for decades, and now the two have teamed up," Laurince added.

"Elaborate," Cetia said, her tone more clipped.

Laurince peered at Myra from the corner of his eye, and she shifted beside the king. She took a deep breath, her chest rising. Then she straightened and tipped up her chin.

"The experiments are two-fold. The first combines Domitius's research with Sebastian's advancements." Myra dropped her gaze to her hands that dug into her thighs, creasing the fabric of her cotton trousers.

She gulped. And when she raised her head, Kallie could have sworn she saw the faint trace of a tear.

A drop of sympathy rose in Kallie's throat, but she swallowed it.

"Domitius has found a way to create humanoid creatures that follow his command," she breathed.

"And the second?"

"The second--"

The doors flew open, and a flushed guard ran through the throne room, their boots clapping on the floor.

"Your Majesty," the guard called out in between heavy breaths.

"What is the meaning of this interruption?" Cetia thundered.

"I--I bring a letter."

"A letter from whom?" she demanded.

"The King of Ardentol."

A cold sweep of tension ripped through the room. Kallie's legs shook, and Graeson wrapped an arm around her, keeping her steady.

"What does it say?" Cetia snapped, her patience having run thin.

The guard quickly scanned the room, hesitating.

"Well?" Cetia commanded, her hand gripping the arm of her throne.

The letter shook in the guard's hand, and the woman swallowed hard. "The King of Ardentol has declared war upon Pontia and Tetria for the abduction of King Rian and Princess Kalisandre."

EPILOGUE
KAGE

AT THE EDGE OF THE MEZZANINE, KAGE STOOD, HIS HANDS CURLING around the railing and his attention fixed on the floor below. The ample space beneath the castle's marble floors had been wiped clean of the mazes he used to train Kalisandre.

But he had no more use of the mazes.

It had been months since the wedding and since the Pontians had taken Kalisandre from him.

She should have been back by now. She should have cut their throats and done away with them already.

If the handmaiden had done her job right, that is.

He should never have considered the handmaiden strong enough. When Kalisandre came around asking more probing questions, he could see his influence on her slipping.

He had not been granted an ability, but the gods were cruel that way, forcing those who deserved powers the most to work the hardest for it. Thus, he had no option but to trust in the girl's abilities.

According to the seer, the handmaiden had been blinded by love.

Love, he thought, a sneer rising on his lips. *How ridiculous.* Preposterous, really.

He made a promise to himself years ago that he would never let such a frivolous and fragile thing have that kind of power over him. He promised he would never let it weaken or destroy him like it had so many.

And he would be damned if he let someone else's love and bond for another do so now.

If the seer believed his chances of winning the upcoming war were slipping away, he would change the fates.

After all, he had defied his fate before. He could do it again.

The sound of creaking armor stirred him from his thoughts. Glancing over his shoulder, he found one of the guards hurrying toward him, breathless and wide-eyed, holding his helmet in the crook of his arm.

"What is it, Kolen?" the king asked, annoyed by the interruption.

The guard skirted to a stop a few paces in front of Kage and promptly bowed before speaking, "Sir, the king and the handmaiden have escaped."

Kage froze, every muscle in his body growing taut. His jaw flexed, his teeth grinding together to an almost painful degree.

Behind him, Lundril, the captain of his guard, let out a low curse.

The seer had not mentioned this chain of events. If she had kept this from him, what else was that wretched woman keeping from him?

It seemed another visit was due.

His grip around the iron railing tightened, threatening to break it in half.

"How?" Kage demanded.

Lundril stepped closer, his hand on the hilt of his sword.

"One of the guards assisted them in their escape," Kolen said, his voice trembling slightly.

Kage snapped, then. He spun around, seizing the guard by the collar and yanking him closer. The guard's helmet fell to the floor with a crash.

"You let a traitor into our midst?" he spat.

The metal armor bit into Kage's skin as his fingers curled tightly around it, but the pain only fueled his anger.

"I didn't know. He--" the guard stammered, the whites of his eyes enlarging, his expression soaked with fear.

Good, he thought. *His fear shall motivate him.*

"Who?" he asked.

"Our men are looking into it as we speak, Your Majesty," Kolen said as he struggled to stay standing, his toes barely skimming the floor.

With an exasperated grunt, Kage released him.

The guard nearly collapsed on the floor, the joints of the armor screeching as they rubbed together. Kolen, at least, was smart enough to kneel at the king's feet.

The guard hung his head in penance. The back of his neck stung with a brilliant red mark where the collar had pressed into his skin. "I apologize. If I had been there, perhaps--"

"Save your breath on your excuses and apologies, Kolen," Kage said, cutting him off. He signaled for the guard to stand. "It is a waste of my time."

Grabbing his helmet from the floor, the guard rose to his feet. Clearing his throat, he straightened and flattened his expression. "I am already gathering a squad to go after them."

Kage flicked his hand. "Don't."

"Your Majesty?" the guard breathed, confusion curling his brows. "I'm sorry, I do not understand."

The king exhaled, the anger slow to release from his body.

Leaning his hip against the railing, Kage ran a hand down the front of his jacket, smoothing out any wrinkles. The beginning of a plan was already forming in his mind.

This was what he did.

This was what had gotten him this far. When a problem arose, he shifted. He adapted.

"I said *don't*," he repeated.

Was it really so hard to find competent men? Soldiers who would listen?

It was a pity Kalisandre had slipped through his hands so easily. She had been so...pliable.

At last, there was nothing he could do about that.

For now, anyway.

The guard swallowed.

"Let them go. Let them scurry off like rats into the night, searching for salvation," Kage said, turning back to the railing and formulating his plan. Yet as he watched the shadows dance over the magnificent sight below, he could still hear the guard's anxious breathing behind him.

"Why are you still here?" he demanded, peering at the guard from the corner of his eye.

"There is...uhm...another matter," the guard muttered.

"Spit it out then, Kolen."

His patience was thinning with every minute that passed. There was work to be done, yet this conversation persisted far longer than he desired.

"The boy," the guard said, his voice failing to hide his disdain for the latest enhancements the boy had received.

But beneath the contempt, Kage detected a hint of envy. Kolen had not been chosen to undergo the same transformation as Mynhos. Didn't the guard understand he had other plans for him?

"What about him?" Kage asked.

The guard shifted on his feet. "The traitors were able to harm him in their escape."

His jaw ticked. "Where?" Kage demanded.

"In the throne room, Your Majesty. The staff is already working to clean up the mess."

Kage scoffed, his nose twitching. "I do not care about the mess. *Where* was he struck?"

"Through the heart, My King," Kolen said quietly.

Kage pursed his lips and ran his tongue over his teeth.

For nearly two decades, Kage had searched for someone who bore a gift similar to Mynhos's. When the seer had finally informed him of the child's birth, Kage knew he had to find him. However, the child's parents were more cunning and resourceful than he expected. Somehow, they had gotten wind of the king's interest in the boy, so they ran.

They hid like the little rodents they were. But Kage had dug them out of their hole.

No one could escape his grasp for long.

Over the past nine years, they had tested the boy's healing abilities in various ways. A cut to his face would heal in a matter of minutes, seconds even depending on how deep the wound was. A missing digit took a few days to grow back. When he had chopped off his hand months ago in front of the boy's sister, it had taken a little over a week to regrow. The process was gruesome and grotesque, even Dr. Thorne had nearly gagged as he watched the new bones form.

It was absolutely riveting. A sight to behold, truly.

However, they had yet to sever Mynhos's head or stab him in the heart--blows too fatal for even Kage to suggest attempting before they were sure Mynhos could survive it. Especially not before they extracted what they needed and found a way to harvest his gift.

The boy's sister--an unexpected prize Kage had not expected to come across nine years ago--proved to be immensely helpful with that issue. Although her escaping had never been something he wished to happen, he had planned ahead just in case.

Since she had been imprisoned, the guards had taken several vials of her blood. They had already used most of it, however, to help speed up the transformation process for the others.

The girl, after all, was slow to perform the experiments, her power not strong enough.

Although, now that she had escaped with the young king, Kage wished they had been able to retrieve more vials of her blood.

He would need to accelerate his plans even more, it seemed.

"What has Dr. Thorne said of his injuries?" Kage asked, returning his attention to the guard.

Metal creaked as the guard shifted on his feet. "The healer was killed in the escape," Kolen admitted quietly.

"Has this been confirmed?" the king asked, his words clipped.

"Yes, Your Majesty. Although his apprentice is still assessing the damage."

Kage hummed. "I will confirm this myself."

"Of course, My King."

"Has the apprentice looked at the boy?"

"The guards have brought his body down to the cells for him to look at, but he has not offered his assessment yet."

Kage nodded. "Very well," he said with a flick of his hand, dismissing the guard.

Kolen hesitated for a second before bowing low and taking his leave.

When the guard disappeared down the hall, his footsteps no longer audible, Lundril stepped closer.

"What would you like to do, Your Majesty?"

Kage rolled his hands around the railing, his grip tightening around it as he shifted his weight forward and peered down.

Below, rows of bodies stood in perfect formation. Several higher-ranked soldiers moved through the rows, some awkwardly maneuvering around the glorious wings of the men in the front rows. Their torches cast light on the faces of the new additions to his ranks. Not a trace of fear shone within their blood-red eyes.

And as the king marveled at their beauty, the wings of the beasts fluttering and the power reverberating among them, Kage couldn't help but smile.

"We continue as planned, Lundril."

Soon, he would unleash them.

Soon, the seven kingdoms would be his.

Then, he would at last prove to the world what true power was.

⚜

Read the final book in the series today:
The Kingdom's Reckoning.

Want to stay updated about upcoming releases, ARC opportunities, and more? Be sure to subscribe to Neena's Newsletter.

Author's Note

Thank you for reading *The Throne's Undoing,* the third book in the "Of Fire and Lies" series!

Kallie's journey is by no means a straight line. Parts of the road crumble before she can even take a step forward. She is forced to rebuild, time and time again.

However, this is not her ending. Not yet.

If you enjoyed this book, please consider leaving a review on Amazon or Goodreads. Reviews are so important to authors and help readers find books that are a good fit for them!

ACKNOWLEDGMENTS

This book—this *series*—would truly be nothing without the support and encouragement of so many incredible people in my life. I am incredibly grateful to be surrounded by such amazing friends, family, and colleagues. Because of them, I am who I am today. Because of them, this series is what it is. Words cannot express how thankful I truly am. But alas, I'm going to try anyway.

As always, first, to my husband, Nathan, you have supported me from the beginning of this journey and have never stopped. Thank you for always pushing me to be better and to take risks (and for letting me hide in my writing cave for hours).

Gabby, thank you for always being willing to hear me ramble and for letting me spoil things for you. Your support knows no bounds, and I am so grateful for your friendship.

Jess, thank you for pushing me to make this book the best it could be and for asking me the hard questions, even when I didn't want to hear them.

Chloe, thank you for seeing Myra for who she is and for pushing for her story to shine in this book.

Thank you to my family, whose unwavering support I am forever grateful for.

Thank you to my friends, near and far. Whether we talk every day, during the (somewhat) annual Michigan football game, or at another gathering, your support does not go unseen.

Thank you to the entire writing community I found on TikTok

and Instagram. You all inspire me every day. Thank you for always lending a helping hand and providing encouragement.

Thank you to my editors, Kay and Ashley. I value your praises and critiques more than you know.

Thank you to my cover designer, Bianca, for creating a stunning cover yet again.

Lastly, to you, the reader. This series started as a wishful dream, but it has become so much more because of you. Thank you for reading and for sticking around.

With love,
Neena

ABOUT THE AUTHOR

Neena Laskowski lives in Michigan with her husband and their two pets. She earned her master's in Secondary Education and bachelor's in English and Classical Studies from the University of Michigan. When she is not reading or writing about morally grey characters, you can find her camping, painting, or spending time with her family and friends.

For upcoming ARC opportunities and to be among the first to see cover reveals, character art, and more, be sure to join Neena Laskowski's newsletter, found on neenalaskowski.com, or follow Neena on social media.